Dedication

To Natasha

Forever young

the forever place

Michelle Montebello

The Forever Place

Michelle Montebello

Please note that Michelle Montebello is an Australian author and British English spelling has been used in this novel.

ISBN: 978-0987641656

Editing by Lynne Stringer at
Australian eBook Publisher and Marcia Batton
Book design by Swish Design & Editing
Cover design by Kris Dallas Design
Cover image Copyright 2021

Even the darkest night will end and the sun will rise.

~ Victor Hugo, *Les Misérables*

A Note From The Author

The Forever Place explores topics of alcoholism, domestic abuse and self-harm which some readers may find sensitive. It is also filled with love, hope and recovery.
If you choose to read on, I hope you enjoy Marley's story.

Michelle

the forever place

Chapter 1

Dawn. Last drinks called.

Lavender streaked the sky, and we sensed the rising sun. Work was a breath away and there was urgency now to reach home; so little time left for sleep. The trance lifted. The bar emptied. The lights flickered on. Night creatures emerged from the darkness, bleary-eyed and wretched, desperate for salvation. *We will sleep, we will wake, we will do it all again.*

I'd been called things before; reckless, an alcoholic. I didn't expect people to understand the complexities of my world; why I drank before work, why I stayed out until sunrise, why I washed away the horrors the only way I knew how. It was their innocent faces I couldn't bear to see. The questions they asked me in the small hours.

Why did you?

How could you?

Time had passed and still, I didn't have the answers, only the silver scars of my battle wounds.

Austin was beside me now, reaching out to entwine his fingers through my waist-length hair—a man I loved in my bed and possibly outside it. We saw things every day that shocked and dismayed—shook hands with the depraved, believed their stories, defended them in the highest courts. We lived for them, craved them, set them free.

Invincible. We were the wild ones.

'Bar's closing,' he said, grabbing my coat. 'Ready to go?'

I kicked back the rest of my vodka martini and reached for my handbag. 'I'm ready.'

Outside the bar, on a Melbourne street slick with rain, Austin helped me into my coat. His brown hair was dishevelled from running his hand through it too many times, and his dark eyes were glassy from the alcohol. He retrieved his phone from his trouser pocket. 'I'll book us an Uber. You can stay at my house tonight. We can tram it back in the morning.'

I swayed slightly, reaching up in my Dior heels to kiss his lips. 'If I do that, we won't get any sleep.'

'I see nothing wrong with that.' He smiled into my mouth, then kissed me back. I tasted mint, but also scotch. My senses fired with the thought of undressing him, of him undressing me. He smelled warm and of cologne; deeply sexy.

I reluctantly pulled away. 'I have to go home. I need to sleep.'

'Catch the Uber with me. I'll drop you at your place.'

'I'm in the opposite direction. And my car is down the road. I have my laptop and paperwork in it. I can't leave it in the city.'

'Do you need a pick-me-up for the morning?' He reached into his pocket and withdrew a small, clear bag, pressing it into my hand.

I glanced down at the powder with longing, wishing it were Friday night so I could enjoy the high then sleep off the comedown. But it was only mid-week, and I had a client meeting at ten and an afternoon in court. Alcohol was one thing, snorting a line before work was something else entirely. That little bag of fun would have to wait.

I begrudgingly returned it to his hand. 'Save it for the weekend. I have Dexedrine.'

He took the bag, pushed it back into his pocket and kissed me goodbye.

I left him outside the bar to wait for his Uber and walked to my car, parked in a laneway close to our firm. Light rain sprinkled my cheeks and the cold air forced me to retreat into my Ted Baker coat. My heels barely gripped the slippery pavement. I felt guilty. I should have offered him a lift home, but it would have added twenty minutes to my journey, and I couldn't risk a different route while drunk behind the wheel.

There were exactly twelve streets from the city laneway to my St Kilda apartment, a fourteen-minute drive in pre-dawn traffic. I knew by heart where the police lay in wait and what times they chose to do so, the backstreets they haunted and the thoroughfares they patrolled. I knew because some of my friends were police officers and, after a night of drinking, they became loose-lipped and informative. I took this knowledge and used it to my advantage so I could drive home intoxicated without being caught.

I reached my car and paused to consider my reflection in the driver's side window. Green eyes, pale hair, a striking face. Some would call me attractive, but now, at five in the morning, all I looked was haggard and worn. I blinked away my unflattering image and unlocked the door, climbing in and setting the heat to high to thaw my chilled fingers. Daybreak was pushing through the clouds, turning them pink. I needed to get home before the sun rose or I would lose those few precious hours left of sleep. I swerved away from the curb and rolled along the laneway, my headlights carving a path through the rain.

Navigating the wet streets, exhaustion took hold, the kind that came when I'd pushed myself too far. I reached a major intersection on the outskirts of the city and yawned. My eyes grew heavy and I relented, closing them for one indulgent second. Or was it longer? I couldn't tell, even though I was still driving through the intersection.

Everything happened quickly. I was careening through the cross street, my eyes like lead and my brain sluggish. And although I was dimly aware that my traffic light was red and I should have stopped, my foot was still on the accelerator. Still going.

It was too late by the time I saw the silver sedan coming from the right. His traffic light was now green, his headlights blinding, and we were on a collision course. As I flew into his path, I instantly realised my error, but time was a trickster, and I could not stop or slow or swerve.

I was certain I heard distant screaming, felt my hands leave the wheel to protect my face, heard the crunch of metal as the other car slammed into me. Glass shattered over my head. My door crushed and folded into my ribs. My airbag exploded, snapping my neck back.

Then there was silence, eerie and still, as our cars came to rest.

And my traffic light turned green again.

Chapter 2

'It was an accident,' Austin said. He sat by my bed, holding my hand, his eyes as sober as mine were. The effect of the alcohol had long since worn off. 'It could have happened to anyone.'

'It shouldn't have happened. That's the point.' I settled back against the pillow in the emergency ward and closed my eyes.

I'd walked away with a laceration to my forehead, two fractured ribs and whiplash. I wasn't sure how the occupants of the other car were, only that when the fire brigade had been freeing me from my car, I'd caught a glimpse of them, a man and a heavily pregnant woman, being helped from their vehicle. They'd looked pale and shaken, the man able to walk but the woman placed onto a stretcher, the shape of her swollen stomach visible through the blanket, as blue and red lights flooded the street. I'd watched them through my shattered windscreen until they were in the ambulance and it was screeching away, sirens blaring, towards the nearest hospital. Then I'd turned my head and vomited my last martini out the side of my mouth and down the twisted wreckage of my luxury Porsche.

After a bleak winter sun had finally risen and peak hour traffic had banked up around the intersection, I'd been whisked away too, to the emergency department to be assessed. By then, my phone had been full of frantic missed calls from Austin wondering why I hadn't shown up for work.

'Have the police taken your statement yet?' he asked.

I opened my eyes and he blurred back into vision. 'A brief one at the scene.' I winced with pain through every word. There was no way to get comfortable. 'And a roadside breath test. I returned a positive reading and they placed me under arrest. As soon as I got here, I had a mandatory blood test. The police will be back later to take a full statement.'

'Well, when they get here, don't say anything. Don't talk to them unless I'm present and can counsel you.'

'I know. I won't.' I shook my head. 'I'm such an idiot. Why didn't I just catch a ride with you?'

Austin shrugged. 'It was a mistake. Don't worry about it. It's just a drink driving charge.'

'It's not just a drink driving charge. I also ran a red light, and I could have killed a couple and their unborn child. It will go to court and I'll lose my driver's licence. I could be deregistered from practising.' The criminal defence lawyer who needed defending. The irony.

'You won't lose anything. It's your first offence. We'll sign you up for a driving program or something. Stop panicking.'

I scoffed. A driving program. A punishment that hardly fit the crime. I'd barrelled drunk and asleep through a red light and careened into a young pregnant couple, almost killing them. And here I was with Austin, discussing ways to exploit the legal system to my advantage.

Shame sunk me deeper into the pillow and I closed my eyes, lying there until I became aware of the weightlessness around my wrists, then they flew open. 'Where are my bangles and watch? Have you seen them?'

He pointed to a table beside me that was out of my view. 'It's okay, they've been here the whole time, behind you.' He scooped them up and handed them to me.

'Thank you.' I hurriedly slipped them on—my Rolex and bangles of all different styles—arranging them so they covered my flesh.

Austin watched me, and I knew he wanted to say the words. To tell me that it was time to let the past go. His eyes were sad and I looked away, not wanting to hear it, not wanting my secrets to rush upon me the way they often did. I couldn't face that tonight, not after what had happened.

A few hours later, Austin stood and adjusted his tie. 'I have to get back to work.'

'I'm sorry,' I said, opening my eyes, for I'd dozed off. 'You've been away for hours. You'll be catching up all day.'

'It's fine.' He smiled. 'Can I come by your place tonight?'

I nodded, wincing again as a sharp pain stabbed through my ribs. 'Did you tell Paul and Brian what happened?'

'I spoke to them after you called. We've rescheduled your meetings and I'll cover you in court this afternoon. Just get some rest.' He bent to kiss me, to smooth back my hair and touch my bandage tenderly. 'See you soon.'

'Bye,' I said, watching him leave.

Five minutes later, the doctor arrived. 'Right,' he said, glancing over my medical record. He was far too young for the stern and disapproving way he glanced down his nose at me. 'A nurse will be in to take your vitals again. How do you feel?'

'Like I've been in a car crash.'

He gave a satirical snort. 'Well, you were lucky, all things considered.'

'How are the people from the other car?'

'I'm not allowed to give you that information.'

'Not even to tell me they're okay?'

'They're okay,' he said dully. 'How are your ribs?'

'Sore.'

'And the head?'

'Same.'

'Your whole body is going to hurt for a few weeks. But as you have no concussion and the rib fractures aren't serious, I'm going to discharge you after the police return to take your statement.'

He left my bedside and I must have dozed off again for, sometime later, I was gently shaken awake by a nurse who'd appeared with two uniformed officers. Their faces slowly morphed into shape as I wrestled my eyes open. I recognised them instantly and my stomach lurched. They were the usual crew I drank with after work and I was certain by dinnertime, I'd be the talk of the station.

They asked me a series of questions but without representation, I declined to answer. They weren't surprised, and we agreed to speak again when my legal counsel was present. They informed me that my blood alcohol level had registered a mid-range scale and that they were going to charge me with serious driving offences.

I'd expected all this, for I understood the process. I'd spent my entire adult life defending charges like these for people. But now the shoe was on the other foot and I was as implicit in a crime as the lowlifes I represented.

After the officers left, I waited for my discharge papers to arrive, sinking back into the pillow, taking long, unsteady breaths. When I closed my eyes, I saw the faces of the young couple I'd hit, the shock in their eyes as my Porsche hurtled towards them. I saw other faces too, skidding past my eyelids, ones that haunted me when I was sober. I'd been running from them for two years now, ever since *that* day. Their memory only dimmed when I had a drink in my hand. And so that's what I did to numb their hold over me.

I drank.

Chapter 3

I was discharged from the hospital a few hours later in my day-old, dishevelled Burberry suit, smelling of sweat, vomit and alcohol. The Porsche was a write-off, but it was the paperwork inside I was most concerned about—folders of documents and photographs I should have taken straight home last night. Instead, I'd flirted with recklessness and now those files had to be collected from the police station where sensitive and confidential details of my clients' cases had most certainly been breached. A defence lawyer's entire caseload in the hands of the opposition? I didn't want to think about it.

The taxi I'd ordered swung to the curb and I climbed carefully into the back, shutting the door. Every breath I took was like a thousand knives piercing my ribs. The driver was blessedly silent on the way to the police station as traffic moved with us, and a cold, light drizzle, the same one I'd catapulted through the night before, fell onto a grey and wintery Melbourne.

It was hard to ignore my body as it cried out for a drink. Even after everything I'd just endured, I still wanted one. I tried to silence it by looking out the window or concentrating on the abrasions on my hands where the Porsche's windows had shattered over me.

Was this what rock bottom felt like? When you drove your out-of-control car through a red light and almost killed someone? When you drank and got behind the wheel because you thought you were above the law? Despite the drinking and drug-taking, I was usually steady, controlled, unwavering. I walked a tightrope that few people could, and I stayed the course, rarely faltering. But there, in the back of the taxi, with its worn seats and smell of old kebabs, my carefully controlled world had collapsed.

At the police station, avoiding the officer's eyes, I collected my personal effects—laptop, paperwork, and car keys, noticing work files and photographs clumsily slotted back into folders. They'd either been flung around during the crash or someone had rifled through them with intent. I'd never know, and I was too tired to question them about it.

The taxi drove me home and I let myself into my apartment, setting my box of effects on the coffee table and gingerly slipping off my Diors. I ran a shower, flinching as the hot water stung the cuts on my hands and face. Strands of my long, pale hair were matted with blood and I cried out in agony as I lifted my hands to wash it, shampoo the colour of rust swirling down the drain.

I dried and dressed in tracksuit pants and an oversized jumper, then headed to the pantry where I kept a shelf of liquor that would make any bartender envious. I poured myself straight nips of vodka and kicked them back until my whole body relaxed, and I worked up the courage to call my father.

He answered on the third ring. 'Hello, sweetheart.'

'Daddy.' My voice quivered despite an attempt to sound stoic. 'I'm in trouble.'

There was silence except for the sound of his scotch glass being set down on his mahogany desk. I remembered how the smell of that scotch used to tickle my nose as a child, an eighteen-year-old Macallan, aged in double barrels, which he still drank to this day. Even as a kid I'd been drawn to its malt scent.

'What happened?' he asked.

'I drove while drunk. I collided with another car. There was a pregnant woman inside.'

'Are you all right?'

'Yes.'

'And the woman?'

'She's okay.'

'Have you given your statement yet?' His voice was full of authority. He wasn't my retired father anymore, grey at the temples and softer around the edges. He was the father I remembered from my childhood, imposing, terrifying, factual, even when all I wanted at that moment were soothing words and a hug.

'Just a brief one at the scene,' I said. 'But Dad, I'm scared. I screwed up. I'll go to court, and my career...'

'What was your blood concentration of alcohol?'

'Mid-range.'

I heard a relieved breath. 'That's good. Not too high and it's your first offence. The magistrate will show leniency if you convey remorse.'

I'm not sure what I'd expected from this call, but there was no chastising or berating my stupidity like a normal parent would do. Maybe that's what I needed—a hard lecture to pull me into line, for someone I loved to intervene and tell me I'd disappointed them, that I should accept whatever punishment came my way. But my father was his usual methodical self.

'I could have killed someone,' I whispered, my body trembling as I realised all over again what nobody else seemed to acknowledge. 'She was heavily pregnant.'

I heard him collect his glass and drink from it again. 'But you didn't, so let's move on. You need to focus on the charges and how you're going to defend them.'

***

Austin arrived later that night with two six-packs of beer and a box of pizza.

'Didn't think you'd feel like going out tonight.' His eyes strayed to the bandage on my head and the cuts dotting my skin. 'Ouch.'

I took the pizza box and walked slowly into the kitchen, my ribs protesting with every step. 'Thank you. This is perfect.'

'How are you feeling?'

'Like I've been run over by a bus.'

'Did the hospital give you a prescription?'

'Just Ibuprofen and to see my regular doctor if the pain doesn't subside after a few weeks.'

'Nothing stronger?' He looked as disappointed as I'd felt when they'd refused to give me more than an over-the-counter pain killer. 'Well, I dropped into the police station on the way over.' He settled onto a bench stool as I collected plates and napkins. He was still in his suit and had the shadowed look of someone who had hardly slept in the past thirty hours. 'They want to question you again tomorrow at nine. I'll pick you up from here and we'll go down together.'

'Have you heard anything more about the pregnant woman from the other car? I called the hospital earlier, but they wouldn't release any information.'

'No, I haven't.'

'I think they kept her in for observation.'

'I don't know.'

'I want to send her flowers. Or say sorry, at least. Her name's Kristy, right?'

Austin rubbed his hand over his jaw and sighed.

'What?' I asked. I could feel it coming, the lawyer about to lecture me on what a bad idea that was. I knew it too, all the reasons why I shouldn't engage with her before this was settled in court.

'You know you can't. It's like an admission of guilt. You haven't even given your full statement yet.'

'I don't plan on fighting the charges, just so you're aware.'

'How do you know *they* didn't run a red light? Or were speeding? Or the husband fell asleep at the wheel? Or he was on his phone and distracted, and he careened into you?'

'Because I know.'

'No, you don't.' Frustration crept into his voice. 'Have you verified any angle of this case yet? Have you read the police reports, reviewed the other driver's statement, watched the CCTV footage? You've assumed guilt based on a patchy memory and the fact that you were over the limit. That doesn't make you guilty of *all* charges.'

I shook my head, more to block out what I knew was reasonable logic.

'Will you just give me a couple of days to look over everything?' he said. 'Don't send flowers. *Do not* say sorry. Just wait, okay?'

I conceded with a nod and let the subject drop, putting slices of pizza onto our plates while Austin twisted the lids off two beers and handed me one.

'What did Paul and Brian say?' I asked, taking a long sip, the bracelets around my wrists jangling.

'Paul's worried about you.' Austin sipped too. 'But Brian's not happy.'

'I expected as much.' With careful effort, I climbed onto a bench stool beside him to eat. Paul Clifford and Brian Dunbar were the partners and directors of the law firm I'd worked at for the last ten years—Clifford, Dunbar and Associates. We were the most successful criminal defence firm in Melbourne, and I knew how disappointed they would be in me for what had transpired overnight. Their brightest lawyer, known in the industry for being so shrewd that she never lost a case, was about to be charged with a string of serious driving offences. I dreaded the conversation I would have with them in the morning.

'Are you going to take a few days off?' Austin asked, wiping his mouth with a napkin and pushing his plate away.

'If I can. I'm not sure how mobile I'll be with two fractured ribs.' My whole body felt like it had been put together wrong.

'How about we go away this weekend?' he suggested, placing his hand on my thigh. 'I'll get the crew together. We can go someplace warm, have a couple of boozy nights on a beach. We'll keep it casual. What do you say?'

'I don't know.' I shrugged. 'I'm not really in the mood.'

Austin sat back as if I'd stung him. 'Marley Kincaid, not in the mood for a party? Since when?'

'I'm allowed to feel bad. I hit a car with a man and his pregnant wife inside. I could have killed them.' My voice rose defensively.

'They're fine. And so is their kid. We would have heard if anything had happened. You're worrying for nothing.'

'Maybe, but I'd still like to say sorry. Not right now, but at some point.'

Austin shook his head. 'You need to separate yourself from them or you're going to get attached. You remember what happened last time you let a case get under your skin.'

It was my turn to feel stung and I flinched, my eyes falling to my wrists, but he didn't notice. He slid off the bench, collected his beer and padded into my bedroom, yawning. I found him in there later, tie loosened, shoes off, lying on top of the covers, snoring softly, as comfortable as if it were his own bed. And it was, I suppose—a second home for him.

We'd wake and have sex later. It was how our relationship had been founded, drunken one-night stands late after work until it developed into some semblance of a connection. He was right for me in all the wrong ways; drawn to each other like moths to a flame. Were we soul mates? No. Would I marry him one day? Probably not. But we were each other's here and now and that was all we needed.

I decided to let him sleep; sleep away the night that was. Wash it away as I couldn't, as if it had never happened. Austin had always been good at that, more so than me. I laid a blanket over him and slipped quietly from the room, closing the door, before stepping out onto my balcony with another beer and two sleeping pills to watch the waves roll over South Melbourne Beach.

The moon was glossy and glowing in a dark sky, casting syrupy patterns across the water. The sound of the beach soothed me, rhythmic and resolute. It looked the same as it always did and yet, I was completely changed, as though I'd been flung from steady ground into an earthquake. Or perhaps I had been the earthquake, thrown suddenly onto steady ground.

I eased myself into a chair, then washed my pills down with beer, wincing with the effort, for every breath hurt. I tried to remember the moment my life had spiralled off course. Was it before or after the Wagners? I'd always been predisposed to a drink, like my father, and his father before him. But just like them, I'd known my limits and how far to push myself. The edges of sobriety hadn't always been so blurred.

Lately though, I had lost my way. Last night was testament to that, and all the other nights when I'd felt too invincible for my own good. Two years ago, the world lost a young mother. Last night, it had almost lost another one. What would it take for me to stop?

I stared down at the bangles around my wrists, parting them to view the skin underneath, tracing silvery scars that crisscrossed pale flesh. My battle wounds. How I'd tried to outrun the past, to end the guilt, to meet my maker.

The Wagner family flashed before my eyes and I squeezed them shut, taking a long gulp of my beer, draining the bottle, until their faces disappeared.

Chapter 4

Two Years Earlier

On a Monday morning, grey with fog, I sipped my second coffee of the day and sighed as I skimmed through my schedule.

A domestic abuse case at nine, a break and enter at nine-thirty, a misbehaving celebrity in lieu of lunch, and a manslaughter charge with my afternoon espresso. It was the cumulative cycle of miscreants that filled my days. I analysed their crimes, listened to their excuses, loathed them with one breath, then defended them with the next. Most people asked why I'd chosen this path. Some even called me cold-hearted. It wasn't always easy to explain, other than to say I had lived and breathed criminal defence since I was a child.

'If you represent someone within the boundaries of the law, no matter how terrible their crime, you cannot be considered amoral,' my father used to say as I sat on his lap and watched him review case photos. 'Everyone is entitled to a defence, Marley.'

'What if the person you're defending did a bad thing?' I pointed to the image of a man wielding a knife. 'Like that. Would you still defend them?'

'Of course. We do not ask them if they are guilty.'

'Why not?'

He swirled coppery liquid around in his glass, ice cubes clinking, before taking a long drink, his brows knitted. 'Because at the end of the day, it's not about whether the defendant committed the crime, it's about what the prosecution can prove.'

'But there's a photograph of him being bad.'

'Yes, but it's just a photograph,' he said. 'Can it be proved, beyond reasonable doubt, that he is guilty of all charges? That is the question.'

This had not made much sense to me at the time, but because little was considered off-limits in my house—not crime photos nor details of the acts—I quickly learnt that criminal law was rarely black and white. You could bend it and twist it and colour it grey to achieve the best outcome for your client. There was a lot of ambiguity to be found in that grey. Society called it abhorrent. My father called it 'testing the evidence'.

Belinda, the receptionist, knocked on my office door, interrupting my thoughts. 'Marley, your nine am client is here.'

I nodded and stood, straightening my suit jacket. 'Send him in.'

Karl Wagner, the CEO of a large tech company, had been accused of beating his wife. I'd already ordered the brief of evidence from the police prosecutor and had reviewed the details the night before in preparation for our meeting. He was facing charges of aggravated assault, intimidation with intent to cause fear, and property damage. The police had served him with an apprehended violence order. He'd been released on bail, Austin representing him at the mention where he'd pleaded not guilty before a magistrate.

I had barely gulped down the last of my coffee when Belinda returned with him. He strode into my office with his assistant, wearing a black designer suit and shoes that smelled strongly of leather. There was a compelling presence about him that was hard to ignore. His hair was silver at the temples, and he had intense blue eyes and attractive features that on any other day I may have considered exceptional to look at.

Karl and his assistant, a young, serious-looking man, took a seat at the round conference table where I greeted clients.

'Can we get you some tea, coffee, water?' I asked.

They declined.

Photographs had accompanied the brief and I spread them out on the table so we could discuss the incident. I'd learned to compartmentalise my work a long time ago, to keep my heart closed to the things I saw. I studied them now, seeing not his wife's injuries, but rather evidence and how we might build our defence around it.

There was bruising to Katiana Wagner's face—a swollen eye and cuts along her cheekbones and lips. There were also photographs of injuries Karl had sustained, some minor abrasions that appeared to be nail marks.

I'd noted in the police's fact sheet that, aside from the recent altercation, they had never been called to Karl and Katiana's home for a domestic occurrence, even though Katiana stated this was not the first time she'd been hit.

'Why don't we start at the beginning?' I said to Karl. 'Tell me what happened the night your wife sustained those injuries.' I collected my pen and poised to take notes.

'I arrived home at nine in the evening from work,' he began. He had a surprisingly soft voice, articulate and aloof. 'Katiana was home with the children. When I walked through the door, she flew into a rage.'

'What was she upset about?'

'An affair she thought I was having. She thinks when I travel for work, that I'm away with other women.'

'Are you?' I asked.

'Of course not. I'm working. She's happy to enjoy expensive holidays and designer clothes but accuses me of being unfaithful when it's *her* lifestyle I'm supporting.'

I scrawled several points of interest on my notepad—*hardworking, family man, unfairly accused of having affairs*, then I glanced up at him again. 'What happened next?'

'We argued, she called me a liar, threw a vase at my head then attacked me. She clawed at me with her fingernails. You can see from the photos the marks she left.'

I nodded because I'd already studied them, the abrasions that resembled fingernail marks on Karl's arms. 'Yes, I saw that she'd scratched you.'

'She was kicking and screaming, completely out of control. I had to defend myself.'

'And is this how she sustained the bruising to her face? You were acting in self-defence?'

'Yes.'

I made a note to work this point thoroughly because a magistrate would question whether her injuries were consistent with Karl defending himself. 'Then what did you do?'

'Finally, she calmed down and I went to check on the children sleeping upstairs. I was concerned we'd woken them.'

I glanced down at the fact sheet. 'It says here that Katiana called the police fearing for her life.'

'Yes. When I left the room, she called the police.'

'What state was she in when you left?'

'What do you mean?'

'Was she angry, terrified, remorseful?'

'She was remorseful, apologetic. I told you, she'd calmed down.'

'She was calm and remorseful, yet she still called the police and told them you'd punched her.' I didn't need to believe him. I didn't need to know if he'd beaten her. I needed his testimony to withstand the prosecution's interrogation and, just then, Karl Wagner's story fell apart.

He sighed, as though I was an annoyance. 'She was angry too, about the affair she thought I was having. She wanted to punish me.'

I made further notes, then glanced up at him, meeting his gaze directly. 'I realise these questions are difficult, but we need to prepare the best defence possible. Charges of aggravated assault come with a jail term and the prosecution will push for this.'

He closed his eyes briefly and nodded. 'Yes. I'm sorry. I understand. I'm under a lot of pressure.'

'How long have you and Katiana been married?' I asked, glancing at the clock. My next client was due to arrive soon.

'Six years,' he said, shifting on the seat, as though trying to regain composure.

'And how old are your children?'

'A boy and a girl. Three and five.'

I studied the reports in the brief again. 'I can see here that you were granted bail by the police, then you entered a not-guilty plea at the mention.'

'That's correct.'

I leant back in my chair and pressed my fingertips together. He watched me closely, as most clients did, trying to catch an inkling as to what their future held. They viewed me as their golden ticket to freedom. 'Mr Wagner, based on the evidence prepared by the police, I recommend that you change your plea to guilty.' He began interrupting but I held up my hands. 'It's your first offence and the magistrate will be lenient towards you. We may avoid jail time this way.'

He shook his head and I saw the agitation building, the denial. A familiar wave of frustration washed over me. I represented clients like Karl all the time. They committed felonies, then assumed I could wave a magic wand and make all the repercussions disappear.

'I have a reputation, a company, a board of directors to answer to,' he said. 'It's bad enough I have the AVO hanging over my head.'

'If you don't change your plea, the magistrate will be tough on you. The prosecution's case is strong—your wife's injuries, her statement, what the police observed when they arrived on the scene. Domestic violence charges are difficult to defend.'

He shook his head. 'I'm not changing my plea.'

I sighed, my patience wearing thin, and it was only nine-thirty in the morning. 'I advise you to reconsider. There will be considerable risks if you don't.'

Karl exchanged a look with his assistant, who raised his eyebrows. He returned his cold stare to me, leaning forward, his expression hard. 'Let me be clear, Miss Kincaid, because perhaps you didn't hear me the first time. I didn't do anything wrong. I'm not changing my plea. So just do what I'm paying you to do.'

***

After Karl and his assistant had left, Paul joined me at the conference table, like I'd expected he would. He was the best partner I'd ever worked for, supportive, involved, and we had a strong working relationship born of mutual respect. I didn't share the same kind of relationship with Brian. He lacked Paul's warmth and enthusiasm which made him harder to connect with on a personal level. Everything was about the firm, reminding me of my father in many ways. Perhaps that should have made him relatable, but I'd spent my life with a man who'd favoured the law over his family and as an adult, I did not automatically gravitate to that same clinical disposition.

Paul sat down at the table, an eager expression on his face. 'How did it go?'

'He won't change his plea,' I said.

Paul sighed. 'I'm not surprised. He feels strongly that he acted in self-defence.'

'Well, the evidence suggests otherwise.'

'And he knows the risks?'

'I explained them to him, but he doesn't seem to appreciate the seriousness of them. I don't need to tell you how detrimental it would be to his case if he refuses my advice.'

Paul nodded slowly, sitting back in his chair. 'Look, Marley, Karl Wagner is an important client of ours. He's well known in the media and he's paying us a lot of money to represent him.'

'Then maybe a barrister would be more pertinent to his case.' My voice rose and I tried to quell the exasperation I felt. No good could come from taking it out on Paul.

'Well, he asked for you personally. You've come highly recommended, so you're keeping him. A win here would be great for your career and for our firm.'

It would have been easy to be flattered had I not had every wealthy criminal seeking my representation. I had a high success rate in court and a reputation that preceded me, but it also meant that the expectations of clients were so unrealistic at times that it was a constant battle to align them with reality. Nevertheless, I loved the law, and I thrived on a challenge, a perpetual thrill that pulsed in my blood.

'The police prosecutor will throw everything at this,' Paul continued. 'You'll have a fight on your hands.'

'I would expect nothing less.' I gathered the photographs and case notes together, needing to prepare for my next appointment. I was fifteen minutes late and I grimaced, thinking of the domino effect it would have on all my other appointments that day.

Paul stood and pushed the chair back under the table. 'Just keep him out of jail, Marley. That's the aim.'

I loved working with Paul, but sometimes he thought I had a magic wand too.

***

The morning of Karl Wagner's hearing, we gathered in the busy magistrates' court before a magistrate I knew well. I wasn't a favourite of the Honourable Norman Daly's, despite my impeccable courtroom etiquette. He was gruff and would often bark at me, and my stomach tightened as I contemplated the uphill battle Karl and I faced that day, Paul's words ringing in my ears. *Just keep him out of jail.*

Katiana Wagner and the police prosecutor sat across the courtroom, closest to the witness box, as Karl and I took our seats near the dock. The prosecutor was a young man with thick glasses and a shock of dark hair that fell over his eyes. He shuffled paperwork around nervously as dozens of people filled the gallery behind us, seeming to add to his agitation. His presence surprised me because I knew everyone from the prosecutor's office, but I had never seen this man before. When he introduced himself to the magistrate as Liam Grant, I realised it was his first day in court, and the first time Daly had met him too.

Beside him, Katiana sat rigid, her spine straight, sad eyes staring forward, all traces of her bruising gone. She was beautiful, with ivory skin and black hair, but she was slight and timid, looking terrified as Karl Wagner's gaze bore into her.

'Try not to look at her so much,' I said to him in a low voice. 'It comes across as predatory.'

'I just want to get her attention,' he said. 'Maybe she'll realise how ridiculous this is.'

'It's best if you keep your eyes forward.'

The hearing commenced and the court officer called the prosecution's first witness—Katiana. She climbed into the witness box beside Daly, and Liam Grant rose and began his questioning. His technique was uncomfortable to watch as he fumbled and sweated under the hawk eyes of the magistrate. It was obvious that he was anxious, perspiring profusely and stumbling over words. I almost felt sorry for him as I recalled my own first time in court and how I'd stuttered through cross-examination. He knocked paperwork off the desk during questioning, then wasted precious minutes retrieving it, shuffling it back into order, while Daly snapped at him.

'Hurry up, Mr Grant. You're my first case and I have plenty more after you.'

'I apologise, Your Honour.'

'Don't apologise. Just move it along.'

Katiana was even less compelling on the stand. It was difficult not to feel compassion for her as Liam guided her through a shaky testimony, her recollection of the night unconvincing. When it was my turn to cross-examine her, despite feeling the thrill I always felt when I questioned a witness, I was hit with an unfamiliar wave of self-reproach for what I was about to put her through.

'Do you often accuse your husband of having affairs?' I asked her.

My first question seemed to stun her, and she glanced at Liam for help, but he seemed equally stunned, as though they hadn't considered this line of questioning in their preparation.

'Yes or no,' I said.

She swallowed, shifting in her seat. 'Um, sometimes.'

'Has he ever given you any reason to believe he's been unfaithful?'

'He goes away often,' she murmured.

'Do you mean he works hard to support your lavish lifestyle? Is a dedicated husband and provider for your family?'

Her eyes found Karl's and she seemed to shrink a little. 'Well, yes, I suppose.'

'On the night of the incident, did you accuse him of having an affair?'

She lifted her chin. 'I only asked him—'

'Yes or no, Mrs Wagner.' I took no pleasure in making her suffer more than she had, in watching her testimony crumble before the magistrate, but like Daly, I had to move this along. I had another court case after this and an afternoon full of client appointments.

'Yes.'

'And when you lost your temper, did you attack him with a vase?'

'That's not how it went—'

'Mrs Wagner,' Daly said gently but firmly. 'You've been reminded several times to answer yes or no.'

She sighed helplessly, dropping her gaze to her lap. 'Yes.'

'Did you claw him with your fingernails?' I was relentless, asking only the questions I knew answers to, skirting around Karl's obvious assault, leading the witness in a way the prosecution was not allowed to do.

'Yes.'

'And he acted in self-defence?'

She shook her head vigorously. 'All I did was ask him if he'd been with another woman. He put his hands around my throat, then punched me.'

'Objection.' I spun around to Daly. 'I request that the court strikes that from the transcript. The witness did not answer the question as it was asked.'

'Sustained. The witness's last comment will be struck from the transcript.' Daly stared down his nose at Katiana. 'Mrs Wagner, please refrain from further outbursts. Just answer the questions you are asked.'

I continued my cross-examination. Katiana was almost inaudible by the end of it, and Daly had to ask her several times to speak louder. The poor woman was terrified—of the court, of her husband, of me, and I was starting to feel the prosecution's case fall to pieces.

When it was Karl's turn to sit in the witness box, he was as confident and articulate as he'd been in my office, stepping through his version of events with methodical precision. Our time on the stand was swift and flawless, and Daly gave me a rare nod of approval.

After our closing arguments, Liam Grant sat back and breathed deeply, mopping his sweaty face with a tissue. Katiana sat beside him, rigid again, her sad, solemn expression returning. I glanced at Karl. He looked composed and I knew he felt it too, a thread of hope. Then Daly handed down his verdict of not guilty and Karl broke into a wide grin.

There was little time to deliberate, though, as the court officer called the next case and people stood to take our place. I quickly climbed to my feet and packed up my paperwork.

'You mean I'm free to go?' Karl asked.

'Yes. The prosecution was unable to prove beyond reasonable doubt that you caused her injuries intentionally,' I said. 'We were lucky today.'

'No, *you* were amazing. I can't thank you enough.' He shook my hand, unable to hide his triumph. 'What about the AVO?'

'The court has little jurisdiction over AVOs,' I explained. 'You will need to serve the full two years, I'm afraid.'

'So I can't see my wife or children?'

'Your wife, no, but we can arrange visitation for your children.'

His jaw twitched. I ignored him, placing the last of my paperwork into my leather tote and zipping it up. It wasn't the place to have this conversation. We needed to vacate the desk.

'You realise if that AVO remains enforced, my position as CEO becomes untenable. I'll be fired by the board,' he said in a low voice, leaning in closer than I felt was comfortable.

But I refused to be intimidated, so I faced him, staring back into those cold blue eyes. 'I'll set up a meeting so we can discuss the next steps, okay? For now, you should celebrate this victory.'

He stared at me before giving me a reluctant nod, then glanced back at Katiana. She was still seated beside Liam Grant as he clumsily stuffed his paperwork into his briefcase.

'Move faster, Mr Grant,' Daly barked. 'We haven't got all day!'

***

It had been a while since I'd been out. Usually, I worked long days and late nights, then on the weekends, I caught up on housework and went to the gym. I'd almost become a recluse, Austin teasing me mercilessly about it until one Friday afternoon, after a gruelling day in court, I relented and agreed to meet him.

I stared out at the city skyline from a table at our favourite bar as Austin set a martini down in front of me and dropped into a seat. 'I heard a rumour today.'

'Oh, and what was that?' I asked.

He shrugged with feigned nonchalance. 'That you're being considered for partner.'

I dipped my head, unable to help my smile. Ever since the Wagner hearing three weeks earlier, when I'd been filmed by the media exiting the courthouse with Karl victorious, I'd been inundated with work and had forgotten to mention the meeting I'd had with Paul and Brian. They'd been ecstatic at how I'd handled the case, Karl passing on his special thanks with an expensive case of Armand de Brignac. I'd been called in immediately afterwards to discuss consideration for partner.

I cast Austin an apologetic look. 'I meant to tell you. I forgot all about it. It's been crazy lately.'

'We tell each other everything. I'll try not to be offended.'

I leant across and kissed him until he relented with a chuckle. 'I'm sorry. Forgive me.'

He kissed me back. 'You're forgiven. You pulled off the impossible with that Wagner case. You deserve to make partner.'

I shook my head. 'It was Liam Grant's first day in court and the victim was unreliable. I'd hardly call it a fair fight.'

'Call it what you want, but Paul and Brian couldn't be happier.'

I sighed, remembering Katiana Wagner in the witness box, the way her eyes had darted fearfully around the courtroom, Karl watching her with his predatory gaze. I still thought about her. Although I could leave most cases behind, she'd stuck with me, like a rain cloud I couldn't shake. 'I still feel bad for the wife. She was a nervous wreck. She couldn't string two words together.'

He ran his fingers along my shoulder. 'You know you've got to put cases like these behind you. They're tough, but you can't let them get under your skin.'

I did know, but despite being conditioned from a young age by my father, I wasn't as resilient as I liked people to believe. 'He still has an AVO and, to my knowledge, hasn't breached it. So that's something.'

'He might breach it. Or she might just go back to him and the cycle will continue.'

'I hope not.'

He shrugged. 'I guess if she didn't, we'd be out of a job.' He pushed the martini into my hand. 'And on that note, work talk is over. It's time to relax.'

It took me several drinks to finally do that, but somewhere between the first martini and dawn, my shoulders loosened, and I forgot about work. We stayed out all night, friends joining us later, as we danced from one bar to the next. When the sun climbed over the city the following morning, Austin and I stumbled home to my apartment, kicked off our clothes and collapsed into bed, falling instantly to sleep.

But it felt like only minutes had passed when a distant ringing sounded in my head, shattering that sleep. I opened my eyes, unsure where it was coming from, then tried to roll away from it. It persisted, louder and louder, threatening to split my head apart, until finally Austin elbowed me and mumbled, 'Your phone.'

I groaned, then hung off the edge of the bed, tugging my handbag closer and fumbling inside. I pulled my phone out and glanced at it. It was seven am and I had four missed calls from Paul and two from Brian. I sat up and pushed my hair aside, the thump of a migraine pounding at my temples.

'Who is it?' Austin asked with bleary, half-opened eyelids. 'Don't they know it's Saturday morning?'

'It's Paul and Brian,' I replied, my mouth like cottonwool. I needed water.

Austin's eyes were open now. 'What do they want?'

'I'm not sure.' I dialled Paul's number and he answered on the first ring.

'Marley, where are you?'

'At home. Why?'

'I need you to come into the office now. Don't talk to the media or the police or anyone else on the way. Just get down here.'

My heart picked up pace. 'What's happened?'

I heard the deepest, saddest sigh I'd ever heard from Paul. 'Karl Wagner strangled his wife last night.'

Fingertips of ice-cold disbelief slithered along my skin. The hairs on my arms rose and the room tilted, not quite righting itself again. '*What?*'

'It happened at their house. I'm assuming he breached the AVO and went over there. There was no sign of a struggle. Katiana may have let him in.'

A response wouldn't register in my mind or find its way to my lips. *Karl strangled his wife. No sign of a struggle.* Katiana. Those sweet, innocent children. That monster. The contents of my stomach leapt, and I had to force vomit back down as I broke into a cold sweat.

I was aware of Austin getting out of bed and pulling on clothes, for I knew he'd heard what Paul had said. But I was immobile, my breathing ragged.

'Marley, did you hear me?' Paul was saying. 'Marley?'

'Yes, I—'

'You need to come to the office now. The media are all over it and they've been calling the firm. We're going to have to prepare our response.'

'Where are the children?' I asked.

'They've been taken into child protection.'

'And Karl?'

'Dead. He shot himself afterwards. Apparently, the children saw everything.'

25

I dropped the phone and swayed on the edge of the bed. I heard Paul calling my name again, saw Austin pick up the phone and talk to him. I rode waves of panic, then nausea, still drunk from the night before, but oddly sober. Surrealism collided with reality, like someone had swung a sledgehammer into the back of my head while I was dreaming. Karl may have beaten his wife, but would he have killed her? He couldn't have. I would have known if he was a psychopath.

Austin finished talking to Paul, then dropped to the bed beside me, his eyes wide. 'Jesus.'

I had no words, nothing that could fix what had happened, nothing that would give those children back their mother. Nothing to absolve my part in this. Katiana's death had been entirely preventable, but I'd sealed her fate. I'd given Karl his freedom.

Austin put his arms around me, but I didn't sob. I just leant into him, numb. 'You'll be all right, Marley,' he whispered into my hair.

'I can't breathe.' I clutched at my chest.

'You're okay. Take slow ones.'

'What have I done?'

'You haven't done anything.' He grasped my hands and made me face him, his expression firm. 'This is not your fault. It's just what we do.' He pulled me close again as though he needed to believe it himself. I could feel his entire body trembling against mine. 'It's just what we do.'

Present Day

My only sibling, Anna, lived in Kallista, a town in the Dandenong Ranges, southeast of Melbourne, with her husband and three children. It was quaint and pretty, with mountain forests for backyards and a charming little shopping village, but the pace was slow, the streets far too quiet, and I was always happy to visit and be on my way again, back to the rush and grit of the city.

Fifteen minutes from her house, I stared out the window of the Uber. My beloved Porsche was a heap of twisted metal in a wrecking yard in Melbourne and two weeks on from the accident, I was still getting around in the one thing I'd always loathed. Public transport.

The police had charged me with drink driving, reckless conduct endangering life, running a red light, and speeding. I knew those officers well. Sometimes we drank together after work; I'd even dated one of them briefly and now, suddenly, they were all business.

Paul and Brian had asked me to take leave from work until my court appearance, to get my head in the right space and to, in not so many words, 'dry out'. I'd taken their advice, avoiding wild nights out with friends, favouring quiet evenings at home with Austin and a bottle of Jack Daniels instead.

I leant my head against the back seat and took a deep breath, fighting the familiar craving for a drink that always seemed to stir in my salivary glands. Anna wasn't a drinker, nor was her husband, Tom, so I often brought my own bottle of wine when I visited, setting it down on their table, ignoring Anna's withering look that suggested she would have preferred a gift of flowers or homemade jam instead.

The Uber pulled into her driveway, tiny rocks crunching underneath the tires. Their house was a renovated nineteenth-century cottage that they'd been adding to for what felt like forever. Originally two bedrooms with a modest kitchen and lounge room, it now boasted six bedrooms—each room added after Anna fell pregnant—three bathrooms, split-level renovated kitchen and dining, and a lounge room with its original fireplace. Inside was cosy and Anna-like, with deep plum walls, rich timbers and thick rugs—a place to come home to and sink into its embrace. But somehow, I always felt out of sorts there, like I didn't quite belong. I loved my sister, but our lives were vastly different. I had my city apartment, designer life and sometimes-boyfriend; she had her adoring husband and a home in the mountains filled with children. We were worlds apart and I was the first to admit I only made the trek out to see them when I needed something.

The front door opened, and my three nieces came charging out onto the front verandah, waving excitedly. All under five, all a handful, but when Anna followed, her swollen belly with child number four protruding through her dress, she glowed as if they were no fuss at all.

I quickly assessed my reflection in a compact mirror, checking for bruises that had almost healed and adjusting my bangles to cover my wrists. I thanked the driver and collected my bottle of wine and a large box of sugary, gourmet cupcakes, then climbed out, trying not to wince so obviously at the pain in my fractured ribs.

The girls were upon me in an instant, a gaggle of golden pigtails and skinny little limbs circling my waist. 'Aunty Marley!' they yelled.

'Hello there.' I couldn't avoid their clutches, grimacing through the agony instead, as their arms knocked my ribcage. 'You're all growing too fast.' Mia, Aubrey, and Jasmine were a bundle of energy, so close in age I'd lost track of how old they were. 'I have cupcakes for you.'

I bent and opened the lid of the box for them to see. Chocolate and vanilla cupcakes covered with icing and sprinkles were met with oohs and ahs.

'We don't really load them up on sugar like that,' Anna said, stepping down from the porch and waddling to the car, her hands resting on her stomach. 'Those cupcakes look like they could give an adult a toothache.'

'Yes, but I rarely see them,' I said, closing the lid. 'It's a special occasion.'

'Then maybe you should visit more.' She gave me a stiff smile and took the box of cupcakes. 'They can have one after lunch. How was the drive?' She did a double take at the Uber reversing out of the driveway. 'Where's your car?'

'In for a service.' I hurriedly handed her the bottle of wine. 'This is for you.'

She accepted it before glancing at her stomach, her lips pursed. 'How thoughtful. You shouldn't have.'

I grimaced. The last time I'd seen Anna, she hadn't been so obviously pregnant, and the offer of wine hadn't seemed so stark. 'Sorry. Next time I'll bring something you can actually enjoy.'

'All we want is to see you more.' She gave me a pointed look before turning to waddle back towards the house.

'You can visit me too, you know,' I said, as I fell into step beside her.

'I know. But it's harder for me to get into the city as big as I am now and with three girls in tow. And your apartment is hardly child-proof. Besides, it's easier for you to visit us. You have more time on your hands.'

And there it was. The assumption made of all single, childless women. If you didn't have children, you must have all the time in the world, for a woman's life couldn't possibly be full if it weren't bursting at the seams with kids.

'I hope you're hungry,' Anna said. 'Tom's cooking up a storm.'

I followed her into the house, my nieces tearing past us down the hall towards the television in the family room, their footsteps thunderous on the polished timber floors. The house smelt comfortingly, as it always did, of rose-scented oil and baking, and in the colder months, smoke from the lit fireplace in the lounge room.

My brother-in-law, Tom, was at the kitchen bench chopping potatoes and pumpkin on a board, wearing an apron. He looked up and smiled when we entered. He was ten years older than Anna, his temples peppered with the first hints of grey. He had kind eyes and a temperament to match. I couldn't think of a nicer person for my younger sister.

'Hey, stranger.' He set the knife down, wiped his hands on his apron and ventured around the side of the bench to kiss my cheek. 'It's been a while. Did you come alone?'

'Yes, just me.'

'You didn't bring Austin?' Anna's eyes challenged me.

I lifted my chin. 'No. I didn't ask him.'

'Can't say I'm upset,' she said. 'He's a bit obnoxious for my liking.'

'He's a lawyer. We're all obnoxious.'

'He's not good for you.' She shrugged. 'But anyway, it's your choice.'

Tom gave me a contrite smile and patted my arm. 'We're just glad you're here.'

'Something smells nice.' I changed the subject, slipping out of my coat and setting my handbag down on the floor. I slid onto a stool at the bench.

'Roast lamb and vegetables,' he said.

'My feet are so swollen these days, I can't stand and cook for too long,' Anna explained ruefully. 'Tom does most of the cooking now.'

'This pregnancy has been harder than the others,' Tom said. 'The baby is heavy and sits lower. Anna has her hands full all day with the girls while I'm at work. Cooking's the least I can do.'

Something fond passed between them as Tom placed his hand gently on Anna's stomach and she smiled adoringly at him. I looked away, feeling like an intruder in their private moment. I loved my life, the freedom and simplicity of it, but I'd be lying if I said I didn't yearn, just a little, for what they had, the companionship and intimacy of a soul mate, the warmth and familiarity of someone to come home to. The love and stability of a forever partner.

'So, what do we have here?' Tom pointed at the wine bottle.

'A present from Marley.' Anna gave him a bemused smile as she set the bottle down on the bench, along with the cupcakes.

'Nice.' He studied the label as though he were an experienced connoisseur. 'I'll have a small glass with you, Marls.'

'Shall we open it now, then?' I was already fidgety from the lack of alcohol in my system combined with the reason I'd come to see them today. I wasn't looking forward to the conversation we would inevitably have.

Anna frowned while Tom looked surprised, but he quickly hid it, ducking back around the bench to the kitchen cupboards. 'Ah, okay, sure. Let's have a glass before lunch.' He reached into a cupboard for two wine glasses and set them down in front of me.

I poured the wine, a three-hundred-dollar merlot from Margaret River, knowing they'd never appreciate the value in such a drop. I felt their eyes on me, hoping they wouldn't see the tremor in my hands that usually preceded a stretch of hours without a drink. And I hadn't had one since breakfast. Normally I would have packed a few pre-mixed bottles of gin and soda in my bag for the journey, but I hadn't wanted Anna to smell alcohol on my breath.

'Cheers,' Tom said, picking up his glass and holding it high. 'To family.'

'To family,' I echoed, knocking back a gulp.

Anna slid heavily onto the stool beside me. She shifted several times trying to get comfortable. 'The kicking is relentless.'

I glanced at her stomach. 'Will this be the last?'

She shrugged and smiled at Tom. 'Maybe. We'll see.'

I chuckled and shook my head. 'How did I miss the baby gene? You must have got my dose.'

Anna chuckled.

'You look uncomfortable,' I said. 'Nothing about pregnancy could entice me to want to have a child.'

'But it's different when you're growing your own baby in there.' Her expression softened. 'I can't explain it. Only that you have to be a mum to understand. One day I hope you get to experience it.'

I took another sip of my wine and thought about the pregnant woman I'd hit with my Porsche, how I'd almost extinguished that experience for her. I knew my face had paled for Anna was staring at me.

'What brings you out here?' she asked. 'I was surprised you wanted to visit, to be honest.'

I glanced at her, then at Tom, acutely aware that they were both watching me. I swallowed another gulp of wine, pouring myself a second glass, knowing that the conversation I'd been dreading was about to happen. 'I had a car accident.'

Anna's eyes narrowed. 'A car accident? Is that why you caught an

Uber all the way here?'

'Yes.'

She stared at me and I wasn't sure if she was concerned or angry. 'When did it happen?'

'One night after work. A couple of weeks ago.'

'Are you okay?'

'I'm fine. Two fractured ribs and some cuts and bruises. It was...' I squirmed. 'It was my fault.'

Anna pulled her lips into a thin line. 'Were you drunk?'

I nodded, feeling as small as a naughty child being berated by her mother.

Her frown deepened. 'Was anyone else involved?'

This was the bit she wasn't going to like. 'Yes. I ran a red light and collided with another car. Inside was a man and his pregnant wife.'

Her sharp intake of breath was audible as her hands flew to her stomach.

'They're both okay,' I said quickly. 'So is their unborn child. They've been released from the hospital.'

Anna's hand shot across the bench to the wine bottle. She snatched it up, slid off the stool quicker than any heavily pregnant woman should and walked to the bin, throwing it in with such vehemence, I thought she'd broken it. Her face was so red that Tom put his glass down and pushed it away too.

'Let me get this straight,' she said, her body trembling with barely concealed anger. 'You got behind the wheel drunk, sped through a red light and hit the car of a pregnant woman and her husband?'

'Technically they hit me.' I grimaced at her expression. 'But yes, that's the size of it.'

Anna stared at me. 'What the hell is wrong with you?'

I recoiled. 'It was an accident.'

'An *accident*?'

'Love,' Tom said, 'calm down.'

'This is classic Marley!' she cried, throwing her hands up. 'Only thinking of herself.' She turned to me again. 'Were you so selfish you couldn't catch a taxi home? Was your apartment so far you couldn't afford it? No, you had to climb behind the wheel rotten drunk and almost kill a woman and her unborn baby.'

'I had paperwork in the car, my laptop. I couldn't leave it in the city,' I argued feebly. She was right of course. I *was* selfish.

Anna put her hands on her hips and bent slightly, taking deep gulps of air. When she straightened, her look of disapproval was wounding. 'I'm pregnant, Marley. Doesn't that mean anything to you when you do these stupid things? Do you not think, what if I get behind the wheel drunk and kill a family, just like my sister's? Does that never enter your mind?'

I didn't want to tell her it didn't. That my head was so cluttered with other things that I rarely considered anyone else. I hung my head shamefully, staring at the few drops of wine left in my glass, wondering how on earth I was going to get the bottle back out of the bin without infuriating her.

'So, is that why you're here? To tell us you had an accident?' she asked.

'Actually,' if the stool could have swallowed me whole, I'd have let it, 'I need a character reference. It's for court, to assist with a more favourable sentence.'

Anna stared at me dumbfounded, her mouth gaping open. 'I haven't seen you in months and you come knocking for a character reference?'

I shrugged and nodded.

'Does Dad know about this?'

'Yes. I called him the day of the accident.'

She scoffed. 'So as usual I'm the last to know.' She held up her hand to stop me from saying any more. 'Don't talk. I can't even look at you right now.' She turned and stormed out of the kitchen.

Tom cleared his throat. He was always the diplomatic one, jumping to my defence when I didn't deserve it, but this time, there was no mistaking the disappointment in his eyes. I felt even worse than I could have possibly imagined.

'I'll go after her,' he said, pushing the vegetables aside.

'No, let me,' I said, climbing off the stool and reaching for my coat. 'I'm the one she needs to yell at.'

'Just try not to get her too worked up,' he said. 'We're not ready for this baby to come yet.'

I cringed apologetically, but he didn't notice. He'd already returned to the vegetables, a worried, distracted look on his face.

Chapter 6

I found Anna sitting outside on the back step in the cold. Her stomach was so large that she was forced to sit with her legs apart, leaning back on her hands.

'Are you going to be able to get up again?' I asked, attempting a joke, something to break the ice. She was livid and I'd made her feel that way, as though her life choices were insignificant, and I had little respect for them. When she didn't answer, I tried a different approach. 'Are you cold? I can get you a coat.'

'I'm fine,' she murmured.

I lowered myself onto the step beside her, feeling worse when I saw her tears and how she'd attempted to wipe them away, leaving streaks through her makeup.

'You're so like Dad,' she said, taking a small, shaky breath. 'He loves a drink. Grandad too. You all have that same thirst for the bottle.' She glanced at me. 'When was the last time you visited Dad?'

I had to stretch my mind back, which obviously meant it had been too long. 'The anniversary of Mum's death.'

'Which one?'

I squirmed with shame.

'Did you know, I visit him on the third weekend of every month, without fail? Tom and I pack the kids up and we drive over. We spend the whole day with him.'

'I didn't know that,' I said.

34

'I've done everything right in life. I'm still doing it,' she said wryly. 'I married, I gave him plenty of grandchildren, I've never caused him or Mum any grief. I visit Dad every bloody month and still, it's not enough. You're the golden child, with your seedy lifestyle and drinking problem and God knows what else.' She swiped at her cheeks as fresh tears spilled onto them.

I didn't know what to say because there was truth in it. I'd never had to make the same effort Anna had. I was the firstborn and so like my father that it had somehow elevated me to favourite status. It wasn't until now, watching my sister, that I realised how aware of it she was and how it hurt.

'My hormones are crazy,' she said, shaking her head. 'I'm sorry. Pay no attention to me.'

'Dad doesn't favour me over you,' I said weakly, the attempt to make her feel better falling short.

'Of course he does!' she replied, getting upset again. 'Grandad was a criminal lawyer. Dad was a criminal lawyer. You became a criminal lawyer. I just got married and had a bunch of kids. Nothing too exciting.' Her voice turned cynical. 'Even after what happened to that poor woman, Dad still couldn't be disappointed in you. Oh, because you were just doing your job, right?' She scoffed. 'Why did you even defend that guy? Why didn't you let him go to jail?'

I bit my bottom lip and turned away, my soul so full of regret, I couldn't look at her. They were questions I asked myself every day.

Why did you?

How could you?

'You could have worked that case a hundred different ways. You could have persuaded him to plead guilty. Instead, you gave him his freedom. Freedom he didn't deserve.'

'I did try! I wanted him to plead guilty.'

'You didn't try hard enough.' She took a deep, steadying breath. 'You're drinking more, aren't you, because of what happened to her?'

I gave an imperceptible nod, even though I rarely acknowledged it myself.

'Are you doing other things? Drugs, prescription or otherwise?'

'No,' I lied.

'Well, I don't believe you. You have a problem, Marley, and I've been aware of it for some time. I'm not just your stupid baby sister who keeps pushing out kids. I have eyes and a brain, and I can see what's happening to you, how much weight you've lost, how we don't hear from you anymore. And frankly, I'm sick and tired of being your mother. You're the eldest. You should be looking out for me, not the other way around.'

Once again, there was irritating truth to her words and I closed my eyes to them, not wanting to hear. Because when someone else sees you for what you are, a woman who's beautiful and flawless on the outside but can barely hold it together on the inside, a little of that bravado cracks.

'So, you need a character reference from me?' Anna said.

'Yes, please. Austin's putting my case together. I have court next week.'

'I'll write it for you if you do one thing.' She turned her piercing green gaze on me, eyes that were so like mine. 'I want you to go to rehab.'

I choked on my saliva. '*Rehab*? What for?'

'Because you're an alcoholic and you need help.'

I shook my head vehemently. 'I don't need rehab.'

'You do.'

'You're making this out to be bigger than it is,' I argued. 'I like a drink every now and again. Big deal. Who doesn't?'

'It's more than a drink every now and again, Marley. You have a problem. You nearly killed a couple and their unborn child. If you want a character reference from me, you're going to have to enter a clinic.'

I went from feeling sorry for her to despising her. Austin had told me in no uncertain terms to come home with one. That my whole case rested on the character testimony of an upstanding citizen, like my family-orientated, pregnant sister. It would strengthen our defence, demonstrate that family and children were a priority for me and that I was remorseful for my error of judgement. But rehab for a character reference?

'No way,' I said, my chest tightening at the thought. 'Rehab would destroy my career. Those inpatient programs can last months.'

'I'm sure the criminals you defend can find someone else to tell their excuses to.'

I felt my frustration boil over again. 'You don't even know what you're talking about!'

She sighed, running her hand through her yellow curls. 'Marley, you need to do *something*. Go to AA meetings then. I want you to make a good go of getting clean or I won't support you.'

'Those programs don't work if you're still surrounded by temptation.' And I was no fool. Austin and my friends were the worst temptations of all, but the thought of giving them up was as overwhelming as drying out.

'Then go away for a couple of weeks to get your head in the right place. Start the process of withdrawing so you can come back, attend the meetings and give yourself the best possible chance.'

I couldn't believe I was having this conversation with her. Where would I go? Where could I possibly outrun impulse?

She fell silent, chewing her bottom lip with a pensive expression. 'I saw a documentary on television the other night about an island where people are so healthy, they live to well over a hundred.'

I smirked. 'Okay.'

'I'm serious. They follow a mostly plant-based diet—fruits, vegetables, grains, and legumes, with small amounts of chicken, fish and red wine.'

'Red wine!' I exclaimed, pouncing on the words. 'See, even the healthy people are drinking.'

'They drink in moderation, Marley, as part of a healthy diet,' she said. 'The average life expectancy is a hundred and five there. They are literally the healthiest people on the planet. Extremely low rates of cancer, heart disease and stroke, and almost no dementia. They exercise, eat well, grow their food and enjoy a long life.'

'And how does any of that help me?'

'You could go there, rent a house for a couple of weeks and adopt a clean lifestyle. Eat well and enjoy nature. Get fresh air into your body and get the toxins out. Stay away from alcohol and drugs, then come back and do the AA meetings.' She was talking quickly, looking at me with such hope that my anger at her self-righteousness began to ebb.

'You want me to give up drinking in a place that drinks red wine?'

'They have restaurants and shops there. Alcohol on the island is going to be inevitable, but it won't be like Melbourne, where you'll find a pub on every corner. It will be easier to manage. And since you won't go to a clinic, I don't see what other choice you have. You'll just have to make it work.'

I sighed. I couldn't go to a place in the middle of nowhere and eat organically and pray all my problems would magically disappear. If I were going to do something about my life, I would need a complete overhaul, to drastically detox every aspect and not just spend a couple of weeks on an island eating vegetables and avoiding red wine. And because an overhaul felt too mind-boggling and my body was already crying out for its next drink, I'd as good as dismissed the idea.

If it wasn't for the character reference.

'So?' Anna asked, still looking at me.

'You're assuming the judge won't send me to jail.'

'If that's the case, so be it. But if you do walk free, I want you to go.'

Her insistence only frustrated me more, but what choice did I have? 'Fine. If I agree to go to this island, you'll write me the reference?'

'Yes.'

'A good one?'

'Glowing.'

Tom appeared at the back door, wiping his hands on a tea towel. 'Everything all right out here?'

Anna smiled up at him. 'Everything's fine. Come help me up.'

Tom flicked the towel over his shoulder and trotted down the steps, positioning himself in front of Anna and helping her to her feet.

She groaned but eventually lifted.

'The girls have eaten lunch and ours is on the table,' he said.

Anna kissed him. 'What would I do without you, my love?'

They walked hand in hand back into the house and I followed them, feeling more sober and alone than I had in a long time.

***

Lunch was torturous. Usually when I came to visit, the conversation was livelier. There would be an open bottle of wine on the table that I'd help myself generously to, and I'd talk politics or law with Tom while my sister listened quietly. That day, I was the one listening as they talked, sulking for my expensive merlot, which was still in the bin, and the ultimatum my sister had delivered on the back step.

Anna, in contrast, was happier than I'd seen her all day. She chirped

38

cheerily about schools for the girls and Aubrey's ballet class and the vegetable garden she wanted to start. Tom ate his lunch with a puzzled expression, watching on cautiously at this odd reversal of roles.

Before I left to go home, I spent time with my nieces. The eldest, Mia, led the way, taking me on a guided tour of all their bedrooms, showing me their collection of dolls and ballet outfits and books. I adored the girls and loved being with them, but my skin was beginning to crawl and all I wanted to do was get back to Melbourne where I could have a few drinks and not be judged for it. Where I could spend the remainder of the day finishing the bottle of vodka I'd opened that morning.

I was irritable by the time Anna walked me out to wait for the Uber.

'I googled that island while you were with the girls,' she said as soon as we were alone on the driveway.

'You're actually serious about this?' I shook my head as the Uber pulled in. 'You won't write me a character reference unless I go to this place?'

'That's right,' she said, shooting me a challenging look.

'Jesus Christ, Anna!'

'It's up to you, Marley. That's my condition.'

I sighed loud enough for her to know I was truly annoyed. 'Fine. What's it called?'

'White Cedar Island. It's east of the Canadian mainland, in the North Atlantic Ocean. It's remote. I mean, further east than Nova Scotia. Out in the middle of the sea.'

'Oh, wonderful.'

She grabbed my hands and held fast to them. 'You need this, Marley, because if you stay on the path you're on, you're going to hurt someone or yourself. And I can't have someone like that in the girls' lives.'

I recoiled. 'What's that supposed to mean?'

'It means I'll cut you out if I have to, to keep them safe.'

My mouth fell open, dumbfounded. 'I'm not dangerous, for Christ's sake.'

'No, but you make stupid decisions when you drink.'

This was no longer about the character reference. She would prevent me from seeing the girls, and while I wasn't in their lives often, the thought of the few visits I made being reduced to nothing cut deeply.

I watched the Uber as he rolled to a stop beside us. 'How are we going to do this? If I book the plane ticket, will that make you happy?'

'As soon as you've booked a ticket and a place to stay on the island, I'll email the reference to you.'

I rolled my eyes.

'But you have to stay a minimum of two weeks. No getting there, turning around and coming straight back or I'll never speak to you again. And I want you to have an AA meeting lined up as soon as you land back here.'

'It just gets better,' I muttered. 'You know I'll probably get fired for taking more time off work.'

'You never take time off. You have loads of annual leave. They can't fire you for that.'

'Whatever.'

She touched my arm gently, a maternal look on her face. I shook her off, then climbed into the Uber and put my seatbelt on. As we reversed out of her driveway, she waved at me, but I ignored her. I childishly turned the other way, anxious to get back to Melbourne, where a whole shelf of liquor awaited in my pantry.

***

Later that night, balancing my laptop and a bowl of Pad Thai from the downstairs noodle shop on my lap, I searched for White Cedar Island on the web. I found the documentary Anna had referred to and watched the first five minutes of it. It was a small island east of Nova Scotia, Canada, in the North Atlantic Ocean. It had a population of two thousand people and was dotted with a village and small houses cut into rugged, forested hillsides. It was beautiful and wild and must have had something in the water, for the people there were known to live well past a century.

With extraordinary vitality and the lowest cases of common diseases, it was considered one of the healthiest places on Earth. A blue zone. Years earlier, scientists had carried out a study on blue zone locations, their objective to prove whether genetics or lifestyle was the key contributor in those remarkably healthy people. Studies of the hearts, lungs and brains of one-hundred-year-old inhabitants discovered they were functioning as well as those of an eighty-year-old, and that it was attributed almost solely to their lifestyle and diet.

I slurped on my puddle of oily Pad Thai and sipped my wine, staring at the screen. Maybe Anna was right and time away would be good for me, but I wasn't convinced this was the answer to my problems. At times, I wasn't convinced I even had any problems, and until I could decide for sure, I couldn't fix them. I didn't want to fix them.

My mobile on the lounge beside me rang and I picked it up, glancing at the screen. It was Austin. 'Hey.'

'Hey.' His voice was drowned out by music and conversation. 'Did you get back from hick town okay?'

'The Dandenong Ranges is hardly hick town,' I replied, transferring my laptop to the coffee table.

'Anywhere outside of Melbourne is hick town.'

I chuckled. Anna was right. He *was* obnoxious.

'Did you get the character reference?'

'Not yet, but she's preparing it. On one condition.'

'What's that?'

I didn't need to be in the same room to know what his expression would look like when I told him. 'That I go to rehab.'

He gave a derisive snort that I could easily hear over the music. '*Rehab?*'

'Well, not rehab, per se. She wants me to go away for a couple of weeks to a remote island and detox.'

'You're kidding, right?'

'I wish I were.'

There was disbelieving silence on the line, then, 'If you're granted conditional release, you can do a driving course or an outpatient program at worst. You don't have to relocate to an island in the middle of nowhere.'

'I know that. But she won't give me the character reference unless I book the plane ticket and a place to stay. If I'm free to go after all this, I'll go to the island.'

This time he scoffed. 'You can't be serious. She does know this will kill your chance of ever working with Paul and Brian again, right? They've only just started considering you for partner again after the Wagner case.'

'I'll speak to them.'

'Just say you'll go, get the character reference off her, then back out.'

'That's a rotten thing to do.'

'Not really.'

'She'll never talk to me again.'

'She'll get over it. Who does she think she is, anyway?' He sounded as affronted as I'd felt earlier. I understood his apprehension, the threat of our happy, co-dependant bubble bursting. But in those hours since I'd left Anna's, my anger had subsided. Now I just felt lost and defeated, like I'd felt after the accident, spiralling towards rock bottom, and riding a roller coaster of emotions on the way down.

'Are you still there?' he asked.

I was brought back to the call, my Pad Thai and wine still on my lap. 'I'm here.'

'What are you doing right now?'

'Eating dinner.'

'Come to Halo Bar. Everyone's asking for you.'

I glanced at the clock. It was eight on a Saturday night and I was sitting in my pyjamas on the lounge. I had spent few nights like this in my adult life. 'I don't know. I'm not sure it's a good idea.'

'I'll get you home safely.'

'It's not that. I'm still in pain.'

'You haven't been out since the accident.'

'And your point is?'

He sighed his frustration. 'Fine. Can I drop around later, then?'

I smiled. Obnoxious and as wrong for me as he was, he was the only person who understood me, all my flaws and weaknesses, our minds working in the same way. I wanted to see him, craved his nearness and his arms around me. Loneliness was a crushing thing and I'd been there before. Had felt the weight of it as I'd lay on the cold tiles of my bathroom floor wishing my days would end after Katiana died. I didn't want to be swallowed by it tonight. 'Yes, please,' I said. 'Whenever you can.'

'I'll be there after midnight.'

And I would lie awake until he got there, trying to keep my anxious thoughts at bay.

Chapter 7

I'd always been an overachiever. University had been less about studying and more about socialising. Excellent grades had come naturally to me and I'd never had to try as hard as my peers. Perhaps that was part of the problem—I was egotistical, gifted with a high IQ and I had the pulse of the law pumping through my veins, making me the apple of my father's eye, to the torment of Anna.

So when I called her the morning after our lunch to tell her I'd rented a small cabin on White Cedar Island, her happiness felt like the slap in the face she'd been waiting all these years to deliver.

'You sound pleased,' I said sourly. 'I guess you got what you wanted.'

'I'm not doing this to punish you.' Her voice was sincere, which only irritated me more. 'I'm doing this because you're my sister and I love you. I want you to live a long and healthy life.'

'It feels like you're getting back at me for something.'

She snorted. 'Don't be ridiculous. For someone so smart you can be really dumb.'

We ended the call and, a few minutes later, the character reference for my court appearance dropped into my inbox with a resounding ting.

The car accident had halted my world. I wasn't permitted back at the firm until after my court hearing and, to idle the hours away, I spent my days inside drinking or walking along the beach outside my apartment. I seemed to float with no structure or routine, time blurring into late nights and later mornings.

I'd hoped in this time to have gained perspective, to catch up on sleep and get my head in the right space, but old demons had a way of haunting quiet spaces and more often than not, I was driven back to the liquor shelf in my pantry, where I could drown out the past.

On some level, I knew I needed change and Anna's suggestion was a sensible one. On the other hand, when I was consumed with craving or needed to chase the ghosts away, I wondered how on earth I was going to survive two weeks on that island without a drop of alcohol.

***

We'd heard the day before that the magistrate presiding over my case was known for his leniency. It was the news I'd hoped for and Austin was buoyant when we met at the courthouse on the morning of the hearing.

'I can't believe we've got Halliday,' he said, his eyes wide with relief. 'I thought for certain we'd get Morag.'

I was warmed by his optimism and grateful for his support, but the nerves in my stomach weren't so easily quelled. By the time we were seated in the courtroom, I was sweating in my demure, fifteen-hundred-dollar Chanel suit, clenching and unclenching my hands. Despite having spent hours in that room defending clients, the shoe was on the other foot now and it was hard to feel anything but vulnerable.

The husband and wife I'd collided with were seated in the gallery and, on several occasions, attempted to catch my eye. I caught them in my peripheral vision but refused to meet their stares, stealing surreptitious glances instead when their focus had shifted to the magistrate.

They were younger than I remembered. Kristy Cameron was pretty with long, brown hair and freckles. She was still in the later stages of pregnancy, huddled close to her husband, with his arm protectively around her. I wasn't surprised to see them there, hoping for a just sentence, a harsh penalty to fit my crime, but whether they would get it was a different story. I may have been nervous, but Austin and I were defence solicitors. If anyone knew how to exploit the legal system, it was us.

***

'It couldn't have gone any better.' Austin clinked his beer bottle against mine and settled onto the bar stool with a wide grin.

We'd left the court with a victory, to the disbelief of the Camerons, who'd looked far from pleased. Because it was my first offence, I was found guilty without conviction, my driver's licence suspended for six months and an infringement notice issued that would hardly leave a dent in my bank account. I wasn't required to complete a driving course or enter a rehabilitation program, just a two-year good behaviour bond and my practising certificate was safe from deregistration by The Law Society.

I'm certain the Camerons had hoped for something more dramatic, like handcuffs and jail time, and maybe that's what I deserved, but I couldn't help feeling relieved by the outcome.

I took a large sip of my beer. 'The Camerons looked devastated. I hope they're okay.'

'Who cares? Would you rather have been sentenced to rehab or jail?' He slid out of his suit jacket and loosened his tie.

'Of course not. I just don't think there were any winners today.'

'*We* were the winners,' he said. 'And that character reference your sister wrote, brilliant! Everything just fell into place.'

I played with the label on my beer bottle, trying to work up the courage to tell him what I'd been avoiding all morning. Finally, I blurted it. 'I'm going away.'

His eyes narrowed as he stared at me. 'To that place? Not this again, Marley.'

'I made a promise to Anna and I'm going.'

'When?'

'Tomorrow morning. My flight is at eleven.'

'Are you kidding?' He scowled like a child.

'It's just for two weeks,' I added quickly, 'to get her off my back. I've already told Paul and Brian. They weren't thrilled, but they agreed I've had a heavy caseload the past couple of years and I've worked myself into the ground. And the Wagners, well... I never took time off after that. A couple of weeks can't hurt, right? And I do have a lot of leave to use.' I was babbling because he was still looking at me as if I'd grown horns.

'I just don't see the point,' he said with a huff. 'No one's forcing you to go to rehab. Why would you go?'

'This isn't rehab. And I'm going because Anna wrote me the reference. I won't go back on my word.'

'She overreacted. Tell her you changed your mind. She'll get over it.'

'I can't do that.'

He sank back into the stool and ran a hand through his hair with a frustrated sigh. 'You've been handed the Holy Grail of sentences and now you're throwing it back in my face. Why did I bother working so hard on this?'

I leant forward and took his hands in mine. He was taking this personally, as though I didn't appreciate his efforts or was choosing Anna over him. We were a team and our lives had been so thoroughly entwined since we'd left university, that I wasn't sure where mine ended and his began. We were each other's oxygen and now, I was tugging on the lifeline.

'Come with me,' I said.

He laughed, although it sounded hollow. 'Yeah, right. Because Paul and Brian would allow that.'

'Just for a week. It won't be so terrible if we're there together.'

He glanced at me; one eyebrow raised. 'Where is this place, anyway?'

'It's an island east of Canada, in the North Atlantic Ocean. It's called White Cedar.'

'Do they have resorts there? Bars, nightclubs, beach parties?'

I didn't want to tell him it was one of the healthiest places on Earth. 'Not sure.'

'Sounds boring. We should do Bali instead.' He let out a long breath to emphasise his misery. 'This is screwed up.'

The misery was contagious, for I was starting to feel it too. I'd already spent weeks indoors, trying to behave, and White Cedar felt like another attack on my existence, an attempt to wrench my freedom away.

'Does your dad know you're going?'

'I spoke to him last night. He thinks Anna's being a bit over the top but isn't entirely opposed to the idea. The quicker I go, the quicker I can come back.' I forced a smile. 'And it doesn't mean we can't celebrate tonight.'

He perked up a little after that as we finished our beers and he left to go back to the office. I went home and packed for the trip, hurling clothes begrudgingly into my suitcase, cursing my sister's name with every garment I threw in. Pride was the only thing preventing me from reneging on my promise, because I didn't want to give her the satisfaction of being right, that I couldn't stop drinking any time I wanted to. I was in control. I would go to that island, stay dry for two weeks, prove her wrong, then come back and live my life however I pleased.

Later that night, Austin met me at my apartment, and we caught a cab to a nightclub in the city. As the drinks went down, I shrugged off the Camerons and embraced our win in the courtroom. I was free; I'd dodged a bullet. I was invincible again.

With Austin by my side, we got messy. We drank, snorted every conceivable thing up our noses and stumbled back to my apartment as the sun rose over Melbourne. If my saintly sister was going to guilt-trip me into spending two weeks on an island in the middle of nowhere, I wasn't going without a bang.

Chapter 8

A flight from Melbourne to Nova Scotia was not entirely straightforward. I had a layover in Auckland, which lasted four hours, followed by another in San Francisco, then Vancouver, before the plane finally crossed the Canadian mainland to arrive at Halifax Stanfield International Airport in Nova Scotia.

Shortly after leaving Melbourne and somewhere over the Tasman Sea, I'd started to feel the effects of my poor decision to party the night before. I came down with a vengeance, twitching and dozing in my business-class seat with the bleary-eyed, gaunt look of someone who hadn't slept in days. My dreams were warped, darting rapidly beneath my eyelids, and I was hovering somewhere on the edge of drug-fuelled oblivion, neither asleep nor awake.

I gave Anna's meddling the evil eye for the entire thirty-six-hour trip. If it weren't for her, I'd be tucked in my bed, sleeping off a fun night, Austin beside me, the shades drawn tight to block out the sun until we could emerge under the cover of darkness again like night creatures. And while I was grateful for the reference she'd written for me, and the victory it had secured, my body was beat, and my brain was too saturated with the substances I'd consumed the night before to feel anything but irritated.

Nova Scotia was pleasantly warm when we touched down and the summer's day was bright as I disembarked. Sleep had been gracious on the last leg of the journey and, before landing, I'd woken mildly refreshed, quickly knocking back three vodkas in succession, something to place under my belt before I started the next two weeks. I refused to leave the plane entirely sober.

Outside the airport, near the cab terminal, I set down my luggage and consulted the notes I'd made. If nothing else, I was organised. I knew a cab could transport me to Halifax Harbour in twenty-five minutes where I would need to catch the boat to White Cedar from one of the wharves. The journey from there to the island took one hour and ten minutes, and boats departed three times a week. I knew this because the woman I rented the cabin from, Madame Noelle Bisset, had sent me the instructions on how to get there.

Look for a green and white boat carrying supplies to White Cedar, she had written in her email. *The gentleman you want to find is Harry. Sails on Monday, Wednesday, and Saturday.*

I sighed. It wasn't a lot to go on, but I wasn't concerned. It was Saturday and if I'd already missed the boat, I'd reserve a hotel room nearby, wait out the days until I found Harry, then sail out with him. Halifax Harbour was brimming with energy when I got there, vibrant bars and restaurants livening up the waterfront, a hedonistic nightlife lying in wait, and I decided there could be no harm at all in not finding Harry for a day or two.

I asked the cab driver where the supply boat for White Cedar left from and he dropped me at precisely the correct wharf. Before I opened the cab door, I saw the green and white boat bobbing on the water, a small craft that had seen better days. Green paint flaked from its side and its name was almost worn from the hull, *Pour Toujours*.

I paid the driver and collected my suitcase, which he'd set down on the sidewalk, tugging it behind me as I made my way towards the wharf. The sun was glaring off the water, too bright for my sensitive eyes, and I squinted against it from behind my sunglasses.

A weathered man with a shock of white hair and a white beard, reminding me of Father Christmas, was inside the boat, bent over, taking inventory of cargo.

'Hello,' I called out as I approached. 'Are you Harry?'

'The only Harry around here,' he replied gruffly, not glancing at me.

'I'm heading to White Cedar Island,' I said. 'A woman there, Noelle Bisset, said I could catch a ride with you on one of your supply runs.'

Harry finally looked up and studied me, eyes travelling from my suitcase to my expensive sunglasses and designer trainers. 'You're not from around here. How do you know Noelle?'

'I'm renting a cabin from her. Have you already been out there today?' I held my breath, hoping he'd say yes.

He returned his gaze to the cargo. 'Not yet. I'm leaving here at two. You can wait in that bar over there and have lunch.' Without lifting his eyes, he pointed to an establishment next door called The Sea Merchant. 'When you see me wave, you get back down here. I'll leave on time with or without you.'

Any hope of staying in Halifax drained and I begrudgingly thanked him, tugging my suitcase back towards the sidewalk and The Sea Merchant. There was a lunch crowd when I got there, but a couple were vacating a table on the deck, overlooking the port, so I claimed it, sliding into a chair where I could keep an eye on Harry.

I ordered a steak and two beers and stared out across the water. Halifax Harbour was beautiful, with boats of all sizes coming and going. The boardwalk below heaved with summer visitors, seagulls wheeling through the air, eyeing cups of hot fries and sticks of cotton candy.

Austin filled my thoughts and I wondered what he was doing. It was one am Sunday morning back home and I had no doubt he'd be out. Maybe at Halo Bar, maybe somewhere else. I closed my eyes and inhaled a wave of salty air, as homesickness rushed over me.

I'd been entirely flippant about coming, determined to prove to Anna that while I may have lost my way, I didn't have a problem. I could stop drinking any time I liked. But as I drained those beers and realised they could well be the last I had for two weeks, the familiar crawl of anxiety began to slip under my skin.

I wasn't sure what awaited me on White Cedar Island, only that craving was an insidious beast. It would come, as it had before; I'd be a fool to think it wouldn't. And while I hated admitting it to anyone—not Austin or Anna, or even myself—I was worried what the long, lonely nights on this island would bring. What would happen to my body and mind if I couldn't douse my thirst with a drink, couldn't block out the voices that took up residence in my mind?

I had six Xanax in my suitcase to get me through the first nights; the only amount I could bring without arousing the suspicions of customs officials, but beyond that, I had only my will power. And I wasn't sure how far that was going to get me.

***

A few minutes to two, Harry waved at me from down on the boat. With the bill already paid and another four beers away, I quickly snatched up my suitcase and hurried off the deck of The Sea Merchant and down to the wharf to meet him. I was sufficiently drunk, feeling so good I could have sailed to the Arctic.

He took my suitcase and heaved it onto the boat with a grunt, then offered me his hand so I could climb in too. I manoeuvred past the boxes and crates of supplies and settled in the cabin with him.

The boat pitched and groaned with the rising tide. I gripped the back of the seat, aware that we hadn't left the wharf yet and I was already hanging on.

'Don't mind this old lady,' Harry said. 'She looks old but she's seaworthy enough.'

'What does her name mean?' I asked.

'*Pour Toujours*?' He started the engine, setting it into reverse and backing us away from the wharf. 'It means "forever" in French.'

The boat shuddered as Harry turned us towards the mouth of the harbour.

'Forever?'

'It's an ode to White Cedar and the people there,' he said.

I nodded as he accelerated, the wind whipping around the cabin, sending my long hair flying. I smoothed it down, holding fast to it. 'And all this cargo? Is it for the people on the island?' I asked above the noise.

'Yep,' he said, concentrating on steering. 'Mostly medical supplies, clothes, stationery for the school, any purchases that the residents order online. They have their own shops of course—a village square— but sometimes they like to buy from the mainland.'

'How about food?'

'I deliver the essentials,' he said. 'Tea, coffee, milk, flour, also the mail, those kinds of things. Then there's a major air delivery every month to bring bulk supplies for their stores. A lot of the folk grow their food too. They're a self-sustaining community.'

We sailed around McNabs Island and past Eastern Passage, out into the vast North Atlantic Ocean where there was nothing but endless blue. The waves were choppier there, the air cooler, and the boat pitched and dropped over roiling waves as the mainland grew smaller behind us. I wondered just how far we would travel into deep nothingness, for we still had an hour to go, and we were already in open water.

Harry seemed to read my mind and gave me a curious look. 'It's an odd choice for a girl like you, coming all the way out here.'

'I suppose.'

'It's not a place that tourists visit often. It's too remote; a blue zone, you know.'

'Yes, I read about the zones.'

'They're regions in the world where people thrive into their hundreds. Most blue zones are remote from mainlands—isolated, untouched by western civilisation. It's one of the secrets to their longevity.'

I turned in my seat to glance behind us and the first hints of anxiety nudged at my consciousness. Nova Scotia had shrunk to a tiny smudge on the horizon. A cold finger of panic slid down my spine, making me sweat suddenly.

What was I doing? I couldn't go to that island. I contemplated asking Harry to return the boat to Halifax, but we were well into the trip and he'd think I was crazy. I supposed I could always get there then turn around and come back with him. I wasn't a prisoner; I didn't *have* to stay. I could spend two weeks in Halifax instead, in that lovely harbour with all those bars and restaurants, before flying home. No one need know. A tiny white lie to keep the peace.

But Anna's words reverberated in my ears as loudly as if she were sitting beside me. *No getting there, turning around, and coming straight back or I'll never speak to you again.*

I scowled as I remembered her ultimatums to cut me off if I didn't change my ways. If she ever found out I'd lied to her, it would spell the end of our relationship.

But two weeks on this island without alcohol and my pills, without Austin and all the things I desperately craved? It was an impossible ask, one I was already convinced I couldn't fulfil.

Chapter 9

The beer I'd had at the Sea Merchant fizzled into oblivion long before we reached the island, and I grew even more agitated as I sobered. A speck of land appeared on the horizon, growing larger as we drew closer until we finally reached its shores. Harry navigated the boat into a peaceful bay, hemmed by golden sand that I would have liked to lie on had I not felt so jittery.

'Welcome to White Cedar,' he said, flashing me a proud grin from beneath his bushy beard. 'This is Eternal Bay. The island is full of beaches like this. You'll want to explore them while you're here. The water is as clear as you'll find anywhere in the world.'

'Great,' I muttered.

'See if you can get to a few before summer ends. It's mild now, but the weather will change soon like the flip of a coin.'

I won't be here long enough to experience it, I thought.

'Winter can be brutal,' he went on as though he hadn't noticed my surliness. 'Rough seas, blizzards, icy blasts from the Arctic. It creates fog and heavy swells and a hell of a lot of storms. All that oceanic fury; I wouldn't dare sail in it. Everyone just pretty much bunkers down when that happens.'

'Sounds delightful.'

'But when it's calm, it's one of the most beautiful places on Earth,' he said above the roar of the engine. 'The forests are pristine, full of white cedars and pines. They make an almighty sound when the wind rushes through them. Take the walking track to the other side of the island while you're here. There's a lighthouse and you can see the humpbacks migrate from Bermuda right about this time.'

We approached an old pier jutting out into the water, light waves slapping against its pilings. I could see a few figures standing together talking and a milky-coated Labrador lying on the warm planks. Harry steered the vessel in with ease until it was parked alongside the pier, and he shut off the engine. The men waiting shouted hello to him, then they helped position the ramp so we could disembark.

Harry left the cabin first and I followed, taking my first tentative steps outside. My oversized sunglasses were no match for the fiercely bright sunshine that rained down. Everywhere I looked I saw rugged wilderness and hilly forests and wide-open ocean. There was too much space, too much earth, and my heart clenched with longing for Melbourne's concrete jungle.

I followed Harry down the ramp, my shoes hitting the pier, and the milky Labrador I'd seen earlier climbed to his feet and trotted over to nudge my hand. I gave him a pat, his coat soft and his eyes adoringly large.

'That's Duke,' a voice said.

I turned and found a man standing behind me. He was tall with hair and eyes as rich as the colour of hazelnuts. His arms and legs were tanned from the sun, his shorts and shirt casual, and he wore navy boat shoes. He smiled broadly and I forced a smile back.

'I'm Lachlan.' He stepped forward and stretched out his hand. 'Noelle asked me to collect you and bring you up to her cabin.'

'Marley Kincaid.' I shook it, then readjusted my bangles, slipping my wrists behind my back.

'Ah, an Australian?' he asked.

'From Melbourne.'

'You're a long way from home, Marley from Melbourne.'

I felt like I'd been catapulted to another planet.

'Noelle mentioned you were staying for two weeks. What brings you to the North Atlantic?' he asked. He was friendly, his Canadian accent betraying a hint of French. He reached for my suitcase as Harry rolled it down the ramp.

I didn't answer. My head was on the verge of exploding and I was bone tired. I'd been travelling for an eternity and small talk was the last thing I felt like engaging in. What I really wanted was to dart back into that boat and return with Harry to Halifax. As I watched the men offload boxes and supplies, it took every ounce of my will power to keep my feet planted on the pier.

'That's Anton, Gilbert and Emile. They're locals,' Lachlan said, pointing to the men helping Harry. All looked elderly but surprisingly capable, as they handled heavy boxes with the agility of someone Lachlan's age. 'Anton's wife, Louise, runs the supermarket in the square. You'll get to know her soon enough. Gilbert is married to Freda; she runs the cafe. Emile's wife is Fabienne; she works at the doctor's surgery. Everyone knows everyone here. Small island.' He grinned.

'Right,' I said, not at all interested.

'Anyway, we should go. Noelle's waiting for you.'

'When will Harry be back?' I blurted.

He seemed surprised by the question. 'Next Monday. Why?'

I shook my head. 'Nothing. I might have to leave sooner than planned.'

He didn't enquire further, and I was grateful. We said goodbye to the men on the pier, Harry giving me a wink and a salute. Lachlan took the handle of my suitcase and rolled it behind us, whistling for Duke as we reached a road that rose steeply upwards.

While we walked, Lachlan chatted politely, but I barely listened. I was already looking forward to Monday when I could catch a ride back to Nova Scotia with Harry. Anna's ultimatums had become a dull murmur in the background, overshadowed by my desperation to stave off the hellish detox I knew was coming.

'This is where the name of our island comes from. We have forests full of them.'

I glanced up, aware that I was being spoken to. 'I'm sorry?'

'White cedars,' Lachlan said. 'Actually, these are eastern white cedars. You can also get northern and red cedars too, but the eastern ones grow in abundance here. In spring, the whole island smells of them.'

I looked to where he was referring, the forest to our right that bordered the road, full of deep green cedars that rose like pyramids, bunched together, the light breeze rustling their leaves.

'The wind rushing through them is like nothing you've ever heard before,' he said with a fond look. 'Its name, arborvitae, means tree of life.'

I tried to appear interested, nodding and making sounds at the appropriate times, but I was fixated on reaching that cabin and swallowing enough Xanax to knock me out until Christmas.

'So, you're from Melbourne,' he said.

'Yes.'

'The city itself?'

'Close enough.' I was starting to feel out of breath from the continual incline. It had been a long time since I'd been to a gym. 'How much longer until we get there?'

'It's just over the hill. You're not tired already, are you?'

'No,' I snapped. His unwavering cheerfulness irked me.

Lachlan cast me an amused look.

'Why are we walking anyway?' I asked. 'Don't you have cars on this island?'

'We do, but the island isn't that big. Mostly we just walk everywhere.'

'Is that your secret to living a long life? Walking everywhere?'

'One of the secrets. But people have to stay longer than two days to learn them all.' He grinned mischievously.

I fixed my eyes ahead. I really didn't feel like flirting or whatever it was that he was doing. I supposed he was just being friendly, but my armpits were clammy, my shirt was stuck to me and my eyes and throat itched from lack of sleep. I needed a stiff drink, then a shower and sleep, in exactly that order, but unless the cabin had a well-stocked mini bar, which I doubted, I was only going to manage two of those things.

We passed several quaint houses along the way, with neat gardens and wrap-around timber verandahs, as well as a school. The island was more civilised than I'd expected and, when I turned to look behind me down the hillside, I could see a small village at the bottom that had several shops and buildings. The view from where we stood was breathtaking, the island green and the sea turquoise.

I was standing on a speck in the ocean, entirely small and insignificant, a striking contrast to my larger-than-life existence. I should have been buoyed by all that nature and clean air, with the ocean wrapping itself around me and the breeze stirring the leaves of the cedars, but I felt off, like I was having an out-of-body experience, and I knew I was only hours away from starting withdrawals.

When we rounded a bend and Lachlan announced that we'd reached Noelle's house and the cabin I was to rent, I went slack with relief. An elderly woman was waiting for us on the porch of her house, slightly stooped and with grey hair, but when she stepped down onto the flagstone path with surprising vitality, she looked anything but frail.

She reached us and gave me an appraising glance. 'I am Noelle.' Her accent was French, and she was half the size of Lachlan, who stood tall beside us.

'My name is Marley. Thank you for renting me your cabin,' I said.

She nodded gruffly, then turned and led us along the path to a smaller structure five hundred yards from her house. It was a quaint log cabin, which Lachlan explained was constructed of cedar, with a verandah, dark red door, pretty gardens of labrador leaf and cardinal flower, and a tall masonry chimney that extended from the ground up the side of the house. It was lovely and I almost forgot my troubles as I took it in.

'This is it,' Noelle said, as we climbed onto the verandah and Lachlan heaved my suitcase up behind us. 'My husband built it for our daughter but...' She trailed off. 'It has hot water, a working fireplace, television and kitchen. I maintain it every day. I also stocked the fridge and cupboards with a few things to see you through until you get down to the village. Louise's store closes at four. You won't make it there in time today so you can go tomorrow.'

'Can I get a phone signal on the island?' I asked, retrieving my phone from my pocket and holding it up, noticing the lack of bars.

'The signal can be patchy in the cabin and there's no Wi-Fi,' Lachlan said. 'You can make calls and check emails from the village.'

Despite the prettiness of the house, I tried not to sigh so obviously. All my usual comforts, the things I took for granted every day, were leeching from my grasp. Phone signal, internet access, alcohol, and the fact that I may be forced to cook in order to survive until Monday unless that tiny village had good take-outs.

Noelle pushed a key into the lock and turned it, swinging open the door. She dropped the key into my hand. 'There you go. All the appliances are easy to use, and the beds are already made up. Extra linen and towels are in the linen cupboard. If you have any questions,

I'm just next door.'

'Thank you,' I said, closing my fingers around the key.

Lachlan wheeled my bag over the threshold and into the foyer, turning to face me. 'If you're hungry later, you should come to Noelle's. We usually have dinner there.' He gave her a wink and I could see their firm friendship in the way she shook her head at him, unable to completely hide her smile.

'That's kind of you,' I said. 'I'm pretty tired, though.'

'Sure.'

They said goodbye and left the foyer, and I closed the door behind them. From the window, I parted the curtain and watched as Lachlan walked Noelle back to her door, then waved and started off down the road. I wondered where he was going, what his life was like, if he had a girlfriend or wife and where he lived on the island. He'd been friendly on the walk to Noelle's, and I'd been horribly rude.

Feeling low and out of sorts, I let the curtain fall and turned to survey the cabin around me. It was as if someone had left the window open, allowing the outside to spill in. There were beautiful log walls, a stone fireplace with a lumber pile, a leather lounge and dark cedar floors. I took my suitcase with me and explored, finding a kitchen at the back, as well as two bedrooms, both beds fully made with soft linen in earthy florals. The bathroom was dated but clean and Noelle had placed folded towels on the vanity with pinecones on top.

I chose a bedroom, one that looked out over the forest behind the cabin, left my suitcase there and returned to the kitchen. A quick survey of the fridge and cupboards turned up a loaf of fresh bread, a bowl of fruit, some sort of home-baked muesli slice, almond milk, and a tub of cashew butter. I groaned. Lost amidst my anxiety about coming here was the recollection that this was predominantly a vegan island.

A further check confirmed Noelle had not left me a drop of alcohol anywhere. Not a welcome bottle of wine or a few beers. I threw open every door, clutching at hope, my heart sinking when nothing could be found.

I leant against the bench, my head in my hands and tried to marshal my panicked thoughts into order. I had two choices. I could run down to the village in search of the grocery or drug store, even though there was a good chance both were already closed, or I could give drying out a chance, ride it out with my stash of sleeping pills.

I hadn't chosen a life of dependency. I didn't even particularly want it. It was just something I'd slipped into without realising. The more I drank and the longer it continued, the worse I felt when I tried to stop. Impulse had always been stronger than me. Or maybe I was just weak and full of excuses.

I lifted my head from my hands, took a deep breath and went in search of the pills in my suitcase. That night, I wouldn't succumb. I would send myself into a boundless sleep. I would avoid compulsion and muster some grit. And when I woke in the morning, I'd be that one step closer to Monday and Harry.

***

It was midnight when the sweating started, soaking and profuse.

Despite drugging myself, I woke to a dark room several hours later, drenched and tangled in the bed coverings. I spent a few minutes trying to orientate myself before it came to me—Halifax, the boat, White Cedar Island, Lachlan and Noelle. I was in the cabin I'd rented, and my last drink had been eleven hours earlier. My body was withdrawing.

I switched on the lamp next to the bed and sat up, pushing the blankets and sheets away. My head was foggy from the pills, my throat so dry I could have drunk the North Atlantic. I reached for the glass of water I'd set down beside the bed earlier and gulped it back. It reached my stomach, settled like lead, then came back up again. I ran for the bathroom, retching into the toilet.

I should have felt better afterwards but I didn't, as I slumped back against the wall, sweat trickling down my neck. My hands were trembling, and my heart raced faster than I was sure was safe. I'd attempted to quit alcohol twice before and I knew the physical symptoms could last for days. I also knew that every attempt to quit had been harder than the time before. It was called 'kindling', when the withdrawal symptoms became progressively worse with every attempt. This time my body wasn't letting go so easily.

I sat on the cold tiles of the bathroom floor, my head against the walls, my eyes closed against the discomfort. I saw Katiana Wagner and her children, the woman I'd hit with my Porsche, the hurt in Anna's eyes, my mother, who was gone now, and my beloved father, who I hardly saw. All my regrets were there—every despicable one.

Alcohol had a way of diluting them, ravaging the guilt until it became more bearable. I could block out my mistakes by drinking them away, assuage my guilt, dampen the consequences. But now, my guard was down, and my defences were crippled.

I was as exposed as a newborn baby, with nowhere left to hide.

Chapter 10

On my first full day of withdrawing, I hardly got out of bed. I dreamed—or perhaps hallucinated—that Austin had arrived. He let himself into the cabin, climbed in beside my hurting body and whispered, 'Why are you doing this to yourself?'

He wasn't there of course; I was alone and, as the hours morphed into each other and I alternated between insomnia, fever, and vomiting, I had to wonder the same thing. Why was I putting myself through this torment? What was it all for? Because I couldn't see the end. I couldn't see the light and I couldn't see the tunnel. All I could see was hopelessness.

The jetlag wasn't helping, my pills were gone, and I hadn't had a drink in twenty-four hours. Perhaps the only thing that prevented me from running down to the village and finding a liquor store was my fear that the locals would see me as some sort of desperate animal and, deep down, my pride was still worth something.

I managed to get through Saturday night, then Sunday. I didn't leave the cabin and I hardly ate, although there was a knock at the door at lunchtime on Sunday and later, on the verandah, I found a plate of freshly baked dinner rolls and a pot of soup that smelt wholesome and spicy. I figured it was from Noelle but, as generous as the sentiment was, I couldn't stomach it. Instead, I lay in bed with my racing heart, feeling utterly miserable, willing the time to pass as quickly as possible.

Then Monday came and I still felt sick but awash with relief, for

Harry was sailing in again. By that afternoon, I'd be back in Halifax in a bar somewhere, my hands wrapped tight around a glass of vodka. I packed my suitcase early and waited impatiently on the lounge. At two o'clock, I left a thank you note for Noelle, along with the cabin key under the front mat, then scampered down the hill to the pier at Eternal Bay.

My joints were aching, and I was sweating uncontrollably as the bay finally slid into view. As breathtaking as it was, as crisp as the ocean air felt in my lungs, I couldn't relish in it. I couldn't even dwell on what Anna's reaction would be when she found out I'd left. I just didn't care.

When I reached the pier, seagulls were squawking high above and a small boat was being loaded onto a trailer on the boat ramp, a group of older men bent over tubs of fresh fish, buckets of bait and fishing tackle. I recognised them as the ones who had helped unload Harry's boat the day I'd arrived—Anton, Emile, and Gilbert.

As I pulled my suitcase up onto the planks, Anton glanced up and waved. I waved back, then leant against one of the pilings, scanning the horizon for a sign of Harry's boat. After a while, Anton put down a box of tackle and trotted over to me.

'You're not waiting for Harry, are you?' he called out as he approached.

He was lean and spry and at least seventy. Wisps of white hair covered an almost bald head, and he wore shorts and a tank top that showed brown arms leathery from the sun.

'Yes, I am,' I replied as he came closer. 'I'm catching a lift with him back to Halifax.'

'Not today, you're not. Harry won't be back for another week.' He held his hand out. 'Not sure if you remember me. I'm Anton.'

I shook it but was still trying to make sense of what he'd just said. 'Harry's not coming back today?'

'He had a family emergency. His elderly mother went into hospital. He'll be back next Saturday.'

'Next Saturday? But that's another week away.' Although I was standing out in the open, I felt everything cave in on me. 'I have to get back to Halifax.'

He gave me a confused look. 'Aren't you staying in Noelle's cabin for two weeks?'

'Yes, but something's come up.' I swallowed hard, my throat as dry as sandpaper. The gentle sun was suddenly scalding, and I looked around the bay in panic. 'I don't know what to do.'

'I can give you a lift into the village if you like, or back to Noelle's.'

'Um.' My mind struggled to work. I couldn't think straight. 'Okay, yes, to the village, please.' It was better to accept the lift because I had no clue how to get there on my own, and I didn't want to go back to Noelle's. Once in the village, I could search for a travel agent or a tour company who ran boats back and forth to Nova Scotia. There had to be one.

Anton took my luggage and placed it in the rear of his truck while I climbed into the passenger seat. He told Emile and Gilbert he'd be back soon, then jumped in beside me.

'Are there any boats I can catch back to Halifax?' I asked as he started up the truck.

He raised an eyebrow. 'That desperate to leave, are you?'

I wasn't going to explain my reasons for wanting to go home to this man, so I frowned. 'Don't worry.'

We bumped along the road for five minutes while he made pleasant conversation, then he slowed and parked the truck at the top of a street that led into a village of shops.

'Here you go, Main Street, and the square is just ahead. This same road continues to the other side of the square. If you follow it, it will take you to Noelle's.'

'Thank you.' I climbed down from his truck.

He did the same, walking around to the rear of the vehicle to collect my luggage and set it down on the sidewalk. 'Anytime. Good luck with that boat. *Au revoir.*' He chuckled, climbed back into his truck, and drove away.

I shielded my eyes from the sun as I glanced up the street towards the village. It was quaint and surprisingly busy. A little further along, the street spilled into a large, paved town square with potted flowers around the border and a chess game in progress in the middle. There was a bank and grocery store, a real estate agency, a French restaurant, and a café, where locals sat beneath white umbrellas sipping coffee.

I tugged my suitcase behind me and entered the square, passing a modern apothecary, a health food shop, and a botanic skincare store. I scanned the shopfronts, my heart quickly sinking when I'd completed two full laps of the square and hadn't come across a travel agency or a tour company. There was also no bar, and I wondered what time the restaurant would open so I could buy a bottle of wine.

I trudged out of the square, continuing down Main Street, and stopped at the front of the hospital, a beige building with neat gardens and a set of large double front doors. An information sign erected in a bed of blue geraniums listed the services offered inside—inpatient, emergency, dental, medical practitioner, and pharmacy.

I thought of my empty Xanax packet and knew that if I was going to be stuck on White Cedar for the next week with nothing left in my arsenal, I'd need a prescription.

I walked to the doors and pushed them open, following the sign down the corridor to the medical practitioner's rooms.

An older woman at the reception desk glanced up when I entered. 'Hello, can I help you?'

'I'd like to see a doctor please?' I said, rolling my luggage up to the counter.

'Is it an emergency?'

'Sort of.'

'I mean are you critically unwell?'

'Oh. Not really.' Although that was debatable. 'I just need to see a doctor.'

'That would be Dr Tremblay then,' the woman said politely.

'I don't have an appointment, though. Can I still see her today?'

'Of course. You can see her right away.'

I nodded, impressed. Even with an appointment back home, you never saw anyone 'right away'. A whole day could be wasted sitting around in waiting rooms, flipping through old magazines.

'Now, I can tell you're new here,' she said with a smile, 'so I'll get you to fill in this form.' She handed me the customary medical form that preceded a visit to a new doctor. 'And what's your name? You'll be next to see her.'

'Marley Kincaid,' I replied.

She typed my name into her computer and I took the questionnaire, attached to a clipboard with a pen, and sat in the waiting room to fill it out. The questions were the routine kind—name, address, date of birth and medical conditions. But then I came to the section that asked about alcohol and drug dependency and if I took regular prescriptive medicines. I chewed the end of the pen, wondering how much to disclose. While my own doctor happily wrote prescriptions for anything I asked for—a relationship I'd built and nurtured over time—a new doctor could potentially be full of questions.

The door to the doctor's office opened and a tall woman in a cream suit and with neat grey hair stepped out. An elderly man followed, and she patted his shoulder affectionately. 'Good work, Gerard. Come back to see me in six months for a full check-up, but otherwise, you're in perfect health.'

Gerard thanked her and left. Doctor Tremblay consulted with the receptionist for her next patient. I was the only one in the waiting room so I quickly ticked no, no, and no to the questions about drugs and alcohol, then stood and handed the clipboard with my form back to the lady behind the counter.

'You must be Marley Kincaid,' Dr Tremblay said, intercepting the clipboard and sweeping her eyes over my answers.

'Yes, I am,' I said, giving her my biggest smile. This woman didn't know me and initially, she might be wary, but I was a master at manipulation. Small-town doctor, trusting, hardly worldly. She would be no match for me.

But Dr Tremblay looked anything but dazzled. 'This way, please.'

I followed her into her office overlooking Main Street. Her walls were covered with framed certificates and her shelves lined with medical journals. She sat in the leather chair behind her desk and I sat across from her, hiding my clammy palms in my lap, and giving her my prize-winning smile again.

'So, Marley,' she said, referring to my form, 'you arrived two days ago from Australia?'

'That's correct.'

'And what brings you all the way here?' Her gaze was cold, not like the warm exchange she'd had with Gerard, and I knew she was sceptical of me.

'A kind of mini-sabbatical,' I explained. It was only half the truth. 'I'm taking a break from work. I'm a lawyer and I've had a busy caseload this year.'

If she was impressed with my story, she didn't show it. 'There are plenty of islands near Australia. Why this one?'

'My sister saw a documentary about blue zones and thought this would be a good place for me to completely unwind.'

'I see.' She raised an eyebrow that told me she was unconvinced. 'So, what is it I can do for you?'

I took a deep breath, my speech prepared. 'Well, I've just come off an exceptionally long flight and I'm struggling with jetlag and sleep. Also, my doctor back home prescribed Xanax for me before I left but I forgot to bring the box with me. It's still sitting in my bathroom cabinet. Silly me. Not that I take it often, but he has asked me to take one if I have sleep issues.' I crossed my legs and gave her an airy wave of my hand.

'Interesting,' she said. 'Well, I'm sorry to disappoint you, but I do not prescribe narcotics or benzodiazepines of any kind.'

I blinked, wrong-footed by her response.

She returned to my form. 'You answered no to regular drug and alcohol use.'

'That's right.' My smile faded, along with my control of the session. I hadn't expected her to be so scrupulous.

'How often do you use alprazolam or diazepam?'

'Hardly.'

'What about other prescriptive drugs? Illicit drugs? Alcohol?'

I began to fidget, the treacherous sweats returning. My skin under my clothes was saturated.

'You wrote no to the questions on the form, but I can see you are visibly affected by the symptoms of withdrawal.'

'That's a bold assumption to make,' I said, irritation creeping into my voice. 'You haven't even examined me.'

'It's a calculated observation based on years of practice. I'm not a stranger to treating patients with these symptoms. Trembling hands, profuse sweating, restlessness. Do you think you've been calm and motionless this whole time? You've hardly stopped moving your legs since you sat down. You keep hiding your hands, clenching and unclenching them, grinding your jaw, rocking back and forth.'

I gulped, forcing myself to sit rigidly still. 'Again, a bold assumption to make without an examination. I happen to be sleep-deprived from jetlag.'

So much for winning over the small-town doctor. She was clearly no fool and, unlike doctors in the city, she had all the time in the world to argue her point. There was no tick of the clock or a long line of patients waiting outside, forcing her to write a prescription and hurry me out the door. And had I really been rocking back and forth, grinding my jaw, pretending to be calm but failing miserably?

I took a deep breath, ready to argue my case and my rights, to demand another doctor, to admit myself to emergency if that would get me a script of Xanax or Klonopin or something.

'How many days in are you?' she asked, logging onto her computer. To my surprise, I saw her screen fill with a prescription template.

I sighed, ready to admit anything if it meant she would prescribe me medication. 'Twenty-four hours completely sober.'

'Day one. Congratulations. And what substances are you withdrawing from?'

I gave in. 'Alcohol, mostly. Some prescription drugs like Xanax and Dexedrine.'

'Illicit drugs?'

'Cocaine and MDMA occasionally.'

She nodded, then stood, reaching for her stethoscope. She listened to my heart, then took my blood pressure, checked my eyes and ears, and felt around the glands in my throat.

'Your heart rate is high, your blood pressure too. Extended substance abuse can cause hypertension but, after quitting, I would expect your BP to return to normal within a couple of weeks. Still, we should keep an eye on it. Is this your first attempt?'

'I've tried twice before, about a year ago. I only lasted a day or two.'

'Withdrawal is difficult, and the initial physical symptoms can be trying,' she explained. 'Your body is used to producing increased amounts of serotonin and dopamine to counter the depressant of the alcohol and it's still flooding your body with dangerously high levels. It'll take a good week of no substances for that to settle down.'

She returned to her seat and began typing. 'I'm going to prescribe a few different things for you which, in the long run, will be more beneficial than a cocktail of prescriptive medicines.' When she'd finished typing, she hit print and the printer beside her beeped to life, delivering the prescription into the tray. She handed it to me, and I glanced at it.

Fresh air. Sleep. Good food. Exercise.

I glanced at her in horror. 'Is this some kind of joke?'

'It's not a joke. It's what you need to get better,' she said calmly.

'What I need is for you to treat my symptoms. With medication. That's your job.'

'I will not prescribe you synthetics. I want you to complete the full week of detox without substance, otherwise, you're simply swapping one dependency for another.'

'A real doctor would give me a proper prescription!' My voice rose with my frustration and I was sure the receptionist outside could hear me.

'Then you are more than welcome to return to the mainland and get a second opinion. But while you are on this island and I'm your doctor, that's what I prescribe. You can take some paracetamol to ease your suffering in the meantime.'

'*Paracetamol*?' I scoffed. I wanted to strangle her. I wanted to climb up onto her desk, wrap my hands around her neck and throttle a script out of her.

Her printer beeped again, and she handed a second page to me. 'I want you to return to the main lobby of the hospital and find the nurses' station. I'd like a full blood count. I can already tell you're anaemic and I'm guessing your liver enzymes are high too.'

'This is bullshit,' I muttered, snatching the blood referral and prescription and shoving them into my pocket.

'You'll need to come back and see me in a week's time.'

With any luck, I'd be off this island in a week. I'd be back in Halifax, my veins soaked in vodka, booking the next flight home, and giving Anna a piece of my mind. She'd condemned me to this place and now I was in the throes of withdrawal without so much as a pill to help me through it.

I made a point of standing abruptly so that the chair teetered for a second before righting itself. 'I don't want your so-called help.'

She raised an eyebrow, then stood too and opened the door for me. 'Let Fabienne know on your way out that you'll be seeing me on Monday. She'll keep an eye out for your blood results.'

I stormed out, not bothering to speak to Fabienne or visit the nurses' station to have my blood drawn. I didn't even thank Dr Tremblay. I grabbed my suitcase, still sitting upright in the waiting room, and left.

Chapter 11

I exited the hospital, tugging my suitcase behind me, finding my way back to the square. The air smelt of coffee and the chess game was still in progress, attracting a small crowd. The breeze had picked up, carrying the sounds of children's voices as they trickled down the hill after school.

I leant against the wall of the health food shop and let go of my luggage, sweat dripping down the inside of my shirt and my limbs shaking. I was entirely bewildered by the situation I'd found myself in, far from home, withdrawing and with no prescription or way off the island. It was enough to make me want to curl into a ball in the middle of the square and weep.

On some level, I knew it was my own terrible choices that had brought me here, but I was so angry at the world that I found other places to allocate blame instead—the pregnant woman I'd collided with. It was her fault I was here, and Paul for assigning me the Wagner case; Karl Wagner, because he'd murdered his entire family, and Anna of course because she'd blackmailed me into coming. Even Austin was to blame. He should have tried harder to talk me out of it.

When my stomach began to cramp and I grew nauseated, I knew I had to get back to the cabin and into bed. I turned towards the hospital once more, remembering that Anton had said the main street would lead me out of the village and up towards Noelle's. I could only pray I wouldn't get lost somewhere in those hills.

I was passing the café when I sensed a ball of white fur charging towards me. I was already tetchy, and I jerked in surprise as the dog came to a screeching halt in front of me, his wet nose nudging up against my fingers.

Duke.

Lachlan ran towards us from the other side of the square, covering the distance in seconds. 'I'm so sorry,' he said as he approached. 'He bolted for you before I could call him back. He doesn't bite.'

I took a deep breath, my heart still thumping in my throat, and bent to pat Duke. 'No, it's okay. He just startled me. I wasn't expecting it.'

'He can get a little excited. He's eight going on two.'

Duke was still at my side and his fur felt soft as I ran my fingers through it. He was a beautiful dog, warm and friendly, and for a moment, I forgot my pain and sank into his spell, crouching low to wrap my arms around him. He nuzzled into me and licked my face, huge chocolate eyes turned up to me, his reverent stare making me smile.

'He likes you,' Lachlan said.

'He's gorgeous. I've always wanted a dog, but it's hard when living in the city.' I gave Duke one last cuddle, then stood and grabbed hold of my suitcase handle again.

'Can I help you with that?' he asked, pointing to it. 'You're not looking for the pier, are you?'

'I was down there earlier. Harry's not coming.' My voice wobbled. 'I was going to catch a ride back with him to Halifax, but I saw Anton and he said he won't return for another week. He's dealing with a family matter.'

Lachlan nodded soberly. 'Yes, I'd heard.'

I was glad I was wearing my sunglasses because I almost burst into tears. Lachlan reached for my suitcase and steered me closer to the café tables, out of the way of the school children who had reached the square.

'Apparently, his mother went into hospital,' he said.

'Yes, that's what Anton told me. Is there another way off the island?'

He raised an eyebrow at me. 'Depends how badly you need to get off. We could always ask the navy to come and get you.'

My spirits lifted. 'We can do that?'

'I was kidding.'

I slumped, deflated again.

'Unfortunately, we're in the middle of nowhere. Ferries and planes only come out once a month. Harry is our regular mode of transport to and from the mainland. Is there a reason you need to leave urgently? I mean, White Cedar's not a bad place to be stranded for a while.'

I shrugged miserably. 'I just really want to go home.'

He nodded and I knew he felt sorry for me. 'Why don't we grab a coffee? My shout. The Wildflower Cafe makes an excellent cappuccino.'

I shook my head. I was wired and exhausted and not great company. 'Maybe another time. I need to get back to Noelle's.'

'Then let me walk you. I was heading back home anyway.'

He grabbed the handle of my suitcase, whistled for Duke, who'd found a gaggle of school children to cuddle with, and we left the square. Back on Main Street, we passed the hospital and I threw Dr Tremblay's office window a contemptuous glare on the off chance she was watching. I wasn't accustomed to emotional outbursts like the one I'd had in her office and I was annoyed that she'd driven me to act that way. I wanted—*needed*—medication, and her unwillingness to help me meant I'd added her to my list of people to blame.

We left the village and began climbing the hill. It wasn't long before my legs were burning, and my lungs struggled for air. Duke remained close by. He had a lovely temperament and walked alongside us obediently, casting Lachlan occasional glances to check for a signal or a change in tempo. Every now and again I'd feel his wet nose nudge my fingertips as I walked to remind me that a scratch behind the ears wouldn't go astray.

'How long have you had Duke?' I asked.

'Since he was a puppy. I was in Montreal visiting my team there and somehow, I came back with this little guy.'

'He's beautiful.'

'He's a truffle hunter,' Lachlan said. 'Well, technically, he's a Labrador Retriever, but he sniffs out truffles on my land.'

'You grow truffles?'

'Just up the road from Noelle's. I have my house and office there too, although my team are on the mainland.'

He leant down to scratch Duke fondly behind the ears and I took the momentary lull in conversation to study him. He was tall and lean, with brown hair that caught the sun at certain angles, turning it chestnut. His eyes were strikingly hazel, like the colour of the forests, and he had a dimple in his right cheek that deepened at the first hints of a smile. I deduced that he was in his early to mid-thirties, the same age as me.

He caught me staring and I quickly glanced away, avoiding his gaze by pulling my phone out of my back pocket and turning it on. I'd turned it off the day before in a fit of frustration when I'd struggled to receive a signal in the cabin. Now, as I glanced at the screen, it lit up with a series of beeps.

Four texts and two missed calls from Anna, one text from my father and one from Paul, an accumulation of people trying to reach me. My heart sank when I noticed the lack of missed calls from Austin.

'Friends and family missing you back home?' Lachlan asked, watching me.

'Mostly my sister,' I said, shoving the phone back into my pocket. I was about to lose signal again and would have to call her later. 'She's a mother. Unfortunately, it means she tries to be *my* mother.'

'That's not such a bad thing, having someone love you like that.'

It wasn't often that I was lost for words, but Lachlan seemed to have done what I'd struggled to do for years—summarise my relationship with Anna in a way that wasn't cynical. I'd never thought of her meddling as love before, only as jealousy, punishing me for being the kind of person she wanted to be but never could be. Successful, sociable, the favourite child.

Perhaps that was as distorted a theory as everything else in my life, for Anna didn't seem unhappy. She had an adoring husband, children she loved and wanted more of, and a beautiful home in the mountains. She longed for nothing that I had—not the career or the money or the designer clothes, only my acceptance of the path she'd chosen.

We continued walking, the sun disappearing behind a cloud then returning swiftly to light up the hills again. The rays felt good on my skin, the hairs on my arms rising as if reaching for the warmth.

'What do you do for work?' Lachlan asked.

I was brought back to the conversation where he was looking at me expectantly, and I wondered for how long I'd slipped into thought. 'I'm a lawyer.' I didn't elaborate on what kind, for a criminal lawyer often drew raised eyebrows and a preconceived opinion of them.

'And is your family in Melbourne?'

'Not Melbourne exactly. Anna lives southeast of the city and my father lives further south on the Mornington Peninsula. He was a lawyer too, but he's retired now.'

'And does your sister practice law?'

'She's a stay-at-home mum. She has three daughters with another baby on the way.'

The conversation was light, and it was easy to become distracted from my sweating palms and gasping lungs. Lachlan adjusted his pace to suit my slower one, but I was taking such painfully small steps up that hill that we were hardly moving.

He explained how he'd arrived with his mother ten years earlier on the island, having come from Montreal. He said he understood the shock of leaving a large city behind to face an almost timeless community like White Cedar.

'But it was the best decision I could have made. And my mother is the happiest she's ever been.'

I didn't ask him what had compelled him to make such a decision. He didn't ask me either and I felt a mutual respect for our privacy.

We turned at an intersection, the roads deserted except for a few people walking. Thick forest seemed to pervade everything. It was in people's front and backyards, it climbed around the hills and up the clifftops, it hugged the village and the school—maples, cedars, and birches. And just as Lachlan had said it would the day I'd arrived, the wind was rushing through the white cedars, the sound breathtaking and formidable.

'Is there really something in the water here?' I asked.

Lachlan glanced my way, an eyebrow raised. 'Is that what you've heard?'

'I did some research before I came,' I said. 'White Cedar is a blue zone. It's considered one of the healthiest places on Earth. What's the secret?'

'Okay, you *have* done your research. But if I told you all our secrets, they wouldn't be secrets anymore,' he said grinning at me.

'You said if I stayed longer than Monday, you'd tell me.'

This time he laughed, and it was such a hearty, satisfying sound that despite my lack of breath and the pain in my limbs, I found myself smiling too.

'Yes, I did say that,' he said. 'Well, we don't have a fountain of youth or an eternal spring hidden away, as most people think. I believe it's a combination of three things. We eat well, we move our bodies, and we live happily.'

'That's it?'

'You sound surprised.'

I shrugged. 'I thought it would be a little more complex than that.'

'For a lot of people, that balance can be difficult to achieve,' he said. 'We mostly eat a plant-based diet here. Some people are strict vegans, like Noelle, others are a little more relaxed. We eat fruits and vegetables, lots of grains and pulses, some fish and red wine, no red meat. But if someone wants an egg or cow's milk in their coffee, it's not a big deal. Louise sells some animal products in her store and people buy them.

'And everyone walks. We have cars and mopeds, but we all prefer to use our legs to get to places. White Cedar is full of hills and we walk them every day. It builds resilience. Old age is not an excuse to stop moving your body here.'

'Wait, no red meat?' I asked, still fixated on his earlier comment. 'No hamburgers or steaks or beef kebabs? No pepperoni pizza?'

'None at all.' He laughed at my horrified expression. 'Look, I get it. I'm a city boy at heart. I was born and bred in Montreal, so giving up red meat when I arrived was a shock to my system too but now, I don't even think about it. I still occasionally order a steak when I go back, just because I can. But I don't miss it. And I think I feel better without it.'

'So you eat well, you move your bodies, what about the third thing? Living happily? That's a broad statement.'

'But perhaps the most important of all, even above exercise and good eating.'

I gave him a dubious look.

'All right, a question for you,' he said. 'Have you ever felt lonely? Have you felt isolated and detached, even though your life seems full?'

His question triggered a flood of unexpected emotions because while my life was constant and colourful and I was always surrounded by people, I *was* lonely. Desperately so. I shouldn't have been for I had Austin and my friends who I could call on any time, yet I didn't know how to confide in them when I felt down, when the ghosts became too much, or my heart felt heavy. There was Anna and my father, I supposed, but I pushed them away at every conceivable opportunity, so when it came down to it, who did I have?

'Loneliness is a silent killer,' he said sagely. 'We're an all-inclusive community here. No one feels left out no matter how young or old they are. The kids sit with the adults and the elderly at our parties. They dance, talk, laugh, tell stories together. There are no nursing homes and the elderly reside in their own houses. More importantly, they look after themselves. We don't take away their independence or exclude them because they're old.'

I considered his words, never having thought of it like that before. 'And you think that's why disease is so rare here?'

'I do, but not just disease. Dementia. It's almost unheard of in blue zones.' He switched my luggage handle to his other hand as we continued walking. 'It's because our social life holds the key. Everyone has a purpose here and no one feels useless. All our elderly residents are in the best possible mental state. Not only do they live a long and healthy life but, when they reach the end, they are as sharp as ever.'

'So why can't this be applied on the continents? It sounds like a no-brainer.'

'It's harder, I suppose, in densely populated areas. Everything moves faster, people's lives are busier. They live by the clock. But at the end of the day, everyone is responsible for their own well-being. If you want to make the change, you don't have to live on an island to do it.'

'Granted, but if you live in a city, it's impossible not to live its fast pace,' I argued.

'Perhaps,' he said. 'But now I've seen what can be achieved with my own eyes, it doesn't take major change to incorporate some simple adjustments into your life. Eat healthier, walk on the weekends or during your lunch break. Spend time with family. Eat a meal together. When was the last time you saw your parents or had a Sunday lunch with loved ones just for the hell of it?'

I bit my bottom lip to avoid answering. Since my mother had passed, I'd slipped further from their fold. I begrudgingly squeezed in visits to Anna, and I almost never saw my father. They were too lenient with me and I exploited it, accepting it as an excuse not to try because partying Saturday night then getting up early with a hangover on Sunday to visit them held no appeal.

Although maybe Lachlan was right. I lived the fast pace of the city because I'd been unwilling to live any other way. I craved it, wanted the rush of it in my veins so that I hardly slept, drank ridiculous amounts of alcohol, ate terrible food, and never exercised. I also didn't have children or a reliable community I could count on. All my friends lived the fast life too, which meant I was probably on a collision course to a miserable existence or an early grave.

'I'm not saying everyone should dash out and adopt our lifestyle,' Lachlan said, 'but this way of living has merit. That's why it's a blue zone because whatever the people are doing here works.'

'I do need to change my life,' I said, surprised at my candour. 'I'm just not sure how to.'

Lachlan nudged me playfully. 'If you stay longer than a week, maybe you'll find out.'

I rolled my eyes at him.

We reached Noelle's property and Lachlan walked me to the front door of the cabin. I was surprised to find a dish of baked vegetables on the porch with a pitcher of fresh juice and more homemade dinner rolls. The key was still under the mat, as was my note.

'Noelle must have known Harry wasn't coming back too. She doesn't miss a beat, does she?' I said, gathering everything up in my arms.

'She knows more than you think she does.'

I unlocked the door and turned to him. 'Thank you for walking me back.'

'It was my pleasure.' He angled the handle of my suitcase towards me so I could free one hand and take it. 'Although, Marley from Melbourne, please try to stay put now. Your luggage is heavy, and I'd prefer not to walk it up that hill a third time.'

I cringed with apology, but his smile was wide.

'See you around? Don't be a stranger.' He winked then turned, trotting back down to the road, Duke galloping after him.

I stepped inside and closed the door, depositing Noelle's latest meal on the kitchen bench before rolling my luggage into the bedroom. I sat on the edge of the bed and took a deep breath.

I hadn't expected to be back here and yet here I was, still on the island with six days of painful detox ahead of me. And if I made it that far, I would start a psychological battle, fighting every conceivable thought of relapse. Yet somehow Lachlan's words had imparted a missing sense of perspective. I wanted to live a good life. I wanted to be healthy in mind and body. I didn't want to catapult through my days like my out-of-control Porsche.

I had to dig deep, ride it out, dredge up willpower from rock bottom and not give in. The next week would be the most testing, but I was on this island. Harry wasn't coming back yet and perhaps that was the universe guiding me.

You can do this. You will *do this. You will fight because you want to be healthy.*

Maybe this island had the answers. Maybe it didn't. Maybe everything I needed I already had. All I had to do was draw on it.

Chapter 12

Over the course of the next week, Noelle delivered a new meal each day—dishes of earthy lentils and soul-warming bean casseroles, pearl barley salads and colourful soups. At any other time it would have smelt delicious, and I would have been tempted to try some, but I was hot and cold with fever and my tongue tasted like I had been licking batteries. The most I could stomach were the bread rolls she left and a little water. The rest of her food sat in the fridge or on the bench, untouched.

She left me other things too—crossword puzzles and adult colouring books with pencils. I had to wonder if she was aware of my suffering. I wasn't sure how she could be, but I felt her presence watching over me and it made those days of withdrawal feel somehow less lonely.

On my fifth day of sobriety, after a week of little sleep and perpetual misery, I woke feeling mildly stronger. The tremors in my hands had ceased, the fog in my brain had lifted and my stomach had settled. I felt almost human again, like the person I used to be, back in my early twenties when drinking hadn't pervaded my every waking moment.

I glanced into the mirror that morning and the person who stared back was not the person who had arrived here. Once pale skin was now brighter, my hair less limp and the breakouts and dark circles I used to cover with makeup had cleared. I'd surprised myself, convinced that each detoxing day would get the better of me, but somehow, I'd persevered, locked away in the cabin, fending off pain and boredom and cravings in a strange carousel of time.

I opened the front door and, for the first time since I'd arrived, I sat on the steps of the verandah, turning my face to the sun. The flood of morning warmth was glorious, my skin tingling from the rays. My stomach grumbled and I rubbed it, smiling. It felt like aeons ago that I'd had an appetite. I was slowly coming back to life and my body wanted sustenance.

There was a rustle in the yard next door, and I turned in the chair and found Noelle tending to her roses in her front garden. She waved at me and I waved back.

'Beautiful morning,' she called to me in her French accent.

'Yes,' I answered, wondering if there was a way to disappear politely back inside without offending her. I wasn't ready for neighbourly conversation.

'Have you run out of food yet?' she asked.

I squirmed. So she *had* noticed I'd been locked away in the cabin. I wondered who else on the island had realised I'd been less than sociable. Lachlan?

She put down her shears, gathered up the roses she'd cut, placed them into a basket, and beckoned with her head. 'Come with me.'

I hesitated. I was still in my pyjamas and looked bedraggled. I would have liked to have changed clothes and run a brush through my hair, but she'd already left the garden and was on her front verandah. When she turned and raised her eyebrows at me, fierce blue eyes expectant, I rose from the step, dropped down onto the flagstone path that connected our front yards and padded across to her.

Her house was bigger than the cabin, and she led me inside to a large living area with a wood fireplace, a cream couch, powder-blue gingham curtains and a high vaulted ceiling. An antique chandelier hung from exposed beams. After a few steps in, I was transported instantly to the French countryside, except when I glanced outside the living room window, I saw directly down the hill to the deep blue of the North Atlantic.

Beyond the living area were the kitchen and dining rooms, quaint and rustic with light oak cupboards and galvanised tin vases full of roses that I knew were from her front garden. They were on every conceivable surface—beautifully coloured petals with perfume that tickled my nose. Her home reminded me of Anna's—of comfort and warmth and cooking.

Of toasty winter fires and lemonade summers. Of putting down roots where they couldn't be easily dug up.

'Were you the one leaving me food and crosswords?' I asked, dragging my eyes away from the rooms to look at her.

'*Oui,*' she said.

I smiled. 'Well, thank you. That was kind.'

She made a gruff noise, setting her basket of roses down on the kitchen bench.

'Your home is beautiful,' I said.

'I've lived on this island all my life.' Noelle reached for a vase by the sink, filling it with water and placing the roses inside. She arranged them and, when she was satisfied, found space on a sideboard, and set the vase down. 'My parents had a house further up the hill where I was born. Then I married my husband, and we built this home. It was just a kitchen, bathroom, and bedroom back then. We extended and renovated over the years.' Her gaze was wistful as she glanced around the room.

'Do you live by yourself?' I asked, taking a seat at the kitchen bench. During my withdrawal, I'd been conscious of people visiting Noelle and of her going out for walks, but I'd yet to become aware of anyone else living here.

'I do. My husband died four years ago,' Noelle confirmed sadly. 'My dear Samuel slipped away quietly in his sleep one night. He was a hundred and four, mind you. That same day he'd been out chopping wood and planting apple trees with no idea that it would be his last. He never said he was in pain, and it wasn't a heart attack or anything like that. He was just ready for eternal sleep.' She sighed, her eyes full of nostalgia. 'We never got a chance to say goodbye, but if I can go as quietly and peacefully as that, I'll be a happy dame.'

My heart grew unexpectedly heavy with her loss. She seemed a strong and capable woman, her mind sharp and her armour tough as nails, but her eyes held a depth of sadness that touched me. I was curious as to her age, although I didn't want to be rude and ask. I suspected she was in the vicinity of that elusive century.

'And what about you? Are you married?' She opened the fridge door and pulled out apricots, berries, and almond yoghurt, then moved to the pantry for vanilla pods, ground cinnamon, honey, nuts, and oats.

I glanced at the things she piled on the bench in front of me, that little mountain of goodness, and I swallowed down my disappointment. I was hungry and what my stomach yearned for was a greasy bacon burger. 'Ah, no. I'm not married. There's sort of someone back home, but...'

'If you have to finish that sentence with a "but", it mustn't be serious.' Noelle took no prisoners, it seemed, yet I found her bluntness refreshing. 'Are you hungry?'

'Starving.'

She opened a drawer and collected a knife, followed by a pestle and mortar from a cupboard. 'Then you will help me make breakfast. You can slice the apricots and crush the nuts.'

I stared at her.

'You do know how to prepare food, don't you?' she asked, assessing me with her sharp eyes. 'How to chop, crush, grate, slice?'

My cheeks flamed and all I could think was how well Anna and Noelle would get along. 'I mean, I guess. How hard can it be?'

She grunted her disapproval.

'I don't really use my kitchen,' I explained. 'I dine out or order in.'

'You don't cook your own food?'

'I'm busy and I eat on the run a lot. Sometimes I skip meals.'

'*Mon Dieu*,' she muttered in French, her eyes sweeping to the heavens. 'That can't be good for you. No wonder you're skin and bones.'

'I eat fruit salad... sometimes.'

'*She eats fruit salad sometimes.*'

I grimaced.

Noelle shook her head. 'Child, you need to be kind to your body. It's the only one you have.' She gestured to her head, then her heart. 'Come, I'll show you what to do.'

I climbed off the chair and went to stand beside her and, for the next hour, she showed me how to prepare breakfast. I piled the nuts into the pestle and mortar and crushed them—almonds, cashews, and hazelnuts. Next, we combined them with the cinnamon and sugar in a bowl and poured warm coconut oil, honey, and vanilla over the top. We mixed it together and spread it out onto a tray, which Noelle placed in the oven.

As our granola baked, we prepared the fruit, washing berries and slicing apricots, and she made me a glass of fresh orange juice which was the most refreshing thing I'd ever tasted. We spoke only a little as we made breakfast. She didn't badger me with questions, and I was grateful for the silence. And when we did talk, we spoke of food and cooking. She said she would show me her vegetable garden one day and that I was welcome to pick anything I wanted from it.

By the time the granola was ready, my stomach was growling so loudly, Noelle heard it and chuckled. When she opened the oven door, the smell of toasted oats and honey engulfed the kitchen.

We spooned the granola into bowls, topped it with the apricots, berries and almond yoghurt, and sat at the table across from each other to eat. It wasn't my breakfast of choice. I would normally eat white toast slathered with butter and a cup of coffee whilst running out the door or, on a morning when I was particularly hungover, I would eat something extraordinarily greasy to quell the hollow pains a night of drinking had given me.

But I was surprised now at how hungrily I ate that little bowl of wonder. The granola was wholesomely crunchy, and the blueberries burst in my mouth. What I marvelled at most was the joy I found in sitting to eat. I wasn't rushing food down or eating on the run. It was simple, peaceful, and unhurried.

Afterwards, I helped Noelle clean up the kitchen, then she walked me to the front door. As I stepped out onto her verandah, flooded with morning light, I asked her for the recipe.

'There's no recipe,' she said. 'I just use whatever ingredients I have that I know will make me feel good.' She shrugged. 'That's all.'

I smiled at her uncomplicated approach. 'Well, thank you. Your granola was lovely.'

She reached for my hand and patted it. 'Sometimes it's not about what we eat, but who we eat with. Thank you for having breakfast with me.'

Chapter 13

After eating at Noelle's, the quiet of the cabin held no appeal, so I showered, dressed, and walked down to the village. Breakfast had given me a surge of energy, and I was eager to go grocery shopping. Maybe I'd cook dinner that night. I already knew I wanted to replicate Noelle's apricot granola for breakfast tomorrow.

The village square was busy that morning, but the pace was relaxed. It seemed everyone on the island was out enjoying the day. People worked, but they also seemed to find time for a morning coffee, an extra-long lunch, an afternoon swim, or a chat near the chessboards. It was Friday and the sun was gloriously warm, so I spent time strolling past shop windows.

A bookstore caught my eye and I walked in, browsing the shelves, then purchased four new books. Feeling accomplished, I stepped back out into the sunshine with my shopping bag, only to be bowled over by a huge ball of snowy fur. Duke.

'Hey, boy,' I said, bending to pat him. He licked my face, happy to see me, and I laughed as my loose hair fell around us.

Lachlan trotted over. 'Sorry,' he said, grimacing slightly. 'He seems to have a habit of nearly bowling you over.'

'It's no problem,' I said, standing and pushing my hair back. 'He's a good boy, aren't you, Duke?' I patted him again and his tongue fell out, a big dog grin on his face.

'You look well,' he said, glancing over me. 'And out of the cabin, I see.'

I blushed at the fact he'd noticed. 'I wasn't feeling well, but I'm better now. And very hungry. I need to buy some food.'

'Ah, you'll want Louise's then.'

He turned and began walking. I realised that he wasn't going to simply point out Louise's store, but was going to take me there, so I followed. There was nothing rushed in his demeanour, like he had other things to do—a job or errands—and what had originally unsettled me about the island—that slow, almost dormant pace—was starting to feel less disconcerting.

Out the front of Louise's, Duke dropped to what seemed a customary position by the door to wait, and Lachlan led me inside.

A woman who I deduced was Louise, was sitting by the cash register, flipping through a magazine. When she glanced up and noticed me, her eyes widened. 'Oh, hello.' She jumped off her stool. 'You must be the girl Harry brought in last week.'

'This is Marley,' Lachlan said.

'It's nice to meet you.' I held out my hand to her.

Louise snapped it up, shaking it so enthusiastically I thought she'd take it right off. 'Aren't you a pretty thing? Lachlan said you were beautiful.'

'I said you were... mildly attractive.' But his cheeks flamed red.

'It's not often we get visitors from the mainland and certainly not this close to fall,' Louise continued, her red curls bouncing with every word. 'So you're from Australia? Melbourne? How exciting. Such a long way from White Cedar. What brings you here to our tiny island? Visiting anyone? Thinking of moving here?'

Lachlan grabbed a basket from the stack, placed a hand on my shoulder and steered me away from the counter. 'Marley's going to do some shopping now. We'll be back soon.'

I giggled as we left a flushed and giddy Louise behind. When we were safely down an aisle and out of earshot, Lachlan cringed. 'I'm sorry about that. People get a little excited when new folk come to town.'

'It's fine,' I said. 'She was sweet. Everyone has been welcoming.' Except for the doctor, I wanted to add, but didn't.

'The community is great if you can handle everyone knowing your business.'

'I think it's nice. Where I come from, people don't care enough.' My stomach grumbled and I clutched it, embarrassed. 'Oops. It's been doing that a lot lately.'

'We better find you some food, then.'

He carried the basket and I placed items into it—rolled oats, sugar, coconut oil and a variety of nuts. I tried to recall what else Noelle had put into her granola that morning, but then I remembered that there was no recipe, that she'd added whatever made her feel good, so I reached for apples, berries, and raisins.

I placed other items in too—bread, pasta, tomatoes, and olive oil, eager to try my hand at cooking later. When I tossed in butter, milk, and a small tub of chocolate chip ice cream, all made from cow's milk, I threw Lachlan a sheepish grin. 'I know. Not exactly plant-based.'

He laughed and held up his hands. 'Hey, I'm the worst vegan around here. Eat whatever makes you feel good.'

We continued through the aisles, pausing in front of a shelf that stocked a range of truffle condiments.

'Wild East Truffles,' I said, picking up a jar of truffle oil and glancing at the logo on the label. 'Are these yours?'

'Yes.' He looked so pleased with himself that his dimple deepened in his cheek.

'Wow, I'm impressed.'

He bowed. 'Thank you.'

'I'll take one of each, please.'

He grinned. 'Louise will be happy.'

Our light-hearted banter continued, and I hadn't realised that we'd made our way to the shelves stocking the alcohol until it was too late. My smile fell away. I'd been entirely focused on food that I'd neglected to prepare myself for the possibility the store would sell liquor.

'I recommend this burgundy here,' Lachlan said, pointing to a bottle of red wine. 'It's the best on the island if you enjoy wine. They're a client of mine, actually, from the Niagara Peninsula.'

I gulped, staring at it all. Vodka, wine and beer. Bottles of them, pressed together in neat rows. My throat grew dry, my fingers twitched, my thoughts became confused and desperate, a battle of wills.

Reach for one. Do it.

Five days sober. Don't do it.

How I longed for the crack of a lid or a cork being popped, of crystal clear or velvety liquid tumbling into a glass, of bringing the glass to my lips and taking that first exquisite sip.

I was a week into my sobriety, but I knew it was minuscule in the grand scheme of things, that I had a long way to go before I could easily resist a drink. Right there, every fibre of my body told me to lift my hand and reach for a bottle. The longer I stood there, the weaker my resolve became.

'Marley?'

I heard Lachlan's voice as though from far away. When I glanced up, he was staring at me. 'Are you okay?'

It was enough to jolt me, like a circuit breaker, and I nodded. 'Yes... yes. I'm fine. I'm done here.'

I moved quickly away from the shelf, darting down an aisle as Lachlan followed. I couldn't meet his eyes; I didn't want to see the questions there. I concentrated on placing one foot in front of the other until I was back at the front of the store where Louise was waiting.

She was still flushed with exhilaration when we appeared. Lachlan arrived beside me and without saying a word, we took the items out of the basket and Louise tallied them up. I paid, then we collected a bag each, said goodbye to Louise, and stepped back outside to where Duke was lying in the sun.

Lachlan looked uncertain and I threw him a contrite smile. 'Sorry for acting weird inside. It was very hot.' I couldn't tell what he was thinking or if he believed me. His forehead was crinkled with confusion. 'And I'm still jet-lagged,' I added quickly.

'Ah,' he said, as though that finally explained it.

I let out a relieved breath, but it didn't stop my face growing pink from the mortification of it all. The last thing I wanted to do was parade my drinking problem around on my sleeve for everyone to see. I was grateful when my phone beeped in my back pocket, providing a distraction.

I retrieved it to glance at the screen. It was Anna. 'My sister,' I said, holding it up.

'Do you want to sit somewhere and call her?'

'No, that's okay.' Her texts were frantic, asking if I was all right, for I'd not returned anyone's calls or messages since I'd been on the island. I quickly texted her, letting her know I was fine and that I'd call soon, then shoved my phone back in my pocket. 'I'll call her later. The ice cream in my bag will melt soon.'

'Back to the cabin then?'

'Yes.'

We walked towards the end of Main Street with Duke at our heels, nudging my hip to serve as a reminder that he was there. As we strolled, I let my fingers drag through his fur, which he seemed to like.

We passed the council chambers—a quaint peach building with neat garden beds and hedgerows. Lachlan explained that it was where the mayor worked, as well as many of the younger locals who had chosen to remain on the island rather than explore the outside world.

'It's about as corporate a job as you can get here,' he said. 'A lot of teenagers gravitate to it when they leave school.'

A young woman sat outside on the edge of a garden wall, eating a sandwich. When she saw us pass, she quickly cast the sandwich aside, evidently embarrassed at having been caught eating, dusted her hands and lap and stood, waving eagerly at Lachlan.

When he returned the wave, she grinned broadly then shyly, dropping her head so that her mousy brown hair covered her face.

'A friend of yours?' I asked as we continued.

'That's Celeste. She's just... a girl.'

'Just a girl? She looked sweet on you,' I teased.

'If my mother had it her way, we'd be married already.'

'Oh, dear.' I shook my head and laughed. 'I see what you mean about everyone being in your business.'

'There is literally nowhere to hide.' He groaned. 'I mean, don't get me wrong, Celeste is nice, but someone's either right for you or they're not and, deep down inside, you can tell.'

The village was behind us now as we climbed the hill to Noelle's. The ocean delighted us with its colour the higher we went, glimpses of cobalt peeking through the trees. My lungs began to struggle for air again and, just like the week before when I'd climbed this same hill with Lachlan, he slowed his pace to match mine so that we fell into an easier stroll.

'You must be looking forward to Harry sailing in tomorrow,' Lachlan said. 'You can be on your way home again.'

'Yes, I suppose.'

As excited as I was to return home, I was under no illusions that life outside the island would be full of temptation. It would be waiting for me the moment I stepped off Harry's boat in Halifax—the bars and restaurants, the alcohol on the plane, Melbourne... Austin. I'd worked hard for my week of sobriety and it saddened me that there was a very real chance it could all be lost within the next few days.

Lachlan was watching me intently. 'You suppose?'

'Well, I haven't always been kind to myself or the people who love me. Coming here was a way of pressing the reset button. I'm worried about going home and not having made any significant progress on that front.' I knew I was being ambivalent, but Lachlan gave me a reassuring smile.

'When my mother and I first arrived, we also had to press the reset button. We had to start completely over. It wasn't easy, especially for her. She struggled to give up on a life she was used to, even though it wasn't a good life. But stepping away can often restore perspective. I truly believe that.'

'I need to do more than step away,' I said. 'I need to strip everything back and start again. And perhaps I need to spend the time to do that.'

'Then that's what you should do. Maybe leaving tomorrow is not the answer.'

The same thought had occurred to me that morning when I'd woken. How badly did I want my sobriety? Because I was almost certain I'd relapse if I went home now. I'd attempted to quit alcohol while living in the city before and, as much as I loved Austin, he'd never been supportive of it, always tempting me back. He was the worst lure of all.

We reached Noelle's cabin and I was disappointed at how quickly we'd arrived. Despite the breathlessness, I'd enjoyed walking with Lachlan. He radiated a kind of calm and positivity that was infectious.

On the verandah, he handed me the grocery bag he'd been holding and smiled. 'You better get that ice cream into the freezer or you'll be drinking it like a milkshake later.'

I laughed. 'Thank you for walking me back up here. I'm sure you have a million other things to do today.'

'Not quite a million,' he said, smiling. 'And not half as fun as this.'

I wasn't sure why I grew pink, but I did. I dropped my gaze to the bags in my hands, aware of his eyes on me.

'Be sure to stop in and say goodbye on your way down to the pier tomorrow,' he said. 'My place is on Deerfield Avenue, just around the corner from Noelle's. You'll see the Wild East Truffles sign out the front.'

'Okay,' I said, raising my eyes to meet his.

He stepped off the verandah and onto the flagstone path with Duke at his side. 'Well, have a good rest of your day.'

'You too.'

I watched them leave, heading back down the hill until they disappeared around a bend. I gathered up the shopping bags and unlocked the front door, stepping across the threshold. I had a decision to make about whether I left the island with Harry tomorrow.

Part of me desperately wanted to go home, but if I was completely honest with myself, it was for one reason only. To drink. I wanted the comforts of my self-indulgent life restored.

On the other hand, I could stay the full two weeks as I'd promised Anna. Try to give myself a fighting chance. Try to convalesce just a little more before I returned to the city. But would two weeks be enough? Would I need more? If I couldn't be trusted in Louise's store, what hope did I have in a city full of temptation? Perhaps I should leave now and accept the fact that I wasn't strong enough.

I battled on like this for the remainder of the day.

I should go.

You're not ready. You should stay.

No, I really should go.

The thought process alone had me crying out for a drink.

Chapter 14

The next morning, after replicating Noelle's apricot and berry granola for breakfast, I dressed and was about to set off for a walk when she called to me from her front verandah.

'It's Saturday,' she said. 'Aren't you going home with Harry later?'

I lifted my hand to my eyes and squinted against the sun. 'I'm going to stay the original two weeks if that's still okay.' I'd deliberated over it all evening, rereading Anna's texts, so full of the kind of love I'd never noticed until now. Until I'd stripped away the substance and it was just me and my clear, rational thoughts. She wanted me to get better. *I* wanted to get better. The decision had been easy after that.

There was the hint of a smile from Noelle, then she nodded her approval and waved me over. 'Come. I will show you my garden.'

I followed the flagstone path into her front yard, and she led me around the side of her house through a white wooden gate to the back. The same path continued through an orchard of peach, apricot, orange and apple trees, plump and colourful fruit hanging from the branches. She led me past trellises of peas and beans, past sprawling vines of cucumbers and tomatoes, and stalks of golden corn, past patches of strawberries and huge bunches of lettuce. Her garden was extraordinary and, if it weren't for the tree line of the forest in the distance, I would have assumed there was no end to it.

The smells were indescribable—bursts of lemon balm and basil, the sweetness of pomegranates and figs, the cool scent of mint that sprang up everywhere.

The flagstone path continued around the yard, weaving alongside picket fences and vegetable beds, taking me on a journey I hadn't expected to embark on. I'd had no idea this garden existed right next door for I couldn't see it from any of the cabin windows.

'This is incredible,' I said, but the words somehow fell short. The garden was more than that. It was colourful and full of life, with so many things to gape at that I wasn't sure where to focus my attention. Gnomes, birdbaths, a replica windmill, a miniature well and, of course, all the fresh produce one could ever want. There were things growing in that garden that I could only hope to name.

'Do you like it?' Noelle asked, but the glimmer in her eye suggested she knew I did, that it was a special place that softened the steeliest of souls.

'It's like nothing I've ever seen before.' Anna would have loved it. She'd always talked about having a large vegetable garden, but pregnancy after pregnancy had kept her occupied and she'd yet to get around to it. I resolved to take photos with Noelle's permission and send them to her, maybe even help her build it when I went home.

'I have herbs in recycled wine barrels over here,' Noelle said, leading me to a spot beneath an orange tree where she grew basil, parsley, thyme, oregano, and rosemary. 'I would grow more of everything, except it becomes too much to maintain.'

'How do you it all? It's a lot for one person to look after.'

'Lachlan and his mother, Ivy, help me. And I cook, so nothing ever goes to waste. Plus, what's mine is yours. Everyone is welcome to harvest from my garden if they are happy to pull a weed or two out in exchange.' She dropped to her knees in a way that belied her age next to the sprawling stems of a Lebanese cucumber plant. 'My cucumbers are ready. Help me pick them.'

I knelt beside her, pushed up my sleeves and watched tentatively as she parted the broad leaves to find cucumbers underneath. She twisted a cucumber from its stem, snapping it off, then glanced at me as if to ask what I was waiting for. I replicated her action, parting the leaves, which were unexpectedly spikey, to find a well-sized cucumber underneath. I reached for it, its skin prickly, and pulled it away from the stem as she'd shown me, adding it to the pile by our knees.

'Do you have children?' I asked her as we worked.

'I had one. A daughter.' She didn't look up as she spoke, her nimble fingers parting the leaves in search of the fruit. 'Her name was Danielle. She died many years ago, though.'

I glanced at her, my heart as heavy as when she'd told me her beloved Samuel had died. 'I'm sorry to hear that.'

Noelle paused, then she nodded resolutely. 'She suffered as you do, *ma chère.*'

I froze, an uncomfortable prickling sensation running down my neck, as I sensed she was more attuned to my situation than I'd first thought.

'Her poison was heroin. She discovered it on the mainland as a young adult. She discovered many things there that she shouldn't have, and she was never herself again.'

My soul wept for Noelle, for Danielle. While I'd always dabbled in recreational drugs, I'd never tried heroin because I was too afraid it would take one use and my impulsive nature would latch onto it, spelling the end for me.

'The cabin was for her,' Noelle continued. 'Samuel and I built it so that she could return to the island and get well. And she did. When she was twenty-eight, she came home to us.'

A small bead of sweat formed on her upper lip and brow, but Noelle didn't halt. In the short time I'd known her, I'd come to realise she was a resilient woman, no matter what hardships life had cast.

'But she only stayed for a week. Just when I thought she was over the worst of it, temptation struck and she caught the supply boat back to the mainland. We discovered that afternoon that she was gone. It was the last time we ever saw her.'

'What happened to her?'

Noelle took a long breath now, sitting back on her haunches, wiping the sweat from her face with her apron. She glanced at me, sorrow in her eyes. 'She overdosed in an alleyway in Fredericton that same night. She didn't have identification on her, so she was a Jane Doe for a while until they identified her and located us. We went to the mainland, cremated her there and brought her home to White Cedar. We scattered her ashes in the ocean and under my rose bushes in the garden.'

I understood now why Noelle so lovingly tended those roses, why there were vases full of them all around her house. It was her way of keeping Danielle close—her spirit in the petals. 'Did you and Samuel have other children?'

She sighed. 'It wasn't easy for Samuel and me to conceive. Danielle was unexpected; a blessing, but she wasn't meant for this world. Or maybe she wasn't meant for the mainland. We always encouraged her to spread her wings, to travel and experience life. Maybe that's where we went wrong.' She shook her head soberly.

I placed my hand on her shoulder. 'I don't know much about children or what's right for them, but you weren't to blame for what happened to Danielle. This island is lovely but there's a whole world out there, good and bad, and you couldn't have kept her here forever.'

'It was the sixties and seventies,' Noelle explained, 'and perhaps, in hindsight, I should have known it was inevitable, the age of free love and drugs. But I wasn't worldly, so I didn't know what life was like out there. I'd lived my entire life here, as had Samuel. Maybe that's why I understand you. You are like my Danielle. Same demons, different poison.'

It all made sense now, the hearty meals she'd left on the step, the crossword puzzles to keep me occupied, her unwillingness to collect the letter and key from under the mat when I'd tried to leave that day with Harry. She'd understood all along what was happening to me.

'I know of your struggles.' She glanced at me earnestly and I met her gaze. 'I saw that haunted look on your face when you arrived, the tremor in your hands, the way you locked yourself inside while you dealt with your detox. I know the cycle well. I've seen it before.'

I wasn't much of a crier. I rarely allowed emotion to surface, a coping mechanism I'd adopted after the Wagners. But there, in that glorious backyard filled with the sights and smells and sounds of everything nature could conjure, I felt it break through me. A single tear slid down my cheek and I hurried to wipe it away, but Noelle caught my hand.

'Let yourself feel, *ma chère*. Let your tears out. How can you heal otherwise?'

'But I'm afraid,' I whispered. 'And when I'm afraid, I drink.'

'Then don't live your life in isolation. Share your burdens with us so we can carry the weight for you. The load will feel lighter.'

She gave me an encouraging smile and, although I didn't feel like I'd shared much, an unspoken bond formed between us, out there by her cucumber vines. She patted my hand. 'Now, help me up. I am a hundred years old, after all.'

I laughed softly, climbing to my feet, and helping Noelle to hers. As spritely as she moved sometimes, I saw glimpses of the old woman she was in the hunch of her shoulders or the stiff way she moved her joints and I wondered if she carried Danielle's fate on her shoulders more than she should. Like I carried the fate of the Wagners on mine. We all had our burdens and we carted them around in different ways. Sometimes they made us stronger. Sometimes they broke us. Sometimes we drank them into oblivion.

We bunched the cucumbers together and carried them into the house. Noelle asked if I'd stay for lunch, but I promised dinner instead. I wanted to walk, to clear my head, so I thanked her for the lovely morning in her garden and for confiding in me, before heading down the flagstone path to the road that led to the village.

When I arrived, I found a bench outside the bookstore to call Austin. I hadn't spoken to him all week—the longest we'd ever gone—but now, more than ever, I longed to hear his voice. To know that he missed me and to share with him the good news of my progress.

I pulled out my phone and scrolled through my messages and missed calls. Lots from Anna, a few from my father, another from Paul but again, dishearteningly, nothing from Austin. I pushed down a rush of hurt, certain that work had been busy, that he'd been in court and that he was generally hopeless at keeping in touch. Excuses perhaps, but the alternative was that he'd forgotten me and that was too hurtful to contemplate.

I mentally calculated the time difference. It was midnight Saturday in Melbourne. When I dialled, the call rang several times before diverting to his voicemail. I left a message, asking him to return my call within the next hour if possible, for I'd still be in the village to receive it. I hung up, waited twenty minutes, strolling around the square and past shopfronts, before I tried calling again. It went through to voicemail once more, so I hung up. A second later, I received a text from him.

Busy. Call you later.

I blanched. *Busy? Call you later?*

I knew what it meant—he was in a packed bar somewhere, the noise was deafening, he was in drunk conversation with someone and he'd be unable to hear me. But shouldn't I be a priority? Shouldn't he be excited and want to call me back straight away?

Insult washed over me, making my stomach clench. I knew I was being sensitive. I was the one who'd left him behind, after all. I could hardly expect him to stay in every evening and pine for me. But I was alone and far from home, and to hear his voice would have meant everything, a familiarity I desperately needed. I didn't want to hear that he was too busy for me, that life was carrying on without me, as though my absence had hardly caused a ripple. If I were to be completely honest, I'd hoped that he would have been miserable without me, that hearing of my progress would have inspired him to take the same journey.

I pushed my phone into the back pocket of my jean shorts and took a deep breath, trying to concentrate on the shopfronts once more, but I couldn't seem to get that infuriating text out of my head.

Would it have killed him to take five minutes out from his partying?

Why didn't he try to call me before today?

Has he even noticed I'm gone?

Amidst all the muttering inside my head, I didn't remember walking across the square and into Louise's shop. My feet seemed to have carried me without a conscious directive from my brain. I only realised I was inside once it was too late and I was standing in front of the shelves of alcohol, the beast inside me telling me to pick up a bottle, take it to the cash register and pay for it.

I shouldn't have been there. Just one drink would undo all my hard work, but I couldn't stop myself. I was struggling with Austin's dismissal and feeling forgotten. A crushing sense of loneliness engulfed me, and I reached for the vodka, closing my fingers around it, the glass cool against my palm.

Every fibre in my body was joyous at the thought of that liquid hitting the back of my throat, burning my oesophagus, landing in my stomach with pleasurable force. I'd have it with ice. I'd make a martini. I'd drink it from the bottle until I couldn't see straight.

'Hey, honey!'

I jumped so high at the sound of Louise's voice that I let go of the bottle and knocked over a stand of pretzels beside me.

'Oh, I'm sorry, love,' she said. 'I didn't mean to startle you.' Her eyes were warm, her hand steady and reassuring on my back.

I fell to the ground, hot with humiliation, trying to gather up packets of pretzels strewn across the floor.

'Let me take care of that,' she said. She helped me straighten the stand and stack the packets back on it. 'No harm done. Were you looking for something in particular?'

'Yes, I...' I swallowed hard, glancing at the bottles again. I wanted that vodka. I wanted it to cloud my mind and fill me with confidence, so I knew how to deal with Austin. But somewhere, through the barrage of cravings, my sobriety was screaming, *Get out of there.*

I shook my head. 'I mean... no. I don't know.'

Louise looked confused. 'Honey?'

'It's all right.' I forced a helpless smile. 'I think I'll just go.'

'Oh.' Louise looked completely bewildered now. 'Okay. well, if there's something I don't have on the shelf, I can always order it for you.'

'No, really, I'm fine. Sorry.' I hurried away from her, back down the aisle, bursting out of the shop and into the sunshine again. I didn't walk, I ran all the way down Main Street, past the council chambers and the hospital and up the hill to Noelle's cabin. I didn't stop until my lungs were bursting, my legs were shaking, and I'd put as much distance as possible between me and that vodka.

Chapter 15

I was trembling all over by the time I reached the cabin. I poured myself a glass of juice, grabbed one of the new books I'd bought from the bookstore and sat out on the verandah, trying to distract myself in words. But the image of that vodka swallowed my every thought. It felt like day one again when I was desperate and wanting, and I'm sure I didn't imagine the withdrawal cramps in my stomach or the battery taste in my mouth.

Somehow, as afternoon crept across the island, my racing heart slowed, and my eyes grew heavy until I dozed off. I came to again when I heard someone calling my name.

'Marley, you will come for dinner,' Noelle called from her side of the yard.

I sat up, closed the book that was still open on my lap, and rubbed my eyes. 'Oh, hi.'

'Yes, you will come,' she affirmed with a nod. 'Be here at four o'clock.' Then she disappeared into her house.

I shook the sleep from my head, positive I wasn't dreaming, then broke into a grin. I was slowly getting used to Noelle, the way she summoned rather than asked when she wanted something. I liked that about her; an authority that felt comforting.

Realising it was already past three, I went back inside the cabin and ran a shower. I washed my hair, then found a blue Greta Constantine dress in my suitcase that Austin had always said brought out the colour of my eyes. I tried not to think of him now and his earlier slight, concentrating instead on getting ready. The dress was a little extravagant for a simple dinner with Noelle, but I was excited. I looked forward to her company and, somewhere between the incident at Louise's shop and falling asleep on the verandah, I'd skipped lunch and was ravenous.

Noelle's house smelled as it always did, of warmth and cooking and love. As soon as I arrived, she slipped an apron over my head and rattled off a list of things she needed from her garden.

'Tomatoes, shallots, carrots, thyme, parsley, potatoes, rocket and green beans. There are scissors and a shovel out there, gloves and baskets and buckets too.'

'Uh.' I looked down at my five-hundred-dollar outfit. 'I'm not really dressed for gardening.'

'Then go home and get changed.'

I shook my head. 'It's all right, I'll live.'

'At least swap those sparkly things for boots.'

I glanced down at my Louboutin sandals. 'These?'

'They won't survive the garden. I have a new pair of rubber boots by the back door you can wear.'

I smiled gratefully. 'Thank you. What are you making?'

'*We* are making garlic beans for entrée, ratatouille for main and chocolate cake for dessert.'

'That's a lot for two people,' I said, not that I was complaining. My stomach was rumbling.

'It's not for two people. I have guests coming for dinner.'

'Guests?'

'Lachlan, his mother and her partner,' she said.

'Oh.'

'And I need to warn you.' Her expression grew serious. 'Sometimes we drink red wine at dinner. I will have jugs of juice on the table, but I cannot control what they will bring with them. Sometimes they bring wine, sometimes they don't.'

I chewed my lip, my stomach constricting at the thought that I was about to be tested, that my carefully constructed bubble could potentially be punctured by something as simple as a bottle of wine on the table. But people shouldn't have to forego their enjoyment because

I couldn't control myself around alcohol. It was a stark reminder that the world didn't stop turning simply because I had. I lifted my chin resolutely as she watched me. 'Thank you for letting me know. I'll be fine.'

'Are you sure? Perhaps this is all too soon. Maybe we should cancel.' She wrung her hands together as concern filled her eyes.

Although I'd broken into a sweat, I didn't want her to see that I was worried. I didn't want my problem to become her problem and start impacting the way she lived her life. Why shouldn't she sit down to a meal with friends and enjoy a drink? Who was I to walk in and expect changes? I patted her arm gently with a smile. 'It's okay, really.'

She stared at me. 'Are you sure? It's no problem to cancel.'

'We're not cancelling. We're about to make all this food.' I gestured to the kitchen bench, already laden with chopping boards and knives and pots. And I *was* excited about cooking with Noelle.

She inhaled deeply, as though still unsure, but eventually relented. 'Okay. Only if you are certain. You can go and get the vegetables so we can start.'

The new boots were by the door, exactly where Noelle said they'd be, and I slipped out of my sandals and pulled them on, then trudged out into the backyard. I wasted no time getting to work in the fading light, looking for all the things she'd asked for. It wasn't long before the hem of my dress was dragging in the dirt and my knees were stained from kneeling. I gathered what she needed, but it took time while I located each plant. Even then I wasn't sure if I was picking the right things.

After an hour, Noelle appeared on the back step. 'I said pick some vegetables, not watch them grow. What's taking so long?'

'Coming,' I called, hauling full buckets and baskets to where she was waiting.

She bent down and rummaged through what I'd collected, then nodded with approval. 'Very good. This will do nicely.'

For the next two hours, we worked side by side, chopping, frying and stirring. I had no idea what I was doing, only that my apron looked like someone had splattered the contents of an entire kitchen pantry over it. Nevertheless, I was enjoying myself, as we drank fresh orange juice and nibbled on the food we chopped.

We talked about Danielle and my work back home and I even told her about the Wagners, stopping short of the confronting details, confessing only that I'd had a hand in an incident that had ended tragically, which had catapulted my drinking into something more serious. In many ways, Noelle reminded me of my mother as she listened, making thoughtful comments without judgement.

Later in the evening, while the ratatouille cooked in the oven and the chocolate cake cooled on a wire rack, we scooped enough garlic beans for a small army onto a platter and set it on the bench. I was laying five places at the table when there was a knock at the door, and Noelle went to answer it.

Nerves settled in my stomach at the thought of seeing Lachlan again and I returned to the kitchen, fussing with the dish of beans, then my hair, then my dress. I took off the apron, realising I still had my boots on, but there was no time to change back into my sandals as voices reached the dining room.

Lachlan appeared in the kitchen, carrying two large glass dishes. His face lit up when he saw me. 'Hey, Marley. It's good to see you again.'

'Hey.' I waved.

'Wow, you look incredible.' His eyes travelled the length of my blue dress, before settling on the green rubber boots. He raised an eyebrow.

I looked down at them and laughed. 'I've been in the garden.'

'Ah, Noelle had you singing for your supper then. She's been known to do that.'

'She did. But I didn't mind. It was fun.'

His hair was wet from the shower, and he smelled fresh like the forest after rain. He wore dark jeans and trainers and a white shirt that showed tanned, muscular arms. I reached for the dishes he was holding, trying not to appreciate the sight of him so obviously. 'Can I take those?'

'Sure. Stuffed eggplants in this one and braised wild fennel with almonds in that one.'

'There's so much food,' I said, uncovering the dishes and setting them on the bench next to the beans. 'There'll be plenty left over.'

Lachlan reached over suddenly, brushing his fingers across my cheek. 'You have flour on your face.'

The intimacy of his gesture took my breath away and I froze. 'Oh, thanks. I didn't realise.'

'No problem.'

He smiled at me, and I knew I'd turned fiercely red. I allowed my hair to drop around my face and spun away in a fluster to collect tongs and serving spoons from the drawers. My back was to the doorway as voices approached. When I glanced up, Dr Tremblay was entering the kitchen. Our smiles vanished as we became aware of each other.

'Ivy, have you met my new neighbour?' Noelle asked, bustling back to the oven.

'Mom, this is Marley,' Lachlan said. 'Marley, this is my mom and Joel.'

I was mortified as I glanced at Lachlan. Dr Tremblay was his *mother*?

'Hello again, Marley,' Ivy said. 'You're looking better.'

Lachlan appeared confused, his eyes darting between us. 'You two know each other already?'

Ivy's lips clamped shut. She was bound by doctor-patient confidentiality, and her eyes grew round with the realisation that she'd said too much.

I frowned at her, struggling to contain my annoyance. 'I consulted with your mother briefly when I arrived.'

Awkward silence fell as everyone's eyes settled on me. I felt like a bug under a microscope.

Mercifully, Noelle clapped her hands together. 'Dinner is ready.'

We all seemed to release a grateful breath as we pounced on the dishes of food and carried them into the dining room. We set the dishes on the table between plates and cutlery and two bottles of red wine someone had already placed in the middle.

Although Noelle had warned they might be there, the sight of those bottles caused my senses to ignite. I was already flustered with the discovery that Dr Tremblay was Lachlan's mother and that I'd have to eat dinner with her, but to also eat in the company of wine was going to test my limits.

Everyone took their seats, except for me, as I spent a few moments finding a spot. I groaned internally when the only empty chair left was between Joel and Ivy, and I was forced to drop into it. Ivy looked displeased, but Joel was gracious as he introduced himself and asked about Australia. He was in his late fifties, jovial and charismatic, offering to spoon beans and ratatouille onto my plate.

But when he reached for a bottle of wine and filled my glass, I sucked in my breath and turned panicked eyes to Noelle.

'Marley doesn't drink,' Noelle said quickly. 'She will have juice instead.'

'Oh.' Joel pulled the bottle back. 'Apologies, Marley.'

I wanted to say it was okay, that since my glass was poured, I might as well have a sip. Just one; it couldn't hurt. But Noelle and Ivy's eyes were fixed on me, and Lachlan was watching curiously, and it all felt too much.

My hands grew clammy, and my throat began to ache, my blood pulsing with the rush of a craving. Even if someone had taken my wine glass away, I'd still have to sit beside Joel while he drank from his. I'd smell it, see the red stain on his lips, hear the whoosh of velvety liquid swirling around in his glass.

I couldn't do it. God help me, I wasn't strong enough.

I cleared my throat, feeling so uncomfortable that I wanted to shrink to nothing and disappear, to wish myself back to my old life in Melbourne. I placed my palms on the table and took a deep breath. 'I'm sorry everyone. I'm not feeling too well. I think I'm going to give dinner a miss and head back next door.'

Lachlan looked surprised. 'Are you all right?'

'A migraine,' I said, clutching my head. 'I've had it all day. I should probably lie down.'

He rose from his seat. 'Let me walk you to the cabin.'

'No, please. Stay and eat. I don't want to interrupt your meal.'

As I stood and placed my napkin on the table, I glanced at the food Noelle and I had prepared and felt a pang of regret. I'd enjoyed my afternoon with her, and I'd looked forward to eating the food we'd made, but my resolve would only take me so far. It was an impossible ask for me to sit at a table and drink juice while others drank wine. I just couldn't.

I caught Noelle's sad sigh as I threw them a hurried goodbye and left the house. I could feel their eyes following me as Lachlan slowly sat again and Joel said softly, 'Did I do something wrong?'

I crept along the path to the cabin and let myself in the front door. After the liveliness of Noelle's home, the cabin was quiet and solitary. I closed the door, walked to my bedroom, and sank onto the bed.

I might have been on the path to sobriety, to a healthier, more fulfilled life, but this journey was a lonely one. There were so few people

I could talk to who would understand or who I could confide in without feeling humiliated and ashamed. I was caught between two worlds—a place I felt most comfortable in and a place I was trying to get to. I wanted to move forward, but forward was terrifying, filled with doubt and memories and the threat of relapse lurking around every corner. If it had not been for Noelle and Ivy's stares boring into me at the dinner table, studying my every move as Joel filled my glass with wine, I would have given in. I would have brought that glass to my lips.

Now, as I stared at the walls of my room, hands clenched around the quilt, trying to fight my cravings, the temptation to throw it all in had never been stronger.

Chapter 16

An hour later, there was a knock at the door. I was still in my Greta Constantine dress, curled beneath the covers in bed reading, trying to lose myself in a world that was not my own. I climbed out and went to the living room to peer through the curtain of the front window, finding Lachlan standing on the verandah.

I opened the door and gave him an apologetic smile. 'Hey.'

'Hey.' He held out a plate of food covered with tin foil. 'I thought you might be hungry.'

'Thank you. You didn't have to do that.' But I was hungry, so I took the plate gratefully and placed it inside on the hall table.

'Feel like company?' he asked.

I didn't want to be by myself, so I stepped out onto the verandah and closed the door behind me. 'Sure.'

We sat on the top step, just wide enough for both of us, our shoulders and hips touching. Silence fell as we watched the North Atlantic Ocean ripple gently beneath a full moon.

'I live on the beach too,' I said. 'Back home in Melbourne. My apartment overlooks it.'

'You're used to living by the water then?'

'Yes, but not like this. There's something different about the ocean here.'

'Maybe it feels vaster because of where we are.'

'Perhaps,' I said. 'Or maybe it's the quiet. There's so much of it. It's easy to forget where you are or to feel forgotten about.'

His eyes were full of questions as they studied me. 'Is that how you feel, forgotten about?'

I shrugged. 'I don't know.'

'By Anna?'

'Not Anna,' I said. He was looking at me expectantly and I knew I was being ambiguous, but I didn't have the words to explain Austin's dismissal earlier and how vulnerable it had left me. How every little challenge felt all the more insurmountable when I didn't have alcohol to pacify it.

'You didn't catch that ride out with Harry today,' he said.

'No. I've decided to stay the full two weeks.'

I caught his smile, soft in the shadows, even when he tried to conceal it by dipping his head.

'You know, when my mother and I arrived here ten years ago, it was because someone had let us down,' he said, glancing back up at me. 'We had to start all over again.'

I watched his expression grow thoughtful as he looked away to stare out at the ocean.

'My father wasn't a nice man. I mean, to me, he was just my dad. But the relationship he had with my mother was unhealthy.'

'In what way?' I asked.

'He was violent,' he said. 'Never in ways that left visible bruises because she was a doctor and had to go to work each day, but in ways that could be hidden under her clothing, so that no one knew what was going on.'

'He was hurting her?'

'Yes. All the time. But it wasn't just physical violence. He restricted her freedom, her access to money, stripped her of confidence. The only place she was allowed to go was to work and, even then, he would drop into the surgery unannounced just to check she was there. He controlled every aspect of her life.'

I had a recollection of Katiana in court, broken and terrified by the abuse in her relationship. I closed my eyes to the knowledge that I'd had the power to protect her but hadn't, even when I'd believed deep down that Karl Wagner was guilty.

'I didn't realise there was a problem until I was old enough to visit friends' houses,' Lachlan continued. 'I'd notice the equality in their parents' relationships and how screwed up mine was.' He made a cynical noise. 'When I became a teenager, I was able to stand up to him and protect my mother. Then, for a few years, everything calmed down. It was like it all just stopped, and life was better.' He hugged his knees closer to his chest, wrapping his arms around them. 'Until I realised he was abusing her when I wasn't home, that he was still controlling her in ways I didn't completely understand as a teenager.'

'How did you find out?'

'I walked into her room one day while she was buttoning up her shirt and I saw the bruises on her stomach. She said she'd knocked herself on the corner of the washing machine until I finally got it out of her that she'd spent money on a new dress, and he'd found out. I couldn't believe it. He was still hurting her, but because I'd grown almost taller than him, he was a coward and would do it when I wasn't around.'

My soul ached for him and for Ivy, who I was sure would be outraged if she thought I pitied her. 'Why didn't she tell you the abuse was still happening?'

'Victims of domestic violence don't just *tell* people what's happening, especially those closest to them. They're humiliated, scared. Just saying it out loud is frightening.'

I thought of what I had put Katiana through, how she'd tacked together a few precious strands of bravery to face her abuser in court, and I'd decimated her with my cross-examination. I shivered, not from the cool night air, but from the agonising twist of guilt in my stomach at what I'd done. For the kind of person I was. Ivy's story was so like Katiana's that I knew at that moment I could never tell Lachlan what had brought me here.

Lachlan glanced down at me, mistaking my unease for the cold. 'It's chilly tonight. Have my jacket.'

I shook my head. 'No, I'm fine.'

'You're not. You're shivering.' He slid out of his jacket, wrapping it around my bare shoulders.

'Thank you.' Although regret was still radiating through me, it was hard not to inhale his scent of pinecones and the ocean. 'How did you get your mother to leave him?'

'It wasn't me, actually. She made the decision on her own. He'd locked her in the house for a week.'

'What do you mean *locked her in the house*?'

'He'd got it into his head that she was cheating on him with a colleague of hers, and he locked her in the house. He had a locksmith arrive to install more deadbolts on the doors and windows so she couldn't get out.'

'Jesus.' I'd witnessed some gruesome stories during my career, and I shouldn't have been appalled, but I was.

'He called her work and said she had the flu, then made her a prisoner for a week.'

'How did she escape?'

'She broke the lock on the laundry door and climbed over the back fence. She ran all the way to my apartment in the city. No easy feat, for she didn't have her car keys or money or cell phone. He'd disabled the modem so she couldn't email anyone. She didn't even have shoes. He'd taken everything. It took her two hours to reach me on foot.'

Not many things shocked me in this world because I'd always viewed the horrors through the lens of defence, but somehow, Lachlan and Ivy's story felt different. This wasn't just another case I'd represented in court. There was no cross-examination or magistrate or due process. This was someone's raw pain. 'So you brought her here?'

He hugged his knees tighter to his chest and I could see he was reliving the past. 'Yes. We knew the first place he'd check was my apartment. And I knew that if he found her, he'd be full of promises and remorse and there was a good chance she'd go back. So, that same night, I drove her to Halifax. We stayed overnight and caught Harry's boat to White Cedar the next morning.'

'And you stayed?'

'Not initially,' he said. 'I travelled back and forth for a while. I had a life in Montreal that I couldn't just disappear from, a job, a girlfriend. I cut my father off, though. I told him I wanted nothing more to do with him. He was persistent, of course, full of apologies.

'In the end, the more time I spent here, the more I liked it. It was just an easier way of life. No stress, no fear, no confusing family dynamics.' He smiled sheepishly in the dark. 'Then the truffle thing happened, and Mom met Joel, and we just stayed.'

It seemed I wasn't the only lost soul to seek solace on White Cedar. Its shores had embraced others before me, had healed wounds and rebuilt lives. Maybe I understood Ivy a little more after hearing her story, the reason she was guarded and protective, intolerant of outsiders.

I was starting to get an inkling of who Lachlan was too. Highly resilient, genuine and incredibly brave. He knew right from wrong, no matter the grey areas. It was the same grey I'd built a career from exploiting. We couldn't have been more different. 'Has your dad ever tried to track you and your mum down?'

'Occasionally, when I go back to Montreal for work and I stay at my apartment, I'll find the odd letter in the mailbox asking us to contact him. But it's been a few years since I've seen one of those. I couldn't even tell you if he was alive now.'

'And that doesn't make you sad?'

'He wasn't a good person.' But even as Lachlan said it, I saw the way his eyes filled with sorrow and his shoulders slumped. Knowing right from wrong was one thing, but you couldn't turn the love off in your heart so easily and I sensed that he wished things had been different. That his dad had been different.

'I guess all has worked out,' I said. 'Your mother and Joel seem happy.'

He gave me an apologetic look. 'I'm sorry that you felt uncomfortable at dinner. I don't know what happened back there or how you know my mother exactly, but I'm guessing you didn't have a migraine tonight.'

He watched me closely and I knew he was expecting candour in return. But how could I tell this perfect guy who saw everything in black and white that my life was a train wreck? That I was selfish and unthinking, and that I defended people like his father every day?

And although I was leaving in a week and I shouldn't have cared what he thought, I did. I liked him and I wanted him to like me too, for reasons I couldn't quite understand.

'Firstly, you don't have to apologise for anything. I wasn't in the mood for socialising tonight,' I said. 'And secondly, I'm here because I need to hit pause on my life. And I'm trying to do that the best way I can while being incredibly homesick and not knowing anyone here.' It was vague, but it was the best I could do without pouring out all the details of the past two years.

He didn't press me further. He just frowned. 'Well now, that's not completely true. You know *me*. And I hope by now we're friends.'

I dipped my head and laughed. 'Okay, you're right, I do know you and yes, we *are* friends.'

The front door of Noelle's house opened, and Ivy and Joel stepped onto the verandah. In the moonlight, I could see his mother searching the yard for him and when her eyes fell on us sitting on the front step of the cabin, she gave a half-wave. 'We're leaving, Lachlan. Shall we wait for you?'

'You go on ahead,' he called back. 'I'll see you tomorrow.'

She opened her mouth to reply, or perhaps protest, but Joel placed a hand on her back and said something in her ear. She accepted this with a slight nod, and they strolled down the path to the road, their silhouettes disappearing into the darkness.

'I should let you get inside,' he said. 'You must be hungry. That food will taste even better warmed up.'

He rose to his feet and I followed, slipping out of his jacket and handing it to him.

'Thank you for bringing me dinner and for lending me your jacket,' I said.

'Anytime.' He accepted it and stepped off the verandah. He smiled at me, and it was so genuine and perfect that I couldn't tear my gaze away from it. 'You have another week here, so don't be a stranger. You don't have to hit pause on your own.'

He gave me one last thoughtful look, then turned and walked down the path, the darkness eventually swallowing him. I opened the door and let myself back into the cabin, closing it behind me.

You don't have to hit pause on your own.

It was remarkable how a person I hardly knew could throw me such a lifeline. He would never understand just how significant those words were. Noelle had offered them too, and it made me realise that there was good to be found here. That I was luckier than most in my predicament. I would relish my time left on the island. I would draw on the kindness and generosity of the people here. I would not let my stay be in vain.

I heated the plate of food, devoured it, then showered and brushed my teeth. Slipping into pyjamas, I had every intention of reading again, but I only managed a few words before I sank into the pillow and fell fast asleep.

Chapter 17

I couldn't remember a time when I'd ever slept so soundly, but the morning after Noelle's dinner, on my eighth day of sobriety, I climbed out of bed feeling fresher than I had in years. It was six am and, instead of going to bed drunk with the rising sun, I woke with it.

I dressed and chopped fruit, blending it into a smoothie that I drank quickly. I was keen to get down to the village and call Anna before she went to bed. I'd yet to speak with her, conversing only in texts.

I'd only been sober a short time, but those precious days of sobriety had given me a surprising epiphany. I hadn't just reached rock bottom; I'd found a whole new depth to it. Every second I stayed dry, each time I didn't have to reach for the Dexedrine, or greet weary, bloodshot eyes in the mirror each morning, I saw the love in Anna's decision to send me here.

After my smoothie, I reached for my phone and a cardigan and walked down to the village. I ordered a cup of coffee from the Wildflower Café and outside, under their umbrellas, I settled into a seat and waited for my order. The sun was fighting for stage time with the clouds. The morning was cool; a reminder that fall was coming. Back home, it would be spring soon, Melbourne emerging from its winter cloak, and my thoughts strayed to Austin. I wondered where he was and what he was doing, feeling the sting of his slight all over again.

As soon as my phone had a signal, I dialled Anna's number. It was eleven in the evening for her, and I cringed at the thought of calling so late. But she answered immediately and sounded awake.

'You weren't sleeping, were you?' I asked.

'I said goodbye to sleep four years ago.' She sighed tiredly. 'No, I'm definitely up. Mia's in our bed with croup. She has a horrendous cough. Anyway, how are you? I tried calling a few times, but I couldn't get through.'

'The signal is patchy,' I said. 'I can't make or receive calls in the cabin. The only time it works is down here in the village.'

'What time is it there?'

'Eight am.'

She snorted. 'Wait, have you been to bed already or are you just about to go?'

'Very funny.'

'Marley Kincaid, my big sister, rising before midday. This has to be a first.' I could see her shaking her head.

'Excuse me, I have a job. I'm up all the time before eight.'

'Yes, but not while on holiday. You'd just be coming in about now.'

'Well, this isn't exactly a holiday.'

There was silence on the other end, then her voice grew earnest. 'I'm sorry. I shouldn't have called it that. How are you doing? You sound well.'

I swallowed down my pride, needing to be truthful. 'I feel... better.'

'Really?' She sounded pleased and a little tentative, like she didn't want to believe it was possible. 'I'm thrilled. When was your last drink?'

'Eight days ago. I don't want to get ahead of myself, but it's the longest I've gone in a while.'

'It must be hard,' she said. 'I mean, you must want one.'

'Every minute of every day,' I said. 'But the people are friendly here. I don't find myself alone too often.'

'You mean they know?'

'Just the town doctor. And my landlady,' I said. 'Her daughter had substance abuse problems a long time ago, so she's been incredibly supportive. She has this garden full of produce, one that you can get lost in. I'll take photos for you. She's even had me over twice to cook.'

'You've cooked at her house?' Anna's voice was wry. 'I'll try not to be hurt by that. You never wanted to cook with us.'

I closed my eyes, feeling the unpleasant rise of regret again. There were so many things to be sorry for. 'I was always hungover. I wasn't in a good place.'

Anna made a sound of agreement. 'Well, you're on the right track now. That's the main thing. Was the detox terrible?'

'Awful,' I said. 'But it's done.'

'And for what it's worth, I'm proud of you. You're the bravest person I know, doing that on your own without anyone there with you.'

I smiled at her words. It had been a long time since my sister had been 'proud' of me. Mostly I'd given her cause to be embarrassed or disappointed.

'So, do they have AA meetings or counsellors on the island?' Anna asked. 'You could start a program before you come home.'

'No, I don't think they have anything like that here.'

'Have you made any friends?'

'A few. Lachlan. Noelle. Louise—'

'Who's Lachlan?'

She'd jumped so emphatically on the word that I was grateful when my coffee and pastry arrived, and I could take a moment to consider my response. 'Just one of the locals.'

'A guy?'

'Well, I don't know any girls called Lachlan.'

'I'm not sure a romance is a good idea,' Anna said gently.

I laughed. 'Who said anything about a romance? He's just someone who lives here. It's hard not to meet everybody. The community is small.'

'Of course,' she said. 'But your time there should be about getting well. A romance or a fling would complicate things.'

'I have one week left here. Hardly time to get romantically involved with anyone. And I do have someone waiting for me back home, remember?'

'Right. Austin.' Her tone wrapped bitterly around his name.

I sighed. 'I know you don't like him.'

'I'm worried that when you come home, he'll tempt you back to old ways.'

'I won't let him.'

'You might not be able to control it. Two weeks away is a drop in the ocean, Marley. You have a long way to go. You need supportive people in your circle.'

She was right, of course. This was only the beginning. The euphoria I felt at conquering the withdrawals would soon wear off and I'd be fighting the same triggers I'd always fought. Change would only be possible if I had supportive people in my life, and I worried that Austin would attempt to sabotage my recovery at every turn because change for me meant change for him too.

'I think when you come home you should start a program and immediately end things with him,' Anna said.

I choked on a sip of coffee and winced as it burnt my throat. 'Um, okay.'

'I'm serious. He's not good for you. I know you've been through a lot together, but this won't work if he's not prepared to dry out as well.'

I couldn't deny that what she said made sense, but Austin was important to me—something that she would never understand. 'Let's take this one step at a time, okay?'

'You need to have a plan for when you leave.'

'I will.'

'You could take an extra two weeks off and come and stay with us. We have plenty of room and the girls would love it.'

'I'll think about.'

Anna's voice sounded resigned. 'I just want you home and healthy.'

I nodded into the phone. 'I know.'

Mia coughed in the background. It sounded like a seal barking and I heard Tom's soothing voice comforting her. For the first time in a long time, I wished I were with them, to help Anna and Tom, and cuddle Mia while she was sick.

'I hope you're feeling well,' I said.

'Only like a whale. I can't sleep and everything I eat gives me heartburn.'

'And you love having babies because...?'

'You'll find out one day, Marley,' she said with a smile in her voice. 'I want to be an aunt too, you know.'

'Don't get your hopes up.'

We said goodbye and I spent another ten minutes enjoying my coffee, then I decided to try Austin again. It was almost midnight by then, and even though he had to work the next morning, I knew he'd be out in a noisy bar. Predictably, his phone rang several times then went to voicemail. I didn't leave a message. Instead, I stood, dropped some money on the table and headed back into the square.

It was Sunday and it seemed everyone on White Cedar was in the village. Louise's store was packed, the café was filling up, and people stopped on the sidewalk to greet each other. I wasn't sure what to do with the day. I felt energetic and didn't want to go back to the cabin simply to sit inside. I thought about taking a walk to the beach to dip my toes in the water. Maybe Anton or Gilbert would be down there. Or maybe I could try to find the lighthouse on the other side of the island.

In the end, I decided to take a walk around the hilly streets to find a view I could photograph and send back to Anna. While those mountainous roads still challenged me, making my lungs and legs burn, I was getting better at climbing them, each day becoming a little easier. Still, I didn't want to get lost up there, so I kept a firm eye on the ocean and the sun to orient myself as I climbed.

Rain had swept through the night before, leaving everything fragrant. The maples and cedars in the forest were heady and a bald eagle cried from above, dipping and soaring through the air. I passed several people out walking, not with activewear and trainers and that determined set of their jaw like their life depended on that one strenuous hour of fat-burning exercise. It was a calm stroll, as though it was as much about the journey as it was the destination. They seemed in no hurry, so I slowed too, taking in the wide ocean studded with sunlight, the green forests wet with rain, and a deer and her fawn who appeared by the roadside to nibble on tree shoots.

Around the corner of a bend, I came to a property with a timber gate. The house wasn't visible from the road, only a canopy of eastern redbuds that led down a pebbled path. It was the small, unassuming sign fixed to the fence that caught my attention. *Wild East Truffles.*

I was certain I'd just stumbled upon Lachlan's place, so I opened the gate and took a few tentative steps inside. I wasn't sure what the rules were on White Cedar Island. People were sociable, yes, and there was an open-table policy, but could you arrive uninvited? I didn't want to catch him unawares, enjoying the company of a woman or worse, with his mother over. The night before had been torturous enough with Ivy Tremblay.

Still, it would be nice to see him, if he were home, so I took my chances, continuing down the path, following it beneath the redbuds until I came to a small building made of timber and glass.

Duke was lying on the verandah. When he saw me, he sprang to his feet and bounded down the path towards me, barking excitedly. He jumped up, placing his milky front paws on my thighs. I laughed and bent to pat him. 'Hey there, boy.' His fur was soft and warm from the sun and I cuddled him close as he panted in my ear.

The glass door opened and there was movement on the verandah behind him. I glanced up to find Lachlan eating an apple, watching me with the widest grin on his face.

Chapter 18

'Hello, Marley from Melbourne.'

I waved. 'Hey.'

'I thought city dwellers slept until midday.'

'Or not at all,' I quipped.

He laughed heartily.

'Actually, I woke early and walked down to the village to call my sister,' I explained, rising from my spot beside Duke. 'I hope you don't mind me stopping by. I came across your place on the way back.'

'Not at all. I was just catching up on emails.'

I raised my eyebrow. 'On a Sunday? Is that allowed on White Cedar?'

He laughed again. 'My hours are flexible. If I have time to kill on the weekend, I'll clear emails. And if I feel like going to the beach on Monday, I'll do that too. But I could use a break now. Would you like a coffee?'

'Sure.'

He indicated that I should follow him. I climbed the verandah steps and he led me onto an elevated timber boardwalk that curved around the building.

'Is this your house?' I asked.

'No, this is my office,' he replied, as we followed the boardwalk past large glass windows.

Through the windows I saw a beautiful oak desk resting on a mahogany timber floor, with bookcases, filing cabinets, and a laptop and printer. There was a leather lounge, a large, mounted television on the wall and a coffee machine. 'Do you work here alone?'

'Mostly yes, although the back rooms have a few extra desks in them. During peak harvest season, some of the ladies on the island help with administration. It doesn't make sense to have staff permanently here, but it does free up my team in Montreal to concentrate on our clients and production. And the locals don't mind. They enjoy it. It's almost a social event for them.'

'How do you manage an office without Wi-Fi? Isn't it non-existent here too?'

He grinned. 'I get Wi-Fi here. And the property is cabled throughout for voice and data.'

I shook my head with a smile. 'I'm completely jealous. I've been lost without my email.'

'You wouldn't be jealous if I told you how much it cost.' He cringed. 'My bank account still hurts.'

I laughed. 'Well, it's a great office space. But doesn't the ocean distract you?' I turned to look back at the North Atlantic shimmering under the morning sun.

'If anything, I find it calming,' he said. 'And I needed the office to be close to the orchards so I can move easily between the two. My house is at the back of the property. This boardwalk will take you everywhere you need to go, from the office to the house, to the orchards, to the outbuildings.'

I hadn't realised how immense the property was until I caught a glimpse of the orchards in the distance, green and sprawling, with rows of trees that reminded me of a vineyard. We continued along the path until we reached a second building—a double storey house with a grey stone façade, a pitched and gabled roof, and white-framed dormer windows upstairs. Downstairs, a row of large picture windows overlooked the property. The boardwalk continued around the exterior of the house and out of sight, so we stepped from it onto a small flight of timber steps that led us to an impressive set of cedar front doors.

'This is my house.' Lachlan said as he pushed through the doors and we walked inside, Duke following at our heels.

'Wow, this is incredible.' My gaze travelled everywhere. It was difficult to pause on just one thing. There was a vast cathedral ceiling and a stone-built fireplace, a twill wool rug and those enormous picture windows that beckoned the outside in. Oversized couches with cushions were inviting and the floors of polished honey timber seemed to extend from the boardwalk. It all felt connected, with nature the starring role.

'Was this already here when you arrived?' I asked.

'No, I had everything built—the house, office, the outbuildings.' He led me into the kitchen, which was surprisingly industrial compared with the rest of the house, with white stone benchtops, grey cabinetry and a large rough-hewn dining table with an antler chandelier floating above.

'What do the vegan locals think about those antlers?' I asked, staring up at them, amused.

'They're faux antlers,' he said, grinning. 'Otherwise, my head would be up there instead.' He tossed his apple core into the bin and moved in front of the coffee machine. 'How do you like your coffee?'

'Cappuccino, one sugar.'

He placed cups on the machine tray and pressed buttons. I heard it purr to life, silky coffee shooting into the cups, followed by hot frothy milk.

'Are you serving me almond or soy milk today?' I asked.

His back was to me, but I saw his shoulders shake with quiet laughter. 'I drink my coffee with cow's milk. Some things I just can't compromise on.'

'Noelle would be outraged.'

'What she doesn't know won't hurt her.' He brought the cups to the bench. 'Shall we take a walk? I can show you the orchards. They're nice this time of year.'

We grabbed our coffees, and Duke and I followed Lachlan out through a sliding door and back onto the boardwalk.

'Was it difficult to build all this?' I asked, looking around as we strolled along the side of the house. 'I mean, the delivery and construction would have been a logistical challenge.'

He shrugged. 'It was, but everyone has to build their house here at some point, so we have the means to do it. Mine was just on a slightly grander scale, which took more time and a hell of a lot more money.' He rolled his eyes. 'But when Anton and I dug up that first truffle by accident all those years ago, I knew if I wanted to make a go of this truffle thing, I'd need a good base here. Up until then, I'd been sharing Noelle's cabin with my mother and I was in a hurry to get out.'

'And you live on your own?' The words had slipped out and I was embarrassed at how they'd sounded, like I was fishing for information on his relationship status.

'Well, I live with Duke,' he said, smiling at me. 'But otherwise, yes, I'm here alone.'

I flushed, then took a long sip of my coffee.

'And you?' he asked. 'Do you live alone in Melbourne?'

'Yes, I do.' It might have been a wise idea to bring up Austin at that point, but I didn't, and I wasn't entirely sure why. Maybe because Lachlan was just a friend and I was leaving in a week, so it shouldn't have made a difference anyway. Or maybe because I didn't want him to know about Austin, which somehow felt deceitful to them both. If he'd asked me if I had a boyfriend, I would have answered truthfully, but even that would have been a strange conversation, for I wasn't sure what Austin was anymore.

The boardwalk curved away from the side of the house and we entered another canopy of redbuds where sunlight cut through the leaves to dapple the path. A few minutes on and we crossed a small stream chattering over rocks on its way down to the ocean. We talked about the island and the people who had become like family to him, then we drifted into a companionable silence that didn't feel awkward at all. Only the sound of the birds and our shoes on the timber boards and Duke's soft panting filled the quiet.

We paused at a set of steps that led down into the orchards, while the boardwalk continued to another part of the property.

'Where does that lead to?' I asked, pointing to its path through the trees.

'It goes to the outhouses. I store equipment and refrigerators there.'

We stepped down the stairs that led into the orchards, where hundreds of trees formed neat rows, the colours of fall so spectacular I was speechless.

'This is where my truffles grow,' he said proudly, leading me along the path through the trees.

'I'm going to confess something,' I said. 'I know nothing about truffles, except that they grow in the ground. I didn't realise you needed so many trees.' But the sight was glorious—the red gold of the leaves, the gentle slope of the hillside, the mild autumn sun as it drenched the landscape. And all the while there was the pervading yet peaceful sounds of nature around us, from the soft rustles in the undergrowth to the twittering of bluebirds.

'You're right, truffles do grow in the ground,' he said. 'They're the fruiting body of subterranean fungi, an underground mushroom if you like, that grow near the roots of trees. But only certain trees can act as hosts. In my case, I found my first truffle under a hazelnut tree, so that's what I've stuck with. I also have some newly planted birches. You can use oaks too, but they take longer.'

We walked down a path lined with irrigation and neatly pruned trees, and Lachlan stopped to touch the leaves. 'The fungi live in a symbiotic relationship with the feeder roots of the trees. When the truffles are ripe enough, they release aromas that animals can detect. That's when we know it's time to harvest. We've already dug out the white summer truffles. I have black Périgords growing now, and they should be ready in December. They're a French truffle.'

'How long do they take to grow?' I asked, lifting my hand to touch the leaves too. They were crisp, and one fell away in my fingers.

'A long time,' he said. 'Anywhere from three to ten years, if at all. It can be hit and miss, which is why you must have a lot of trees to make it a success. This first section here are my originals.' He indicated the row we were in. 'The next batch of hazelnuts are the ones I planted five years ago, and they're growing the Périgords for December. Then the next batch will be ready in June and so on. The birches are my most recent trees, at the far back, and we won't dig around those for another three years.'

I found it fascinating and hadn't noticed until now that the day was slipping by, and it was already afternoon. I'd lost all notion of time, having left my watch in the cabin, and I hadn't checked my phone in hours.

Lachlan watched me closely and I must have had a faraway look on my face for he flushed. 'I'm sorry. Truffle talk is completely boring.'

'Oh, no.' I shook my head emphatically. 'I'm not bored at all. On the contrary, it's fascinating. I was just thinking that I'm always in a rush to be somewhere and now, well, there's nowhere I have to be. I haven't glanced at the time once. It's been nice.'

He smiled, then indicated that we keep strolling. 'I remember what that feels like, living the fast life, always having somewhere to go. Sometimes I miss it, although when I visit Montreal, I enjoy it for about a day or two before I can't wait to get back here. I like island time. I like the culture and the people and the lifestyle. It makes me feel good.'

'Even with your busy truffle empire?' I asked.

'Probably in spite of it. If I were in any other place in the world, I'd be working around the clock. I'd be rushed, stressed, my diet would be terrible. I'd be drinking far too much alcohol. For all its limitations, this island brings out the best in me.' He gave me an apologetic look. 'Sorry, I'm talking too much again. Can you tell we don't get visitors often? We tend to chew their ears off given the chance.'

I laughed; a sound that came from deep in my stomach to bubble up my throat. There was something so perfect about the day that I couldn't quite put my finger on. The walk, the orchards, the company, and conversation. The fact that I was sober, and it had been hours since I'd last thought of having a drink.

'You must get busy in Melbourne,' Lachlan said, turning the topic to me. 'You mentioned you were a lawyer.'

'Yes, that's right.'

'What kind are you? Not the kind that defends criminals, I hope.' He said it light-heartedly, but I couldn't mistake the rise of his brow, as though he were expecting, hoping, I'd say no.

'More like... family law,' I said. But the lie came so smoothly I cringed on the inside.

'Are the cases you work on interesting? I imagine you'd deal with all kinds of complex divorces and custody battles.'

'You have no idea.' I tried not to meet his eyes, even though he was gazing intently at me. I was worried he'd see right through the lies.

'So is that why you came here? To take a break from it?'

I didn't answer. Instead, I watched as Duke ran ahead to chase rabbits out of the orchards. I should have confided in him then about my drinking. The opportunity was there and all it would have taken were a few words to tell him the truth, then the whole charade would be over. But one incident couldn't be explained without the other, so how did I confess it all? The alcohol, the criminals, the Wagners, the collision with the pregnant woman's car. A series of failures linked like dominos knocking into each other. I didn't know how to tell him any of it without seeing the disappointment in his eyes. The same disappointment I struggled with each day.

'Marley?' Lachlan's voice came from a distance.

I'd fallen silent in my contemplation and I hadn't realised minutes had passed. I shook my head. 'I'm sorry. What were you saying?'

'Just that I shouldn't have asked. It's none of my business.'

I forced a smile, my mouth dry suddenly. 'No, it's fine. I just needed a break from work. That's all.'

He nodded. 'I think we all do at one point or another.'

I couldn't be sure if he believed me or if he were dropping the matter out of courtesy, but I was relieved when he pushed no further. My quickened heartbeat slowed, safe in the knowledge that the deepest, darkest, most shameful parts of my life were still buried away.

We reached the edge of his property and the fence that protected his orchards from the wildlife. We spent a moment gazing out through the palings into the forest, which, overnight, seemed to have turned the leaves into a riot of colour with the change of season—the golden needles of the cedars, the dazzling red of the maples and the vibrant orange of the birches. Our coffee cups were empty, and Duke had returned, nuzzling his wet nose against my fingers. I smiled down at him, stroking his soft fur, then we turned and headed back towards the boardwalk.

It was easy conversation all the way to his house. We returned the cups to the kitchen and he led me through the canopy of redbuds again out onto the road. I wasn't expecting him to walk me back to Noelle's, but he did, and we talked all the way up the hill.

'Free for dinner tonight?' he asked as we reached the front verandah of the cabin. 'My mom and Joel are having dinner with friends, so it will just be Noelle and me.'

'Sure.'

'Great. I'll see you next door around seven, unless you want to forage in the garden with us beforehand? In that case, be there at four.'

'Okay!' I grinned as he waved goodbye, and he and Duke jogged back towards the road, disappearing down the hill. I already knew I'd be there at four. And this time, I wouldn't wear a five-hundred-dollar Greta

Constantine dress and Louboutin sandals. I'd wear shorts, a shirt, and my new rubber boots because I planned on getting dirty.

Chapter 19

The next morning, I woke at six to a sun that was barely up. I dressed, made a chickpea omelette using a recipe I'd borrowed from Noelle, and left the cabin, heading down to the village where I was determined to reach Austin if it took me all morning to do so.

As I walked, I thought about dinner the night before and how much fun I'd had with Noelle and Lachlan. I'd trekked next door at four to find them already in the garden, so I'd rolled up the sleeves of an old sweatshirt I'd thrown on and knelt beside them, pulling sweet potatoes and garlic from the ground, and climbing ladders to reach pears and persimmons. We were sufficiently grubby by the end of it, and Lachlan had laughed at one point, pulling apple tree leaves out of my hair.

While we'd cooked, Noelle made us virgin raspberry mojitos. If Lachlan had wondered about the missing alcohol, he didn't comment on it, and we all agreed they were refreshing after an afternoon in the garden.

I reached the village and, although it was early, I was glad to find the Wildflower Café open. I took a seat outside in the sun and glanced at the menu, choosing tea instead of coffee, and a slice of vegan carrot cake. While I waited for my order, I retrieved my phone and dialled Austin's number.

The call rang through to voicemail. I hung up and tried once more, before finally leaving a frustrated text.

Are you ever going to answer your phone?

His reply came back instantly. *I'm out.*

So, he *was* getting my calls and messages. I scowled at his brusqueness, hurriedly typing a response before I lost him again.

All I want is a minute of your time to say hello. I don't think that's too much to ask.

A few minutes passed agonisingly by, then a text dropped into my phone.

Just because you left it doesn't mean the world stops.

I flinched at his words, the resentment and anger in them. It left little doubt as to how he felt about my sobriety. On some level, I wasn't surprised that he'd reacted this way. On another, it hurt because I'd clutched at the hope that he might want to attempt sobriety too. Clearly, I'd been deluded. By coming here, all I'd done was damage us, for if Austin and I didn't have alcohol together, what did we have?

I wanted to fire back an equally wounding remark, the lawyer in me ready for a fight, but as instantly as the desire came, it faded, until all that remained was sadness. A waitress arrived with a tray carrying a tea pot, cup, and a slice of cake. As she set it down, Austin's words delivered another blow to my stomach. *Just because you left it doesn't mean the world stops.*

I did what I probably shouldn't have done while in an emotionally fragile state. I snatched up my phone and stalked his social media pages, desperate to see how he'd been spending his time without me.

There were the usual pictures of nights out—Austin drinking with our close friends. Someone had tagged him in two photos, and I saw a brunette I'd never met before sitting on his lap. They looked out of their mind on drugs and booze, sweaty hair matted to their foreheads, sloppy grins on their faces. In one of the shots, their lips were so close, I was sure they'd locked at some point.

I put my phone down and swallowed the hurt rising in my throat. Austin and I had been close friends since university. In the last few years, we'd shared unspoken exclusivity. He'd been there when the Wagners had died, and my world had collapsed. He was the one who'd found me on the bathroom floor, suicidal and bleeding from the wrists. He'd understood that an attempt like that could be career-destroying, so he'd bandaged me up, stuck a glass of scotch in my hand and together, we hadn't told a soul.

After that, he'd nurtured my ability to cope in ways that might have been wrong, but he'd still been there. And now he was hurting, cheating even, because I'd altered the frail dynamics of our relationship. I could hardly blame him for his fear. If the shoe were on the other foot and I was losing him to sobriety, I'd be fearful too.

Old cravings began to wrap their tentacles around me. Years of hiding my emotions in a bottle had not weathered me to deal with loss and I took a deep breath, trying not to think of alcohol. But the harder I tried to ignore it, the stronger the desire became.

Louise's store was across the square, directly in my line of sight. I could see her opening for the day, knowing that all I had to do was walk across, buy a bottle and I could spend the rest of the morning forgetting about Austin.

I drank my tea, but as lovely as the cake looked, I had little appetite for it. I rose to my feet, dropped money on the table and left the café. I didn't want to go back to the cabin and fight with cravings all day, waiting, hoping, praying they'd pass, so I wandered the square, keeping my distance from Louise's, trying to distract myself.

I stumbled into the botanical skincare shop. Their range was organic and the lady inside was friendly. I was the only one in there and she showered me with her full attention. She squirted the backs of my hands with lotions and let me try on makeup. Everything she offered was light and organic, in stark contrast to the chemical-laden designer brands I'd lathered myself with for years to hide my malnourished skin.

I rewarded her friendliness by spending a fortune, then I left with two full bags and went next door to the modern apothecary. There I bought herbal teas, tinctures of essential oils and aromatherapy candles. I bought more books from the bookstore, then avoided Louise's, buying groceries in the health food store instead.

It was with some relief that when I was about to leave the village and start up the hill towards the cabin, I saw Lachlan. He and Duke were outside the council chambers and he was talking to Celeste. He glanced up as I walked past, struggling under the weight of my purchasing frenzy. He threw Celeste a hasty goodbye and dashed over to me.

'Wow, doing some shopping?' he asked, reaching for half the bags.

I gave them up gratefully. 'Just a little.' Celeste glowered at me and I looked at Lachlan apologetically. 'Sorry, I didn't mean to interrupt.'

'Oh, it's no problem.' He didn't cast a look back at Celeste, who was still standing by the chamber gardens watching us. 'Duke and I were out for a walk and she called us over. It was nothing important.' He glanced inside the health food bag, raising an eyebrow. 'Taking up the vegan thing, I see.'

'Not quite. It was more of an impulse buy.'

We began walking up the hill towards Noelle's. After a frosty start, the day had grown unexpectedly warm and it wasn't long before I had to stop, place my bags down and tug off my cardigan.

'It's Monday. Shouldn't you be working?' I asked him, fixing my bangles in place before tying my cardigan around my waist.

'I felt like a break, so Duke and I took a walk.'

'Celeste looked devastated when you left.' I picked up my bags and we began to walk again. 'I feel bad pulling you away like that.'

He gave a slight roll of his eyes. 'Please don't. My mother is to blame for that. She keeps filling the poor girl's head with ideas.'

'What kind of ideas?'

'That we'd be great together. That she should stick it out a little longer as I'll eventually come around.'

'Have you tried going on a date with her, just to see? You might be surprised,' I said.

'I don't need to go on a date with her,' he said with mild frustration. 'I already know I don't feel anything. It would only encourage her.'

'Have you told her that?'

'Not in so many words.' He ran a hand over his jaw and cringed. 'A few months ago, she tried to kiss me.'

I cringed too. 'Oh.'

'Yeah. Down at the beach. In the water. It was a disaster.'

'What did you do?'

'I pulled away, which obviously hurt her feelings. She cried, then left. I'd embarrassed her, which hadn't been my intention at all. The kiss caught me by surprise. She's only just found the courage to start talking to me again.'

'She's certainly resilient,' I said, impressed with the girl's persistence.

'If you tried to kiss a guy and he pulled away, would you keep trying to get his attention?'

I shrugged. 'Probably not. I'd get the hint and move on.'

'Thank you.' He nodded with such a look of boyish satisfaction that I smiled.

We continued up the hill, but with the weight of the bags, the heat of the day and my gasping lungs, our pace was slow. Eventually we reached the cabin.

'Well, Marley from Melbourne, it's always a pleasure,' he said, depositing the bags on the verandah by the door, then wiping his brow. 'I'm not sure where this heat came from. Last time I checked summer was over.'

'Would you like a cold drink before you go?' I asked, still catching my breath.

'I was thinking of going for a swim instead.'

'Like in the ocean?'

He laughed and looked at the sea behind him. 'Where else?'

'Can I come?' I didn't want to intrude, but I also didn't want to be alone in the cabin with my cravings, and I'd yet to swim in the ocean.

'Sure you can.'

'Great. I'll just be a minute.' I left him at the cabin door and ran to the kitchen, dropping the shopping bags onto the bench. Rummaging through my suitcase in the bedroom, I found my swimming costume and hastily changed, throwing a light cotton dress over the top. I filled a backpack with a hat, towel, and sunscreen, and slipped into sandals, then rushed back to the door. But when I returned, Lachlan and Duke were gone.

I glanced around, puzzled, wondering if he'd changed his mind about having company, but then I heard a whistle from Noelle's yard and glanced across.

'Come and pick something to eat,' Lachlan called, 'or we'll get hungry down there.'

I skipped along the path and into Noelle's back garden. Noelle was there, on her knees, pulling radishes and turnips from the ground. She glanced up at us, first with curiosity, then the hint of a pleased smile.

'What do you feel like?' Lachlan asked.

I walked immediately to the orchards where the fruit trees stood. 'Mandarins,' I said. 'And apples.'

'How about pears?'

I could taste their crisp flesh already. 'Yes, please.'

'I have oranges too,' Noelle said, pointing with her garden spade. 'And strawberries around the corner. They're sweet. *Délicieux.*'

We plucked fruit from branches and patches and stuffed it all into my backpack. Then we thanked Noelle, Lachlan planting a kiss on her cheek. I couldn't resist doing the same, throwing my arms around her, and she patted my arm with a tender smile.

'You're a good girl,' she said softly to me. 'Your heart is pure and so is his.'

My vision blurred unexpectedly with tears. Never had my heart been called pure before, and it swelled so intensely with love for her, I thought it would burst. I hugged her close, feeling her ancient body against mine.

We left the garden and flew down the hill with Duke bounding ahead of us, the ocean beckoning in the distance. We stopped at Lachlan's place on the way so he could change and collect a beach towel, then we ran without stopping, like kids, all the way down to the beach.

Chapter 20

It was midday and there was no one around when we got there. Emile, Anton and Gilbert had already departed after their morning fishing expedition and, aside from a lone figure in the distance walking a dog, the beach was deserted.

'Are you sure you shouldn't be working?' I asked as we stripped down to our swimmers. 'This feels clandestine.' It was a strange concept to be taking a swim in the middle of a working day and, although I wasn't the one working, I still felt guilty doing it.

But Lachlan just laughed. 'It's perfectly fine. Everything's under control. My team know how to find me if they need to.' He grinned mischievously. 'Last one into the water has to cook dinner for the other!'

I was quick, tearing down the sand, but he was quicker, powerful legs overtaking me in no time as we crashed into the water. Duke followed us in but turned back when it became too deep.

I'd always been a strong swimmer but, as Lachlan freestyled easily out into the ocean, I struggled to match his pace after years of inactivity. Nevertheless, I'd forgotten how wonderful it was to glide through the water and I almost didn't mind the effort it took. He slowed down and I caught up, and we swam a long way out. When we stopped to tread water, a fair distance from the shore, I glanced nervously around me. 'We're not going to be eaten by sharks, are we?'

'No, we're all good. Our sharks are vegan too.'

I splashed him playfully, then rolled onto my back to float. He did the same and, for a few minutes, we drifted weightlessly, minuscule drops in an enormous ocean. The sun was beating down and I knew I was probably burning, but I couldn't move, so indescribably calm and motionless that for a few precious moments, my world stopped raging. Thoughts of Austin and my chaotic life left me, and I was at peace.

We stayed out there for an hour, far from the beach, until Duke's barks eventually called us in, and we freestyled back. On the sand, we laid our towels out and sat on them to dry. I grabbed my bottle of sunscreen and we lathered it on our hot skin, unsure if it was going to make a difference. My pale, Melbourne-winter skin was already turning cinnamon.

We dug the fruit from Noelle's garden out of my backpack and ate. Thoughts of work dropped briefly into my head, which cases were being worked on, but it quickly lost legs and faded away, as though it had no place on that beach. Lachlan too, looked like he had the whole afternoon free to spend with me, no other place to be.

'What are you going to cook for me?' he asked, finishing the last of an orange and lying back in the sun, licking his fingers then tucking his hands under his head.

I glanced down at him. Long, muscular legs ran the length of the towel, ending up in the sand. His torso was lean, his chest smooth and tanned, water droplets glistening in the sun. He stared up at me with an equally appreciative look and I quickly turned away, conscious suddenly in my little black bikini.

'Well, I know you prefer a mostly plant-based diet and, while I'm going to do my best to respect that, I can't promise I won't sneak an egg or two in there.'

He grinned. 'I love eggs.'

'You don't happen to like New York steaks too, do you?'

This time he laughed and pulled himself up beside me. 'Whatever you cook will be amazing.'

'I wouldn't be so sure,' I said. 'You should probably eat before you come.'

'Are you certain you want to attempt a vegan menu? It can be tricky. I'd be perfectly happy with a pepperoni pizza or roast chicken.'

'No,' I said firmly. 'I'm going to give it a go. Besides, Noelle would kill me if I fed you a dead animal.'

132

'Yes, you're probably right. You must be missing meat, though. I don't think anyone can be expected to adopt this lifestyle overnight, and certainly not in the short time you're here.'

It was true. I did miss meat and dairy. I missed the oily Pad Thai from the restaurant under my apartment and the greasy pizzas Austin brought over and the kebabs we'd devour after a drunken night. But they were also part of a life I was trying to move past, and while it wasn't easy to give everything up at once, I couldn't deny that Noelle's organic, plant-based eating had me bouncing out of bed each morning.

'I do miss those things,' I said. 'But I'm here and I'm trying to embrace something new.'

'Well, hats off to you. It's not easy to overhaul a diet you've lived on for most of your life. I think you're remarkable.'

I was hardly remarkable, in fact, my baggage was so immense against his flawless existence, I felt like it might sink me. I blushed, hiding my cheeks behind my wet hair, my bangles rattling against my wrists. 'So, when would you like your meal? I'll just need a day or two to put the menu together.'

'Well,' he said, shifting his gaze out to the ocean, 'I have to leave for the mainland tomorrow. I'll be in Montreal with my team for the rest of the week and back on Saturday. We could have dinner then, which should give you plenty of time to prepare.'

'Saturday?' I said, my excitement deflating. 'I'm leaving for home on Friday.'

'Oh.' His face fell. 'I didn't realise. The days have gone so quickly.'

He was right. It was just as I'd found my rhythm that they'd sped up. And now, thinking I still had five more days with Lachlan, I was surprised at how devastated I was that he wouldn't be here. 'So, you're leaving for Montreal tomorrow?'

'I have a charter flight collecting me at ten.'

I nodded, turning my gaze to the ocean while his eyes settled on me.

'Hey, why don't you come?'

I glanced back at him. 'What do you mean?'

'Come to Montreal. You could spend a few days touring the city while I work, and we could catch up in the evenings for a meal. You could fly home from there. I bet you've never been to Montreal before. It's an amazing city.'

His invitation caught me off guard and I wasn't entirely sure why—maybe the fact that he'd invited me 'away' when we hardly knew each other, or maybe, and most likely, it was the idea of being on the continent with all its temptations. How would we enjoy a meal without wine? How would I avoid it without being obvious? Anxious thoughts drenched me in a cold sweat even though the day was warm.

'It was just an idea,' he said, shifting awkwardly on his towel, and I knew he'd mistaken my reluctance for rejection. 'I thought you might like to do something exciting with your last days.'

'No, I mean, I love the idea. Montreal would be great. It's just that I'm starting to get the hang of island life now. I'd like to spend my last days here.'

He nodded and smiled. 'Then that's what you should do.'

'But I won't be able to cook you my amazing vegan dinner. And you *did* win the race.'

He laughed and stood up, helping me to my feet. 'Maybe I can cash in my prize if I'm ever in Melbourne.'

We dusted the sand from our skin and shook out our towels. Duke was inspecting seaweed on the other side of the bay and Lachlan whistled for him to come.

We began climbing the hill back towards the cabin, detouring past Lachlan's house and pausing at his front gate.

'So you leave at ten tomorrow?' I asked.

'Yes.'

'And who normally looks after Duke while you're gone?'

'Sometimes Noelle or Anton, sometimes my mother. He's a bit of a gypsy when I go away, but don't be fooled. He loves it.'

'I could mind him,' I offered. I didn't know the first thing about caring for a pet but decided it couldn't be too difficult. And I loved Duke. I could already imagine him sleeping at the foot of my bed or walking down to the village with me. If I were entirely truthful, it would be like having a part of Lachlan with me after he left.

'Are you sure? I can just leave him with Noelle.'

'Well, if you think he'd like to stay with me, I could have him until Friday and leave him at Noelle's when I go.'

'Really?' Lachlan looked pleased. 'Duke would love that. But if he gets in the way, just drop him at Noelle's.'

'How could he possibly get in the way?' I said, bending to scratch him behind the ears. He leant in closer so that I wouldn't stop.

'I'll bring him over tomorrow before I leave,' Lachlan said. 'That way we can say goodbye.'

My stomach twisted at the thought. I didn't want to say goodbye. I didn't want him to leave. I wanted to spend my last days here with him. 'Sure, that would be great.'

He smiled and waved, then disappeared through the canopy of trees, Duke trotting behind him. I climbed the rest of the way up the hill to the cabin, trying to sort through the confusing rush of emotions.

I was enjoying the island. I thrived on the isolation and didn't want to leave, but knew that, at the end of the week, I'd have to. A life was waiting for me back home—work, Austin, a discussion about that girl and our relationship.

Then there was Lachlan—decent, funny, kind, someone I admired. So why did thoughts of him confuse me? Was it because I liked him more than I should?

I reached the cabin and climbed into the shower, washing the salt away, my skin tingling from the sun. I was exhausted but unable to relax, my fingers jittery. A craving settled on my nerves, making me anxious.

Noelle must have had a sixth sense for she knocked on the door at precisely the time I began to contemplate Louise's little shelf of alcohol. 'You are sad?' she said.

I let out a defeated sigh. 'A little.'

She closed her eyes and nodded. 'It's a shame you have to say goodbye to him tomorrow.'

I straightened in surprise, marvelling at how Noelle could know what was upsetting me.

She tossed me gardening gloves. 'Can you trim rose bushes?'

I caught them, smiling wryly. 'I haven't trimmed a rose bush in my life.'

'*Magnifique!* Today you will learn.'

'But they're Danielle's roses. Are you sure you want me to work on them?'

She raised an eyebrow. 'Are you trying to get out of it?'

'No,' I said, affronted.

'Then come. The sun is setting, and it will wait for no one.'

Chapter 21

The next morning, I woke early, had breakfast with Noelle, then returned to the cabin to wait for Lachlan. He arrived at nine with Duke in tow, who bounded in through the door, jumping up and placing his front paws on my thighs.

I laughed as Lachlan shook his head, smiling. 'Glad to see you won't miss me too much, Duke,' he said. He handed me a bag containing dog food and bowls and pointed to a dog bed just outside the door. 'This is everything you need. Like I said, if he gets too much, just drop him at Noelle's.'

'We'll be fine,' I said. I walked him back down to the road, feeling the last of our time together trickle away. 'How will you get to the airport?' I looked around for the direction it might be in, for I hadn't seen a plane fly in or out since I'd been there.

'I'll walk. It's not far. I just have to grab my bag from home.'

'Well, have a safe flight,' I said.

'Yeah, you too.' His hands were jammed into his pockets, a look of hesitation on his face, like he wanted to say more but couldn't find the words. 'It was great to meet you. It's a shame we didn't have more time to get to know each other.'

I felt it too, the regret of our circumstances—my short stay, his isolated world, the distance between us. 'If you're ever in Melbourne, please call. I'd love to catch up.'

'Likewise. If you're ever in this part of the world again, drop in.' He removed his hands from his pockets and held them out to me. I stepped closer and let his arms wrap around me. I thought it might feel awkward embracing another man like this, but Lachlan's hug was anything but awkward. I let him hold me and I closed my eyes, resting my head on his chest, savouring the moment of being close and subsequently cursing it. In another time and place, this might have been different. *We* might have been different.

When we drew apart, he gave me one last smile and Duke one last pat before saying goodbye and setting off down the hill, back towards his house. Duke yelped and hung his head but followed me obediently inside.

I spent the morning trying to distract myself, cleaning the cabin and washing clothes. Duke followed me around like a shadow, looking as hopelessly lost as I felt. Around mid-morning, I heard the engines of a small plane take off from a runway. I glanced outside the front windows to catch a glimpse of a Cessna soaring over the bay and across the North Atlantic until it became nothing more than a speck in the sky. I had a feeling it would be the last time I ever saw Lachlan. As if to share in my melancholy, Duke nudged my hand with his wet nose, his eyes large and sad.

'I know. I feel sad too,' I said to him.

He whimpered.

'How about we get out of here? I think we could both do with a walk.'

I grabbed my phone and purse, locked the cabin door and we headed down to the village together. The fall air was much cooler than the day before, crisp and full of winter promise. I glanced at the time. It was one am in Melbourne, and I decided I would try my luck with Austin again.

I'd thought about it at length the night before. If I was going to succeed at sobriety when I returned, I needed him to understand what my homecoming should look like. I couldn't have him organising a boozy party in my honour or turning up at my door with alcohol. I needed him to respect what I was trying to achieve because I was the first to admit my resolve would crumble in the face of all that seduction. I also needed to know what had happened between him and the brunette, although I wasn't sure I was going to like the answer.

Duke and I reached the café and he plonked down at my feet while I ordered tea. As the waitress retreated, I saw Lachlan's mother, Ivy, approach with a girl I recognised as Celeste from the council chambers.

'Hello, Marley,' she said, stopping by my table. 'How nice to see you again.' Her smile didn't quite reach her eyes.

'Hello, Ivy.' My nerves were already frayed at the thought of speaking to Austin. I wasn't sure I had the stomach for dealing with Ivy too.

Duke glanced up, wagged his tail, then rested his chin on his paws again.

Ivy gave me a confused look. 'Why is Duke with you?'

'Lachlan left for Montreal this morning,' I replied.

'I'm aware of that, but why do *you* have Duke?' Her tone was crisp. Beside her, Celeste cast me a withering look.

'I offered to mind him while he was gone.' I was hardly a shrinking violet, but Ivy's gaze was penetrating.

'That's an odd offer to make. Aren't you leaving soon?'

'Yes,' I said, seeing instant relief cross her face, 'but I'll be here until Friday and I'll leave Duke with Noelle when I go.'

Ivy turned to Celeste. 'Perhaps you could collect Duke from Marley the day she leaves. You know how to care for him and I'm sure Lachlan wouldn't mind at all.'

'I'd love to,' Celeste said, brightening. 'I'll drop by the cabin on Friday and pick him up.'

'Right,' I said slowly, 'but Lachlan asked me to leave Duke with Noelle. That was our agreement and so unless I hear otherwise from him, that's what I'll be doing.' I knew I was irritating Ivy, but Lachlan had entrusted Duke to me, and I wasn't going to pass him to anyone but Noelle without his permission.

Ivy rounded her shoulders and lifted her chin, steeling for an argument. 'I'm Lachlan's mother, *Marley*. In his absence, I'm sure I can be entrusted to make decisions for him.'

'Be that as it may, Ivy, I'm not handing Duke to anyone without Lachlan's knowledge.' We stared at each other and I could almost see the steam billowing from her ears. Mercifully, my tea tray arrived, and I smiled with feigned apology. 'I'm sorry, I have to make a call. Was there anything else?'

Her eyes narrowed. 'No, nothing else. Come Celeste, we'll be late for work. Good day, Marley.' She patted Duke's head and he reached up and licked her hand.

Celeste didn't say goodbye, she just gave me a curt flick of her hair and followed Ivy out of the square towards the hospital and council chambers.

I let out a breath and pressed my fingertips to my forehead. If I'd had any intention of winning favour with Ivy Tremblay, I'd all but blown it. The woman despised me. It was obvious in every interaction I had with her.

I poured tea into the cup and added a dash of almond milk, then picked up my phone from the table, glancing at the time. It was now almost two in the morning in Melbourne, and I dialled Austin's number, hoping he'd be home and awake.

To my astonishment, because I'd been prepared for another ghosting, he picked up on the second ring. 'Hello.'

'Austin, it's me.'

'Hi.' He sounded tired, his words slurring from what I knew was a night of drinking.

'How are you? I've been trying to call you for days.'

'I've been busy.'

'Yes, I can tell.' I tried to keep my tone in check but the image of the brunette on his lap flashed through my mind with infuriating persistence.

'What do you want?'

'*What do I want?*' I asked, incredulous. 'I've been wanting to talk to you. To see how you are. To tell you how I've been doing. Haven't you been wondering how I am?'

'What's there to wonder about?'

'Okay.' I tried to steady my voice. 'I can tell you're angry and I'm sorry about that.'

'Whatever.'

'God, Austin!' I said, finally exploding. 'What is wrong with you?'

'This whole thing is what's wrong!' he said, his voice rising too. 'Did you ever stop to think how this would change us? I happen to like our life exactly the way it is. What am I supposed to do when you come home? Give up alcohol? Never say the word around you?'

'I don't expect you to do anything,' which was a complete lie because I'd already thought of all the ways he could damage by progress by just being Austin and that for us to co-exist, he would have to change too.

'You're kidding yourself if you think you can just come back here and everything will be fine,' he said.

I tried to keep my voice calm as diners dropped into café chairs around me. 'You knew better than anyone that I couldn't keep going the way I was. I almost killed two people on the road. I was out of control.'

'I also know that mistakes happen. You didn't have to go across the world on some redemption expedition. We could have cut back on the partying together at home. You left me behind, but you know what? The world keeps turning Marley, with or without you.'

'So that's what you were doing with the brunette on your lap? Punishing me? Showing me that your world can still turn without me?' I was starting to shake with anger. How had we got here? One act of sobriety and the fault lines in our relationship were exposed.

I heard him sigh deeply. 'She's just a friend.'

'I know all your friends and I've never met her before.'

'Look, I'm tired. I've had a long day in court. Some of us had to pick up your caseload while you've been on holiday. And by the way, Paul and Brian are expecting you back at work on Monday. So do the right thing and get back here or you're going to get fired.'

'Did you have sex with her?'

'For God's sake!'

'I'll take that as a yes.' I was no fool. I knew what had happened, that he'd been unfaithful, and my heart shattered right there by the café table.

We were silent for a while and I took time to gather my thoughts, hoping he'd tell me no, that I'd misunderstood, but he didn't. 'I'm not sure I can do this anymore,' I said. 'I mean, do you even want to be with me?'

He sighed louder this time and it was filled with such annoyance that I flinched. 'It's two am, Marley. Do we have to do this now?'

'Yes.'

'Well, I'm tired. Not all of us get to laze around on a remote island.'

'Austin, wait—'

But to my astonishment, he hung up. I put the phone down, caught somewhere between overwhelming sadness and white, hot frustration. Austin *was* punishing me. He was resentful and hurt and he'd cheated on me with another woman. I was certain of it. But what had I expected?

That he would roll out the sobriety welcome mat for me? That he'd detox too? That we'd trade in three-day benders for early morning jogs and green breakfast smoothies?

Our entire relationship had been built on a cumulative cycle of parties. I'd never had to think about what that meant until I took it away and now that I had, what Austin and I were left with was little more than broken pieces. I'd given up all the bad things in my life and, without meaning to, Austin had become collateral damage.

I finished my tea, then Duke and I climbed the hill back to the cabin. Instead of going inside, I knocked on Noelle's door, hoping that she was home and not out for her daily walk with friends.

She opened it and took one look at my miserable expression before ushering me inside and sticking a wooden spoon in my hand. 'Stir the broth,' she said. 'It will make you feel better.'

I found a pot of soup bubbling on the stove and did as I was told, Duke plonking down on the floor beside me. Noelle returned to the bench, slicing leek and celery and parsnip. For a while, we worked in silence.

'It's time for seasoning,' she said. 'And can you add the tomatoes?'

I went to her pantry, collected the salt and pepper, and returned to the pot, seasoning the soup before emptying a bowl of diced tomatoes into it. 'I'm going home in a few days,' I said.

'*Oui*,' Noelle replied, still concentrating on her slicing.

'And the one person I'd hoped would support me when I got there has told me he won't.'

Noelle put down the knife and turned to face me.

'I'm not that surprised,' I said. 'Without the alcohol, we're different people. We also work together, so it's going to be horribly awkward.'

She nodded with understanding. 'Maybe it's not the right time to go home then.'

I glanced at her. 'It's kind of impossible not to. I have a job to get back to. I committed to two weeks leave only. Cases are piling up and my colleagues are working overtime to cover for me.'

'Maybe this job is not right for you either.'

I smiled as I stirred the broth. 'I love my job. I worked hard to get where I am today. I'll be up for partner soon. I mean, it's not the easiest career in the world, and I don't always deal with the nicest people, but the law is who I am. It's what I was born to do, what my father and grandfather did.'

She turned back to her slicing. 'Have you not worked hard for your sobriety too?'

I paused my stirring to answer. 'Yes, I suppose I have.'

'That's important also. The question isn't *can* you go home? The question is are you *ready* to go home? Can you finish what you started if you do? If you think you can, then go. But if you need more time, then you should stay. What was the point of coming all this way if not to see it through?'

Her shoulders dropped then, and her voice was sad. 'Given our time again, we would have made Danielle stay longer. For all the times she came home to get better, we let her go far too soon. We should have insisted she not leave until she was strong enough.'

'But isn't it weak of me to hide out here? Shouldn't I go home and tough it out in the real world?'

'It is not the sufferer who is weak, but the world around us that is cruel. There is no cowardice in admitting you need more time.'

I considered her words as I put the lid on the broth and left it to simmer. Was I a match for this world? Could I take it on without alcohol to bolster me?

I knew what Anna would say to this dilemma. She'd tell me to fly home, start a program and move in with her. Paul and Brian would order me back to work. Austin would stick a drink in my hand and tell me there was no future for us if I pursued sobriety.

My brain was flooded suddenly with an inexplicable amount of noise. My head was telling me to leave. *You have a job and an apartment in Melbourne. You need to go home.* But my heart was telling me to stay. *Noelle's right. You're not ready.*

I would have to leave at some point. It wasn't realistic to expect to stay forever, protected in this bubble. But was I willing to jeopardise my career for a few more weeks? Was I willing to jeopardise my sobriety for my career?

Was I ready for any of it?

I shook my head because the noise was palpable, the questions too many, the decisions overwhelming.

Chapter 22

I tossed and turned that night, my brain unable to calm while it analysed and strategised and did all the things it was trained to do in situations like these.

The next morning, after little sleep, I dragged myself from bed and made a cup of tea in the kitchen, glancing out at blue hills through foggy windows. The air was cold, and I stamped my bare feet on the timber floor, marvelling at how suddenly the weather had turned.

As a weak sun climbed into a pale sky, I slipped into warm clothes and left the cabin with Duke at my heels. We trotted down the hill, our breath white on exhale. At the Wildflower Café, I took my usual seat at an outdoor table, Duke plonking on the floor, straight onto my feet. I could feel his heart beating against my ankles. As I ordered tea then picked up my phone to make a call, Ivy and Celeste strolled past. I caught them in my peripheral vision but pretended I hadn't seen them. They pretended too and kept on walking.

The call to Paul rang but went through to voicemail. I wasn't surprised. A glance at the time told me it was late at night in Melbourne, and he was probably asleep. I'd hoped to have this conversation with him rather than Brian, for he'd always been more understanding, particularly after the Wagner case, while Brian offered little empathy. But I was left with no choice. I needed to talk to one of the partners before I lost my nerve.

Brian answered on the first ring. 'Marley,' he said.

'Hi, Brian. Sorry I'm calling you so late.'

'No problem. Just clearing emails and was about to turn in. How are things going? Paul said you were doing well.'

'Yes, I'm feeling much better, thank you.'

'Good. Ready for the office on Monday? We've got a lot of new clients waiting for you.'

'Yes, about that...'

'The team has been struggling with one person down. If you've got time to look over some cases now, I'll email them to you so you're ready for your first day back.'

'I want to stay,' I blurted.

There was silence on the line, then Brian said with confusion, '*Stay*?'

'Yes, just for a couple more weeks.' My heart quickened in my chest. Oh, why couldn't I have had this conversation with Paul?

'Sorry, let me get this straight. We gave you two weeks leave and you're asking for more? Why?'

'Because I need it, Brian,' I said.

'What you need is to get back into the office.'

'And I will. Just not yet.'

'Not yet?' There was an annoyed sigh from him, as though I were testing his patience. 'What's the problem, Marley? You said you were well. Is there a reason you need to take *more* time off?'

'To be fair, I can't remember the last time I took sick or personal leave, even at times when I should have,' I said. 'I'm feeling better, yes, but I'm not sure I'm ready to come back yet.' For a lawyer who spent her days arguing, it was a hopelessly inadequate defence. The truth was, I didn't know how much Brian knew of my circumstance or if he even knew what his solicitors and paralegals got up to every night.

'No one's denying that you've worked hard, Marley. You're our best defence lawyer. And you probably should have taken time off long before this. I'm not completely oblivious to what you all get up to outside of work. If you ask me, a few of the others could take a leaf out of your book. But giving you another two weeks on top of the two weeks you've already been granted is impossible. Plus, you had time off after the car accident. It all adds up.'

'But I really need this.' I was pleading and I could almost see the shake of his head in reply.

'Sorry, Marley. I don't know what to tell you other than to come back and take it easy. Don't go out as much, let up on the alcohol and you'll be fine. You're a brilliant lawyer and you will make partner one day, but I need to know I can count on you. I don't have another two weeks to give you right now. Maybe at Christmas.'

'And if I don't come straight back?' I wasn't sure I wanted to hear the answer.

'Then I'll find another lawyer who can be in the office on Monday.'

I didn't know what to say, only that everything I'd ever worked for rested on this single moment and how I would respond. I didn't want to lose my job and all the successes I'd had under Paul and Brian's guidance, or to throw away hours of work, my blood, sweat and tears down the drain. I didn't want to give up my chance of becoming a partner.

'Well, what's it going to be?' Brian said with irritation. It was late and I knew he wanted to finish his work and go to sleep.

I nodded at his ultimatum. What choice did I have? 'Yes, okay, I'll be in the office on Monday.'

We said goodbye and ended the call, and I sat staring for a long time at my phone. Just like that, the decision had been made for me. I would leave the island as planned, whether I was ready or not.

***

I spent my last few days on the island with Noelle in her garden, harvesting what vegetables we could.

'Winter is coming,' she said, pulling cabbages from the ground. 'And it will be long and dark and cold.' All the plants would fall dormant during that time, she told me, and the ground would freeze over, making it essential that we collect what we could now. Closer to winter, she would cover up the plants to prevent them from snow and frost.

Although I wasn't fond of the cold, I was sad to miss the experience of a white North Atlantic winter, to enjoy roaring fires inside while it snowed or to see Lachlan one last time. So much had been left unsaid between us and I wasn't sure if those words were better left that way or if we needed to hear them. Austin played on my mind too, but thoughts of him left me uneasy and confused.

When we weren't in the garden, Noelle and I worked in her kitchen cleaning the produce we harvested, pickling vegetables or making frozen meals with whatever would spoil early. The distraction was welcome for I'd been fretting over what would happen when Harry returned me to Halifax. Addiction was a cunning creature, and the world beyond was full of lures that I was still no match for.

On my last day on the island, my bags were packed and waiting by the door, and I had a few hours to fill before Harry arrived. I decided to take Duke for one last walk down to the village so I could say goodbye to Louise and the ladies in the other stores. Louise held me close to her large bosom and patted my back in farewell. Although I'd avoided her shop almost every time I'd been in the village, we'd still passed each other often in the square and stopped to say hello.

'Do come back soon,' she said through watery eyes.

'Of course.' It was the standard platitude, for I would probably never return. The distance was too great, and Brian had made it clear I wouldn't be afforded time off again until Christmas.

I left the square and hurried back up the hill to the cabin. Saying goodbye to Noelle proved harder. I wasn't good with emotion and neither was Noelle. We managed a quick embrace before she pulled away, muttering something about turning the heat down on the stove. But I was certain I'd heard a quiver in her voice.

'I'll stay in contact,' I said.

'No, you won't.' She gave me a sad smile. 'Just do me one favour, though.'

'Anything.'

'Send me a letter in three months' time and tell me you are still well.'

My eyes filled unexpectedly with tears and so did hers, maybe because we both knew my run of good health would end the minute I stepped off Harry's boat into Halifax.

She was emotional after that, disappearing into her garden alone, leaving me to say goodbye to Duke inside. He nuzzled against me, giving me a disgruntled bark, as though he knew I was leaving. I held him close, grateful for his company the last few days.

'Be a good boy for Noelle,' I said as he whimpered. 'Look after Lachlan for me.'

I took one last look at Noelle's kitchen, a place that had brought me back to life, then I let myself quietly out the door, tugging my suitcase behind me.

I set off down the hill, the wind rushing past me. The ocean was churlish, the waves dark and choppy, mirroring a slate-grey sky. I reached the pier a few minutes to three and waited for Harry's boat to appear on the horizon. It wasn't long before I heard the acoustic of his engine and saw the familiar shape of the hull approach.

I waved to him and he waved back, steering the vessel closer to the pier and cutting the engine.

'Ahoy,' he said with a gruff smile.

'Hi,' I said.

'I wondered when I'd be taking you back. Holiday over?' He threw a rope to me unexpectedly and I caught it, clumsily tying it around a piling to secure the boat in place.

'Something like that. Is this rope tied well enough?'

'It'll hold,' he said, unperturbed.

'How's your mum?'

He smiled. 'Doing much better, thank you.'

'I'm glad.' I glanced at the boxes of supplies he was carrying. 'Are you unloading all these by yourself?'

'No, the boys are on their way down. We'll unload it together, then you and I can be on our way. Thick fog is rolling in. I don't want to head back too late.'

'Okay.' I tugged my suitcase out of the way and pulled my phone out while I waited for the unloading to begin. There was a signal at the bay and my phone lit up with a text that Paul had sent earlier that morning.

Don't fly out today. I checked with Payroll. You have three months of long service leave. Take it. Paul.

I blinked several times at the screen to make sure I wasn't dreaming. I became aware of Anton and the others arriving to help unload the boat, but I was too gobsmacked to glance up and say hello. And even though it was only five in the morning in Melbourne and Paul would still be fast asleep, I hurriedly punched out a reply.

What? But Brian said I had to be back on Monday.

His response came surprisingly quickly, and I wondered if he'd been only half asleep in the hope of catching me.

Don't worry about Brian. I've spoken to him. Austin will take your cases.

I was so overcome with gratitude that I almost burst into tears on the pier.

Can I call you? I asked.

He replied *yes*, so I dialled his number. He picked up on the first ring.

'I don't understand,' I said.

'Let's just say I'm going out on a limb for you,' he said. 'Finish what you started, then come back and be the lawyer I know you can be.'

'But Austin, the others. Won't it be too much for them?'

'You're entitled to that leave so we can't actually say no. But don't worry. We'll cope. Just concentrate on getting better.'

It was then that I realised Paul knew more than he'd ever let on—the alcohol, the traumatic shock of Katiana's death, my ability to cope ever since. Possibly even my suicide attempt. I couldn't be like Brian, Austin or my father and shake bad things off when they happened. I felt them keenly and Paul had always understood that.

'Thank you, Paul.' I was crying, swiping at my dribbling nose with my jacket sleeve. 'I can't begin to tell you what this means.'

'I think I know,' he said. 'Just promise me one thing.'

'Anything.'

'Use the time wisely. You may not get another chance like this.'

'I know. I will.' It was an extraordinary gift, and I was determined not to waste it.

We ended the call, and I dried my eyes, trying not to yelp with joy as I snatched up the handle of my luggage and began jogging away from Harry's boat.

'Hey! Where are you going?' he yelled after me. 'We're leaving soon!'

'Not today, Harry,' I called over my shoulder. 'I'm staying!'

'What?'

'See you in three months!' I laughed as I left the four men on the pier, scratching their heads and exchanging confused looks. I sprinted back up the hill with my suitcase, not pausing once for breath. When I reached Noelle's house, she was out the front, standing by her roses, just staring at them.

As Duke bounded towards me, she looked up with surprise. 'What in God's name?'

'I'm back,' I said, gasping for air, clutching a burning stitch in my side. 'I'm staying. Three months. Can I rent out your cabin?'

'Three months?' She broke into a huge grin as Duke barked and ran excitedly in circles. 'Well, of course you can rent my cabin. Where else would you stay?'

'Thanks,' I said, still hunched over, my legs quivering from running all the way up the hill with a full suitcase.

'Three months, hey?' Noelle shook her head. 'That's something.'

'And I get to keep my job.'

'I think you're the one worth keeping.'

I smiled, still marvelling that I was somehow back here and not on Harry's boat returning to Halifax. I would need to call Anna and Dad and tell them I was staying. I'd need to reschedule my flights and unpack my suitcase and buy groceries since I'd run down the cupboards. Louise would be surprised, so would the ladies in the other shops. I was elated, my head swimming with all the things I needed to do, but of course, Noelle wasn't one to leave me on cloud nine for too long.

'All right let's not stand here wasting time,' she said, walking back towards her house. 'The fog is coming in and I need you to help me with the compost.'

Chapter 23

The fog settled in that afternoon like I'd never seen before, opaque and rolling. I spent the evening cooking with Noelle, then we sat on the couch afterwards drinking tea and looking through her family photo albums, listening to the thrum of rain on her roof.

I woke the next morning to find the sun was out and the cedars deliciously scented, the ground cold and glistening. Duke and I had breakfast with Noelle, then we went back to the cabin to wait for Lachlan to return home.

He arrived shortly after lunch. I watched through my window as he trudged up Noelle's verandah steps and knocked on her door to collect Duke. When Noelle answered and pointed to the cabin, I saw the moment realisation dawned and he broke into a wide grin.

He jogged down the verandah steps, along the flagstone path and up onto the cabin verandah, knocking on the door. I opened it and Duke rushed past me, jumping up onto Lachlan and licking him.

'Someone's happy to see you,' I said. Deep down, I wasn't just referring to Duke.

Lachlan bent to hug him then straightened, glancing at me with an incredulous smile. 'I thought you'd be on your way home by now.'

'My plans changed. My boss gave me three more months.'

'*Three months?*' He looked so happy that I couldn't help the way my heart swelled in response.

'Have you been home yet?' I looked around for Lachlan's suitcase.

'Yes. I dropped everything there first, then I came here.'

'And was your trip a success?'

'It was. We got a lot done.' He smiled mischievously. 'Want to go down to the bay?'

'Now?' I glanced over his shoulder at the ocean. 'It's freezing.'

'We don't have to swim. But the sun is out. We can walk and I can tell you about Montreal and you can tell me how you managed to wrangle three months extra leave.'

I agreed to walk with him, and we stole next door to Noelle's garden, collecting apples and pears from her trees before heading down the hill with Duke. At the bay, we kicked off our shoes and sank into the cold sand as we ate our fruit. We walked down to the water's edge, the sea numbing our toes, and Lachlan told me about the new business he and his team were attempting to broker—restaurants and wineries up and down the east coast of Canada and the United States, and the new truffle salts he was adding to his range.

'And I want to grow my team too. I want to have offices in France and Italy, maybe even Australia one day,' he said, nudging me.

I tried not to grin so obviously at the idea.

'So what great lawyer tactic did you use to get another three months?' he asked, biting into a pear.

I shrugged. 'It was by pure chance. I was about to climb into Harry's boat when one of the partners at my firm texted me. He said I had long service leave to use and that I could stay.'

'Just like that?' he asked. 'Seems incredibly generous. Any special reason he'd be willing to do that for you?'

His gaze on me was intense and I could see the question in his eyes. *Yes Marley, why would Paul let you stay for three months? What are you going through that would warrant such generosity?*

'I'm entitled to it under Australian law,' I said.

'That's it?'

'And I needed the break.' I looked away from him, out to the ocean because I was worried he would see the real truth in my eyes. 'I was burning out. Paul knew that.'

Lachlan nodded. 'The pressure must be enormous, lots of people counting on you all the time.'

'It's a relentless battle. And that's all I seem to do. *Battle.* In court, in the office, with clients. It's exhausting.'

He screwed up his nose. 'It doesn't sound very enjoyable.'

I shook my head sheepishly. 'I'm being unfair. It's not all bad. Don't get me wrong, it can be stressful, and the hours are long. And I don't always work with nice people. But there's also a sense of accomplishment, like when justice is served, or you help someone who didn't have a hope otherwise.'

He stared at me and I sensed questions on his mind. I was wading into dangerous territory, so I changed the subject. 'Noelle and I have been harvesting and cooking for winter.'

'Yes, we do that on the island,' he said. 'We harvest what we can and cook enough to last the winter. It's futile trying to grow anything in the cold. And there's not much daylight anyway.'

I'd become aware that the days were shortening, that almost overnight everything had seemed colder, that the North Atlantic churned with a ferocity more powerful than it had when I'd arrived just two weeks earlier.

'We mostly bunker down when the blizzards hit,' he said. 'And we ride them out until February.'

'How about supplies?'

'It's difficult for Harry to come regularly, so we increase our ordering in the weeks prior to blizzard season. Speaking of which, the last of our fêtes this year will be held in two weeks.'

'Fêtes?'

'Yes. We have them regularly, but it will be too cold soon, so we need to get the last one in before winter comes.'

'What's a fête exactly?'

'It's like a fiesta—one big party. We hold them outdoors and everyone brings food and there's dancing and music. It's a lot of fun.'

'It sounds like it. Does everyone go to them?'

'Yes, especially this one since it will be the last one for the year.'

Lachlan placed his hand on my back and pointed out towards the ocean. In the distance, black clouds began to churn, blurring the horizon. 'Looks like a storm is coming in. We should probably get home.' He whistled for Duke, who came bounding from the other side of the bay.

At the edge of the sand, we dusted our feet and slipped our shoes back on, then began the return trek up the hill.

'Dinner tonight?' Lachlan asked. His expression was hopeful as we climbed the steps of the cabin verandah.

'Sure,' I replied. 'Noelle's at seven?'

'Or four, if you want to pick your meal from the garden.'

We both laughed, our eyes locking. For a moment, neither of us could tear our gaze away, until I blushed, and he looked down, smiling shyly.

'I haven't forgotten about cooking you a vegan dinner either,' I said. 'You won that race fair and square, and I intend to honour your reward.'

He glanced back up at me. 'A girl of her word. I like that.'

'Just don't come hungry.'

He laughed again. 'I'm really glad you decided to stay.'

I tried not to beam, even though I was cartwheeling on the inside. 'Me too.'

***

The next morning, I woke early to wait at the hospital for a blood test, clutching the blood referral form Dr Tremblay had given me weeks ago. While I waited, I called Anna to update her on my change of plans. She was surprised to hear that I wasn't coming home yet.

'I'd still prefer that you come stay with us and start a program. Isolating yourself on an island is not a substitute for AA,' she said.

'I know that, and I don't mean to hide away. But it's working for me. I've been sober for fifteen days.'

'And that's amazing, Marley, honestly,' she said. 'I'm proud of you, but one day you're going to have to return to the real world. I'm worried you won't know how to do that if you don't prepare now.'

I understood what she was saying, that a program or support group at this stage of my recovery would be beneficial, enabling me to speak with others who were in a similar circumstance. I didn't disagree, but it was one more thing I'd have to get my head around, confiding in strangers, sharing my most shameful secrets with them, being vulnerable and letting them see the real me. 'I'll sign up for a program as soon as I'm back in Melbourne. You have my word.'

'That's three months away,' she persisted. 'Is there any chance you could do a program while you're there? I'm sorry to harp on about it, but I believe it's important.'

I sighed, but not unhappily. I was growing to appreciate her meddling. 'Okay, I'll look into it here.'

'Thank you.' She sighed with relief. 'Have you spoken to Austin?'

I shifted my weight to my other foot, keeping one eye on the nurse's station which had yet to open. 'I have. We're not in a great place right now. He's not supportive of my sobriety.'

'Of course he isn't. Change for you means change for him, and he's not ready to accept that. I can't say I'm terribly heartbroken over it. Maybe staying on the island isn't a bad idea.'

My phone beeped and I glanced down to see a message from Austin landing on my screen.

Brian told me you're staying there. Are you kidding, Marley? Are you fucking kidding? We are done. Done! Forget you ever knew me!

There were a few more expletives and a second text of gibberish, filled with awful words he'd never said to me before. It was like he was screaming at me from ten thousand miles away. He was obviously drunk and even if I wanted to, which I didn't, there would be no reasoning with him, no point trying to explain why I needed to stay. I closed my eyes with a heavy sigh, the last delicate thread of our relationship unravelling.

We were over. Just like fragile glass, the merest touch had shattered us, and I had no energy left to put us back together. What could possibly be salvaged from this train wreck anyway, except for bad blood? We'd had good years—great years, in fact—but Austin was never going to support my sobriety and I would never get over the fact that a week after I'd left Melbourne, he'd slept with someone else.

I said goodbye to Anna, then pushed my phone into my back pocket, closing my heart to everything I'd shared with Austin. I would grieve, yes. I would weep in the small hours for the loss of my best friend, but he'd been right to end it, for no matter how much I turned it over in my head, there was no other way forward for us.

I was relieved when the nurses' station finally opened at nine o'clock. And although I wasn't one for relishing in blood tests, I pushed through the hospital front doors, welcoming the distraction.

***

Pathology processed my blood on-site in a matter of hours, the nurse joking that the White Cedar residents were so healthy, I'd finally given them all something to do for the day.

While I waited for my test results, I bought groceries and visited the skincare shop, where I had the shop assistant prepare an organic gift pack for Anna that I planned to send to her. Then, when I was sure my results were back with Dr Tremblay, I went to sit in her waiting room.

It was just after lunch and I was the only one there. Fabienne, the surgery receptionist, recognised me and smiled. 'She won't be long. She's just on a call.'

Five minutes later, Lachlan's mother emerged from her office and noticed me. She sighed deeply, as though the sight of me had ruined her day, then waved me inside. I took the seat opposite her desk. She closed the door and lowered herself into her chair.

'What can I do for you, Marley?'

'I got my blood test done. I thought I'd come and see you for the results.'

She glanced down her nose at me. 'I heard from someone the other day that you didn't catch the boat back with Harry. That you're staying for three months. Is it true?'

She would have heard it from Louise, who'd heard it from Anton, who'd been down at the bay when I'd told Harry. It wasn't what I wanted to spend our session talking about, but her penetrating stare wasn't going to let me off the hook. 'It's true.'

Her eyebrows shot up. 'Well, I'm surprised to hear it, frankly. Is there a reason why you're staying? Surely you want to get back home and continue your recovery.'

'It's home that I'm avoiding. All my triggers are there.'

She gave me an assessing glance. 'While I admit that you look well and I can tell you haven't been drinking, you still need to enter a program. You can't stay here and expect to make progress. You need professional support. Detoxing is one thing, but you need to treat the psychological symptoms too. We don't have those services available here.'

'I was hoping you might have some other suggestions for me.' It was clear she was torn between her professional obligation to help me and her personal desire to get rid of me.

'All support services are offered on the mainland,' she insisted. 'It would be better if you relocated there for the duration of your recovery. I can put you in touch with a reputable rehabilitation clinic in Quebec City. I can even find one for you in Melbourne. You'd be able to fly home tomorrow.' She gave me a pointed look. 'Unless of course you're staying for another reason.'

I hesitated, wondering what she was implying. 'I'm staying because if I go home now, I'm afraid I'll relapse.'

'So, this has nothing to do with Lachlan? Because he has a nice friendship with Celeste, and I'd hate for anything—or anyone—to come between that.'

I frowned at her inappropriateness. 'You're my doctor. Are you allowed to say that to me?'

She inhaled sharply, her hand flying to her grey hair to smooth it down. A flush crept so fiercely up her cheeks that I almost felt sorry for her. 'I apologise, Marley. No, I shouldn't be saying that to you as your doctor.'

I closed my eyes, then opened them again. It had already been an emotional day and I didn't want to squabble with her. 'Look, everyone has been kind to me and it's not my intention to disrupt people's lives. I just want to get better. That's my focus.'

She gave me a long, uncertain look, then turned to her computer. 'Fabienne passed along your blood work. We should check it.' She typed my name, clicked her mouse, then brought my file up on her screen. She spent a few minutes quietly reviewing the results before turning to me. 'Well, as far as your iron goes, you're still borderline deficient, which is not uncommon in heavy drinkers. Try a supplement or some iron-rich foods. Your liver enzymes are high too. If you stay off the alcohol, that should improve. I'll write a referral for another blood test in a month's time to check both your iron and liver.' She printed out the referral and handed it to me.

I accepted it, folding and placing it in my jacket pocket. 'Dr Tremblay?'

'Yes?'

'I haven't told Lachlan about my problem with alcohol. It hasn't come up, and I'd prefer that it didn't.'

She glanced at me warily. 'If he's just a friend and you're going home eventually, what should it matter if he knows?'

'Because I'm embarrassed. Please, can you keep it to yourself?'

'I'm bound to anyway, Marley,' she said with a wry smile. 'Doctor-patient confidentiality. I'm sure you wouldn't hesitate to sue me if I breached that.'

I stood, glad that we had an understanding but uncomfortable that she thought so poorly of me. I suppose I hadn't given her any reason to like me so far and that, like many others in my life, she might just be another bridge I'd have to mend in good time.

Chapter 24

'Are your eyes closed?'

'Yes.'

'Are you sure? No peeking.'

'They're closed. I promise.' Which was entirely true because when I crashed my elbow into Lachlan's wall, I yelped in pain. 'Ouch!'

'Sorry. Sorry.' He steered me back on course. 'Are you okay?'

I rubbed it. 'You owe me a new elbow.'

It was evening and we were at his house. He'd asked me to meet him there, announcing that he had a surprise. As soon as I'd stepped through the front door, I'd been ordered to close my eyes.

'All right, nearly there,' he said. 'Just this way, watch your step and *voilà!*'

I opened my eyes and gasped in astonishment. His dining table was set for two and crammed with pans and trays and dishes of food. There was pizza covered in pepperoni and sausage, a bowl of chicken salad, and garlic bread dripping with what I knew was real butter. There was pasta loaded with bacon and cream, hamburgers with thick beef patties, tall glasses of cold milkshakes and rich chocolate cupcakes.

'Good Lord!' I exclaimed.

'I hope you're hungry,' he said grinning. 'I wasn't sure what you liked so I went crazy and made everything.'

I gaped at the table, salivating, my stomach rumbling. I had enjoyed Noelle's vegan cooking and couldn't deny that I felt more energised from it but overhauling my diet and drinking at the same time had been especially challenging. 'How did you get all this meat? I'm pretty sure Louise doesn't sell beef or pepperoni in her store.'

'I placed an order with Harry, and he brought it in today. I know how much you've been missing these foods.'

I had to resist the urge to spin around and throw my arms around him. I was overwhelmed by his generosity and if it were not for Ivy's voice in my head warning me away from her son, I might have done so.

'Well, it's getting cold. Let's sit down and eat.'

We took up seats beside each other and I couldn't hide my smile. Everything smelt deliciously greasy. 'You must have been cooking all afternoon.'

He shrugged. 'For the past four hours anyway.'

'I can't thank you enough. But I feel terrible. I was the one who was meant to cook for you. Do you even want to eat this?' I looked guiltily at the fat dripping from the beef patties.

He laughed. 'Sure. There's lettuce and tomato on those burgers too.'

I shook my head at him.

'Seriously, I figured you needed meat more than I needed vegetables. And yes, I can eat all of it. I eat stuff like this when I go to Montreal, so it's not a big deal.'

We dove straight in, piling our plates with pizza and chicken salad and pasta, deciding to share one of the burgers because we couldn't fit another thing on our plates. We sat there, eating and talking, then suddenly Lachlan said, 'Sorry, I haven't offered you a drink yet. Would you like a beer or wine?'

I paused on a mouthful of pasta, before forcing it down. 'I'll just have one of these milkshakes, thanks.'

'Are you sure? I have more grown-up drinks than milkshakes.' He pulled a bottle of wine out of the refrigerator and glanced at it. 'How about this pinot grigio from Leesburg, Virginia?'

Oh God, how I wanted to say yes. It was just one glass. Just *one*. Who would know? Who was here to witness it other than Lachlan? If I exercised control and stopped at one, I could almost pretend it never happened, just pick up afterwards where I left off. And yet, the voice of sobriety seemed to boom louder every day making it harder to ignore. I shook my head emphatically. 'No, I'll just have a milkshake.'

He closed the fridge door and returned to the table. 'I'll have one too. I always go a bit nuts in Montreal when I see my old friends, so it wouldn't hurt to have a night off.'

He reached for the milkshakes and set them down in front of our plates. 'Come to think of it, I remember Noelle telling us at dinner that time that you're not a drinker. Is it the taste you don't like?'

'Sort of,' I mumbled, concentrating on my food so he wouldn't see the way my cheeks had grown pink. I hated lying, especially to him.

'So, tell me about your childhood,' he said, taking a bite of pizza and placing the slice back down.

I let out a breath, grateful for the reprieve. 'Well, I grew up in Melbourne. My mother was a schoolteacher and my father, as you know, was a lawyer too.'

'And do they both still live in Melbourne?'

'My mother died four years ago,' I said, a lump forming in my throat. 'From lymphoma.'

'I'm sorry to hear that,' Lachlan said.

'Thank you. My father quit law shortly after she died and moved to the country to be closer to his brother. But I've long suspected that he regrets not having quit sooner. He let his job consume every minute of his time. Maybe it was easier to do that than face what was happening.' I knew because I had those same regrets. I'd worked my mother's final weeks away because I wasn't able to deal with the reality of losing her. Lost time. That was all I'd been left with because, like my father, I'd thrown away those last precious moments when I could have been with her.

'It must have been a devastating time.' Lachlan's eyes were full of sorrow.

'It was. After Mum died and Dad moved away, I worked harder than ever. I've always done that. Worked myself to the bone when life threw curveballs.'

'And your sister?'

'She and Mum were so alike—born to love and nurture. She took her death hard, especially as Dad and I were always so similar. She felt like she had no one left in the family who understood her.'

'Family dynamics can be tricky,' Lachlan said. 'I have no siblings, well, none I'm aware of.' He smiled. 'But I've always wondered what it would be like to have a brother or sister, the kinds of things we'd get up to, or the fights we'd have.'

I smiled at the memory of the childhood games Anna and I used to play in our suburban backyard. 'She loved playing mums and dads, while I wanted to play cops and robbers. Except I was always the cop, the lawyer, the judge and the prison guard.' I laughed at the recollection. 'Anna used to cry to Mum that I wasn't playing the game right, and they'd go inside and do something terribly domestic like make cookies. I'd jump on my father's computer and type up an affidavit for my make-believe client.'

Lachlan chuckled and wiped his mouth and hands with a napkin, taking a sip of his milkshake.

'Mind you, I was only seven at the time. I was my father's daughter from the moment I was born.'

'What kind of law did your father specialise in?'

I hesitated because the idea of lying to him was becoming exhausting. 'He was a criminal lawyer.'

Lachlan's eyebrows shot up. 'Ah, defending the bad guys.'

'Well, everyone is entitled to a defence.'

He scrunched up his face as though disagreeing. 'I'm not so sure about that. I think what they're entitled to is a prison cell for the rest of their lives.'

This was exactly why I didn't tell people what I did for a living. The judgement. The notion that they even had a clue as to what my job entailed. 'Some people do bad things, yes, but they're not beyond rehabilitation. Doesn't everyone deserve a second chance?'

'It depends. Sometimes they're given multiple chances and they blow them. Sometimes their crimes are so bad they don't deserve anyone in their corner.'

'You really see the world in black and white, don't you?' I said, feeling my skin prickle with defensiveness.

'I think the problem with society is there is too much grey. And criminal lawyers take advantage of that. My father went to court once for hitting my mother and *she* lost. If the lawyer who defended my father saw her as a person at all, he wouldn't have defended him so ruthlessly. But what he cared about was money and success with no thought for the victim. Do you think she ever had the courage to go to the police again? No way. Why would she? She just accepted the violence because even the court wouldn't help her.'

I wiped my mouth with a napkin and threw it down on the plate. 'Okay, what about people who come from broken homes, or have mental health issues, or who have just lost their way? They offend and they might even re-offend, but someone has to help them, or they just become a lost cause.'

Lachlan leaned forward in his chair and folded his arms. 'My father was a spoilt, entitled brat who came from a privileged background and not a broken home. He was just someone who thrived on power. And he was given way too many chances to ruin my mother's life. Sorry if my perspective is a little jaded on this, but the court had every chance to find him guilty and still they let him go. And because of that, my mother endured more years of abuse.'

I swallowed hard, staring down at the table. I loved a healthy debate and could argue for hours, but I was achingly aware of how personal this issue was for Lachlan, how real and raw his pain still was, and I couldn't argue with that. It made me bite back my words.

'God, would you listen to us?' Lachlan took a deep breath and shook his head. 'Such a heavy conversation and we haven't even had our cupcakes yet!'

I forced a weak smile. It unnerved me to discuss the law with Lachlan because I couldn't hide from the fact that I was deceiving him. Lying, withholding the truth, twisting it a little. Whatever the case, I wasn't telling him the full story. I was afraid to because if he ever knew the real Marley, it would be a reminder of all the things he despised in this world.

We finished our milkshakes and a cupcake each, and Lachlan walked me home under a clear, cold sky. There were billions of stars splashed across it and I spent most of the walk with my head tilted back, looking at them.

'They're something, aren't they?' Lachlan said.

'I've never seen so many before.'

'Blue zones aren't just about clean living. They have the cleanest skies too.'

'It's incredible.' As we approached the cabin, I rubbed my stomach. 'I think I have a belly-ache.'

'I hope it wasn't my cooking,' he said worriedly.

'Not at all. I literally gorged myself and I'm paying for it. As much as I've missed those foods, I'm not sure my body can handle them anymore.' I looked forward to an almond milk smoothie in the morning and some of Noelle's berry granola.

'I feel like that when I come home from Montreal, like I've gorged myself Christmas-style and then I have a food hangover for the next few days. It takes some good island eating before I feel right again.'

'We better not tell Noelle what we ate tonight,' I whispered, as we reached the cabin verandah.

'I wouldn't dare,' he whispered back.

We stood facing each other in the darkness. I could see the outline of his face, the strong curve of his jaw, his bright eyes as he smiled down at me.

'I enjoyed tonight,' he said.

'Me too. Thank you. No one has ever cooked for me before.'

'I find that hard to believe. I imagine men would be falling over themselves to make you dinner every night.'

I rolled my eyes. 'No.'

'Well, I'd like to do it again. Maybe with not so much meat next time.'

I clutched my stomach. 'That would be nice.'

He leant down and I thought he was going to kiss my lips, but he grazed my cheek instead.

I exhaled, not quite sure if I was relieved or disappointed.

'Good night, Marley from Melbourne,' he said. 'Sleep well.'

I watched him as he and Duke stepped back down onto the road. He turned once to wave before the night swallowed him. I brought my hand up to my cheek to touch the spot his lips had brushed. I wasn't sure if it were the cold night air or the way Lachlan made me feel, but I shivered, realising I'd wanted that kiss to be more than it was.

I opened the cabin door and stepped inside, noticing a folded piece of paper on the floor, as though someone had slipped it beneath the door earlier that evening.

I bent to retrieve and unfold it. In elegant cursive writing was the name of a rehabilitation clinic based in Ottawa. Beneath it was a phone number, a website address, and a small note.

Dear Marley,
This clinic offers an online support program for remote
patients. I think it could work for you. You may use one of my
surgery rooms for the sessions. Good luck.
Dr Tremblay.

I realised then that Ivy had spent considerable time researching programs I could participate remotely in from the island and that the doctor in her wanted me to succeed, even if, as Lachlan's mother, she would prefer I go. But if ever there was an olive branch to be extended, it was this one, and I accepted it gratefully. I would try my hardest not to disappoint her.

Chapter 25

It was the end of September.

Cold winds blew from the north, dense fog rolling behind it, and the whispers of an unforgiving winter on its way. I'd been on the island a full month and I woke that morning, thirty days sober.

Every day that I remained dry was an achievement, but a full month was something I'd never accomplished before. I wanted to celebrate the milestone, to shout the news from the rooftops, but I wasn't sure how, for few people knew about my sobriety. There was Noelle who, when I went next door to tell her, hugged me before wiping away a traitorous tear with the corner of her apron and ordering me to prepare the porridge. Then after breakfast, I walked down to the village to call Anna and text Dad. I texted Paul too, who replied immediately and told me how pleased he was.

Next, I ran errands, having my blood taken again and visiting Dr Tremblay, who told me my liver function had improved. Then I bought groceries at Louise's store, which I was able to do more confidently now. There was no quaking with impulse in front of her liquor shelf. I could walk right by it and tell myself it didn't exist, and sometimes I almost believed it.

What had completely transformed my days and my whole attitude towards recovery, were the one-hour support sessions I participated in three times a week. Dr Tremblay leant me a small room at the back of her surgery where I joined online and in private. Even Fabienne wasn't privy to what I did in that room. For one secluded hour each time, I spoke with my support counsellor, then joined a video group session.

On some level, I'd thought tucking myself away from temptation was the key, but those sessions taught me that recovery was far more than just removing myself from the problem. Self-control was an underrated virtue and I learnt strategies on how to integrate back into society, how to improve or let go of certain relationships, and how to manage the stress of my job.

I filled Noelle in one afternoon as we cooked in her kitchen, preparing the dishes we would take down to the fête the next day. As I chopped onions and potatoes for the stew and she brought together the dough for the bread, I told her about my session that morning.

'My counsellor gave me homework. I need to make a fearless moral inventory of myself.'

'Hmm,' Noelle said, working the dough. 'How do you do that?'

'I take a hard look at the kind of person I am and write an objective assessment of that. It should include character deficits, strengths, weaknesses and what damage my addiction has done to others.'

'That sounds confronting.'

'It will be. I know I haven't always been a nice person, especially when the drinking was bad. I was awful to my sister, I avoided my Dad, I made no effort with anybody unless a party or alcohol was involved, but I'm at a point now where I need to take responsibility for the hurt I've caused.'

'First, you must acknowledge it, then you can fix it.'

'Exactly.'

Noelle nodded her approval. 'This sounds like a good step. What about the people you will lose because you've stopped drinking?'

I thought of Austin and my friends, all of whom were heavy drinkers and recreational drug users. There was no doubt I would need to become more intentional about the people I spent my time with, but I was still hit with a pang of sadness at the thought of leaving them behind. For years they had been my 'family'. They understood the complexities of my job, could empathise with a long day spent in court. They knew *me*. But they fixed their problems with substance, and I'd spent the better part of a month trying to rid my body and mind of it. How did we co-exist moving forward? How did I spend time with them when all they wanted to do was drink their lives away in a bar?

'I'm not sure,' I said truthfully. 'I don't have a lot of friends who aren't drinkers, so I'll be returning to a small support circle. My sister mostly, maybe my boss. There's no one else really.'

'You will always have us.' Noelle smiled softly.

'Yes, but you'll be ten thousand miles away,' I said. 'I don't want to think about leaving you or anyone here. It terrifies me too much.'

'You still have two months to go. A lot can happen in two months.' Her grin was sly as she chopped the vegetables.

***

It was the day of the fête and Noelle and I worked in her kitchen from sunrise, finishing the baking, then packing everything away in casserole dishes and tubs. There were stews and lentils and crusty fresh bread. There was golden arancini stuffed with mushrooms and rice, and crispy fried chickpeas with cucumber and tahini.

I was adding the finishing touches to a platter of glossy artichokes and marinated olives when Lachlan arrived. He sniffed the air eagerly. 'I didn't think Noelle's house could smell any better but today, it does.'

'We've been cooking for three days straight,' I said.

His eyes travelled the length of my floral belted dress and leather boots. 'Wow, you look beautiful, Marley.'

I blushed fiercely. 'Oh, this old thing.' It was in fact a brand-new Longchamp dress I'd brought with me from Melbourne with a palette of browns, reds and greens that reminded me of the White Cedar forests in fall. I'd thought Lachlan might like it, but my cheeks still burned at his obvious appreciation. 'Did you bring the car around?'

'It's out the front. Here, let me take these first.' He collected the loaves of bread and a dish of pine nut lentils and disappeared out the door.

Noelle appeared in a long-sleeved blue dress with tiny rosebuds on it. Her grey nest of hair was set, and she wore thick tan stockings and tan pumps. For once she wasn't wearing her rubber boots or galoshes, and I smiled fondly at her. 'You look absolutely lovely.'

She harumphed, but I knew she'd enjoyed the compliment, dusting away lint from her dress. 'Okay, where are we up to?'

'Lachlan's taking things out to the car now.'

She reached for my hand and turned me towards her, staring solemnly into my face. 'There is going to be a lot of alcohol there tonight. Everyone gets a little silly before winter comes. If you feel tempted, come find me.' Her stare was so serious, I threw my arms around her little body and hugged her tight.

'Thank you.' It was all I could manage. Anymore and the surge of emotion in my chest would reach my eyes, and I didn't want to cry in front of Lachlan.

He reappeared in the kitchen and I took a deep breath before handing him another dish. We eventually loaded all our cooking efforts into the car, piled in around it, and Lachlan drove us down the hill to the square where the fête was being held.

He parked near the hospital and we made several trips back and forth carrying the food. The square was full, and I was surprised at how many people lived on the island, seeing them converge now in one place. There were tables laden with food forming the perimeter, and tables and chairs in the middle for people to sit and eat. There was a dancefloor near the chessboards and fairy lights strung up through the trees. Candles sat flickering on tables, as well as lanterns, and shop lights were on, casting the square in a golden glow.

I followed Lachlan and Noelle with our platters and dishes of food, setting them down on tables wherever there was room. Anton and Louise noticed us and hurried over, hugging us each, and talking animatedly about the dishes they'd brought. Then Gilbert and Freda joined us, followed by Emile and Fabienne. Ivy appeared with Joel to help Noelle uncover the food. She gave me a small, uncertain smile before returning her attention to the platters.

'This is great,' I said to Lachlan as we moved to the side, out of the way of children chasing each other and people bringing more dishes. 'Everyone looks so happy.'

'Wait until they all start dancing,' he said. 'Give it another two hours and a bit more wine. Speaking of which, can I get you a drink?'

My eyes fell on the drinks area. Several tables were pushed together, covered in bottles of red wine and beer and towers of cups. There were bowls of punch too, with fruit pieces and ice cubes bobbing up and down.

'What's in the punch?' I asked.

'Usually just fruit juice. It's for the kids.'

'That sounds nice. I'll have a glass of that.'

'One glass of punch coming right up.' He gave me a warm smile before disappearing into the crowd. Ivy had moved away to talk with friends, so I returned to Noelle's side, helping shuffle dishes around to make room for more, keeping myself busy as I tried to shut out the wine that everyone was drinking.

'Are you okay?' Noelle asked in a low voice.

'I'm fine,' I said. 'I just need distraction.'

'*Oui*,' she said. 'Take those potatoes to Freda. They should go over there with the broccoli.'

Lachlan found me a little while later and handed me a cup of punch. I saw the cold beer in his hand, forcing my attention away from it and sipping my drink.

'Wow, the punch is amazing,' I said, and it was.

'Fabienne makes it every time. It's so good, no one bothers trying to outdo her.'

When it was time for dinner, everyone collected plates from a table and began snaking their way around the square from dish to dish, piling food on, before dropping into the nearest chair. Couples mixed with other couples, the young with the old, friends catching up until it all resembled a mishmash of one big family. I found a chair beside Lachlan, who was sitting next to the mayor. They were talking about the latest developer who had set their sights on White Cedar.

'It's a constant battle keeping them out,' the mayor said, shaking her head. 'Once I let one in, they'll come in droves and our island will be changed forever.'

After dinner, someone put on *Le Festin*, turned it up loud, and the islanders climbed to their feet to dance. While they did, I helped Louise and the other women clear the tables of empty plates and cups.

Afterwards, I searched for Lachlan but noticed him sitting at a table chatting with Celeste. I didn't want to disturb them, so I searched for Noelle instead, who was talking with her friends. As I was about to walk over and join them, someone placed a cup of wine in her hand. She thanked them and accepted it, taking a hearty swig. I didn't want to be the reason she felt bad and put the cup down, so I halted abruptly, turning instead and walking to the edge of the square, far away from the drinks table, where I sat on a bench.

I wrapped my arms around myself and watched the fête from afar. Everyone was enjoying themselves, their lives happy and whole. It was a joy to witness all that love, even though I'd never felt more alone.

Despite its best intentions, sobriety had made me a recluse. It had stolen my confidence, my identity, my ability to cope in social gatherings. I didn't know how to be at parties like this without a drink in my hand. I was certain my counsellor would say it was all part of the journey, but it didn't stop the loneliness from creeping in. I couldn't be around alcohol or around people who drank it, so where did I go? How did I fit in?

Unsure how to deal with the strange sadness that had settled upon me, I decided to take a walk and shake it off. No one would miss me and the idea of the bay at this time of night, where the moon would be shining over the ocean, felt nice. I climbed to my feet and left the fête behind, finding the road that led down to the water.

Once I was there, I kicked off my shoes, sinking into the cold sand. The moon's glow was otherworldly as it lit up the ocean, rippling with the current. Gentle waves broke on the shoreline in frothy crystals, and aside from the distant sound of music that drifted on the air, everything was calm.

I sat there for a while, my mind still, empty of noise. I was so transfixed by the sea that I didn't hear the patter of feet on the sand until they were right beside me, and I glanced up to find Lachlan.

'Hey,' I said.

'Hey.' He plonked down beside me. 'I've been looking for you.'

'Sorry, I thought I'd take a walk.'

'Had enough of the fête?'

'No, it was fine.'

He nodded slowly as though not believing me. 'Everything okay?'

I didn't reply, stretching my legs out instead. I wasn't sure how to explain what I felt.

He scooped up a mound of sand and let it fall through his fingers. 'Are you missing home?'

I shrugged. 'Maybe. I don't know. I feel out of sorts.'

'You know, a part of it may have to do with island fever.'

I glanced at him. 'Island fever?'

'Yeah. When you come from a big city and you get cooped up on an island for too long.'

I shook my head and laughed. 'That's not it. I like the island.'

'Whatever you say,' he said with a teasing smile.

'You and Celeste looked cosy earlier,' I teased back.

He dipped his head, and I caught his embarrassed smile. 'She's a nice girl and I'll never be impolite, but it was just conversation. A little one-sided if I'm honest.'

'You looked pretty into her.'

He laughed out loud. 'Please, don't give my mother or Celeste any more encouragement.'

'Why don't you pretend you have a girlfriend in Montreal? Let her down gently.'

'I've tried. And half the time it's been true. I've had plenty of girlfriends on the mainland. But Celeste, well, she doesn't seem to care. She's persistent.'

Part of me was sorry I'd brought up the topic of girlfriends. Prickling jealousy rose up my neck at the mention of them, which was entirely unreasonable, for Lachlan and I were only friends.

'Anyway, there's someone else I like. Someone I've liked for a while,' he said. 'I'm just not sure how to tell her.'

'Does she live on the mainland?'

'No, she's here.'

'On the island?' I racked my brain, for I was certain I would have known if Lachlan was keen on someone.

'Actually, she's sitting on this beach.'

'She's here?' I looked past him, back across the bay towards the village. 'I don't see anyone else.'

'She's closer than you think.'

Realisation dawned and my heart began to thump against my ribcage.

'You dummy,' he said, shaking his head. 'It's you, Marley.'

I couldn't conjure the words to reply; I was certain I'd stopped breathing. There was no denying that what Lachlan and I shared was magnetic, but while I'd wondered, hoped, that he felt it too, letting him into my carefully guarded world was something else entirely.

His gaze was intense and searching now, as he watched me closely.

171

'I've been wanting to kiss you for a while.'

'You have?'

'Yes.' He smiled. 'So... can I?'

I wanted to say no, that I wasn't good for him, that I had more baggage than the luggage compartment of a jetliner, that I would be leaving soon, and he'd be staying and to start something now would only be detrimental. But all those protests stalled because when he leant in to kiss me, I didn't stop him.

His touch was gentle at first, our lips brushing, a hesitant kiss. But as we grew bolder, his tongue sought mine, and the kiss became deeper, more certain, and we relaxed into it.

He shifted in the sand to face me properly, one hand stroking my cheek while the other found my waist. It was the kind of kiss I'd been afraid of, the one that would bind us emotionally, the one that threatened to undo me, but I couldn't have stopped if I'd tried. Everything about it was perfect, every delicious sensation, every touch of Lachlan's fingertips as they trailed my cheek. I felt it all.

We only pulled apart when another couple dropped onto the sand and began walking in our direction. When they passed us, heading towards the headland, Lachlan gave me a languid smile. 'I can't tell you how long I've been wanting to do that. Since before I went to Montreal.'

I was quiet, still processing what happened.

'Uh oh,' he said. 'Not a good kiss?'

I shook my head quickly. 'No, it was perfect.'

'You have a boyfriend then?' He raked his hand through his hair. 'Christ, I didn't even think to ask.'

'No, it's not that,' I said. 'The kiss was amazing. *That's* the problem.'

He raised an eyebrow. 'That's a funny problem to have.'

'You know what I mean. I'm worried about starting something when our time together will eventually come to an end. Aren't we just making it hard for ourselves?'

Lachlan cringed. 'I better rethink that marriage proposal then.'

I elbowed him, trying not to laugh.

'Look, I don't know where we go from here either, only that I like spending time with you,' he said.

'I like spending time with you too.'

'Okay, so why don't we just call it an awesome kiss for now?

Everything after that, we can take one day at a time.'

It was such a Lachlan thing to say—take it one day at a time, see what happens. He was so entirely relaxed about it that despite my reservations, I found myself relaxing too, nodding in agreement.

'Okay. One day at a time.'

Chapter 26

The following week, I was watching Lachlan chop wood in the forest behind Noelle's property when he turned to me, wiping sweat from his forehead. 'I've been thinking.'

'Uh oh. That can never be good,' I said.

He laughed and leant forward to plant a kiss on my lips. I caught him and pulled him close to me, the kiss deepening until we were both breathless.

'Your nose is cold,' he said.

'So is yours.'

He kissed me again.

The past week had been full of stolen moments like these. Noelle had caught us kissing in her garden and had given us a surprised but delighted look, leaving us to giggle like teenagers when she'd turned her back again. But she was the only one who knew. We'd agreed to remain discreet until we understood what was happening, but there could be no denying that our feelings for each other were going from strength to strength.

'Seriously though,' he said, returning to the pile of wood. 'I'd like to take you on a trip.'

My heart dropped into my stomach. 'A trip? Where?'

'To Alaska to see the aurora borealis.'

'The northern lights?'

'Yes.'

My mind raced, thinking of all the ways I could avoid leaving the island. 'Won't it be freezing up there?'

'That's kind of the point,' he said, raising the axe and bringing it down on a chunk of wood. It splintered apart. 'You need long hours of darkness and clear night skies. It's the perfect season for it.'

I'd been cocooned on the island for six weeks and returning to the mainland and all its temptations was still a daunting notion. I fidgeted, searching for an excuse. 'I don't know, Lachlan. Can't we just stay here?'

'Marley, it's the *northern lights*.'

'I know.' I scuffed the ground with my boot, kicking up brown leaves that had turned soggy from the rain.

'Then what's the problem?'

How could I tell him of my darkest fears, that I was an alcoholic terrified of relapsing? That I'd been here all this time recovering and I'd kept it from him. The lie was bigger than me now. Lachlan was the kindest person I'd ever known, and I didn't want to hurt him the way I'd hurt others. 'Won't people suspect we're together if we go on a trip?'

'Who cares if they do?'

'Well, your mum wouldn't be happy. And neither would Celeste. I don't want to upset anyone.'

He gave an indignant snort. 'We're adults. We can do what we like.'

I stamped my feet against the cold, trying to buy more time. 'How long would we go for?'

'A week. We could fly to Montreal first, grab you some thermals and Mukluks, a good jacket. Then we'd be on our way.'

Thoughts of restaurant dinners drinking wine and sitting in the hotel bar overwhelmed me, but Lachlan's expression was so hopeful, I could feel my resolve crumbling. And it *was* the northern lights. Whatever willpower I'd stockpiled in the past six weeks would have to be enough. I was determined to stay the course, no matter how tempting.

'So?' He stared at me with huge brown eyes.

I gave in. 'All right, let's do it.'

'Really?' A wide grin lit up his face. He dropped the axe and closed the gap between us in two quick steps, picking me up and swinging me around.

***

The morning of our trip was cold and blustery. Lachlan arrived at nine to drop Duke at Noelle's and, as we said goodbye, she hugged me. It was more than a hug though because she knew the significance of the trip I was about to take and how it could change me.

'You are strong,' she whispered in my ear. 'You can do this.'

I saw a fierce tenacity in her eyes that I wanted to lock away someplace safe for when I needed it.

We left Noelle's house and Lachlan drove us in his car across to the western side of the island where the airport was. The runway was wet from overnight rain and the sky thick with heavy clouds, the pilot warning us the flight to Halifax would be bumpy.

We boarded the plane and Lachlan was as excited as I'd ever seen him, chatting constantly, while my insides knotted together like rope. We'd told few people that we were going away, but that wouldn't stop the rumour mill from exploding once word got out. Still, Lachlan seemed unfazed, while I chewed constantly over how Ivy would feel, like I'd betrayed her despite her recent goodwill.

The flight took thirty minutes, the wind throwing our little Cessna around like a kite. I was relieved when the wheels touched down on the tarmac and we rolled to a stop. There was no time to venture out into Halifax Harbour and explore though, for our next flight to Montreal was in an hour. I was relieved about that, and when Lachlan suggested we grab lunch and a beer in the small airport bar while we waited, I pulled him towards the safety of the café instead.

Once my nerves had settled, I enjoyed being off the island and away from prying eyes. We could kiss when we wanted, hold hands and stand with our bodies pressed together as we waited in queues. I knew what we were doing was torturous, that we were destined to rip our own hearts out by the end of all this, for I would leave, and he would stay, but we couldn't seem to help ourselves. What we felt for each other was so intense that there was a need to gorge on it before our time was over.

The flight to Montreal was longer, although less bumpy. We arrived to a dark evening, the last of the scant daylight having slipped away, the air cool as we stepped out of the airport.

'Welcome to my home city,' Lachlan announced proudly. 'Fall is the most beautiful time of the year to visit Montreal.'

He'd hired a car for our overnight stay, and we tugged our luggage in the direction of the rental station. The Lexus was warm and smelled of new leather when we got in.

Lachlan steered us out of the airport carpark and into traffic. 'We'll buy you some proper winter gear tomorrow. My favourite shop is close to where we're staying.' He looked happy behind the wheel, one hand on it, the other resting on my knee. I liked this side of him, taking control, confidently navigating us through busy city streets. I had looked after myself for so long that it was nice to shift gears and be looked after. 'Then our flight to Alaska is at four.'

'It all sounds great,' I said, my excitement bubbling.

'And I hope it's still all right if we stay at a hotel tonight. I leased out my apartment years ago. Sometimes it's free when I'm in town, sometimes it's not. Usually, it's easier to stay at the Birks.'

'Whatever you have planned will be perfect,' I said, smiling at him.

He leant over and kissed me on the lips, making my stomach flip, before returning his eyes to the road.

We reached the Hotel Birks on Phillips Square in downtown Montreal and Lachlan parked the Lexus. We collected our luggage from the trunk and checked in at reception.

Once we were in our room and we'd set our bags down, Lachlan cast me a sheepish look. 'I hope I wasn't being presumptuous in booking us a shared suite. Although I took the liberty of asking for separate beds because I wasn't sure how you felt about it all, I mean, if you wanted to... you know...'

I felt shy suddenly, watching him stumble over the words. It was something I'd thought about since the day he'd asked me to come on this trip, for we'd kissed and touched, but had yet to sleep together. I was far from being a saint and, once upon a time, I would have been bolstered by alcohol and eager to indulge in reckless, drunken sex with him.

But I wasn't drunk or high or coming down. I was sober and it had been a long time since I'd slept with anyone in that state of mind. There was more at stake with Lachlan. I didn't want sex with him to be drunken and reckless. I wanted it to mean something because *he* meant something.

So I shrugged, then nodded, unsure what to say, until Lachlan dropped his suitcase and pulled me close to him, holding me tight. 'We don't need to decide now,' he said, kissing the top of my head, then the tip of my nose.

'I just don't want to rush it,' I said. 'You mean more to me than that.'

He held me closer, and I could feel the soft thud of his heartbeat against my cheek. 'I don't want to rush it either. If it happens, it happens, and if it doesn't, it's fine. No pressure, okay?'

I snuggled into his chest, comforted by his understanding, torn between restraint, and wanting so much more with him.

***

There was no escaping a visit to the hotel bar. It was late and we were both tired, so we ate downstairs. Then, when I was all out of excuses, we moved to the bar for a drink before bed. As we settled into a lounge, the waiter appeared to take our order.

'I'll have a beer, thanks,' Lachlan said, studying the menu. 'A Molson.'

'And I'll have an orange juice,' I told him.

The waiter returned to the bar and Lachlan reached for my hand. 'They have a nice selection of wines here.'

'Do they?'

'Yeah. You sure you don't want to try one to celebrate our trip?'

How could I tell him that for me, it would never just be one drink? That if I started now, I would throw them back until I lost count? That I would still be drinking long after he went to bed, then rose, then went to bed again?

'I'm fine,' I said. I breathed in relief when he let the subject drop, telling me instead about the last time he'd visited the northern lights in Yellowknife and how incredible it was.

'You're in for a treat,' he said. 'Fairbanks is one of the best places in Alaska to view it.'

'Will we definitely see something? I've heard it's a bit hit and miss.'

'It all depends on the conditions—how dark the sky is, what the solar winds are like and if the weather is clear. I've planned it for a new moon and so far, the weather looks good. Fingers crossed.'

The waiter arrived with our drinks. After he retreated again, we sat close, and I felt the weight of Lachlan's hand on my leg, the other around my shoulder. Occasionally, he'd drop a light kiss on my neck, then nuzzle in until I giggled. I almost forgot he had a beer in his hand as we became drunk on each other's company. I was like a twelve-year-old schoolgirl again, experiencing her first crush.

Back in our room, we retreated to our separate beds but somehow ended up together in his, me climbing beneath the covers and snuggling in close so he could hold me. We spent most of the night awake, every kiss, every whisper, every touch agonisingly torturous. He told me he'd never felt this way about anyone before and I told him that I felt the same. We'd only known each other a short time, but Lachlan had become a warm and beautiful part of my new world. I didn't want to think about the day I'd have to say goodbye to him.

Sometime at dawn, after talking the hours away, we almost succumbed to our desires, but I remained strong. What I had with Lachlan was precious and, unlike the rest of my life, I was determined not to stuff it up.

Chapter 27

On my fiftieth day of sobriety, we woke early and left to purchase my new winter gear, before returning to the airport. We boarded our flight and flew out of Montreal in a blaze of afternoon sun, soaring across Canada into Alaska, watching the terrain change from dense housing to wooded hillsides, then to white, glacial mountains.

The hotel driver collected us at Fairbanks Airport. As we walked to his car, I was stunned to feel the frigid cold bite at my skin despite wearing a beanie, gloves, and my new parka.

'How long are you staying?' he asked us as we climbed in, the heater blasting.

'Just a few days,' Lachlan said, removing his beanie. 'We're hoping to catch the lights while we're here.'

'Where are you going to see them?' The driver steered us out of the airport parking lot. He was middle-aged, with a grey, whiskery beard and blue-grey eyes that matched the landscape.

'Borealis Basecamp,' Lachlan said.

'Awesome. I mean, there's never any guarantee with natural phenomena, but if you can catch them, they're a sight to behold.'

'The forecast for the next few nights looks good.'

'And that's what you want,' the driver replied. 'Clear skies. Although a blizzard is due to blow in later this week. Hope you brought layers. It's the only way to survive the cold out here. Lots of layers.'

Lachlan winked at me and I smiled back.

'Daylight is fading fast,' the driver went on, almost to himself. 'By January, we'll only have about four hours of it. In these parts, it's either the land of the midnight sun or days of eternal darkness.' He chuckled as he drove us towards our hotel, chatting about the weather and the challenges of winter this far north, speaking of its beauty and misery as if they were one and the same.

We reached downtown Fairbanks and pulled into a small hotel carpark.

'Here we go,' he said, parking the car and climbing out.

Our breath fogged instantly as we climbed out too, collecting our luggage from him and following him into the foyer to check in.

Once we were inside our room, warming ourselves by the fire, Lachlan pulled me towards him and wrapped his arms around me. 'We made it,' he said.

I shook my head, for it was hard to believe. 'If someone had told me a few months ago I'd be in Alaska right now, I would have laughed.'

'What would you be doing right now if you weren't here?'

'I'd be back at Noelle's cabin.'

'No, I mean, if you were at home.'

I shrugged. 'Working, I guess. Doing the usual things.'

'And what's your *usual* thing?'

I pulled back slightly to look at him, my shoulders tensing. 'Why do you want to know?'

Confusion crossed his face. 'It was just a question.'

'Well, it's an odd question.'

His look of confusion deepened. 'Not really. I'm making conversation and you're getting defensive.'

I breathed, trying to rein in my prickliness. 'I don't know. Just stuff.'

He nodded slowly, never breaking our gaze. 'What kind of stuff? Do you like sport? Shopping? Travelling? I already know you don't like to drink.'

'Shopping, I guess.'

'Okay, that's one more thing than I knew yesterday.'

I smiled weakly at him and walked to my luggage, unzipping it, trying to avoid his stare.

He took a seat on the edge of one of the beds, watching me. 'I'm not trying to pry,' he said. 'I just want to get to know you.'

'You know plenty.'

'I know you're a lawyer, that you have a sister, that your dad practised law too, and that your mum passed away a few years ago. But I don't know who the real Marley is. And sometimes you're like a closed book.' He was smiling, but I could tell he was serious, trying to peel back the layers of who I was.

I collected my toiletries from my luggage and disappeared into the bathroom with them. I could feel his eyes studying me, full of questions that I couldn't answer. It was almost impossible to outrun the old Marley—she seemed to be lurking everywhere I turned, waiting to trip me up. I couldn't get past her and the worse thing of all was that Lachlan couldn't either. He was desperate to know her.

I heard him sigh, get up to stoke the fire, then retreat out onto the balcony. After the glass door closed behind him, I sighed too, wishing I could be the open book he wanted me to be, except my book was like a horror story.

I finished unpacking, then called room service for drinks. Lachlan was still on the balcony when they arrived. I opened the door to hand him his parka and a beer and he gave me a small, appreciative smile.

I settled into a chair beside him, wrapping my gloved hands around a cup of hot cocoa. Sunlight was slipping and the landscape beyond our room was changing. The cerulean sky had turned navy blue and snow the previous day had dressed the Alaska Range in a white coat. Autumn had ravaged the trees so that they were lanky and skeletal and everything with a heartbeat would hunker down soon for a cold and endless winter. We were at the edge of the world in a land of primitive and inhospitable beauty, so bitterly cold I could feel it in my bones, but there was nowhere on earth I would rather have been than on that balcony with Lachlan.

I felt his fingers reach across and wrap around mine. I glanced at him, saw his eyes full of apology and I blinked my own sorry.

'I don't mean to be secretive,' I said.

'I know. And I don't mean to push.' His fingers stroked mine gently. 'I'm just worried that you're going home in six weeks and if I don't find out now all the things that make you who you are, I may never know them.'

'You know all the parts that matter,' I said.

'I want the good, the bad and the ugly.'

How could I tell him that my ugly was beyond fathoming?

We sat that way for a while, our bodies close and our hands held, as the sun sank below the horizon and night tumbled down hard and fast around us.

***

After breakfast the next morning, a shuttle from the Borealis Basecamp came to collect us in Fairbanks. The tension from the day before had dissipated and we were relaxed again as the shuttle carried us north on a fifty-minute journey along powdery white roads, snow piling in drifts along the verges.

It was freezing outside, every blast of wind bringing the frozen, bleak howl of the Arctic with it. Beyond the shuttle's windows, mountains rose in grey and white peaks, and if I'd thought White Cedar was remote and rugged, this felt like the ends of the earth.

We arrived at the basecamp and were shown to the domed fibreglass igloo that Lachlan had booked for the next two nights. We climbed the steps of the igloo onto a wide, timber deck and opened the door. Lachlan grimaced at the sight of the queen bed. 'I promise I requested twin beds,' he said. 'I'll call them and ask for a roll-away.'

I placed my hand on his arm. 'You don't need to do that. There's nowhere to put it. And besides, we *have* slept in the same bed together. I think we can control ourselves.'

'Are you sure?'

I reached up to touch his cheek. 'Of course. I want to watch the lights next to you.'

He bent to kiss me in all the ways that told me he wanted me next to him too.

We had time to spare before the lights arrived, so we explored the basecamp in its white-on-white world, the snow soft and thick beneath our Mukluks.

We ate dinner in the dining room as the sky darkened, but it wasn't until midnight that the first hints of green tinged the sky. We were lying on the bed together, studying the clear ceiling, waiting for their appearance, when Lachlan grabbed my hand suddenly and pointed.

'Look!'

I saw them in that same glorious moment, shimmering ribbons of green light dancing across the sky. We watched them, Lachlan as awestruck as I was, even though this was not his first time.

'It doesn't matter how many times you've seen them,' he said. 'They're always incredible.'

'I don't think I'll be able to sleep tonight,' I said. 'I may never stop staring at them.'

He reached for my hand. 'Come on, let's go outside. They'll be even better.'

It was utterly glacial when we stepped out onto the deck and down onto the snow. The green lights streamed above us, flickering across the aurora belt, casting the ground in an otherworldly glow as silhouettes began to emerge from neighbouring igloos. We were all in wonder, transfixed by the display, and when blue and violet streaks began to swirl amidst the green, there was a collective gasp.

'Beautiful,' I whispered, reaching for Lachlan's hand.

He pulled me close, and I leant into him, thankful that our paths had crossed, and we were here now, together, witnessing this precious natural gift.

It didn't matter that our lips were blue, or our teeth were chattering. In that moment, standing beneath the polar lights with Lachlan on the edge of nothingness, I was euphoric and breathless with gratitude. When he bent to kiss me, I met his lips with an urgency that surprised me.

We stayed outside for the next hour, holding each other, feeling the sexual tension build until we could stand it no longer. We went inside to the warmth of the igloo, unable to help ourselves now, fumbling with zippers and gloves, our hands and lips in a frenzy to make up for lost time. Something had happened under those lights—a need to feel as raw and exposed as the landscape around us. I'd never known a high like this—boundless and wild, in this place where Mother Nature spoke loudest.

Once our parkas were off, we slowed down, taking a breath, peeling away the layers one by one—boots and snow pants and sweaters and long johns. At one point we laughed because there were *so* many layers, it was almost comical. Eventually, we were in our underwear and Lachlan's eyes were on me, intense, his breathing ragged. I shivered, not from the cold, but because I wanted him in that same agonising way.

He took a step towards me and closed the gap, tracing his hands down my cheek and along my collarbone, then down to the curve of my breasts. I tilted my head back and sank into him, his lips roaming my neck, his other hand firm in the arch of my back so that we were one.

'You have no idea how much I've wanted you,' he said. 'But are you sure you want this too?'

'Yes,' I said.

'Because I would understand—'

'Stop talking.'

He grinned and picked me up, wrapping my legs around his waist and walking me to the bed. He eased me down gently and I dropped back onto the covers, taking him with me. We pushed away the last of our underwear until there was nothing left between us. High above, the lights danced, and I was still in awe that we were there, that I was with Lachlan and we were about to make love for the first time beneath them.

And when he moved inside me, I felt all my senses explode. I could no longer tell where he ended and I began, only that somewhere along the way, I'd fallen in love with him. I'm not sure when it had happened. Maybe from the first day I'd met him or maybe it had been a gradual thing, slipping beneath my defences.

Whatever the case, he'd become the air I breathed, and I was hopelessly and beautifully lost to him.

**

We spent another night at Borealis Basecamp, swimming in the hot springs and patting reindeers during the day. At night, we enjoyed the lights. We were oblivious to those around us, living in the moment as though the outside world had ceased to exist.

Even when we returned for our final two nights in Fairbanks, all we knew was our hotel room, the roaring fire and each other's bodies. My thoughts slowed when I was with Lachlan and I was at peace when asleep in his arms. It was a peace I'd never known before, not even with Austin.

185

But love can make you stupid, for this could only end in heartache. In six weeks' time, I would return to my job in Melbourne, and he would stay on White Cedar. We'd yet to have a conversation about what that day would mean, but I knew we were both thinking about it.

Back in Montreal, we caught our connecting flight to Halifax, but we arrived too late for the charter to White Cedar and had to spend the night on the harbour.

Over dinner at a local restaurant, Lachlan's phone lit up with calls, and he switched it off. 'My mother,' he said. 'She probably wants to know when we'll be back.'

'Do you want to call her?' I asked, sipping my lemonade.

'Not really. I'll drop in and see her when I get home. I'm sure she'll have plenty to say about this trip.'

I played with the straw in my drink, trying to push through the anxiety of returning to the island. We'd been in a bubble for the past few days, and it had been easy to forget that the people back on White Cedar would be curious about us now. 'How are we going to do this?'

He gave me a confused look. 'Do what?'

'This. Us. When we get back to the island.'

He took a swig of his beer and set it back down. 'Well, it's nobody's business, so we'll just be ourselves.'

'But your mother and Celeste. They'll want to know.'

'They're just going to have to get used to it, Marley,' he said with a touch of annoyance. 'I'm a grown man. I can be with whoever I want.'

'I know that,' I said, reaching across the table for his hand and closing my fingers around it. 'I just don't want to make things difficult for you. It's a small community and people talk. And we need to be honest with ourselves. I'll be leaving in December. What then?'

He looked down at his empty plate, then back up at me. His eyes were sad. 'I'm not sure. We'll try long distance. I'll come visit you and you'll come visit me. Maybe we can meet up in LA or Hawaii so the flights are shorter. We'll make it work.'

I was worried that the distance would be the thing that would end us, no matter how we tried to meet in the middle. After almost five months off work, it would be a tall ask to convince Paul and Brian to give me more time to fly anywhere in the world.

'All I know is that I don't want this to end,' Lachlan said. 'Not now.

186

Maybe not ever.' He brought my hand to his lips and kissed it, holding it close to his stubbled cheek, his eyes never leaving mine.

I felt the air rush out of me as I held his gaze, my heart swelling and breaking at the same time. I'd never known love like this—all-consuming and formidable, so intense it hurt.

We left the restaurant and walked along the esplanade before heading back to the hotel. Lachlan held me close that night and we filled gloriously long hours exploring each other's bodies. Hours that I wanted to slow down, bottle up and keep with me forever before our time ran out.

'You have well and truly stolen my heart,' he said later as we lay tangled in the sheets, our faces so close I could see his hazel eyes in the dark, unfathomable.

'And you have stolen mine,' I whispered back.

'That will be enough to get us through. To work it all out.'

'Yes, I think so.' Somehow, I believed it too. Maybe it was blissful ignorance or maybe my love for Lachlan was too indestructible *not* to work, but I fell asleep that night knowing that what we had was incomparable to anything we'd ever felt before and that had to count for something.

The next morning, we caught the charter flight from Halifax back to White Cedar, the wheels touching down on the island's runway on a bright, cold morning. When we disembarked the plane, we were both surprised to find Joel and Anton waiting inside the small airport building.

'Rolling out the welcome mat for us,' Lachlan said as we approached them. He was in good spirits, his smile wide.

But their faces were sombre, and I knew instantly something was wrong.

'Your mother's been trying to reach you,' Joel said. 'She sent us up here to wait for your plane to arrive.'

'What's wrong?'

'It's Noelle,' Anton said. His eyes were bloodshot, as though he'd been up most of the night crying.

I grabbed Lachlan's arm as the world tilted.

'What happened to her?' Lachlan grew pale. 'Is she all right?'

Joel swallowed, his Adam's apple bobbing. 'She passed away

yesterday in her sleep.'

I heard the moment Lachlan's breath caught, felt my heart drop sickeningly into my stomach.

'Passed... what?' Lachlan's words were slurred suddenly, as though the sheer energy to conjure them was too great.

'I'm so sorry,' Anton said, wiping his eyes.

'Come on,' Joel said gently. 'We'll take you to your mom.'

Chapter 28

I couldn't remember the drive from the airport to the hospital where Ivy was waiting for us, only that the forests and the cold, calm North Atlantic outside the windows passed by in a blur.

Lachlan was quiet beside me as we sat in the backseat of Joel's car, his jaw set, his eyes blinking back tears. He didn't look at me. He kept his gaze focused outside, his hands in his lap, his shoulders rigid, and I knew he was trying to process the shock.

I was struggling to comprehend it too. *Noelle gone?* It couldn't be possible. It had to be a nightmare that we'd surely wake from. I'd left her in perfect health just a week earlier. She'd been happy that Lachlan and I were taking the trip together, happy about my continuing sobriety, happy that I was staying three more months. We'd made plans to harvest the last of the autumn vegetables and to cover up what might wither when the snow arrived. She'd never mentioned feeling unwell. So how could someone in the place of forever die so unexpectedly?

We reached the hospital and Joel parked the car. It appeared all of White Cedar was gathered outside, talking, comforting each other. They'd lost one of their own and their grief was like a tidal wave, vast and insurmountable.

Joel cleared a path for us through to the front doors. The lobby was busy too. Ivy looked bereft, her usually kempt hair unbrushed, her eyes red-rimmed. Louise, Fabienne, Freda and Celeste were beside her, their voices soft, their arms a protective shield around her. Emile and Gilbert were there too, a look of astonishment on their faces.

They glanced up when we entered, and Ivy walked straight to Lachlan and embraced him as they both cried silently. I stood to the side with my own grief, unsure what to do, an intruder on their private pain.

'I tried calling you,' Ivy admonished him, before shooting me a scathing look. 'It kept ringing out, then you turned it off.'

His shoulders slumped, and I knew he felt guilty for not picking up those calls. 'What happened?'

'She passed peacefully in her sleep the night before last. Joel and I found her yesterday afternoon. We were going to cook dinner at her place but when she didn't answer the door, Joel broke in through a back window and found her in bed.' Ivy crumpled, her entire body trembling. 'She was already gone.'

Lachlan stared blankly at his mother as Fabienne and Louise placed their arms around him and Ivy, then Celeste and Freda followed, tightening the circle of support. Emile patted Lachlan's arm and Joel rubbed Ivy's back. I watched from the corner of the room with no one to comfort or be comforted by, and I thought they must be wondering what right I had to sadness anyway when I'd only known Noelle a short time.

'She'd been there the whole day,' Ivy explained. 'I called the hospital and they sent Dr Childs up with the van. He confirmed her death was most likely from natural causes. She simply went to sleep and never woke up.'

'Where is she now?' Lachlan asked.

'In the morgue, in a viewing room. Some people have already said goodbye. We're restricting it to close friends only.'

'Can I go in?'

'Of course, darling.' Ivy wiped her eyes and nose. 'We'll all go with you.'

I stepped forward because I wanted to say goodbye too.

'Sorry, Marley. *Close* friends only,' Ivy said.

'Marley *was* close to Noelle.' Lachlan's eyes flashed with defensiveness.

'Marley's an outsider. If we let her in over the others, they'll all be up in arms over it. Please, Lachlan.' She pressed her fingertips to her forehead as though to stave off a headache.

I held up my hands. Emotions were running high, and I didn't want them to argue over me. Not here. Not now. 'It's fine. I understand.'

'Are you sure?' Lachlan looked torn between staying with me and going.

'I'm sure. Go and say goodbye. I'll wait outside for you.'

He smiled sadly, then walked heavily down the corridor towards the morgue. They all followed, holding each other, crying into their tissues. When Celeste passed me, she gave me a self-satisfied smirk.

I left the lobby and pushed through the doors to outside. The front garden of the hospital was still scattered with mourners, but most people had moved on. I found a spot on the garden wall and sat, waiting for Lachlan, and it was only then that I realised my hands were shaking and that I hadn't taken a proper breath since we'd left the airport.

Noelle's gone. Now that I'd stopped to process it, it barrelled me over with astonishing force. I swooned, clutching the edge of the garden wall.

'You're the young lady that's renting her cabin,' a man's voice came from nearby.

I looked up and squinted into the sunlight. 'Yes.'

'She was the heart and soul of this island. A good woman.' He glanced up at the hospital. 'She thought the world of you too. Always talked about you.'

I drew a ragged breath, worried that the tears sitting behind my eyes would break free.

'She's with Samuel and Danielle now, and although we'll miss her, we can't begrudge her for wanting that.' He gave me a sombre smile, tipped his cap, and walked away.

It should have given me comfort too, knowing she was reunited with her beloveds in the afterlife, except I needed her as well. Because the sun would still rise and set, the seasons would still cycle and I would still be here, but Noelle was gone. Forever. And I may have only known her a short time, but the thought of never seeing her again caused the ache of loss to roll over me.

I waited for an hour on the garden wall, alone with my grief, everyone else having departed. Lachlan was still in the morgue with the others, and I wasn't sure how much longer they would be down there or even if I'd be welcome in their circle of mourning when they emerged. All my things were still in Joel's car, but I knew there was a spare key for the cabin in Noelle's house, so I lifted myself off the wall and started up the hill.

In the unexpectedness of her passing, someone had left the front door to her house unlocked and I let myself in, pausing in the entryway, feeling her all around me. Her coat and beanie were on the coat rack and her galoshes rested neatly by the door. Her umbrella was standing upright in the corner, everything as it should be, as though she'd just come back from a walk with her friends.

I made my way into her bedroom, stepping over broken glass from the window Joel had smashed to get inside. I saw her robe on the edge of her bed, sheets and quilt askew, and booted indents in the carpet where people had trod as they'd dealt with her body. The room smelt like her—powdery and grandmotherly and full of love, but it was still. So still.

I was trembling by the time I made it to the kitchen. I half-expected to find her standing by the bench chopping vegetables, ready to order me out to the garden or to stir something on the stove. She wasn't there, and the kitchen was clean and orderly, as she must have left it before she'd gone to sleep.

A great, heaving sob pushed its way up my throat and I sank to the floor, pulling her apron from the top of the bench down and holding it close, as though I could imprint her on my soul. I hadn't been here for her final days, to help her, to say goodbye. For a place that prided itself on social inclusivity, she'd died alone in her bed.

I stayed there for hours, unable to stop the tears, feeling her absence like a great gaping hole. The sun moved across the sky, changing the light in the room so that shadows shifted, and the house stirred. Time dragged and blurred and dissolved into nothing.

It was only when the kitchen was finally plunged into darkness that I realised the entire day had slid by. I pulled myself up from the floor, found the cabin's spare key on her key hook and stepped back outside.

I should have gone straight inside, taken a shower, tried to make dinner, but something had switched gears in my brain. My tears dried, my senses fired, and my breathing took on the short, sharp rasps of someone about to be consumed by a full-blown craving.

I hardly remembered walking back down to the village, only that at one point, I vaguely recalled telling myself *don't do it*. But impulse is like pure insanity. There is no rhyme or reason, no negotiating. I was being guided by a force so strong I couldn't have stopped it if I'd tried.

I walked past the hospital. There was no sign of anyone, so I continued to Louise's shop. She was behind the counter when I stepped in and I muttered a brief hello as she looked up from her register.

'Oh, hello, Marley. I was just about to close for the day.'

I didn't respond. I walked past her, directly to the shelf that displayed the alcohol and collected three bottles of vodka. Back at the register, I set them down with more force than I'd intended so that they clinked loudly on her countertop. 'I don't have my money with me. My purse is in Joel's car. Can I put these on an account?'

Louise glanced from the bottles to my face, which I'm sure looked wild and flushed from the hurried walk down here. 'Uh, sure. I'll set one up for you.' As she wrote up my account in her book, she kept glancing nervously at me. 'Are you okay, honey? I know it's been a rough day for us all.'

'I'm fine.'

'Lachlan was in here earlier with the others. They were shopping for dinner. They're going back to Ivy's.'

I nodded impatiently, trying to block out the mention of Lachlan's name.

'I'm heading there myself after I close up. You should come, too. We can walk over together.' She bagged up the bottles with a smile.

'I don't think I'm welcome,' I said.

She smiled sadly and handed me the bag. 'No one should be alone when they're grieving.'

'Well, lucky I hadn't known her that long.'

Louise's mouth dropped open as I said goodbye and left.

I knew I was being unkind, saying hurtful things I didn't mean, but I was angry. Angry at Noelle for dying, angry at Lachlan's circle for shunning me, angry at my grief because it left me vulnerable and afraid. I didn't know what to do with all that sadness, how to let it out, how to accept it. It felt like Karl Wagner had murdered his wife all over again— a different set of circumstances with the same set of emotions.

I hurried back up the hill, determined to get the vodka to the cabin before I changed my mind, as though I was intent now on sabotaging my sobriety, worried I'd talk myself *out* of drinking.

The sun had long dipped below the horizon, the sky bereft of colour but for a few frosty streaks of violet. Using the spare key from Noelle's house, I let myself into the cabin and went to the kitchen. I collected a tumbler from the cupboard, unscrewed the lid off one of the bottles, added ice and poured a decent glass. I sat down at the dining table, just the vodka and me, and I stared at it.

Ten minutes dragged by, slowly, interminably, while I debated all the reasons why drinking would be a bad idea.

Fifty-five days sober.

Lachlan.

Anna.

Noelle.

For God's sake, don't do it!

I grabbed the glass, brought it to my lips, hesitated... then sipped. The first hit burned my throat and I coughed. In the blink of an eye, all my days of sobriety went down the drain. I took another sip and another, reinstating my love and tolerance for it. First the burn, then the warmth, then the light-headedness.

Oh, how I've missed you.

They say addiction comes in many forms, from the desire to satisfy a sweet tooth to the silky bitterness of a caffeine hit, even a first love you can't live without. We were all drawn to something. My weakness was alcohol, and perhaps no matter how hard I tried in life, no matter how many days I stayed 'dry', I would always need it. Like air.

My one great love and my one true loathing.

Chapter 29

I wasn't sure what time it was when I decided to go for a walk. The idea struck me when I was halfway through the first bottle and feeling restless. I was appallingly drunk, alcohol coursing through clean veins and an empty stomach, my mind foggy.

I stepped out onto the verandah, the freezing air stinging my skin, reminding me that all I had on was a thin sweater and jeans. I had no other warm clothes for everything was still in Joel's car, along with my purse and phone.

I hadn't heard from Lachlan yet. If he had tried to call me, I wouldn't have received it anyway, although I felt it was more a case that he hadn't tried. Ivy was keeping him distracted. She'd never liked me.

I held firm to my bottle of vodka and walked down the hill, taking sloppy swigs, zigzagging all over the place, letting the moon's fuzzy light guide me. I arrived at Lachlan's house, letting myself in through the gate and banging on his office door, but he wasn't there.

There were patchy spots in my memory after that and sometime later, I reached the bay, although I couldn't quite remember how I'd got there. I sat drinking on the sand for a while, the moon large and ethereal in a black sky. I thought of Noelle, wondering where her soul was; deep, bottomless thoughts that made me cry.

Minutes passed, maybe hours, and all I could think about was how much I missed her. I'd missed the chance to tell her that I'd survived the mainland. That I hadn't had a drink. That I'd conquered my fear of leaving the island.

Life was full of missed opportunities, moments I should have seized but didn't, things that I could have done differently. I thought of my mother and all the words I should have told her before she died. That it wasn't just Anna that loved her, that I'd loved her too and I was heartbroken without her. That the void she'd left in my life could never be filled.

I laid down on the sand, closed my eyes, felt the world spin, then woke again. I wasn't sure how long I was out for, except that the moon had moved, and the tide had come in. The ocean was now lapping at my feet and I was shivering with cold.

I shrugged at my empty bottle as the sea claimed it, then started back towards the cabin. Along the way, I tripped on driftwood or perhaps something else, maybe the edge of the pier, then tasted blood. It was all over my hands and my head ached the rest of the journey home.

I reached the cabin again but my memory after that was a jumbled mess of puzzle pieces. I was sure at one point I'd vomited all through my hair, opened another bottle, and had a conversation with myself. Mostly it was a blur, but at least I was numb.

Chapter 30

I hid myself away for the next two days, nursing my final bottle. I took my time drinking, making it last, so I wouldn't have to go down to Louise's for more and risk running into anyone, most of all Lachlan.

He'd knocked on the door several times since I'd relapsed, asking if I was all right, but I'd lied and told him through the window that I'd come down with something and was contagious.

I knew he didn't believe me, and that, alongside his grief for Noelle, I'd become another thing for him to worry about, but I couldn't explain to him what was happening to me. It was frightening and uncontrollable. To make matters worse, I was sporting a black eye and a cut lip from my fall on the beach, and it would only raise more questions if I let him see me.

It was afternoon on a day I couldn't name, and I was watching television on the lounge. I was still in my pyjamas, lank hair pulled back into a messy bun, when I heard someone step onto the verandah then pound on the door loudly.

Lachlan.

When I didn't answer, he pounded again. 'Marley, open up. I need to talk to you.'

I groaned quietly, turning the sound on the television down. With any luck, he'd go away. But then I heard a key in the lock and was astonished to realise that somehow, he had the means to let himself in. I turned to see the door open and Lachlan standing in the foyer with Duke.

His eyes swept over me, taking in my unkempt appearance and the dirty plates and glasses on the coffee table. I'm sure he could smell the vomit and booze all mingled together.

'Jesus,' he said, his eyes roaming. Even Duke made a disgusted noise.

'Yeah,' I slurred. 'I needed time out.'

'*Time out*?' His mouth gaped open. 'Are you drunk?'

I shrugged. 'What if I am?'

He nodded slowly. 'I thought you didn't drink.'

'Well, I guess I do. And where did you get that key from anyway? Can't a girl have a little privacy on this island?'

'Noelle lost her spare a few years ago and had another one cut. Then she found it and ended up with two. My mom had the other one.'

'Of course she did.'

Lachlan's eyes narrowed. 'What the hell is wrong with you? Where have you been the last two days?'

I looked down at my hands. The hurt and disappointment in his eyes made my shame so deep I wanted the floor to swallow me. I was wretched. No, worse than that. I was pathetic.

'We're all hurting, Marley,' he said. 'We're all lost without Noelle. You're not the only one who loved her.'

'I never said I was,' I snapped. 'And it was just a few drinks. What's the big deal?'

'This is more than a few drinks. This is some kind of breakdown.'

I laughed out loud. 'Don't you mean rock bottom? I've been there a few times.'

'Huh?'

I rolled my eyes. 'Forget it. I wouldn't expect you to understand.'

He sighed tiredly and I could see that Noelle's death had taken its toll. 'You're right. I don't understand, but right now, I just need to get you to the village. We can talk about this later.'

'To the village? Why do I need to go there?' *For a town intervention*? *A public flogging*? I could already see Ivy lining up.

'Because your brother-in-law Tom has been trying to reach you. When he couldn't get through on your phone, he rang the council chambers.'

I sat upright. 'Tom? Why? What's wrong?'

'Nothing's wrong.' He gave me a soft smile. 'Marley, your sister went into labour yesterday. She had a baby boy. You have a new nephew.'

I crumpled then, the weight of everything I'd done caving in on me. Big sobs came from deep in my soul—for Noelle, for my new nephew, for my lost abstinence and all that I wanted to be as a person but couldn't seem to be.

Lachlan watched from the foyer. He didn't utter soothing words or take me into his arms. He just stood there, impassive, as though processing the scene, the state of me far too perplexing to grasp.

'Come on. I have your suitcase from Joel's car,' he said softly. 'You can get dressed, then call Tom.'

I climbed off the lounge and trudged into my bedroom. I showered and washed my hair, then dressed in warm clothes from my suitcase.

Lachlan watched me as I towel-dried my hair. 'I'm not even going to ask how you got that black eye.'

I nodded sadly because, in that moment, I had no words, just shame. I knew the time was near when I'd have to confess all.

We left the cabin and passed Noelle's house on the way to the road, both of us averting our gaze because the agony of knowing she wasn't there anymore was too much to bear. Even the roses seemed to be missing her, in full autumn bloom, waiting for her to cut them.

The day was cold and fresh as we walked and, although I was still intoxicated, it was sobering to be outside with the wind rushing through the cedars and the briny smell of the ocean drifting up the ridge.

At the Wildflower Café, Lachlan sat me down at a table outside and ordered me coffee and a sandwich. As soon as I received a signal on my phone, he stepped away and I called Tom. Duke plonked himself down on my feet, his body warm against my ankles.

Tom answered on the second ring. 'Marley.'

'Tom!' I cried. 'How's Anna?'

'Fine, everyone's fine,' he said, sounding tired but happy. 'We're all doing great. We've been trying to reach you.'

'I'm sorry. I'm so sorry,' I said. 'I was up at the cabin and I just... my phone...' How could I explain the last two days?

'It's all right,' he said gently. 'You're here now. Anna's next to me. Want to talk to her?'

'Please!'

I heard Tom speak to Anna, heard rustling as the phone was passed to her, then her voice was on the line.

'Hey,' she said.

'Hey,' I replied, wiping tears away because people were starting to stare. 'How are you?'

'A little tired, but otherwise great. I've been up feeding all night.'

'What's his name?'

'Cooper Anthony. He's a tiny thing, but he's feeding well.'

'And the birth?'

'It took us by surprise. I had him on the bathroom floor at home. The contractions came so quickly that Tom had to call an ambulance because there was no way we would have made it to the hospital in time. The paramedics helped Tom deliver his son. It was not what we'd expected and not at all like the girls' births, but it was probably the best labour I've ever had.'

I was a flood of emotions, barely able to speak as she told me how amazing the paramedics had been and how she'd held Cooper in her arms the minute he'd been born, and that she and Tom had been a puddle of happy tears as they'd all sat squeezed into the bathroom for the delivery. She painted such a beautiful, joyous picture that I wished, for the first time ever, that I had been there with her, to be part of the delivery, to watch my nephew come into the world and take his first breaths, to hold him.

'Where are you now?' I asked.

'Back home. Cooper and I went to the hospital for an assessment but we're both fine and we came home last night. He's perfect, Aunty Marley. He's in my arms now, just so perfect.' I could hear the quiver in her words as she fought to hold it together. 'Anyway, enough about us, how are you?'

I was silent for such a long time that she asked me again.

'Marley?'

'Oh Anna, I messed up,' I said.

'Messed up? What does that mean? What happened?' Her voice became urgent and the last thing I wanted to do was upset her.

'I'm fine, really, I just... the last few days...' My words were coming out unevenly and I could hear her talking to Tom, asking him to take Cooper.

'Marley, take a deep breath and tell me what happened.'

'I drank. After fifty-five days, I drank.'

'Oh Marley.' I could hear the sadness in my sister's voice. 'How? Why?'

I lowered my voice, as the waitress set down my coffee and sandwich. 'Noelle died.' Just saying the words made my heart break again.

'Your landlady?'

'My friend.'

Anna was quiet, and I knew she was trying to make sense of it. 'You grew close to her.'

'Yes.'

'She was like a mother figure.'

'Or a guardian angel.'

I heard Anna's sad sigh. 'I'm so sorry. How did she die?'

'Old age,' I said. 'She decided it was time, I guess. From the day I arrived, Noelle understood me. She kept me company, brought me food when I was sick, filled my days with cooking and gardening. You would have loved her.'

'She sounded wonderful.'

'The thing is,' I said, 'I'm not sure I know how to do any of this without her.'

Anna's tone grew firm. 'You do know,' she said. 'You know because at the end of the day, you have done all the hard work yourself. Friendships and support are great, but you and only you kicked alcohol for all those days. And you can do it again.'

'I'm not sure I can.'

'You *can*. I know you're sad and you're missing Noelle, but you must try. She wouldn't have wanted you to drink because of her.' Her voice was desperate now, trying to impart every word into me. She was right. Noelle would have been heartbroken if she'd thought she'd caused my relapse. The thought of it made me sick with guilt.

'You know, I wasn't keen on you staying there beyond the first two weeks because I thought you needed to do this in the real world, but I'm glad you did,' she said. 'I'm glad you have a safe, stable place to get back on your feet and try again. I'd hate to think what would happen if you were here with Austin and your friends.' Soft, sleepy voices sounded in the background. 'The girls have just woken up. They want to hold their brother.'

'Of course.'

'Do you mind if I call you back in a little while?'

'You don't have to call me back,' I said, smiling.

'Are you sure?' Anna asked. 'I won't be long. I'll get everyone settled here.'

'No, go and enjoy your family. I'll be fine.'

'Promise me you won't drink anymore,' she said. 'Promise me that whatever alcohol you have left in your cabin you will pour down the sink. *Promise me.*'

'I promise,' I said.

'Good. Because we're all counting on you. Cooper wants to meet his beautiful, healthy aunt soon. And I want to see you too. I miss you.'

The words made me dissolve into tears again.

Chapter 31

Day one.

I woke the next morning fatigued, the bitter taste of indignity in my mouth, the clock wound back on my sobriety. *Ground zero.* My momentum was lost and all that remained was the fear of starting over.

Day one had always terrified me and there had been a few of them in the past. It was a day of uncertainty, of jittery fingers wanting to hold a glass, along with the real possibility that I wouldn't make it to day two. But I desperately wanted to because, despite letting alcohol in time and time again, I knew I couldn't go on this way. And while I might be a functioning alcoholic and appear relatively normal from the outside, I've done some stupid things whilst under its spell.

As promised to Anna the day before, I poured the rest of the vodka down the sink. It had taken every ounce of will power not to pour it down my throat instead. Yes, day one was difficult, but I *really, really* didn't want to drink anymore.

I showered and dressed, then packed a picnic to take down to the beach. I was meeting Lachlan because he wanted to talk and I wanted to avoid what was coming, so I'd hoped food would dull the edges of an uncomfortable conversation.

I was the first to arrive, so I set up the blanket and spread out the food. I'd intentionally left my bangles at home, my wrists feeling weightless and exposed without them, all my secrets about to be laid bare. The sky was overcast and the tide was coming in, the ocean a grey mass of cold, choppy water.

A few minutes passed, then I turned towards the pier. Lachlan stepped down onto the sand wearing jeans, a jacket and a beanie, the bitter breeze whipping at his clothes. Duke bounded towards me, almost bowling me over with his big paws. I hugged him before he ran off again.

'Hey,' Lachlan said when he reached the blanket. 'What's all this?'

'Brunch,' I said, 'I hope you don't mind. I still owed you a vegan meal.'

He dropped to his knees beside me, looking at the food. 'You made me a vegan brunch?'

'Yes.'

He nodded soberly and I knew he saw straight through the façade. We lifted the lids off quiche and fruit salad, and I unwrapped granola bars. I pulled out a thermos of hot tea, pouring us each a cup, curls of steam instantly snatched by the wind.

'How are you feeling?' he asked, not meeting my eyes, fixing them instead on Duke who was tearing up the bay towards a pod of seals gathered on a rocky outcrop.

'Sad,' I said. 'Humiliated.'

He nodded.

'The thing is,' I put the thermos down and took a deep breath, 'I haven't been completely honest with you. I've misled you about what brought me here and that was wrong of me.' My voice was trembling, and I fought to keep it steady. 'I'm ashamed of what I'm about to tell you. I can't think of an easy way to do it, other than to just be truthful.'

'Then be truthful,' he said.

'I'm an alcoholic.'

They were three simple words and yet they'd always wielded enormous power over me. I'd never known how to say them before, had never truly believed them either, until I'd started my remote sessions with the counsellor.

My name is Marley and I'm an alcoholic.

Lachlan stared at me and I wanted to ask what he was thinking, but the silence was staggering. I knew if I was going to get everything off my chest now, I'd have to keep going.

'I've been an alcoholic for a long time; my entire adult life. But it became particularly bad a couple of years ago after a case I took that ended badly for the victim.'

He blinked several times, and I knew he was trying to process what I'd just said.

'You see, I'm not in family law. I'm a criminal lawyer. I defend criminals for a living. And before you say anything to that,' I said, when he began to interrupt, 'it really isn't as black and white as you think. Some people *do* need me in their corner. Some people are young and stupid, and they make mistakes. Others are wrongly accused and some act in self-defence. So it's not always just about helping the bad guys.'

He looked out towards the ocean.

'But sometimes yes, they are bad, and it's still my job to defend them in court and get them the best possible outcome.'

I saw his jaw tighten.

'Two years ago, a man beat his wife in a domestic incident. He was facing serious charges. I represented him in court, and I was able to get him acquitted. A few weeks later, he killed his wife, and himself, and condemned his children to a life in foster care.'

I hadn't realised my voice had dropped to a whisper or that tears were streaming down my face until the wind ceased for a second and we seemed paused in my moment of confession. Lachlan still wasn't looking at me, his gaze fixed on the ocean, and I knew what that meant. He was wondering how someone he loved could have lied to him like this.

'My life changed after that,' I continued. 'The media hounded me, and I received death threats. I'd walk down the street and be called vile names. But that wasn't what drove me to drink more. It was the guilt that ate at me, that if I'd allowed justice to take its course, maybe those children wouldn't have lost their mother. Because the cruellest thing of all is that I knew he was a monster.' My voice broke on those last words and I drew my knees up to my chest.

I told him then about the suicide attempt and he glanced down at my wrists, void of bangles, his eyes sweeping over the pale slash marks. I told him how I'd run a red light with my Porsche while drunk and almost killed a pregnant woman, and how Anna had intervened, forcing me to come to White Cedar, that I felt better than I had in years, but I was still a long way from being well again. Noelle's death and my relapse had proved that fifty-five days dry was infinitesimal when compared to the rest of my life. And that every minute of every day, I would be running from my addiction. I told him all of this as the ocean pounded the shoreline and churned up the sand, and the clouds grew heavier, blotting out what little daylight there was.

We sat that way for a while, in the raw, bitter wind. Lachlan was quiet and I had no words left. None that mattered. Eventually, he sighed and stood, dusting sand from his jeans.

'Where are you going?' I asked.

'I need some time... to process.'

'Isn't there anything you want to ask me?'

He shrugged. 'Not really. I think you've painted enough of a picture.'

'You can yell if you want.'

'All I want is to be left alone.'

I flinched, knowing he needed space, but also wanting him to react in some way. To ask questions, to shout at me, to tell me I'd disappointed him. Anything but that cold wall of silence. 'Okay.'

He whistled for Duke, then glanced down at me. 'Sorry I didn't eat. You went to a lot of trouble.'

'It's fine.' I forced a smile, but he didn't smile back.

'See you around.' He and Duke started back across the sand towards the road.

I sat and watched him leave from my spot on the blanket, my heart pleading for him to turn around, but he didn't. He walked up the hill and disappeared, and I stayed there alone on that deserted beach, wondering why I kept hurting the ones I loved.

***

The following week, I was sitting on the verandah watching the moon cast an eerie glow across the ocean when someone came walking up the hill towards the cabin. It was Lachlan.

'Hi,' he said when he was closer.

'Hey,' I said.

'Mind if I sit with you for a bit?'

I shuffled over so he could fit on the top step.

We sat in silence for a while, our shoulders touching. I didn't know what to say or how to make it all better, but it was Lachlan who spoke first.

'Sorry I haven't come to see you,' he said. 'I know it's been a week. I had to get my head in the right space.'

'You don't have to apologise,' I said. 'I would have come to you, but I wanted to give you time.'

'It was a lot to take in. And I don't deal with stuff like this too well.' He let out a slow, steadying breath. I could tell the days had not been kind. First Noelle's death, then everything I'd told him. He was tired, as was I.

'Are you okay?' I asked.

'Honestly, I'm not sure. Why didn't you tell me any of it sooner?'

I glanced at him, his eyes large and sad in the dark. 'Because I didn't know how to. It's not a glowing report card. Would you have looked at me differently if I'd told you the truth from the start?'

'I don't know.'

'You would have,' I said. There was no accusation in my tone, just the regrettable reality that we were different people.

'It's the lying that hurts,' he said. 'I could have dealt with the details, but you kept so many things from me that it makes me wonder if I can trust you. To find out that you had a problem with alcohol this whole time, that you'd been struggling while I kept offering you drinks. I mean, I even drank in front of you. Jesus Christ.' He ran a hand through his hair, looking mortified.

'I didn't tell you because I was ashamed. And because I didn't want you to think less of me.'

'But Marley, don't you get it? It's so much worse that you hid it.'

'But your dad and who he was...' I shook my head. 'How could I be the person I am and expect you to want me?'

Lachlan fell silent for a long time, staring out at the ocean. 'I've never felt this way about anyone before,' he said finally. 'And I've never been hurt like this either.'

My heart twisted in my chest. All I wanted to do was wrap my arms around him, to love the hurt away, to hold him close and never let him go. But I'd ruined my chance.

'How long were you sober for?' he asked.

'Fifty-five days.'

'Is that the longest you've gone?'

'Yes. I've reached day two before, but that's it. All it took was a tough day at work or a restless Saturday night and I'd start drinking again. I used to drink during work too. I was so afraid of representing someone like Karl again, that it was the only way I could cope.'

'Did losing Noelle trigger this recent relapse?'

'Yes. I was alone and overwhelmed. I didn't know how to compute my grief or have anyone to share it with. That's not an excuse; I'm not blaming anyone,' I added quickly. 'But for so long I've used alcohol as a crutch to blur away my emotions, to smooth over a bad day, and when Noelle died, I didn't know any other way to deal with it.'

Lachlan nodded slowly. 'I'm sorry I wasn't there for you. Everything happened quickly and I was on autopilot. I should have checked in on you.'

'Please don't be sorry,' I said, reaching for his hand. 'I'm not your responsibility. I should be able to control myself. And besides, you were grieving too. You knew her longer than I did.'

'It doesn't make your pain less worthy.' He glanced at me. 'And you *are* my responsibility.'

My breath caught on his words and I met his eyes, unsure of what he meant. I swallowed and quickly looked away, afraid to hope. 'I'm not sure I'll ever forgive myself for not being here when she needed us most.'

'We weren't to know,' Lachlan replied. 'Obviously, if she'd been sick and we knew the end was coming, that would be different. We wouldn't have gone to Alaska. But we didn't know.'

'So instead, she died alone in her bed,' I said, which had always been my worst fear too. Of living and dying alone because I'd never spent my life constructing meaningful relationships.

'Yes, but the thing is,' Lachlan said gently, 'everyone here dies that way.'

I gave him a horrified look.

'Think about it. No one succumbs to terrible disease like cancer or stroke. They're healthy and they live long, and they leave in the best way possible, peacefully in their sleep. Noelle was ready. And there was no pain or morphine or fear. I would have wanted this for her. Hell, I want it for me too.'

There was logic in what he said. Even if I'd been next door, fast asleep, I still couldn't have saved her, but my heart was broken all the same.

We fell into silence again, deep in thought, the night cold and quiet around us.

'You know, I'd always planned to tell you the truth,' I said after some time. 'About the alcohol and my job, about everything. But there was just so much of it to say and it was all bad, so I didn't know how.'

He glanced at me and I was surprised to see an apology in his expression. 'I didn't make it easy for you to tell me, having such strong views because of who my dad was. He has always cast a long shadow over our lives and in some ways, it's shaped how I perceive the world. Black and white, as you say.' He sighed. 'I don't want to be apathetic or uncaring. I want to be compassionate. You might not realise it, but I admire your ability to see past people's flaws and still want to help them.'

A small tear rolled down my cheek and I brushed it away. It had been a long time since I'd met anyone who saw the good in who I was.

'So what now?' he asked.

'I don't want to drink again. That much I know.' I looked back at the cabin, then across at Noelle's house. 'And I'll probably have to go home sooner than three months. I'm still paying rent here, but that may change once Noelle's will is read.'

'My mother is the executor.'

I wasn't surprised by the news and knew it wouldn't bode well for me. 'Whoever the property passes to, I don't think I'll be invited to stay.'

'You never know.'

'I think I do.' I gave him a sad smile. 'I suppose I do need to get back to work. And I want to see Anna and the children. When I'm here in this cocoon it's easy to forget that there's so much waiting for me at home.'

'I'd like it if you'd stay as long as possible.'

I glanced at him, stunned. 'Really? After everything I did?'

He shrugged, then turned his body towards mine. 'I want you to get better, Marley. And I believe you can do that here.'

I saw the hope in his expression, heard the sincerity in his words, but I was too afraid to trust it. 'Is that the only reason? My sobriety?'

A hint of a smile appeared. 'Maybe I'm not ready to give you up yet either.'

I closed my eyes, releasing a held breath, feeling warmth spread through me. It was more than I deserved. He was more than I deserved. When I opened my eyes again, his face was close to mine.

'The fact that you struggle with alcohol doesn't make me love you any less,' he said. 'It's when you keep things from me that I start to doubt us.'

'I know,' I said.

He reached for my wrists, tracing my scars with his thumb. 'And I never, ever want you to hurt yourself again. Promise me.'

I nodded, blinking back tears, my throat thick with them. 'I promise.'

He smiled softly. Everything I needed in that moment was in his smile. 'So, before we go further, is there anything else I should know?'

'Only that Noelle and your mum knew about my alcohol problem. Your mum lends me an empty room in her practice, and I join online support sessions three times a week. Kind of like a remote AA.'

He raised an eyebrow. 'So, I really was the last to know.'

'Not the last,' I said sheepishly. 'Just not the first.'

He chortled lightly. 'Okay. Anything else?'

I shook my head. Every dark, unfathomable secret had been laid bare. There was nothing left. 'No, you have it all.'

He smiled, then brought me closer still to brush his lips against mine. I folded into his arms as they circled around me, knowing I was entirely unworthy of his love and forgiveness, but unable to resist him all the same.

I knew in that moment that I would fight for sobriety for the rest of my life, that I'd be the best version of myself that I could be, not just for Lachlan and me, but for Anna and my nieces and nephew, for Mum and Dad, and for Noelle.

We stood up and I led him into the cabin where the fire was warm. In my bedroom, without words, we undressed each other, and Lachlan took me in his arms.

'I will be here every day to help you,' he said, brushing my hair from my face and kissing me until my head swam. We stood in the dark, trembling with need. I could see his body in the flickering firelight, strong and beautiful, and I'd never wanted anyone like I wanted him.

He laid me down on the bed and slowly traced his fingers across my skin, kissing my neck, then my breasts. I moaned with the need to have him, but Lachlan was in no hurry, taking agonising time. I ran my hands through his soft, unruly hair and across the stubble that had grown in the past few days. I inhaled him, our lips touching again. He whispered, 'I love you' and I whispered it back, even though the words were too small and inadequate for everything I felt.

I knew with every part of my soul that I would always love him. That Lachlan had ruined me in the most exquisite way. That a love like this came along once in a lifetime, twice if you were lucky. I'd never been in love before. Had never felt it sweep me up, fling me around and wreck me like a hurricane. And although I was on tumultuous ground, I was more stable than I'd ever been.

Chapter 32

Noelle's funeral was held at the small Catholic church high on a cliff overlooking Eternal Bay. Everyone who lived on the island attended, swathed in colour, as Noelle would have wanted. The pews inside filled quickly so that the throngs of people who couldn't get a seat poured out of the building, down the steps and into the church garden.

Noelle had touched many lives and it didn't seem to matter how long they had known her for, she'd impacted them in a profound way. Without her belief in me, I would never have believed in myself, would never have found the strength to face each new day. She'd saved me and I would forever owe her more than just my gratitude.

To maintain the peace, I offered to sit at the back while Lachlan sat at the front with his mother and Joel. I didn't want the day to be marred by Ivy's resentment of me, but Lachlan wouldn't hear of it. He held fast to my hand and led me straight to the front of the church where Ivy's disbelieving eyes bored into me.

'One of these seats is for Celeste,' she hissed.

Lachlan shot her a warning look, and she pursed her lips and fell silent.

After the ceremony, Noelle was cremated, and a plaque installed in the church cemetery beside Samuel and Danielle. Later, when her ashes were ready, we planned to scatter some from the headland, the wind carrying them on the breeze out to sea. The remainder would be laid in the ground beneath her rose bushes, with her daughter.

Ivy hosted the wake at her house, and everyone brought dishes and drinks and extra chairs. I went too, but after an hour of enduring Ivy and Celeste's loaded stares, I decided to leave.

'I'll come with you.' Lachlan reached for his jacket on the coat stand.

'No, you won't,' I said, pulling my scarf around my neck. 'Your mum needs you here. You should stay.'

'But what about you? You're not going to... you know?'

He looked so concerned that I couldn't help smiling. Lachlan had become part-lover, part-stalker lately, casually searching my cupboards for alcohol and watching me like a hawk when we shopped in Louise's store. If it had been anyone else, I'd have found it horribly stifling, but I loved that he was as invested in my sobriety as I was. 'No, I'm not going to "you know",' I said. 'I might take a walk then have an early night.'

'I'll be back at mine in a couple of hours. Want to stay the night?'

'I could go there after my walk, feed Duke and wait for you.'

'Even better,' he said, dropping his house keys into my hand.

That's how we spent the next few weeks. Bunkered down at his house in front of the fire or in bed as the weather deteriorated and the snow came. We spent days lazing around as I cooked and he worked, and we made love in the afternoons and again in the evenings. There were fewer outdoor coffees at the Wildflower or walks along the beach. The air that blew in from the ocean was bitterly cold like Arctic ice and the temperature plummeted.

I was conscious of Noelle's roses in her front garden and her fruit and vegetable patch out the back, for no one had tended to them in some time and the weather would soon spoil them. I raised it one morning in bed with Lachlan.

'I'm no good with roses but I can take care of the backyard,' he said, as he read work emails on his laptop.

'We'll have to get to the roses soon. It's where Noelle and Danielle are. I'd hate for them to ruin in the winter because no one looked after them.'

'I know,' Lachlan said distractedly, typing a reply. 'And we will. Next weekend, I promise.'

***

One freezing December morning, only weeks before Christmas when I was due to go home, Lachlan and I woke early. The reading of Noelle's Last Will and Testament was scheduled for nine at the council chambers and, despite me not having a reason to be there, Lachlan asked if I'd go with him.

'Just for some lawyerly advice,' he said.

I'd figured it was more for emotional support than anything, so I agreed, and we bundled up as warmly as we could and walked down together.

We reached the council chambers on time and found the meeting room. Ivy and Joel were already there, as well as an older man with round tortoiseshell spectacles and a briefcase. Joel gave me a warm hug while Ivy threw an exasperated look.

The lawyer gestured for us to sit. Celeste arrived with glasses and a jug of water, setting them down on the table. She was surprised to see me there, blinking several times in confusion, her expression souring as she left.

'I'm Felix Bouchard, Noelle's lawyer,' Felix said. 'I apologise that it has taken me this long to settle the will with you. I'm based in Halifax and the weather has been terrible. I couldn't get out here.' He pulled a folder out of his briefcase and set it down on the table, placing his palms on it. 'Right, I'm pleased to say that Noelle left her affairs in excellent order. In fact, she'd updated her will just a few weeks prior to passing, so that should make things nice and simple.'

He opened the folder and walked us through the legal process, terms that were familiar to me. Then he moved on to the specific details.

'Noelle has no debts or other balances outstanding, therefore there is no estate residue to settle. Aside from her property on the island, there were no additional assets like a car, boat or second property. There are also no surviving dependants that require guardian care.' He turned the pages over one by one as he read through the items.

'Now to the matter of her funds. Noelle had a sizable nest egg left to her by her late husband, Samuel, that she had barely touched in the past decade. Two hundred and eighty thousand, one hundred and fifty-six dollars to be exact, which has just been bubbling away, building up interest over the years.'

Lachlan let out a low whistle. 'Go, Noelle.'

'Ivy, Lachlan, she has asked that all funds in that bank account be transferred to the two of you. You will be given an equal share—fifty percent each.'

Ivy's eyes filled with tears. She nodded, plucking a tissue from her handbag, and dabbing at them, as Joel placed an arm around her.

'Now, on to her property, which consists of the house and the cabin.' He glanced down at his page, then looked up at me. 'Are you Marley Kincaid?'

I froze as all eyes turned to me. 'Yes.'

'The entire property shall be bequeathed to you.'

Ivy let out a half-sob, half-cry of disbelief. Lachlan and Joel looked dumbfounded.

I struggled to utter a reply. 'To me? Can I see that please?'

'Uh, sure,' Felix said.

I reached for the will and slid it towards me. Sure enough, Noelle had gifted me her island property in full. Not jointly with another recipient, but solely to me. I stared at the typed words as the air in the room began to rush through my ears.

'But how can this be?' Ivy asked through her confusion. 'She'd only known Marley six weeks when she died. Did you put her up to this?' She pointed her finger at me. 'Did you brainwash her into changing her will at the last minute?'

'Of course not!' I was offended that she'd even suggest such a thing.

'She's a lawyer,' Ivy shrieked, her expression furious as she turned to Felix. 'She would have known exactly how to coerce Noelle into this.'

'Mom, Marley didn't do this,' Lachlan said gently. 'It was Noelle's choice.'

'I understand this must be upsetting, but I can assure you,' Felix said, 'Noelle was in her right mind when she made this change. Her instructions were clear. She wanted the island property to go to Marley.'

'Well, I'm the executor of the will and there are others on the island far more deserving of that property than her. What are my rights?' Ivy folded her arms and lifted her chin, steeling for a fight.

'You can contest the will,' I said.

Felix nodded. 'That's right. You can challenge the will in court, but your argument would need to fit a certain criterion. Simply saying that Noelle's decision is unfair won't stand. You'll need to provide proper justification to the judge.'

'It's also expensive and time-consuming.' I turned to Ivy. 'I won't put you through that. I'm not sure why she left the property to me, but you can have it. Take it, it's yours.'

'But it won't be mine, that's the problem,' Ivy argued. 'It will always be yours because the will says so and there won't be anything stopping you taking it back whenever you like.'

'Then I'll reject it,' I said. 'I can do that easily. But it won't guarantee that the property will pass to you. We can't control that. The decision will depend on who Noelle left it to after me.'

'She's also right about that,' Felix said. 'In the event that Marley is unable or unwilling to accept the property, it will pass to Lachlan, as her will states.'

'Then that's where it should go,' Ivy cried.

'I want Marley to have it,' Lachlan said.

'Oh, for goodness' sake!' Ivy clutched at her forehead as though a headache were brewing.

We sat in terse silence as Felix cleared his throat uncomfortably and began to shuffle his papers into a neat pile. 'The reading of a will can often be an emotional event,' he said. 'How about you take some time to think about what we discussed today? I'm happy to schedule another meeting and talk through the next steps.'

Joel rubbed Ivy's arm. 'Let's do that, love. Let's not make any decisions right now.'

She sniffed into her tissue and nodded.

Felix concluded the reading with the last of Noelle's instructions—everything in the kitchen was to remain with Marley, her jewellery was to pass to Ivy, some items of insignificance were to transfer to other beneficiaries, and Samuel's old tools and mementos would pass to Lachlan. Then Felix handed out envelopes to me, Lachlan, and Ivy.

'Noelle has penned a letter to each of you. I don't think she thought her time was up yet, but she was a stickler for preparation. And this might help explain some of her decisions.'

We all stood and shook Felix's hand, and he gave me a reassuring smile as he left the chambers to catch the boat home with Harry.

On our walk back to the cabin, Lachlan and I held hands against the cold.

'You didn't know, did you?' I asked him.

'That Noelle was going to leave you her property? I had no idea. I asked you to come with me because it was going to be a tough day.'

'And you believe me, right, that I didn't influence her decision?'

'God, Marley, of course I do.' He stopped walking and took both my hands in his. 'She left you her place because she wanted you to have it, to have somewhere to go when you needed to. Somewhere that was yours.'

'But your mum's right. I don't deserve this gift. The property should have passed to you or her or someone else on this island.'

'It was enough that Noelle thought you were deserving.' He stopped walking and bent to touch his lips to mine. I kissed him back, grateful for his support and belief, but still unsure how I could accept such a gift when all it had the potential to do was cause more pain.

***

Later that night, we read our letters. Lachlan's was a thick wad of pages and when he let himself out onto the verandah by himself, I knew he wanted to be alone with Noelle's words. So I let him be and curled up in bed with mine. My letter was smaller, only a page, and I sank beneath the covers to read it.

> *Dear Marley,*
>
> *I watched you wash over this island like a tidal wave, angry, broken and confused, and yet, over the past weeks, you've settled like a stream, finding your way gently to the ocean again.*
>
> *If you are reading this, then I have moved on. Please do not be sad. It was time for me to go. I am tired, tired of living without my Samuel and Danielle, tired of all the years... and there have been plenty. I am ready to sleep now but you, ma chère, have your whole life ahead of you. This is why I am leaving you the house and cabin.*
>
> *I know this will cause heartache for others, but I did not want to leave it to someone who would simply enjoy it. I wanted to leave it to someone who needed it. In the way*

Danielle did.

Wherever you are right now, in Australia or on White Cedar, I want you to know that you will always have a place to go when the world becomes too much, if you have tried and stumbled and want to try again. White Cedar will be a sanctuary for you. I want you to cook in my kitchen and tend to my vegetables and love my roses because they are yours now. I know you will find comfort in them as I did.

Please look after Lachlan. He tries to be strong for everyone, but even he needs someone to look out for him.

Take care, my dear child. It fills my heart to have known you.

Pour Toujours,

Noelle.

I didn't realise Lachlan was beside me until he was holding me as we both cried. My heart was broken, the grief resurging as though I were learning again for the first time that she had died. I felt an emptiness inside that was so insurmountable I wanted to drink it away.

'Let's go for a walk,' Lachlan said, as if he knew.

'It's freezing outside,' I said, staring up at him through watery eyes.

'We'll rug up. Come on.'

We climbed into our parkas, scarves and beanies and took Duke with us. We wandered along the hilly roads, not venturing too far, but far enough to let the icy cold air clear our lungs and dry our tears.

'She asked me to look after you,' Lachlan said, holding my hand.

'She asked me the same.' I stopped walking and threw my arms around him, so desperate never to lose him that I felt the need to be as physically close as possible. We stood like that for a while, on the side of the hill, holding each other in the dark.

'What are you going to do about the house?' he asked.

'I don't know,' I said, burying my face in his shoulder. 'If I keep it, I'm going to hurt people, but if I don't, I'm dishonouring Noelle's wishes.'

Lachlan pulled away to look at me. 'She wanted you to have it.'

'But is it fair to keep it if I'm going home soon? It feels like a slap in the face to those who live here.'

There were so many decisions to make, and I was even more

confused after reading Noelle's letter. I missed her and would have given anything to have one more day with her, to ask her what I should do. She would say, 'Take it, *ma chère*! Live happily.' But I was entirely undeserving of that sliver of paradise on the hill, sanctuary or not, and I could understand Ivy's resentment. Still, it was the most generous gift, and had I not felt so distraught at upsetting others, I would have embraced it with grateful arms.

Chapter 33

We were both busy with the truffle farm in December, and although we'd intended to, we hadn't found that free weekend yet to tend to Noelle's gardens. The Périgords needed harvesting before the ground froze and this brought a flurry of urgent activity to the farm. Locals were there day and night, in the office and in the orchards, helping with the harvest, including Ivy and Celeste.

On one particular day, when I'd endured enough of their biting stares, I asked Lachlan if he would mind if I worked at Noelle's instead.

'Of course not,' he said, dropping a kiss onto the top of my head after I found him in the orchards. 'Is everything all right?'

I didn't want to bother him with trivial matters when he was inundated with the harvest and trying to beat the snow. 'Everything's fine. I just don't want her gardens to freeze.'

'Okay, you go. I'll catch up with you later.'

No one had tended to Noelle's property in weeks. There was a coating of dust over everything in her house and the gardens outside were overgrown and sprouting weeds. The grass needed mowing, despite falling dormant in the cold, and the roses were wild and tangled.

I spent an entire day in the back garden, harvesting the rest of the fall and winter vegetables before the temperature plummeted again. I weeded and layered mulch to protect the soil from freezing, then went down to the village to purchase new materials to construct plastic tunnels. I would cover as many plants as possible to help them withstand the snow. Noelle had shown me how to do this months ago and we'd had every intention of doing it this winter.

As the sun went down, I turned the compost bin, then took all the vegetables I'd harvested inside to clean, cook and pickle. My back was aching by the end of it but while the work had been tiring, I'd thoroughly enjoyed it. The only thing missing was Noelle, for what I'd loved most about working in her garden was the time I'd spent with her.

It was after midnight when I fell into bed. Lachlan was staying at his house, having worked late in the orchards, and even though he wasn't beside me, I fell asleep instantly. I woke early the next morning and donned my boots, jeans, and Lachlan's old Montreal Canadiens jersey.

After breakfast, I trudged back over to Noelle's house and stood before her rose garden. The entire perimeter of her front yard was bordered by roses, all in full bloom, pinks, yellows, reds, whites. They'd been there for over a week, and although rose bushes were best pruned in mid to late winter, I wanted to collect the flowers now, then cut back any damaged branches in case rough wind tore them away, wounding the healthy stems.

I found Noelle's gardening gloves and her bypass shears in the shed, then went through the house and located the basket she always used. I returned to the front garden and started at the first bush, cutting cleanly through the stems as Noelle had shown me, and placing the flowers in the basket. I removed the dead and damaged branches, then laid fresh compost and fertiliser over the soil, moving from one bush to the next. I didn't realise I'd missed lunch until the sun was setting at four and my back was aching again.

I took the basket of cut roses inside, found as many of Noelle's galvanised tin vases as I could, and plunged them all into water. As I was placing the vases around the house, I heard the front door open then close again.

'Lachlan, is that you?' I called out.

Ivy stepped into the kitchen, her eyes wide as she looked around the house, taking in the vases of roses.

'Oh, sorry,' I said, wiping my hands on a dishtowel. 'I thought you were Lachlan.'

She placed her handbag down on the kitchen bench, still staring.

'The roses would have died soon,' I felt the need to explain, 'so I cut them and put them in vases.'

She looked dumbstruck until finally she blinked. 'I was coming to do the same thing. I was worried they'd die.'

'I was worried about that too.'

She nodded, the astounded look giving way to sadness, and I knew she was thinking of Noelle. 'What about the back garden? I imagine the weeds have taken hold.'

'I was out there yesterday,' I said. 'I cleaned up the weeds and pulled everything off the trees and out of the ground. Then I mulched and covered as much as I could with plastic tunnelling.'

Ivy walked to the kitchen window and stared out, that surprised look on her face returning. 'You did all this?'

'Yes.'

'By yourself?'

I faltered, unsure if I'd offended her by being out there. Maybe Ivy had wanted to do the garden herself. 'I'm sorry. I wasn't sure if someone else was coming by or if I should just do it. I was worried about the ground freezing and ruining the produce.'

She glanced at me. 'And what did you do with the fruit and vegetables?'

'I cooked and froze meals, then I pickled the rest like Noelle showed me. I made a jam with the last of the figs. If you'd like to take some home, there's plenty.' I fidgeted with the dishtowel still in my hand. I couldn't interpret her mood, whether she was happy that I'd done her a favour or upset that I'd overstepped the mark.

She turned her gaze to the window again. Her voice was soft. 'I didn't realise Noelle had shown you how to do all that.'

'She taught me how to prune the roses and how to maintain the back garden, how to cook and preserve the produce.'

Ivy sniffed, and I wasn't sure if she was crying. She stayed for a long time by the window, staring out, lost in private thoughts. I let her be and returned to plucking vases from cupboards and sideboards and filling them with water.

After a few minutes, Ivy moved away from the window and joined me. 'She has a couple more vases in the top shelf of the pantry,' she said.

I found them and pulled them down, and side by side, we filled them with water and arranged the roses in them, setting them down around the house.

'I was a bit worried about coming today,' she said as we worked.

'Why?'

'Well, I don't know the first thing about roses,' she said with a shrug. 'I know a little bit about the backyard, but the roses have always been sacred because they're where Danielle is scattered. Noelle's never let anyone near them. I'm surprised she showed you how to care for them.'

'It was just a couple of tips,' I said, setting a vase of soft pinks down on the dining room table. 'How to cut the roses properly without damaging the stem, how to clear the dead and damaged branches so as not to promote disease.'

'You were close to her.'

I nodded.

'She saw Danielle in you, someone she could care for like a daughter or granddaughter.'

I was close to tears, so I busied myself filling more vases.

'She cared for me too when Lachlan and I arrived here,' Ivy said. 'I don't know how much Lachlan has told you, but my ex-husband was a brute of a man. I came here battered and swollen and terrified. We stayed in her cabin and she nursed me back to health, showed me how to appreciate life again. I'd lost my mother when I was young, so Noelle was like a mother to me. Taught me how to cook her plant-based meals, how to harvest in her back garden, how to be healthy and sociable. I'd been isolated in an abusive marriage for so long I'd forgotten what it felt like to be around people.'

'I'm sorry that happened to you,' I said.

She sighed, picking up a yellow rose and smelling it. 'It was a long time ago. That's the thing, Marley. I'm stronger now. I've healed. And while I was devastated to learn that Noelle had left this house to someone other than myself or Lachlan, I can see why she did it. She explained it to me in her letter, and I do understand.' She gave me a rare smile.

'It was never my intention to take anything off anyone,' I said. 'I'm more than happy for this house to pass to Lachlan.'

Ivy shook her head. 'Noelle wanted you to have it, and so you should. It wasn't my place to accuse you of brainwashing her and it's not my place to challenge her decision. I was hurt and emotional from losing her and I said things that were awful. I'm sorry.'

I smiled my acceptance of her apology, then my stomach grumbled. I clutched it, embarrassed. 'Sorry, I skipped breakfast and I guess I skipped lunch too.'

She laughed. 'I'm feeling a bit hungry myself. We've been working non-stop in the orchards.'

'I made vegetable stew yesterday. Would you like some?'

'I'll get it out. You finish the roses.'

Ten minutes later, we were seated at the kitchen bench, eating bowls of hot stew.

'This is good,' Ivy said. 'Noelle's recipe?'

'Yes,' I said. 'It's soul-warming.'

'Indeed.'

I wiped my mouth with a napkin and took a deep breath. 'I relapsed.'

Ivy set her fork down on the edge of the bowl. 'Please don't be angry with Lachlan, but he told me. He wasn't sure how to help you and he asked for advice.'

'That's okay. I'm not angry with him,' I said. 'I wanted to come and see you myself, but I wasn't sure if you would want me to.'

Ivy sighed regretfully. 'You should never have to feel uncomfortable about seeing your doctor, Marley. I'm the one who made you feel like that and I apologise. I've been terrible at blurring the lines lately, completely unprofessional.'

'I did put you in a difficult position,' I said. After we fell silent for a few minutes, I looked up from my bowl. 'I do love him, you know.'

She closed her eyes and nodded. 'And Lachlan loves you. He's had a few girlfriends in his time, but I've never seen him like this with anyone before.'

'I don't want to make things harder for you,' I said. 'But if I have this house and Lachlan to keep me here, then I might consider staying long-term.'

She stirred the stew around in her bowl, then set her fork down again, her expression contemplative. 'You know, when I was married to Lachlan's father, I was a completely different person—meek, anxious, fearful. I hadn't realised how isolated I'd become from the world; it was such a gradual thing. It wasn't anyone's fault but my own,' she said sadly. 'I'd allowed it to happen. Bit by bit, my friends stopped calling, my

224

family stopped checking in. And when they did, I pushed them away even more because what went on in my home was so shameful, I couldn't let anyone see. The only thing that kept me going was my son. He was my reason to live.'

'None of it was your fault,' I said. 'Your husband did that to you.'

'I guess what I'm trying to say is that for a long time Lachlan was all I had. I'm better now, of course. I have Joel and friends and a job here that I love, but Lachlan is still the most important thing to me, and I admit, sometimes I meddle. Sometimes I think I know what's best for him, even when I don't.'

She gave me a small smile and I realised this was her olive branch.

'Celeste would have been a nice match for him,' she said, 'but she's young and naïve. She would never have made him happy like you do. I can't stand in the way of that, not when he loves you the way he does.'

I smiled into my bowl, so full of gratitude for her words that my heart almost burst. 'Thank you.'

Ivy took a deep breath, then climbed off the stool and washed her bowl in the sink. She wiped it and placed it back in the cupboard, then collected her handbag. 'Well, it seems like you have everything under control here. I better get back to the orchards.'

I rose as well. 'Maybe sometime soon, you, me, Joel and Lachlan could come here for dinner. We could cook together.'

She tilted her head. 'I think Noelle would have liked that.'

'I think so too.'

She glanced around the kitchen with a renewed look of disbelief, her chest rising and falling with the saddest sigh. 'I just can't believe she's gone. I keep expecting her to walk into the room.'

'I know.'

'You've left a big hole in my heart, *Maman*, more than I can bear sometimes,' she said to the open space. Grief shattered her expression again and she wiped a tear that had slid free. She straightened her shoulders and smoothed her hair, composing herself. 'Well, thank you for the stew, Marley. You know, sometimes it's not about what we eat, but who we eat with.'

Her words threw me back to the first time I'd ever had breakfast with Noelle. 'She once said that to me.'

Ivy smiled. 'She used to say it to me all the time. And I still find truth in it every day.'

She patted my arm gently, then I watched her leave, hearing the door close softly behind her.

Chapter 34

I woke early the next morning, Lachlan and I having spent the night at the cabin. He'd worked late in the orchards, then had walked over at midnight and we'd stayed up until dawn talking about the future.

We'd both been exhausted, and I let him sleep now, in deep repose, naked and beautiful in my bed with the covers draped around his waist. I had phone calls to make in the village, so I dressed quietly and let Duke out with me.

The square was mostly deserted when we arrived, many of the patrons eating inside the Wildflower where the heat was on, the cold outdoor tables only for the brave hearted.

Lachlan knew what I was going to do today, the huge professional risk I was about to take, for we'd discussed it long into the night.

'Are you sure?' he'd asked. 'I want you here with me more than anything, but this is a big decision. I know because I've been there before. I quit my whole life to come here, and it was scary.'

'But you found your way back,' I'd said.

'Yes, but I hadn't studied for years like you did. There was less at risk for me. You've waited a long time to be reconsidered for partner. Aren't you worried you'll have to start all over again?'

'That's *exactly* what I'm worried about. I've come to realise my job and my drinking are one and the same. One doesn't exist without the other. My colleagues, who are my friends, are all heavy drinkers. If I go back to doing the same thing I've always done, I will relapse. I'll have to start over and over.'

Lachlan had reached for my hands, bringing them up to his face as we'd laid under a blanket by the fire. 'I want you to stay, but I don't want you to regret this slow life once the novelty wears off. I don't want you to get bored with me here.'

I'd leant over then and kissed him, trying to smooth away his fears. 'You are *not* a novelty, and neither is my sobriety. I don't think I've ever wanted anything or anyone more.'

The relief on his face had been paramount, and I could only hope that he would never doubt my love for him. I wasn't staying just to get better and because the island was convenient. I was staying because of Lachlan and because ten thousand miles between us was not an option anymore.

I entered the café and looked around for a table. The chatter seemed to deflate as I stood there, eyes cast my way, and I was reminded that everyone on the island was aware that Noelle had left me her property and that *everyone* had an opinion on it. Gossip was still rife that I'd coerced her and most felt that I was entirely undeserving of such a gift.

Celeste was at a table with her friends, all of them turning to stare at me before putting their heads together again to whisper. Even Freda did a double look as I stood there, making no move to help me find a table. I stepped back out into the cold, taking a seat beneath the umbrellas instead, cutting a solemn figure outside as fog coiled around the square. Duke dropped at my feet in that way that he did, his heavy bulk warming my ankles. Freda eventually came out and I ordered tea and a pastry, before working up the courage to call Paul and resign.

'Wow, Marley, I wasn't expecting that,' he said after I finished explaining that I wouldn't be returning. 'What does this all mean? Are you going to let your practising certificate expire?'

'I'm not sure yet. I have six months to think about that.'

'What about partner? We were going to consider you again in the new year. It's everything you've worked for.'

'I know,' I said, feeling a sudden wave of guilt. 'And I'm so grateful for all the opportunities you and Brian have given me, but I have to be honest. If I return to work right now, I won't stay sober.'

He let out a slow breath. 'When you put it like that...'

'I'm sorry, Paul. I know you've gone out on a limb for me, especially with Brian, and it feels like I'm throwing it back in your face.'

'Marley, your health will always be a priority,' he said, 'but I don't want you to toss your whole career away because of one short-term decision. You will be stronger one day, and you may want to return to law, and that might mean having to start as an entry-level associate again. You've worked too hard for that to happen.'

Of course, I'd thought of all that, but having him say it out loud gave me a jolt of uncertainty. In the past, I'd put everything on the line for my career—my sanity, my health. I'd sacrificed more than most. At the eleventh hour, when I was about to make partner, could I throw it all away? Was Lachlan right? Would the novelty of island life wear off someday and I'd become bored?

But then I remembered everything I had here—Lachlan, Noelle's house, a life that was healthy and sober and full of promise. And while I might always love the fast pace of a city, I also loved the nurturing peace of the island.

'So what's the plan?' Paul asked after I fell into silence. 'Are you taking a year off, two years, are you staying there indefinitely?'

'A year initially,' I said. 'I'm going to keep my apartment in Melbourne, but if all goes well, I'll be based here long-term.'

'How will you survive?'

'I have money put away, and I inherited a property here.'

'You *inherited* a property?' He chuckled. 'I'm not even going to ask.'

'It's a long story.'

'They usually are.' He sighed deeply. 'Why don't we do this—you type up your resignation, then hold onto it? I'll give you another three months to decide, without pay. After that time, you can either hand it to me or return to work.'

'But Paul—'

'You're one of our best solicitors, Marley. I don't want you to throw your whole career away for the sake of one year.'

'One year or ten. I haven't decided yet.'

'Let's see if I can't convince you to come back sooner.'

Even from across the oceans, I could picture that glimmer of mischief in his eyes—the master negotiator. I shook my head with a smile. 'All right, fine. I'll speak to you again in three months.'

We ended the call. I wasn't sure how I felt about leaving the door ajar to returning to work. I didn't want to confuse Lachlan with the notion that we were back on borrowed time, but Paul's words had allowed doubt to form at the edges of my decision to resign.

My tea and pastry arrived and as I ate and drank, I called Anna. I told her of my plans and although she was distracted with Cooper in her arms, she was supportive.

'Maybe once Cooper is a little older and the weather improves here, you could come and visit,' I said.

'We could come after Christmas, around March,' she replied. 'We're so happy you're serious about getting well. I never imagined in my wildest dreams that I'd send you there and you'd actually *stay*. I was certain we were going to get into an argument because you'd try to leave after two days.'

'I did try to leave after two days,' I confessed.

'Marley!' But she was laughing as she said it.

After we hung up, I left the Wildflower and dropped into the internet café at the council chambers to type up my resignation. I printed it and tucked it away in my jacket, then Duke and I walked back up to the cabin, where I hoped Lachlan was still in bed waiting for me.

***

Christmas arrived with a blizzard and the whole of White Cedar hunkered down. On Christmas morning, I woke at Lachlan's house, pushed back the covers, and ran to the window to gaze at the snow as it fell in swirls of white. The trees had all but disappeared under a cottony blanket and the frost on the windowpanes was cold enough to freeze fingertips.

I sat there, watching the world crystalise, my hands bunched up inside my pyjama top to keep them warm. Lachlan and I had exchanged gifts the night before after I'd called my father and Anna to wish them a merry Christmas. I'd given him a diving watch that I'd ordered weeks ago, fretting that the weather would hamper Harry's efforts to get it here. Lachlan had given me a white gold necklace with an amethyst teardrop set in diamonds.

'I got it in Fairbanks before we came home,' he'd said as I'd gasped. 'Alaska is rich in amethyst, particularly in the northern parts. I thought the purple went with your eyes.'

230

I'd hugged him so tightly that he'd coughed, and I'd had to let him go.

'When could you possibly have got this?' I'd asked, letting him fix it around my neck.

'When I had to go down and see reception.'

'You bought me this when you went down to see reception?' He'd left the room during our last afternoon in Fairbanks to book our transfer back to the airport and I'd dozed in that time, catching up on hours of missed sleep, unaware he'd gone jewellery shopping too.

As I stared out the window now, sunrise began to emerge under a washed-out sky and daylight expanded with every breath. The world was as white as if I were trapped in a snow globe.

'Merry Christmas,' Lachlan said sleepily from the bed.

I glanced back at him, smiling. 'Merry Christmas. It's snowing.'

'It is. Not the hot Christmas you're used to?'

'Not at all. But it's so beautiful.'

He pulled the covers aside. 'Climb back in.'

I went to him, slid back beneath the quilt and wrapped my hands around his waist, our legs entwining. I loved the way we fit together so well, like pieces of a jigsaw. I knew the perfect place to snuggle into his chest or the kind of ball I needed to curl into when I sat on his lap.

'Your feet are cold,' he said, kissing my nose. 'And your nose too.'

'Can we stay in bed all day?'

'For a little while longer. We'll have lunch with my mom and Joel later.'

'How much later?'

'*Much, much* later,' he said, drawing me closer.

He rolled on top of me, and I felt the weight of his body on mine, sure and protective, as though the outside couldn't reach us. His hands found the places that always made me weak, and I moaned softly, arching my back, which pleased him more. And when he pushed inside me in that agonisingly slow way that stole my breath, when I felt his entire body tremble against mine, I knew that no matter what, I'd be irrevocably tied to him forever.

'You make me so happy,' he said after we'd both recovered. 'Do you have any idea how I feel about you?'

His words made my heart squeeze and I pressed myself into his arms. 'I feel the same.'

'I want to spend every Christmas with you,' he said. 'Every minute of every single day for the rest of our lives. Your decision to stay means a lot to me.'

I was yet to tell Lachlan that I hadn't officially resigned because I didn't want him to doubt my commitment to him. Paul had asked for three months and I would grant him that, but it was merely a formality I was waiting to expire. 'Are you sure you won't get bored with me?' I asked.

'Marley from Melbourne, you are anything but boring.'

I swatted him and laughed.

'So, what's your plan for Noelle's house? Will you move into it soon?'

'I think I'll stay in the cabin for now and just maintain the house,' I said, tracing my fingertips along the muscles in his arm. 'It doesn't seem right moving in there, even though it's the bigger building of the two.'

'Because it still feels like Noelle's house?'

'Yes,' I said. 'It hasn't sunk in yet that she's gone. And it's still too raw for people. I don't want to upset anyone by moving in there when the cabin is perfectly fine for me.'

'You could always move in here.'

His expression was so serious my heart flipped. 'You would let me move into your fancy house?'

He shrugged lazily. 'It was Duke's idea. He's the boss around here.'

I laughed. 'I had this idea of setting up the cabin for Anna and Tom for when they come to visit. The girls could share a bedroom and I could buy bunk beds and toys for them. I could renovate it a bit, make some small changes, freshen it up, buy a cot and baby things for Cooper. It would make travelling with the kids easier knowing that they have everything they need waiting on the other side.'

'While they're using the cabin, you could stay here.'

'Duke did make a nice offer.'

We stayed in bed for a while longer, making plans until we could ignore the clock no more, then we climbed out from the covers and spent the next hour talking over coffee.

Life with Lachlan was a beautiful thing and I wanted more of it every day. I wanted to wake to him each morning and close my eyes to him each night. Our love was surreal in some ways, vastly different from the relationship I'd had with Austin, where I'd mistaken wild, intoxicated co-dependency for love. What Lachlan and I shared was wholesome and pure, and it wasn't unrealistic to consider a long life here with him.

My resignation letter came to mind, sitting on the kitchen bench at the cabin, signed and folded away in a sealed envelope. I was determined now, more than ever, that I would send it to Paul.

Chapter 35

The new year came and went, disappearing in a landscape of white. Most days, the North Atlantic was ferocious and turbulent, but Lachlan and I would walk down to the bay with Duke when the weather permitted, layered in our winter jackets and scarves, holding each other's gloved hands against the wind.

Lachlan was still occupied with work, processing and shipping out the Périgord harvest. Needing to keep busy too, I worked in Noelle's garden, doing what I could to ensure its survival in the cold months. Lachlan also showed me some of the company's bookwork and I spent several mornings in the office helping him with administration.

The days were slow with little to fill them, and I was looking forward to March when Anna and Tom arrived so that my days would be full again. I was eighty-nine days sober.

By the end of January, I could feel the subtlest shift in weather. Snowstorms became less frequent, and daylight seemed to linger just a little longer. The ground began to thaw, and streams trapped beneath shelves of ice began to flow again towards the ocean. Although the days were still bitingly cold, hungry animals began to wake, emerging from their hibernation to forage for food.

I was down at the bay one Wednesday afternoon, taking Duke for a walk, when I saw Celeste waiting on the pier. It was Harry's day to sail in but even so, it was unusual for her to be down there greeting him personally. She lifted her head and saw me walking towards her along the sand. Her lip curled churlishly, and I sighed. Sometimes the island felt too small for both of us, and I was happy to skirt around her, taking the long way back to the road and up to Lachlan's house to avoid speaking to her.

'If you've got time, I wouldn't mind your opinion on this,' Lachlan said as I walked into his office.

'Luckily, time is something I have plenty of.' I stood on my tiptoes to run my hands through his unruly hair. 'You need a haircut.'

He slipped his arms around my waist. 'I'm growing it out.'

'I could cut it for you.'

He stood back to look at me properly. 'You must be bored if you're offering to cut my hair.'

'Well yes, I am bored. I've run out of things to do. But I would do a good job.'

He laughed at my earnest expression. 'I'm not sure I'm brave enough to find out. How about you look over a contract for me instead?' He turned to his desk, collected a stack of papers bound together by a bulldog clip and dropped them into my hands. 'Our lawyer is on holiday and I thought you could glance over it in his absence.'

'Corporate law isn't my specialty, and Australian law is different from Canadian, but I'm happy to look.'

Lachlan made coffee while I curled up on an armchair with the contract. I spent the next thirty minutes reading and underlining sections that I felt were significant, feeling purposeful and productive, my brain getting a long-overdue workout. It had been months since I'd put it to use in this way.

Afterwards, we sat together at his desk and I took him through my notes.

'Thank you,' he said, giving me a grateful kiss. 'I like having a lawyer for a girlfriend.'

'You should let your company lawyer take a look anyway, just in case.'

'Sure.'

I lingered by his desk as he turned his attention to his laptop. 'Have you got any other contracts for me? I could go over them, make some notes, or I could do something else. Invoicing maybe?'

'Not at the moment.' He gave me an enquiring look. 'Is someone starting to miss work?'

I shrugged, trying not to let him show that I was, just a little.

He stretched, finished his coffee, then shut down his laptop. 'I might run down and get a haircut before the village closes.'

'Okay. I'll head home and get dinner started.'

'I'll meet you there. I won't be long.'

We left each other at the nearby junction, and he headed down the hill to the village as I continued up towards the cabin. The sun had set early behind dark clouds and I could hear the distant rumble of thunder rolling in from the north.

Closer to the cabin, I noticed a figure standing on my verandah. There was a suitcase by their side, and they were holding their phone up to the sky as though trying to get a signal. When I recognised who it was, who had travelled thousands of miles from my past to be here, everything within me ground to a halt.

Austin looked past his phone and saw me standing on the road. He dropped his hand and grinned broadly. 'Hey, baby.'

I was so shocked I could barely breathe.

'Happy to see me?'

I walked closer to the verandah, pausing at the bottom step to stare up at him. No, I wasn't dreaming. Austin was standing on my verandah. 'What are you doing here?'

'I missed you, so I came to see you.' He held his phone up again. 'Doesn't this shithole have reception?'

'Austin,' I said, firmly this time. '*What* are you doing here?'

He sighed loudly and dropped his hand again. 'Paul said you wanted to resign. I came to tell you that that was a stupid idea. That you've worked too hard to quit. That I want you to come home now with me. Enough of this.'

'You came all this way to tell me that?'

He shrugged. 'I'd tried calling and emailing but your phone was always off, and you never got back to me. So I just came.'

It was true. I hadn't been in the village for weeks, preferring to avoid the whispers of Celeste and the others. I hadn't turned my phone on all that time. Anna, Dad, and anyone else of significance knew how to get hold of me via Lachlan, so there was no other reason to check my messages every day.

Austin coughed and wiped his forehead with the sleeve of his sweater. Even though it was freezing, his skin wore the sheen of imminent withdrawal, his hands trembling and eyes anxious. 'Where can I get a drink around here?'

'There's no alcohol in this cabin.' I climbed the steps, pushed past him and unlocked the door. 'And you can't stay here.'

'Why?' he said, tugging his suitcase and following me inside.

'Because we said everything that we needed to say to each other months ago.'

'Where else am I supposed to go?'

'Back down to the village. Ask the ladies at the council chambers for a room to stay.'

'That Celeste girl? She told me to come up here. She's the one who encouraged me to fly over. Said I could stay with you.'

Celeste. That's why she'd been standing on the pier. She'd been waiting for Austin to arrive with Harry. She'd orchestrated this whole thing. It was why Austin was now standing in my entryway in his Ralph Lauren cable knit sweater, looking completely lost and perspiring profusely.

The sky rumbled above us and fat drops of rain plummeted to the ground. Austin coughed again and took a wheezy breath.

'Bloody hell,' I muttered. He was going into detox. I couldn't send him back out in this weather while he was withdrawing, with the village closing and nowhere to stay. 'Fine. Come in.'

'Thanks.' He rolled his suitcase into the loungeroom and glanced around. 'Wow, you traded in Melbourne for *this*?'

'Stop being obnoxious,' I bit back. 'I like it here, okay?'

He held up his hands in surrender. 'Okay, okay. Jesus.'

I sighed, glancing at him. He looked like a wreck. Jetlag and detox were a wicked combination, and I remembered my first night here all too well. 'When was your last drink?'

He glanced at his watch. 'I knocked back a few in Halifax. Maybe five hours ago.'

'You're going into detox.'

'No shit.' He wiped his forehead again. 'I'll need something soon.'

'There's no alcohol in this cabin,' I reiterated. 'Or prescription drugs or anything else. And all the shops except the restaurant are closed.'

237

'We can go down there and get a drink.'

'No, *we* can't.' And watching Austin now, with his sallow skin and quivering hands, I wasn't even tempted. 'I've been sober for eighty-nine days. But do what you want. Just don't go down there and be a menace. This isn't the city. I don't need you making a spectacle of yourself.'

He groaned with frustration. 'Just bloody come with me. I have no idea how to get anywhere around here.'

'I'm not going to buy alcohol with you. I already told you, I don't drink anymore. Besides, I have someone coming over.' I avoided his eyes as I said it.

He did a double take. 'You mean a guy? Are you seeing someone else?'

I really had forgotten how arrogant he was. 'You make it sound like I'm seeing both of you at the same time. You ended our relationship months ago. Do you remember when you told me we were done?'

'Yeah, but I didn't mean it. I was drunk and lashing out. You'd left me, then you wanted to change us, how we were. I was angry. You know we say things we don't mean when we're not thinking straight.' He took a step towards me, his arms open.

I stepped back, shaking my head at him. I could smell the alcohol on his breath even though it had been hours since his last drink, could smell it in his hair and on his skin, could see the need for it in his eyes. Austin was everything I'd disentangled myself from. As much as I would always care about him, would want him to live a long and healthy life, I couldn't go back to the way we were. I didn't love him enough to be pulled under again.

'No,' I said resolutely. 'We *are* done. I have a life here and I'm happy. I've met someone who means a lot to me. You made a mistake coming here, expecting us to pick up where we left off.'

'Is it the drinking?' he asked. 'If it's the drinking, I'll quit too. I'll detox now, tonight. And that thing with the brunette, that's all it was. A thing. She didn't mean anything to me. I was angry and I wanted to hurt you...'

I watched his eyes dart around, saw his tongue run over his dry lips, trying desperately to impart moisture. I knew his heart was racing and in a matter of hours, the fever would come.

'I feel awful about everything.' He took my hand and held it, his sad, desperate, bewildered eyes meeting mine. 'I just want you to come home. Come back to work. I want us to be a team again, you and me. I miss you.'

I pulled away, pointing to the bathroom and spare bedroom. 'You can take a shower. There are clean towels in the linen cupboard. I'll make you some soup and tea, then you need to get into bed. Tonight's going to be rough.'

He nodded and dragged his suitcase into the bedroom. I heard him unzip his bag, rustle inside for toiletries and clothes, then the shower squeaked on.

I walked into the kitchen and placed my hands down on the bench, taking several deep breaths. Of all the people to arrive on my doorstep, it had to be Austin. It wasn't hard to put two and two together. Austin had called the chambers when he couldn't reach me and had spoken to Celeste. He'd probably told her everything she'd been waiting to hear, that we had a past, that Austin wanted me back, or maybe that we were still together. And in an act of revenge, without consulting me first, she'd given him instructions that had led him straight to me.

I lifted myself off the bench and went to the fridge, pulling a pot of soup out that I'd made the day before. I warmed some in a bowl, cut a few slices of bread and boiled the kettle for chamomile tea. He was going to turn his nose up at all of it, but I didn't care. If he didn't like it, he could leave in the rain and find another place.

I was pulling cutlery from the drawer when I heard a knock on the door, and it took me a few seconds to realise it must be Lachlan. I groaned inwardly. I hadn't made a start on dinner yet and explaining that my ex-boyfriend was in my shower was not going to be easy.

I opened the front door. Lachlan was standing on the verandah, saturated from the rain.

'God, you're soaked through. Where's your umbrella?' I pulled him inside, but he tugged out of my grip.

'Is it true?'

'Is what true?'

'Is your boyfriend here?'

I stumbled over a reply. How could he possibly know about Austin already?

'Your boyfriend, Marley, and don't lie to me.'

I swallowed, taking a deep breath, trying to steady my voice. 'Okay, yes, Austin is here. But it's not what you think.'

'Oh, really? Because I just ran into Celeste down at the village. She told me everything; she's telling *everyone* everything. That this guy has arrived to take you home. That you didn't quit your job and you're going back to it soon.' He looked through the doorway past me.

I stepped out onto the verandah, pulling the door shut. 'Lachlan, please. Slow down. This is as much as a surprise to me as it is to you.'

'Where is he now?' Lachlan's jaw was set, his eyes narrowed. He was upset and I was worried what that meant.

'He's in the shower. It's a long story.'

'*He's in your shower*?' Lachlan shook his head.

'Okay, just calm down. I can explain everything.'

'Damn it, Marley,' he said. 'When will you stop with the lies? Why didn't you tell me you had someone waiting for you at home?'

'Because I don't,' I said, my voice rising. 'We ended it months ago.'

'When?'

I fought to remember exactly, my hesitation making me look guilty. I understood now what it felt like to be a witness on the stand, pelted by a defence lawyer during cross-examination. 'I don't know. Before you and I had our first kiss.'

'And who ended it?'

'He did.'

'*He* ended it? Not you?'

'Yes,' I admitted. 'But we weren't in a good place and it was only a matter of time before I did it anyway.'

Lachlan took a deep breath, running his hand through his hair. It was still unruly, and I realised that he hadn't had it cut yet. That he'd been down in the village all this time with Celeste gleefully filling him in. 'What about your job? Did you resign?'

I stared down at my feet and shook my head. I felt horrible. 'No. I was asked to think about it for three months.'

'You left the door ajar on the off-chance you might get bored here and decide you want to go back to work?'

I looked up. 'No. I did it out of courtesy because Paul asked me to take my time. It was a big decision.'

'I get that, but why didn't you tell me? Why am I finding out, once again, by accident?'

'Because I didn't want you to think I was having second thoughts.'

Lachlan scoffed, shaking his head.

I placed my hands on his sweater and pulled him towards me. 'Please, understand, I didn't tell you that I didn't resign yet because I didn't want to confuse you. But my resignation letter is typed and ready to be sent. I haven't changed my mind about that. And I didn't tell you about Austin because there's nothing between us anymore.'

'Clearly, he thinks there is if he's turned up here.'

Tears sprung to my eyes. I watched as his jaw grew tighter and he kept shaking his head at me. He was livid, and I was losing him.

'I thought there wasn't going to be any more secrets between us,' he said. 'But here we are again and you're keeping things from me. I asked you months ago if there was anything else I needed to know, and you said no.'

I swiped at the tears that ran down my face. 'Because I didn't know how to tell you any of it.'

'Or you didn't think you'd get caught. Like the drinking and the career choice, all of which we could have worked through if you'd just been honest with me from the start. But as usual, Lachlan is the last to know.'

I was crying now, devasted that I'd hurt him, that nothing I said now would make a difference.

'Is he staying the night?'

My shoulders slumped. 'Yes.'

'You're going to spend the night here with him?'

'Not in that way. He's an alcoholic,' I explained. 'He's already started detoxing.'

'Then leave him here and stay at my place.'

I knew he was testing me, and I should have said yes, that I would leave Austin to fend for himself while he withdrew, but I couldn't. I didn't have the heart to abandon him when he was about to face the most hellish night of his life. 'I can't,' I said. 'But as soon as he's strong enough, he's going straight back home. I promise.'

Lachlan let out a breath. 'Wow, Marley, okay. I know where your priorities lie.'

'He's got a rough night ahead. I can't just leave him here while he suffers.'

'He's not a baby. He did this to himself.'

'Don't be like that.'

'How do you expect me to be?' He yelled the words at me, and I knew in that moment that we'd turned a corner and we might never make it back.

I watched him step off the verandah into the rain, then storm off down the road, angry and hurt. I could hear Austin move into the doorway behind me, his teeth chattering, rugged up in a blanket.

'Is everything all right out here?'

'Fine,' I snapped.

Austin flinched. I wanted to rage at him, to tell him this was all his fault and to send him back where he came from, but I didn't have any words left. I was utterly defeated by it all.

'Sorry,' he said.

I looked at him properly, forlorn and wretched under that big blanket, and I remembered how it felt to be alone and suffering, to sit inside those walls and detox without anyone to support me. It was the loneliest feeling in the world. I let out an exhausted sigh, my anger deflating. 'Forget it. How do you feel?'

'Like I've been run over by a bus.' He reached for my hand and held it, running his fingers gently over my knuckles. 'I'm serious, Marley. I'm going to give this a good go. I'm going to be healthy and sober and do everything right by you. You'll see.'

I pulled my hand away. I didn't want to hear it. It was too confusing. 'I'll find you some paracetamol.'

Chapter 36

I hardly slept that night. Austin's insomnia and the despair I felt over Lachlan kept me awake. As I laid there in the dark, I thought several times about going to Lachlan's house, but Austin was close to climbing the walls, twitching and moaning as detox wore him down, so I stayed.

The next morning, having dozed off as dawn was breaking, I woke to silence. The rain had moved on and a bleary-eyed sun lit up the curtains. I pushed the covers aside, pulled on my robe and stepped out into the lounge room as someone was opening the front door.

It was Austin, carrying a tray of coffees and a paper bag full of pastries from the Wildflower.

'Good morning,' he said cheerily, setting everything down on the bench. 'I bought coffee and pastries. I tried to find bacon and sausages for a fry up, but nobody sells it.'

'It's a vegan island,' I said.

'Oh.' He scratched his head. 'Well, I got pastries instead. Sorry, I can't eat any more of that soup. I need normal food.'

'Freda's pastries are vegan too.'

'They are?' He groaned. 'For God's sake.'

I stared at him incredulously because I could smell the alcohol on his breath. 'Have you been drinking?'

There was an infinitesimal pause as he laid the pastries out on a plate. 'No.'

'Don't lie to me, Austin. I can smell it, and there's no way you'd feel that cheerful if you were still detoxing.'

He stopped setting out the pastries and sighed. 'I can't spend another night like that. I felt sick the whole time, with the worst stomach cramps. I couldn't sleep. Surely there's got to be a better way to do it. With medication. Or maybe I could taper down to avoid the withdrawals, try to wean myself off bit by bit.'

'You know that doesn't work. We've tried it before.'

He slumped against the kitchen bench, shoulders sagging, looking defeated. 'Going through withdrawals wasn't what I had in mind when I got off the plane here,' he said. 'I thought I'd arrive, and you'd want to have a few tequilas on the beach or sit in a bar with me, at least. I guess I didn't want to believe that you'd actually quit.'

It was hard not to feel pity for him. I wasn't the girl he once knew and I could understand how that would have turned his life upside down, like I'd pulled the rug out from under him. I almost felt guilty for my sobriety until I remembered how hard I'd worked for it. 'If you're not ready to quit, then there's no point trying.'

'I'm ready. I just wasn't ready *yesterday*. That was unexpected.' He gave me an embarrassed smile.

'So, you'll try again?'

'I want to,' he said. 'But I'm not sure if this is the right place for me to do it. Maybe I'd do better if I were back home in Melbourne. In my own house and my own bed.'

'You need to break the routine. A change of scenery made all the difference for me.'

He stepped forward and placed both his hands on my shoulders. 'Then that's probably what I need. Either way, I'm going to give it another try. And when we're back in Melbourne, we can go to AA meetings together and spend quiet nights in. We can wake early and do whatever it is normal people do.' He laughed nervously. 'The idea of it freaks me out, if I'm honest, but I'm willing to follow your lead.'

We shared a pastry in silence as his words of expectation hung heavy on my shoulders, as though his entire chance at sobriety depended on my cooperation. I didn't know what to do with that, what it all meant. It gave me hope that he was considering it, but did I want to be part of his recovery in such a significant way? I had a life here with Lachlan. I'd moved on.

Too many things were happening at once and Austin's presence in the cabin grew suffocating. While he was distracted with the channels on the television, I dressed and quietly left, stepping out into a cold morning glistening after a night of rain.

I walked down to Lachlan's house and let myself in through the gate. When I reached his office, I saw him at his desk, propped up on his elbows, staring off into the distance. He saw me in his peripheral vision and quickly dropped his gaze, pretending to busy himself, shuffling papers and disengaging his screensaver.

'Hi,' I said, letting myself in.

'Hey,' he replied, avoiding my eyes.

'How are you?'

'Fine. You?'

I sat down opposite his desk. 'I hardly slept.'

He chewed his lip, then nodded. 'Yeah, me either. How's your friend?'

'Let's just say day one didn't eventuate.'

'Relapsed already, huh?'

'He wasn't ready.'

'Well, maybe you shouldn't be around him.' Lachlan's expression darkened and it was clear he was still upset. 'If he's staying there and drinking, that's going to put all kinds of temptations in front of you.'

'I know, but I want to see him get well. I want him to give it another try.'

'That's not your decision to make.'

'No, but he is considering it. And that's something.'

'What do you mean? He's going to do it here?'

'It's a possibility.'

Lachlan's eyebrows lifted. 'Last night you said he was going straight back home once he felt better. Now that he's drinking again, he must feel better. So why can't he go home?'

'He would have to wait until Harry comes back anyway.'

'Charter him a flight.' Lachlan's voice rose.

I flinched at his tone, so exhausted I could barely think straight.

Lachlan sighed and ran a hand through his dishevelled hair. 'Marley, I'm confused. Your boyfriend or whatever he is turns up, completely blindsiding me, you say there's nothing between you anymore and yet now you're trying to talk him into staying.'

'I'm not trying to talk him into staying. I just want him to get better.'

'If he were just an ex, why wouldn't you send him on his way so he can recover back in Melbourne?'

'Because he needs support. I needed it too and I know how scary it can feel to attempt it alone.'

'Or are you still in love with him?'

I shook my head, but the words I desperately needed to reassure him with wouldn't come. Why did I hesitate? Why didn't I tell Lachlan what he wanted to hear? I didn't love Austin, not in the way I loved Lachlan. But I still cared about him. How could I explain the complex and tangled history of co-dependency we'd shared, the highs and lows we'd ridden? Turning Austin away now, as much I knew was the right thing to do, was also like tearing my heart out.

But Lachlan was still staring at me, and I knew I owed him an explanation. 'I care for him, that's all. We've been through a lot together.'

It was the wrong words, for Lachlan's jaw hardened and his eyes narrowed. 'I get it.'

'You wanted me to be honest with you and I'm trying.'

He made a disbelieving noise. 'Okay.'

'What do you want me to say?'

'I want you to say that you want *us*. Completely. With no other guy in the picture. Is that too much for me to want?'

God, what was I doing? I was so confused and the two of us so completely broken, that I wasn't sure how we'd got to this point or how we would ever make it back. 'I'm sorry,' I said. 'It's you I love, but he needs me right now.'

Lachlan nodded, then swallowed. His eyes were full of emotion. 'Then I guess you need to decide who is more important. Because sobriety is a lifelong commitment and he's going to need you for a long time. So how does that work? What does that mean for us?'

'I don't know.' I stared at him, at the quiet lines around his eyes that deepened when he smiled, at the day-old stubble that clouded his jaw, at the lips that had known my body so intimately.

'I'll make it easy for you because clearly you're struggling,' he said. 'Maybe we should take some time out.'

'You want to have a break?' I asked in disbelief.

'Yes.'

'For how long?'

'As long as it takes. We both need time to think.'

'I've put my whole life on hold to stay here.' My voice quivered and tears gathered on the brim of my eyelashes. 'I'm about to resign from my job and sell my apartment. If you don't want this relationship, you need to tell me now.'

'You're the one calling the shots, Marley.'

I felt the air rush out of me and the room tilt. I couldn't believe what I was hearing, that this could well be the end of us.

I turned before the tears spilled, before deep sobs from way down in my soul overwhelmed me, and I left the office. I ran back through the canopy of redbuds and out onto the road where I stopped. I didn't want to return to the cabin to listen to Austin's drunken, jaded optimism, so I turned and walked down to the bay to sit on the sand.

Maybe I'd been a fool to stay the night with Austin, choosing his convalescence over Lachlan. Maybe Lachlan had been wrong in asking me to choose. Maybe Austin shouldn't have come in the first place.

I stared out at the beautiful, wild North Atlantic, missing Noelle and Anna, and my mother and father. Missing my nieces and Cooper and Melbourne. Missing a life that might have been precarious and unhealthy but at least it was predictable, for I'd had a job, a purpose, a place to go every day.

Then there was Lachlan. Sweet, kind, generous Lachlan, and my heart broke all over again at the thought of him not being in my life.

I stayed out on the beach for hours, long after the sun began its descent towards the horizon, then I dragged myself back to the cabin. Austin was inside wearing an apron, his hands covered in flour. He'd found an old vegan cookbook Noelle had leant me months ago and was trying his hand at vegetable pie.

'I think I've done the pastry right,' he said when I walked in.

I could smell alcohol on his breath, realising he'd been drinking while I was gone, but I didn't have the energy to fight with him. 'I can't believe you're cooking a vegan meal.'

'Taste it first before you congratulate me.'

I gave a weak smile.

'Rough day, hey?' he said.

'Something like that.'

He nodded, then handed me a freshly squeezed orange juice. 'I just finished my last drink. I'm not having any more tonight. I'm going to try detoxing again, and I'm going to try my hardest this time.'

'Okay.' Tears welled in my eyes, and I put the juice down and leant against the bench, great heaving sobs pushing their way from my chest.

Austin wiped his hands on a tea towel and placed his arms around me, pulling me close. He didn't say anything. He just held me while I cried for Lachlan, for a decision I was inevitably going to have to make. I was trapped between two worlds, one I desperately wanted to be part of and another that I belonged to, each pulling me in a different direction. And I had no idea how to move forward.

Chapter 37

I didn't see Lachlan for the rest of the week. As much as I'd wanted to, to make sure I hadn't dreamt a nightmare where I'd hurt him and he'd ended things, I kept my distance and gave him space. Instead, I stayed close to the cabin while Austin detoxed, enduring sleepless nights as he retched and moaned and swore the hours away.

Austin had always been a heavier drinker than me, a heavier everything—illegal drugs, prescription pills, alcohol, and I knew he was barely hanging on, that if I weren't in the cabin with him to talk him out of drinking, he would have relapsed by now.

I prepared nutritious meals he didn't eat, just as Noelle had done for me. We did crosswords and puzzles, and I watched over him, reminding him every day that he would feel better if he just stayed the course. That sobriety was within his grasp, he just had to hang on a little longer.

On day seven, he turned a corner. I woke to find him sitting on the verandah as I had done all those months ago, stomach growling, breathing in the fresh forest air under a cornflower-blue sky.

'How are you feeling?' I asked, sitting in the seat beside him.

'Better,' he said with a smile. 'Clearer in the head. The acidic taste in my mouth is gone and I'm hungry. Damn hungry.'

I laughed. 'I'll make you breakfast.'

As I stood, he reached for my hand, looking up at me and squinting into the sunlight. 'Thank you, Marley,' he said. 'I know what you gave up to stay with me this week. I want you to know that I won't let you down.

This is it for me. I haven't been this sober in years, and I won't ever forget the sacrifice you made to help me.'

I gave him an uncertain smile. I hoped it wasn't mere platitudes he was delivering, something to make me feel better, for I had given up my whole world to see him through the dark days. I wanted no thanks, other than for him to be sober forever.

I made him pancakes for breakfast, then I went for a walk by myself to the bay. I passed Lachlan's house, hoping I'd run into him, but his gate was locked, and he was nowhere along the stretch of road that led down to the water. When I arrived at the bay, I saw Anton, Emile and Gilbert hauling their morning catch onto the pier and I waved to them. Only Anton waved back, half-heartedly I thought, and when I strolled down to the boat, he was the only one to give me a forced smile.

'Good catch this morning?' I asked as Emile and Gilbert ignored me.

'Not bad,' Anton murmured.

We fell into silence as I watched them work.

'Have you seen Lachlan today?' I asked after a while. 'I thought he might be down here.'

'Lachlan?' Anton stopped unloading boxes of fishing tackle onto the pier and straightened. 'He left.'

'Left? To go where?'

'Montreal. He packed up a couple of days ago. He's planning to spend two months there.'

I felt my whole world tumble down around me. '*Two months*?'

'He said something about work commitments, but we all know why he left.' He stared down his nose at me disapprovingly. 'You've got that boyfriend of yours living in Noelle's cabin.'

I let out a frustrated sigh. 'He's not my boyfriend. Did Lachlan tell you that?'

'Not Lachlan. He didn't say anything. Celeste is the one telling everyone.'

I glanced at Emile and Gilbert. They wouldn't even look my way, carrying on instead with unloading their fishing rods. 'Is that what everyone thinks? That I lied to Lachlan about a boyfriend and now I'm living with him in Noelle's cabin?'

Anton resumed his unloading. 'Pretty much. Small town, big whispers. Hiding with him up there hasn't helped.'

I could only imagine the hotbed of gossip that was happening right now in the village, what people were saying about me. That I was staying in the cabin with Austin, and it had driven Lachlan away. That I'd defiled Noelle's gift with my treacherous ways. My entire world suddenly felt extremely small.

I muttered a thanks and turned to leave, heading back along the road towards Noelle's. Tears blurred my vision, my heart shattering into a million pieces. Lachlan had left. He hadn't said goodbye, he'd just left, his quiet farewell far louder than any words he could have spoken.

I thought about all the opportunities I'd had to tell him I loved him, to make him understand he was the one I'd chosen and not Austin. That my empathy and good intentions were not a substitute for our relationship. That I'd simply been helping a friend through what would be the darkest, most trying days of his life. But empathy won you no favours. It only forced heart-wrenching sacrifices.

I reached the cabin, but instead of going inside, I walked up to Noelle's front door and let myself in with my key. I sat on a stool at her bench and laid my head down on the cool stone. I could almost feel her beside me, hear the rustle of her skirt and smell the lavender of her powder.

The question isn't can *you go home? The question is are you* ready *to go home?*

She had uttered those words in this very kitchen, all those months ago, when she'd been alive. Back then, I hadn't been ready to go home. It had been during the early days of my recovery and the thought had terrified me. Now, I wasn't so sure home was a terrifying place.

My tears fell, dropping onto the bench, the loneliness silent and biding. And I knew that the tide was turning. That without Lachlan on the island, and with the entire village against me, my time here had come to an end.

***

On my one-hundredth day of sobriety, Austin and I waited on the pier for Harry to arrive.

The day was mild, a soft breeze lifting the flaps of my jacket and tossing the ends of my hair around. Seals had returned to gather on the rocky outcrop on the far side of the bay. It reminded me of Duke and how he loved to bound across the sand to where they lay, barking at them and being barked at in return.

I hadn't seen him in weeks, hadn't had a chance to say goodbye; something I would have liked to do. But he was staying with Ivy while Lachlan was in Montreal, and I wasn't certain I was welcome there. There was no avoiding seeing her though when I called into the surgery the morning of my departure to drop off Noelle's keys.

'The house and cabin are both clean and all the gardens are in order,' I told her. 'The ground has mostly thawed, so it should be ready for spring planting.'

'Thank you, Marley,' she said crisply.

'Once I'm back home, I'll make arrangements to have the property transferred into your name.'

'I'm more than willing to pay you what it's worth.'

I shook my head. 'Please, I don't want money for it. It shouldn't have been gifted to me in the first place. I'll set things right when I get home.'

She nodded and took the keys, setting them down on her desk.

'How's Lachlan?' I asked, unsure if I should ask or if she'd tell me.

'He's busy with work. There will be a lot of new business coming in now that winter is almost over. It makes sense for him to be located with his team.'

'I've tried calling him. I left him a few messages too. He won't answer.'

'Maybe he's not ready to.' Her lips were pursed, her back rigid, and I knew she'd grown wary of me again, that all the trust we'd built over the last two months had inadvertently collapsed.

'I'm sorry for everything that's happened,' I said. 'I didn't mean for Lachlan to leave.'

Ivy shrugged sadly. 'He's hurt. Perhaps he should have stayed and tried to sort it out with you, but Lachlan feels things deeply. He always has and he always will. He runs from trouble because his father taught him to be afraid.'

'I never wanted to be the one to hurt him,' I said. 'I care about Austin but he's not the love of my life. He's someone who needed my help, just as I needed help all those months ago. If people had turned their backs on me, I'd still be drinking.'

She gave me a rare sympathetic smile. 'Helping a sick friend is admirable, but I don't need to tell you how unhealthy co-dependency is.'

I dropped my gaze. 'I know.'

'You were put in a difficult position,' she said. 'And, despite the gossip, we are aware that what Celeste did was underhanded, enticing that Austin boy all the way here. It's not her job to give out personal information for her own gain or to meddle in other people's affairs. I've already had a word with the mayor.'

'I agree but I don't want her to lose her job.'

'You don't have to be noble with me. It's the least she deserves.' Ivy frowned. 'Little does it matter, though. We can't change what has been done and goodness knows you're all the island is talking about. Perhaps it *is* best if you leave. Small town rumours can be brutal.'

I'd hoped in some way that she'd try to talk me into staying, that she'd tell me it wasn't all that bad and maybe offer to speak to Lachlan on my behalf, but instead, she called the visit to a close and gave me an awkward hug.

'I wish you all the best with your recovery, Marley,' she said. 'Do send me word on how you are going.'

I promised I would and left her surgery, skirting the village and heading straight to the pier. I didn't say goodbye to Louise or Freda or any of the ladies in the other stores. Even Fabienne had given me a stiff smile on my way out.

Down at the pier, at a few minutes to three, we heard the rumble of Harry's boat as it glided into the bay.

'I was just starting to enjoy this place,' Austin said, looking back towards the forests behind us, as the wind stirred the trees.

I glanced back too but my eyes blurred with tears and I had to turn away. I couldn't look at the rugged forests or the beauty of the hillsides or the clouds that graced the tips of the maples and white cedars. Saying goodbye was as painful as I knew it would be because it was so much more than just a place I'd enjoyed. My heart was here, my sobriety and my forever. *Lachlan.* I kept my eyes forward, focusing on the deep blue and the sight of Harry's boat as it came closer, steeling myself for the gut-wrenching moment when I'd step aboard and leave.

He moored to one of the pilings just as Anton arrived to help unload the cargo.

'You're not going to run away on me again, are you?' Harry said to me. His voice was gruff, but I saw the smile beneath his beard.

I shook my head sheepishly. 'No, this is it. I'm definitely leaving today.'

He handed boxes to Anton. 'All right then. I don't have much to unload. We'll be on our way soon.'

Ten minutes later, the boat was cleared, and Harry helped Austin drag our suitcases on board. When Anton tipped his cap to me, I stepped forward and threw my arms around him. I'd caught him by surprise, but he hugged me back.

'Take care of yourself,' he said.

'You too,' I said, pulling away. 'Say goodbye to Louise for me. Tell her I'm sorry I didn't stop by.'

He gave me a sad smile. 'She always liked you.'

Austin's hand was on my back. 'Ready?'

I nodded and gave Anton one last wave goodbye. We climbed aboard Harry's boat and settled inside the cabin. I remembered the first day I'd come to the island, sitting in this same seat, loaded with alcohol, then panicking as it drained from my system and we sailed into the unknown.

All these months later, I was a different person. In many ways, I was whole again and better for knowing the people who lived here. For loving them and living their peaceful ways. For spending time with Noelle during the last precious months of her life.

And as we pulled away from White Cedar Island, I thought of Lachlan, who I would never forget, for all the days and nights I had left on this earth.

***

We spent one night in Halifax before our flight departed for home the next morning. I'd booked Austin and me separate rooms at a small bed and breakfast. He sulked about it, then he sulked again when I suggested we eat in the dining room rather than going out. He wanted to visit a restaurant and a string of bars he'd seen the previous week when he'd flown in, insisting he wouldn't drink, that he just wanted to be around people. But I knew what temptation could do to a recovering alcoholic and I didn't want to tempt fate. The physical detox may have been over for Austin, but he still had a long battle with psychological triggers challenging him at every turn.

I managed to keep us both indoors that night, and the next morning, we woke early and caught the first of many planes home. We'd been in the air an hour when I unclipped my seatbelt and went to queue for the bathroom. When I returned to my seat, the flight attendant was setting down two gin and tonics onto our tray tables.

'Who ordered those?' I asked a little too sharply.

The flight attendant straightened and gave me a prickly look. 'Excuse me?'

'I did,' Austin said. 'One for you, one for me.'

'Well, you can take them back, thank you,' I said to the attendant.

She shot a hesitant glance between us. Austin let out a frustrated breath. 'God, Marley. It's just one drink. What's the big deal?'

'The big deal is we are recovering alcoholics,' I said, loud enough for the entire section of business class to hear. But I didn't care. I would call Austin out if it meant he would give those drinks back.

He pulled me down into my seat. 'Will you be quiet?' he hissed. 'What the hell is wrong with you?'

'You can take both drinks back,' I said to the attendant again. 'We'll have a Coke or juice.'

'Do what you want but I'm keeping mine.' Austin snatched his glass off the tray table as though he feared I would dive over the armrest and seize it.

The attendant lifted mine from my tray table and, with another dubious glance at us both, she disappeared back down the aisle.

'If you drink that, you will have to start all over again,' I said. 'All that hard work down the drain. And you might feel good for a few hours, then you'll just feel ashamed.'

He shook his head and rolled his eyes. 'Whatever. It's one drink and everyone on this plane is drinking. We have thirty hours of flying to go. When did you become such a killjoy?'

He brought the glass to his lips and took a sip, closing his eyes in what I knew was a moment of pure pleasure. I looked away. I didn't even want to be next to him.

It was in that single defining moment that I realised I couldn't fix Austin. I couldn't 'make' him sober. He had to do this on his terms, for himself. He had to dig deep and stare down rock bottom and maybe he'd have to hit it a few times before the desire to give up was strong enough.

Either way, it was his journey to take, and I could no longer be a part of it. I'd tried to help him, had sacrificed Lachlan and my stay on White Cedar for him, but Austin was still a long way from wanting sobriety. Perhaps that was selfish of me, to desert him in his time of need, but I had to distance myself if I was going to break the chain of co-dependency. We weren't a team. We were each other's downfall.

And if I remained in his life, he would lead me to relapse again and again.

Chapter 38

Nothing in my Melbourne apartment had changed and yet, at the same time, everything had. There was dust and a stale smell, and a pile of mail that Anna had slipped under the door, but my Dior heels were still by the door where I'd last kicked them off, and a Prada handbag and coat were strewn across the lounge where I'd flung them after my final night out with Austin in the city.

The view from my balcony looked the same, waves gently breaking over South Melbourne Beach. But as beautiful as it was, it was hard to ignore the way it seemed tainted now. The sand was alight with garish neon signs from storefronts and the sound of the waves were suffocated by car horns bleating their staccato warnings. The smell of sesame oil from the noodle shop downstairs, mixed with the greasy meat of the kebab stall on the corner, turned my stomach so that I had to close the windows. All that noise and energy was an attack on my senses, and I longed for the clean smells and soothing sounds of the island.

I'd left Austin at the airport. Even though we would have passed through his suburb on the way to mine, I couldn't share a cab with him. I didn't want to spend a minute longer in his company while he babbled a confused mix of drunken apologies and pleas to go out and party.

'We're back, baby!' he'd yelled at startled onlookers while we waited for cabs outside Melbourne airport.

The stench of liquor on his breath had been overpowering as he'd steadily knocked back alcoholic drinks on the flight home. It didn't revolt me as much as it did tempt me to want to drink too, and I knew I couldn't be around him, so I'd stuffed him into a cab, given the driver his address and asked him to take him straight home.

I tugged my luggage into my bedroom and unzipped it, pulling clothes and toiletries out, walking around my bathroom and lying down on my bed, trying to reacquaint myself with a life that now felt foreign. Really, I was just putting off the inevitable, what awaited me only a few feet away in the kitchen. I knew I would have to go in there sooner or later and deal with it.

Eventually, I dragged myself off my bed and walked in, switching the light on and pulling open the pantry doors. High up on the shelf, like old toxic friends, was my stash of alcohol. Bottles of wine and tequila, champagne, vodka, bourbon, and gin. Shot glasses and cocktail shakers and my collection of liqueurs. On some level, it was incomprehensible that I once replenished this shelf on a weekly basis, and yet some part of me wanted to reach up, unscrew a lid, pour a glass over ice, and drink it back like it was happy hour.

I wrapped my hand around a bottle of vodka and pulled it down. This bottle of crystal-clear liquid was my ultimate weakness, the pinnacle of my cravings, the one that undid me every time.

I unscrewed the lid, brought it to my nose, closed my eyes and sniffed. The fumes burned my nostrils, tingling my oesophagus. I let out a steadying breath and went to the sink. Before I could talk myself out of it, I poured the entire contents down the drain. I returned to the pantry and selected the next bottle, a three-hundred-dollar champagne, then a bottle of gin, then bourbon, then a Yarra Valley wine. Next was a brand-new orange liqueur, a crème de menthe and coffee liqueur. I turned the tap on and let it all run down the sink, thousands of dollars' worth of alcohol. After it was gone, I reached for the cocktail shakers, swizzle sticks and shot glasses and tossed them into the bin.

By the end of the ordeal, I was spent. I thought I'd feel empowered, like I'd conquered some great feat, but the feeling never came. Maybe it would later. For now, I just felt hollow, like it was another love I'd had to let go of. At least I'd safeguarded the apartment from all the triggers that lurked in the shadows.

I made a cup of tea, then went to the bathroom, undressed, and took a long hot shower.

***

The café around the corner from the firm was as chaotic as I remembered. This part of Melbourne City was always abuzz, full of law firms, financial institutions, and tech companies, with a steady stream of people that flowed through the café often.

When I arrived, I found Paul at a table at the back.

'Hey, you,' he said, standing to embrace me.

I hugged him close. 'It's good to see you.'

He pulled away to take me in properly. 'You look amazing. Fresh and bright-eyed.'

I smiled. 'The time away was good for me.'

'I can see that. Sorry, this was as quiet a spot as I could find. I hope it's okay.'

'It's fine. No problem.'

We took our seats and placed our orders for coffee.

'So how's life at the firm?' I asked.

'The usual,' he said. 'We've taken on that huge youth camp case that's been in the media lately. The one where the camp staff were accused of running a paedophile ring while the children stayed there during the holidays. Intimidation, torture, sexual abuse. The crimes they're being accused of are horrific and some are even factually impossible. The prosecutor's case is full of holes, not to mention none of the alleged torture victims have once visited a hospital for their injuries. Their stories keep changing too. I think the parents have put them up to it. Sour grapes over something.'

Our coffees arrived and I raised mine, taking a sip.

'You must have heard about it. It's been all over the news,' Paul said, raising an eyebrow at my lack of comment.

I shook my head. 'No, I haven't been keeping up with the news.'

'Well, if this goes to trial and we lose, we're looking at a grave miscarriage of justice. I want you back on the team. This case is yours. I don't see how we can lose with you on it.'

Once upon a time, Paul's words would have inspired something in me—a challenge, a burning desire to win, that fire in my belly for a courtroom battle—but as Paul watched me with eyes full of expectation, that inspiration barely sputtered. All I felt was empty inside.

'Well?' he asked. 'What do you say?'

I shifted on my seat, took a deep breath, and pulled my signed resignation letter out of my handbag. I slid it across the table towards him.

He stared at it, blinked, then sighed resolutely. 'So that's it?'

I nodded. 'Yes.'

'You're certain about this?'

'I am.'

'Do you need more time to think about it? It's a big decision, Marley, everything you've worked for.'

I placed my palm over the letter and slid it closer towards him, pushing it under his hand. 'I don't need any more time to think. It wasn't a decision I made lightly but I've made it.'

I'd spent hours over the past week, walking along the beach behind my apartment, weighing up all the odds. I had come to the realisation that I was a different person. That Lachlan and Noelle and White Cedar had changed me. That sobriety had given me a new perspective. That I would always love the law and hoped to incorporate it again into my life in some capacity, but in this moment, I couldn't go back to doing what I was doing, the lethal carousel of long working hours, the drinking, drugs, and self-shame. And I wasn't sure I believed in what I did anymore.

Paul stared down at my letter, folded beneath his hand. When he glanced up, I saw sadness there, but also understanding. 'I've known you a long time, Marley, and while I'm saddened by your decision, if you think it's the right one, then it probably is. I wish you nothing but the best. You'll always be a great lawyer, and you would have made an even better partner. If you ever change your mind...'

I nodded, close to tears, trying desperately to hold them back in the busy café. It was the end of an era.

'So, what's next for you?' he asked, placing my resignation letter into the pocket of his suit jacket.

'My apartment is on the market and I've had a couple of offers. I've packed up most things. A lot of my furniture will go into storage.'

'Where will you live?'

'I'm going to stay a few months with my sister, Anna, in Kallista. I want to spend time with my nieces and help her with my nephew. I'm thinking about starting a community garden somewhere, maybe a program to help recovering addicts. I'd like to extend it to domestic violence victims too, and their children. I could teach them about organic growing and how to cook using the produce. From the garden to the table, so to speak.'

'Sounds interesting. A vastly different lifestyle from what you're used to, though.'

'Not really,' I said. 'On the island, I did a lot of gardening. I rather miss it—the smell of damp earth and compost, the vegetables and manure and getting utterly dirty. And I *miss* cooking.'

'Good grief!'

We both laughed at the image I'd painted, so far removed from the girl Paul had known.

'What about Austin?' he asked.

I sighed sadly. 'I've had to be firm. Get clean or we cannot be friends.' It had broken my heart to say those words to him, to sever ties with such a demand, but I'd hoped by doing so that I'd given him something else to fight for. And save my own soul from relapsing.

'Austin's out of control,' Paul said. 'Frankly, I'm not sure how much longer he'll be with us. If he doesn't quell the partying or enter rehab, I don't see a future for him at our firm.'

'Maybe that will be enough to convince him,' I said.

'I hope so. He's a good lawyer. We don't want to lose him, but he will force our hand.'

We parted ways shortly after, promising to stay in touch. And, unlike the usual farewell cliches, I knew we would always be friends, that in this new and sober world of mine, I would value less the expensive accessories and more the love and support of the ones I held dear.

***

Packing up my apartment was harder than I thought. There were many memories here, some good, others painful. I felt it in the dim light cast by afternoon shadows and in the dusty corners after the furniture was carried out. I felt it in the now-empty kitchen and the echoing floorboards, and the balcony that had witnessed my tears.

I was everywhere in that apartment, all of it, the light and the dark.

Now I hoped to leave as a better person. Someone who had more to offer the world. Someone who had made her fair share of mistakes and who would always struggle with redemption, no matter how much time had passed.

As I left that day, my apartment already sold to a hopeful city newcomer, I gave it one last sweeping look. We'd been through a lot together. That apartment had seen more of my pain than anyone. Then, without meaning to, Lachlan fell into my head, something that happened a lot.

Although weeks had passed since I'd left White Cedar and there had been no contact in that time, I still wondered where he was and what he was doing, if he thought about me often. My heart ached at the way we'd ended things, so abruptly, with little said of the things that mattered. When I felt particularly down, I thought of him more, of our lost opportunity, the one that got away.

On my journey to Anna's house, with a rental car full of suitcases and boxes, I stopped at the cemetery before leaving the city. The day was beautifully bright, the whisper of autumn wind blowing golden leaves from trees.

I purchased a bouquet of flowers from the cemetery florist and laid them on Katiana's grave. I sat with her for a while, my heart full of apology. It was so weighted with sorrow that my tears fell on her headstone. Her life had been cut tragically short and, while I hadn't been the one to kill her, I had sealed her fate and her children's that day. I'd robbed them of a mother, robbed *her* of all those wonderful years with them. She should have been able to watch them grow and marry and have children of their own. Her absence would leave a gaping hole in their lives and my shame at the part I'd played would take a lifetime to heal, if ever. Wherever Katiana was today, I prayed for her peace.

After I left the cemetery, I stopped at another florist in Camberwell and ordered a delivery of flowers to be sent to Kristy Cameron. Paul had helped me locate her home address through old case notes. I'd learnt that after my collision with her husband's car that fateful night, she'd gone on to deliver a healthy baby girl. Some wrongs could never be made right, but closure was to heal, and remorse was as powerful an apology as any.

I wrote her a note and slipped it across the counter to the florist to add to the bouquet. I knew Kristy would understand who the flowers were from, for my name would be forever etched in her brain.

> *Dear Kristy,*
> *Sorry will never be enough for what I did to you all those months ago.*
> *I never meant to hurt you and your family.*
> *It's a regret I will live with forever.*
> *Marley.*

Then I climbed into my car and drove to Anna's.

A Year Later

I finished changing Cooper's nappy, dressed him again, then pulled him off the change table and into my arms. He grinned toothily at me and a string of nonsensical babble left his lips. When I heard an unmistakable *Marwey* amidst all the sounds, my heart exploded, the way it often did when he said my name.

'Oh, little one, you are going to steal hearts one day. Do you know that?'

He chuckled, throwing his arms around my neck.

I sighed. 'You already have mine.'

Down in the kitchen, I handed him to Anna, who slid him into his highchair and set down fingers of toast on his tray. He was almost eighteen months old, and I was blessed to have been a part of most of his life. I was ashamed to admit that it was more time than I'd ever spent with my nieces while they'd been babies.

'Aubrey's bag is ready for nursery,' Anna said. 'Tom will be down soon to take Mia to school. Would you like a smoothie?'

I'd converted Anna and Tom's breakfasts from toast to green smoothies and granola bars. And whilst I had dropped some of the island's vegan ways, we still ate healthily, the kitchen always full of produce I'd harvest from the gardens.

'You stay with Cooper. I'll make them,' I said.

Amidst the whirr of the blender, Tom and the girls arrived in the kitchen and there was the comforting sound of instructions and chaos. Cooper always took delight in having the family in the room with him, where he could sit in his chair and clap and observe. I felt a little like that sometimes, proud to be part of this family. It was a joy to help my sister and Tom as they raised their children and I was grateful that, for now, until I found a new place to set down roots, they were happy to have me too.

'Okay, Miss Aubrey, are you ready for nursery?' I kissed the top of her head and collected her bag and my smoothie. She reached for my free hand and glanced up at me with a mop of blond curls bursting to free themselves from her pigtails. 'Goodness, you'll be at big school with Mia before too long.'

'Please,' Anna said with a groan, 'it's too depressing to think about.'

'When can I go to nursery?' Jasmine asked, the youngest of the girls.

'Next year,' her mother said, picking bits of Cooper's mushed toast off the floor. 'When you're a bit bigger.'

Jasmine gave an unsatisfied sigh, then disappeared into the next room to put cartoons on the television. There was a flurry of kisses and hugs and bags being slipped onto backs as the rest of us prepared to leave.

'I'll see you this afternoon,' I said, collecting my car keys from the key hook. 'Remember, I'm making that pasta dish tonight. The one the girls love.'

'Honestly, I don't know how I ever managed without you,' Anna said, with a tired but grateful smile.

I felt a sudden well of emotion, for I felt the same way about her, and I had to turn away to fuss with Aubrey's bag straps to clear the lump in my throat.

We left the house, farewelling Tom and Mia as they reversed out of the driveway. I secured Aubrey in her seat and, two minutes later, we were at the nursery, where I left her in the care of her educators, driving on to reach the gardens shortly after.

Autumn had arrived the previous week with typical Melbourne chill. The air was growing colder, but not bitingly like White Cedar or Alaska, and the ground would not freeze in a way that restricted winter sowing. I parked my car in the small parking lot on the property I'd purchased a year ago—an acre of land with a small cottage and barn on it.

The sign for Amethyst Healing Gardens was askew and I straightened it fondly before climbing the timber steps to the front door. I unlocked it, allowing the frosty morning air to follow behind me and disturb the dust motes. My social workers, Jillian and Mick, hadn't arrived yet, nor had my farmhand, Bill, and the cottage was quiet as I parted the curtains and checked the day's diary.

Our usual group was attending the afternoon session—a mix of rehabilitated drug addicts and young domestic abuse families who were in safe housing. But the morning sessions were for newcomers to the group. I could see that we had two sexual assault victims from the trauma and recovery centre in Greensborough arriving at eleven, and a teen who aspired to be a horticulturist but who was staring down the barrel of several break and enter charges.

I made a cup of tea and thought about all the people who had passed through these gardens since I'd started the program. Many had found a path to healing here when all other programs had failed or when they'd needed something less rigid to temper the seriousness of their way forward. A distraction. An escape from normality, or perhaps to it.

Two-hundred and forty days sober. That's how long it had been since my last drink. It would have been five-hundred and fifty-two except I'd had a relapse ten months ago in a bar in Melbourne when I'd visited the city courthouse to register the program. A slip-up, a lost battle with old memories, a pub door opening and the sounds and smells of inside overwhelming my senses.

I'd battled shame and embarrassment afterwards, had even tried to keep it a secret from Anna until I'd been overcome with guilt and had finally told her. I've learned to pick myself up and move on after episodes like that, to brush away the setbacks and embrace 'day one' again.

I leant against the windowsill and stared out across the property. The Forever Garden, in honour of Noelle Bissett, was closest to the cottage, beautifully cluttered with beds of cabbage and carrots, pumpkin and potatoes. In spring, there would be vines of colourful tomatoes and cucumbers, stalks of bright yellow corn and trellises of green peas and beans.

Further along was Katiana's Orchard, filled with trees of apple, orange, lime, pear, and mandarin. Next to the orchard was a herb garden, named after my late mother Elaine, the smells of basil, mint, lemon thyme, parsley and rosemary carried easily on the breeze, filling the cottage rooms with their scent.

Further down the back was a barn with chickens and two cows and, inside the cottage, a kitchen where we made jams and bread and cakes from all the produce. The children loved cooking, and we had aprons and child-friendly utensils. They would take their baking home if there was any left after we all sat down at the table to eat.

The place was serene, one of healing, somewhere to escape to and learn and be at peace. It was exactly how I had envisaged it all those months ago, and now that it was a registered program with the courts, people could come here and be recognised for their rehabilitation, take new skills back into the community and find solace after trauma.

I heard a car pull into the gravel carpark and glanced at the time. It was not quite nine, too early for our new group to arrive, which meant it was most likely my social workers. For some reason, my hand reached up to the purple amethyst around my neck, still fastened securely since the day Lachlan had slipped it on, feeling its cool weight suddenly against my throat.

The door opened, clipping the small bell at the top, sending a chime through the cottage.

'Jillian, Mick, is that you?' I called. 'You're just in time for a cup of tea.'

I was met with silence and I turned from the window, my breath catching at the sight of the person standing in the office doorway.

It was Lachlan.

Neither of us spoke for a long time. He looked haggard, as though he'd been travelling for many days, week-old stubble on his face and eyes grey from jetlag. He wore jeans and a sweater, his brown hair thick and dishevelled.

He smiled. I was so stunned to see him that I'm not sure if I smiled back. We were caught in a moment where time stopped, and I was certain I wore the surprised look of someone who had just seen a ghost.

'Hey,' he said, with a slight wave of his hand before jamming it back into his jeans pocket.

'Lachlan.' It barely came out a whisper. 'What are you doing here? It's been over a year.'

He took a deep breath and stepped inside my office. 'I'm touring vineyards in Victoria for the truffle business. I thought I'd look you up and pay you a visit.'

'You came all this way for vineyards, and you thought you'd look me up?'

He hesitated, as though he wasn't sure he should say what was on his mind. 'Actually, it was the other way around. I wanted to pay you a visit and I thought I'd tour vineyards while I was here.'

My heart cautiously soared. Most people would think the sequence of his plans made little difference, but they meant everything to me.

I studied him closely, unable to take my eyes off him. Thoughts of him had filled every waking moment since I'd left White Cedar. He'd crept into my heart during the lonely hours of the night and haunted me in my dreams. There had never been anyone since him, and now here he was. I was glimpsing him in the flesh and not just through the haze of memory. I could hear his voice, watch his eyes as they watched me and feel his smile warm my world again. Nothing had changed. I still loved him.

He glanced around the office, his eyes settling on the window outside. 'You started a healing garden?'

'Yes.'

'Called Amethyst?'

I touched the stone at my throat again. 'Yes.'

'And the firm?'

'I quit.' I was still staring at him, trying to convince myself that he wasn't a mirage, that I hadn't dreamt the past few minutes. 'How did you find me?'

'It wasn't too hard. After I realised you'd changed your number, I took a chance and googled your name. I saw your Facebook page for this garden.' He winced slightly. 'You didn't change your number because of me, did you?'

I smiled and shook my head. 'No. I changed it because I needed to leave some people in the past.'

I hadn't spoken to Austin since I'd left him at the airport, other than to tell him he wasn't welcome in my life until he'd changed his. He'd hurled insults and abuse at me, calling me a blackmailer. It hadn't changed what I'd come to realise. Austin would never get better if I kept making excuses for him. So, I'd changed my number and only a select few had the new one. Austin could have found me if he'd wanted to, for Lachlan easily had, but he hadn't and that spoke volumes. He wasn't ready for recovery. It saddened me deeply, for all I wanted was for Austin to be healthy, to know the glorious feeling of sobriety, but that wasn't my choice to make.

I was still holding my cup of tea and I placed it down on my desk, trying to calm my trembling hands. 'Can I get you a drink, something to eat? You've been travelling for hours, I imagine.'

'No, I'm fine. And yes, it was a long flight. I literally stepped off the plane a few hours ago, hired a car and came straight here. I'm still not sure which side of the road I drove on, but I made it.'

Despite the shock of seeing him, of being flooded with a million emotions, I laughed. 'Would you like to take a walk then? I can show you the gardens.'

'I'd love to.'

We stepped out the back door just as I heard Jillian and Mick's cars pulling into the carpark. From where we were, I could see them walking towards the front steps, folders and laptops and coffees in hand, chatting. I waved and they waved back before disappearing inside to prepare for our morning group.

We reached the first garden and Lachlan touched the signpost as I opened the gate.

'The Forever Garden,' he said, a soft smile touching his lips. 'You made this in honour of Noelle.'

'I did,' I said. 'Come on, I'll show you.'

We walked around Noelle's garden, Lachlan bending to inspect potatoes and to touch the sprawling pumpkin runners and broccoli heads. He was quiet, his eyes fond, until finally he straightened and sighed. 'I'm sorry about the way we left things.'

'Me too.'

'I'm not even sure I know what happened. We were swallowed by the moment and before we knew it, we were over.'

'I never wanted us to be,' I said, looking up at him. Once upon a time I would have been too afraid to tell him how I felt, to be vulnerable in such a way, unless I'd been drinking. Time and sobriety, no matter how many times I'd stumbled, had instilled strength.

He nodded slowly. I saw his Adam's apple shift as he swallowed his emotion. We continued walking along the path between the beds of vegetables, the cold winter mist rising off the mountains in the distance.

'It's beautiful out here,' Lachlan said, stopping and taking a deep breath. 'It reminds me of White Cedar. Crisp, clean air, the smell of the forests.'

'It took me a long time to appreciate it,' I said. 'Years, in fact. And a whole lot of sobriety.'

'And now?'

'I'm two-hundred and forty days sober.'

I watched as he did the math. 'A relapse?'

'Briefly, about ten months ago. I went into the city for a day and...' I stared down at the ground with humiliation.

But Lachlan's voice was kind. 'Two-hundred and forty days is amazing, Marley. I'm proud of you.'

I glanced up and we shared a soft smile.

'Do you live close by?' he asked.

'Yes, with Anna and her family, just around the corner. I started the healing garden because I felt the need to give back in some way and criminal law wasn't the place for me to do that anymore.'

'I read up on this garden on the internet,' he said. 'Only in operation for a year and a huge success. You've healed a lot of pain.'

'It's been healing for me too.'

We reached Katiana's Orchard and I let us in through the gate. We strolled down the path, pausing every now and again to observe the variety of trees. 'Lachlan, why are you really here?'

He gently ran his fingers along the leaves of a dwarf lemon tree, taking a while to answer, as though struggling for the right words to explain. 'What Celeste did was wrong,' he said. 'She shouldn't have stirred up trouble and started rumours like that, and we shouldn't have listened. Everything happened so fast but once we got to the bottom of what she did, people felt bad about the way they'd treated you. Anyway, she was fired from the mayor's office for breaching privacy and is about to move to Vancouver for the summer with her friends. With any luck, she'll stay there.'

I appreciated his words, but he still hadn't answered my question. 'Is that why you came all this way? To tell me about Celeste?'

He jammed his hands into his jeans' pockets. 'Not just that.'

'What then?'

'I don't know. Everyone misses you.'

'*Everyone* misses me?'

'All right, fine, *I* miss you. I miss you so much it hurts.' He met my eyes and I saw my pain mirrored in them, the long, lonely months without him, when I'd felt as though a part of me was missing. 'I wake every day and it's a struggle because you're not there. I thought I'd go to Montreal and forget about you, but that didn't work. I went back to White Cedar and that only made it worse. I'd sit in Noelle's garden and just feel miserable, missing you both. I tried to get on with my life, to leave you to yours, but I can't seem to move forward.'

I turned away to stare out across the property, at hazy blue hills turning green. I'd missed him too, so much that it had felt like physical pain. My heart wanted to hear the words, to believe in the possibility of us again, but my head was cautious, too used to picking up the pieces when they were locked in battle.

I heard him take a steadying breath. 'What I'm trying to say, and not very well, is that I can't live my days without you. I've tried for a year and it's not working.'

'What are you asking?' I said, finally looking at him.

'I don't know. I... I guess I need to know if you feel the same way.'

My breath caught as I whispered, 'Of course I do.'

His shoulders relaxed in visible relief.

'But Lachlan,' I said, shaking my head, 'if you're here to turn my world upside then leave again, please, don't. I'm not strong enough for that. I couldn't—'

He stepped forward suddenly, his arms around me, and he lowered his head, dropping his lips onto mine. The power of that one, unexpected kiss, so like our kisses from a lifetime ago, when we'd been too naïve to think the world couldn't catch us, took my breath away.

He pulled away slightly and smiled, kissing my cheeks and the top of my head, and pulling me into him. 'God, you feel good.'

I held him too, as I breathed him in, familiarity sparking to life all the things I could never forget about him. 'I can't believe you came back to find me.'

'I had to,' he said. 'It was a risk, not knowing if you still felt the same way or if you'd moved on with someone else.' He pulled back suddenly.

'You're not with someone else, are you?'

I laughed. 'No. There's been no one since you.'

He beamed at the words and I couldn't stop smiling too. I was aware that Jillian and Mick had taken up post by the window and were watching. Their curiosity must have been irresistible for they'd always known me to be a solitary person and not someone who kissed random men in the gardens. I grabbed Lachlan's hand and pulled him out of their view, towards the barn to see the cows and chickens. We talked about everything, about the year that had gone by and the vineyards he was scheduled to see next week, and how the business had grown over the past twelve months. I told him about Anna, Tom, and the children, about the different people who came through the program and about my recovery, the counselling sessions I still attended regularly.

As we walked back towards the cottage, he pulled me into his arms again and kissed me unreservedly, as though too much time had already been lost. I wasn't sure what would come of all this—if he would stay in Melbourne or return to White Cedar. I was still trying to process that he was here. We lived oceans apart, led separate lives on different continents, and had businesses to consider. Was our love enough to bridge the distance? It was impossible to know in the single hour we'd spent walking the gardens.

'My mom asked me to give you something,' he said, reaching into his jacket pocket. He pulled out a set of keys that I recognised instantly as the ones belonging to Noelle's house and the cabin.

I took them tentatively. 'She's giving me back the keys? Why? I sent her the paperwork ages ago to transfer the property into her name.' And despite several reminders, Ivy had yet to sign it.

'She wants you to have it, as Noelle intended.'

I gaped at the keys. 'Is she sure? She loves that property.'

'If my mother thought for a second that she should have it over you, believe me, she would have signed the paperwork ages ago,' he said. 'She's hoping it will give you a reason to visit one day. As do I.' His smile was slow and prepossessing, and it was difficult to tear my gaze away from it.

We had reached the back steps of the cottage again and we climbed them, turning to look out over the gardens. My gardens. Beautiful and peaceful and powerfully healing, full of new beginnings.

'You know,' he said, looking down at me. 'There's just one thing this place still needs.'

'What?' I asked, almost defensively, for I thought it was perfect.

'Truffles,' he said. 'Right there, behind your mother's herb garden.'

'Truffles?'

'Yes. You've got the room. We could start with a few trees.'

'Truffles,' I whispered again. A slow smile spread across my face.

I knew in that moment what he was saying. That while there was love, there was hope. That if we could withstand the test of time, we were worth fighting for. And that oceans and distance and the past were no match for us. There were a hundred ways to be lost in this world, but there were also a hundred ways to be found. And we'd found each other.

'Yes,' I said. 'You could be right.'

Epilogue

Vibrant summer sunsets had at long last arrived, leaching gold into the North Atlantic. A pod of humpbacks frolicked in the water, migrating north to feed in Greenland's icy seas. White peaks formed off ruffled water as the tide dragged lazily out. The ocean heaved, the waves sighed, seagulls squawked.

I watched the afternoon descend into a lavender dusk from Noelle's verandah, the forests around her property brimming with deer and birdsong and tiny creatures that rustled in the undergrowth. Duke was sprawled out across my feet, a spot he'd always preferred to the floor, and Lachlan stepped through the door with glasses of iced tea, placing them down on the table before taking up the seat beside me.

He reached for my hand and we shared a smile that conveyed more than words ever could. Our commitment to each other.

I was eighteen days sober.

I'd had a relapse before returning to the island when Lachlan and I had made plans to spread our time on both White Cedar and in Melbourne. I'd been nervous about coming back here and leaving the garden in Anna and Tom's hands, even though it was just for three months. The relapse had been small—a few vodkas in a pub in the next town along, and I'd dragged myself home, confessing all to Anna in a flurry of tears and slammed doors and crippling shame.

Are relapses ever *small* though? It doesn't matter if it's a sip or a whole bottle, it's still all those hard-earned days of sobriety down the toilet. It's facing day one again, with the taste of failure in your mouth.

I'd come to accept lately that I'll never be perfect. And that's okay. I will struggle with alcoholism until my last breath. I will relapse again. I will make poor choices and I will deal with the consequences. Lachlan grapples with his demons too. He doesn't trust or communicate easily, shutting down after we have an argument. The lawyer in me likes to work through the issue, argue both sides, debate and conclude. He doesn't so much, preferring to let our arguments die a quiet death, with many things left unsaid.

We will find our way together in this world, learning all there is to know about each other. We will do it here on White Cedar for half the year and in Australia for the other half. We will do it beneath the Northern Lights in Alaska when the whim takes us, and in Montreal, when Lachlan's work calls. We will always navigate together, wherever our journey takes us.

'The roses are ready for cutting,' Lachlan said, breaking my reverie.

I glanced at him, then out across Noelle's front garden, at the roses in bloom. 'I'll start on them tomorrow.' There were so many of them, and soon Noelle's house would be full of their colour and perfume.

While on White Cedar, I lived with Lachlan at his house. But as the view was better from Noelle's at the top of the hill, we came up here for the sunsets, made iced tea and sat on her verandah. Sometimes we cooked in her kitchen and invited Ivy and Joel for dinner. *My* kitchen, I supposed, for Ivy never did sign that paperwork. Instead, she visited often, dropping hints about grandchildren and marriage. Lachlan and I weren't in any rush. There was a lot to keep us busy. And we were renovating the cabin, a few minor changes to modernise it so Anna, Tom, and the kids could visit.

'Thank you, Noelle.' I hadn't realised I'd whispered the words until Lachlan looked across at me and squeezed my hand, and the breeze stirred in response, rustling the leaves of the cedars.

Forever. It was both time and place, physical and abstract. It was the love in our hearts that would always live on, for the ones who had passed and those who were still with us. It was the memories we tried to bottle, never to forget, despite life marching on.

Forever was in the trees we touched and the earth we sowed in, the wind we whispered to and the sea air we breathed. That is the true forever because the ripples of our mark on this world would always be felt, for the ages to come.

I glanced across at Lachlan, my heart so full of love for him that it was impossible to put into words, even for someone like me, the kind of love that could never be articulated in a way that would do it justice. And when he leant across the table to brush his lips against mine, I knew he felt it too.

Our course was set, across stormy seas and perfect summer days. Under starlit nights and snow-capped forests. Wherever our lifetime of adventure took us, we would always have each other. Through every challenge, great or small.

Forever.

Also by Michelle Montebello

The Quarantine Station

BLURB

The rules were crystal clear. She broke them all...

1918 ... When Londoner, Rose Porter, arrives on the shores of Sydney with little more than her suitcase, she is forced to take a job as a parlourmaid at the mysterious North Head Quarantine Station. It's a place of turmoil, segregated classes and strict rules concerning employee fraternisation.

But as Rose discovers, some rules were made to be broken.

2019 ... Over a century later, Emma Wilcott lives a secluded life in Sydney. Still reeling from a devastating loss, her one-hundred-year-old grandmother, Gwendoline, is all she has left. Suffering the early stages of dementia, Gwendoline's long-term memories take her wandering at night and Emma realises she is searching for something or someone from her past.

Emma's investigation leads her to the Quarantine Station where she meets Matt, the station carpenter, and together they begin to unravel a mystery so compelling it has the power to change lives, the power to change everything Emma ever knew about herself.

Set during the First World War and the height of the Spanish Influenza pandemic, The Quarantine Station is a captivating story of people who will love, no matter the cost.

The Lost Letters of Playfair Street

BLURB

A lover's game. A chest of clues.
Come find me. I'll be waiting...

1929: On the night of her engagement to austere banker Floyd Clark, Charlotte Greene meets enigmatic Sydney Harbour Bridge engineer, Alexander Young. Their encounter is brief, but their attraction instant.

Alex invites Charlotte to play a game with him, one of daring clues and secret meeting places. She accepts and they embark on a thrilling lover's chase across the city.

But with her arranged marriage to Floyd looming, will she have the strength to let Alex go?

Present Day: Paige Westwood is helping her boss establish a publishing company in his newly purchased Playfair Street house in The Rocks, Sydney. In the attic, she discovers a chest of old clues that lead the reader on a journey across the city.

Paige contacts the former owner, Ryan Greene, who explains the clues belonged to his great-aunt Charlotte, who once lived in the house, but who mysteriously disappeared in 1929.

Together, they follow Charlotte and Alex's clues to unravel a fascinating tale of lies and intrigue, of two lovers bound by hope, but also by deceit. Can they solve the mystery of Charlotte's disappearance or has all hope been lost to the past?

Beautiful, Fragile

BLURB

We'd hurt each other, my soulmate and me...

Faith James is found on a remote beach in the south of Spain with a head injury and no recollection of how she got there. Recovering in hospital, she is desperate to return to her twenty-five-year-old, single life in Sydney.

But Faith has lost ten years of memories and her world becomes unrecognisable.

Her husband, Will, arrives to collect her, and she is told she has three young children waiting at home in London.

So begins the emotional journey to reclaim the life she's forgotten, learn how to be a wife and mother, and mend a broken marriage. She wants to remember everything...

But are all memories worth fighting for, even the ones that hurt?

Author's Note

As is always the case with my books, I dive headlong into research before and during the writing process. Researching blue zones was one of my favourite parts of this story. At the time of writing, there are five original blue zones in the world—Ikaria (Greece), Sardinia (Italy), Okinawa (Japan), Nicoya (Costa Rica) and Loma Linda (California, USA).

According to research, the inhabitants of these regions live a decade longer than the rest of us and experience extraordinary vitality and social happiness, making their lifestyles some of the healthiest on Earth.

In *The Forever Place*, White Cedar Island has been created as a fictitious sixth blue zone. Many positive attributes of real-life blue zones have been adopted for White Cedar, but its inhabitants and lifestyle are mostly fictional and drawn from my imagination. If you find blue zones as fascinating as I do, you may wish to visit www.bluezones.com. I'd like to extend my special thanks also to Maura Mackey, who lent me her time and wisdom on all things Canadian.

To bring to life Marley's struggle with alcoholism, I was privileged to be able to speak to several people who suffer from this disease. They wish to remain anonymous, but I thank them for their courage and candour. I was moved by their stories of hope and eternally grateful to them for trusting me to share their personal struggles through Marley's voice. I also found several blogs relating to alcohol addiction extremely useful.

I extend my sincerest thanks to Maddison Michaels, Penelope Janu and Leanne Lovegrove for assisting with the scenes regarding Marley's drink-driving charges and the Wagner trial. These three women were incredibly gracious with their time, wisdom, and experience, and I am deeply appreciative of their patience with me. Any errors are, of course, my own.

My love and thanks also to Rania Battany, who has the most amazing produce garden. You can find all her gardening tips and stories on Instagram under @ranias_garden. Thank you, Rania, for helping me bring Noelle's garden to life. I dedicate her little piece of paradise to you.

Acknowledgements

I always thank my family first—Brett, Eve and Connor—for without their love and support, the books I release would not be possible. They gift me time, patience, and understanding, and they put up with the second great love of my life—writing. Special thanks also to Carmen, Joe, Michelle, Rhonda, Joanie, Roger and Paula for being so supportive and letting me talk about stories.

Thank you always to my long-time editor, Lynne Stringer, who guides me so patiently through the panic of fixing intricate structural problems, and to Marcia Batton, close friend and editor, who I can count on to find anomalies, even after the manuscript has been reviewed dozens of times.

Love and thanks to my close circle of friends, Liz, Joanne, Bianca and Erika, and especially to Natasha Booth, who I have known *forever* and who this book is dedicated to.

To many in the book world who I consider dear to me—Phil and Craig, Philippa Clark, Helen Sibbritt and Tanya Nellestein, my heartfelt appreciation for your support, kind words and long lunches.

To Kris Dallas, my talented designer, who *always* creates a stunning cover, and to Kay Osborn from Swish Design & Editing for the beautiful interiors that make my stories come to life on the pages.

Finally, to my readers, thank you for investing in another book of mine. I can't tell you what it means to have you along on this journey. You are kind, enthusiastic and you experience the highs and lows with me. I wish I could personally thank each and every one of you. Know that you are special to me.

Connect With Me Online

Check these links for more books from Author
Michelle Montebello.

NEWSLETTER

Want to see what's next?
Sign up for my Newsletter.
https://michellemontebello.com.au/newsletter/

GOODREADS

Add my books to your TBR list
on my Goodreads profile.
http://www.goodreads.com/author/show/
17208833.Michelle_Montebello

AMAZON

Buy my books from my Amazon profile.
https://amzn.to/2LzG4Aj

WEBSITE

http://www.michellemontebello.com.au/

TWITTER
http://www.twitter.com/Michelle_Monteb

INSTAGRAM
http://www.instagram.com/
michellemontebelloauthor

EMAIL
michelle@michellemontebello.com.au

FACEBOOK
https://www.facebook.com/
michellemontebelloauthor

Book Club Questions

1. Blue zones are undoubtedly the healthiest regions in the world. Were you previously aware of blue zones? What, if any, of their lifestyle choices would you adopt or already have?

2. Do you feel Marley should have done more to ensure justice was served for Katiana Wagner? It's clear as a criminal lawyer that she had a professional obligation to defend Karl's charges. How important was her moral obligation to protect Katiana?

3. Did the story challenge your perspective on alcoholism? Did you learn anything new about the illness?

4. Should Marley have confessed her secrets (her alcoholism and profession) to Lachlan sooner? Or was she right to conceal them for fear of losing him? What would you have done in her place?

5. Do you feel Marley was entirely responsible for her addiction? Or do you believe her childhood, career, and other external factors played a role?

6. To attempt sobriety, Marley relocated to White Cedar Island. Do you believe this would have been easier or more difficult than attempting sobriety in a rehabilitation clinic? When answering,

consider the differences between the two, in terms of access to treatment and support, and the availability of alcohol.

7. Do you think Ivy Tremblay acted professionally in her sessions with Marley, or was she too conflicted to treat her properly?

8. Marley's relationship with Austin was complex. Could she have done more to support him through his detox and sobriety? Did she treat his fear of her abstinence appropriately?

9. Which character did you enjoy the most and why?

10. Which scene in *The Forever Place* affected you most? What emotions did it evoke?

About the Author

Michelle Montebello is a writer from Sydney, Australia where she lives with her family. She is the internationally bestselling author of *The Quarantine Station, Beautiful, Fragile* and *The Lost Letters of Playfair Street.*

Her books have won numerous awards. *The Lost Letters of Playfair Street* won the 2020 Australian Romance Readers Association Awards for Favourite Contemporary Romance and Favourite Australian-Set Romance.

The Quarantine Station and *Beautiful, Fragile* were shortlisted in 2019 for Favourite Historical Fiction and Favourite Contemporary Romance. Michelle has twice been shortlisted for Australian Author of the Year.

When Michelle is not writing, she has a keen passion for reading, tennis and travel.

9 780987 641687